Written by Stephanie Cooke & Insha Fitzpatrick
Art by Juliana Moon

Etch
Houghton Mifflin Harcourt
Boston   New York

For all of #TeamNoChill.
Stay weird <3

hmhbooks.com

The text was set in Amescote.

Color by Whitney Cogar
Lettering by Andrea Miller and David Hastings
Edited by Lily Kessinger
Cover and interior design by Andrea Miller

Library of Congress Cataloging-in-Publication Data
Names: Cooke, Stephanie, 1986– author. | Fitzpatrick, Insha, author. |
Moon, Juliana, illustrator.
Title: Oh my gods / by Stephanie Cooke & Insha Fitzpatrick ; art by Juliana Moon.
Description: Boston : Houghton Mifflin Harcourt, 2021. | Audience: Ages 10
to 12. | Audience: Grades 4–6. | Summary: When Karen leaves New Jersey
to spend time with her enigmatic father on Mount Olympus, she is shocked
to learn that her junior high classmates are gods and goddesses, and
that one of them is turning people to stone.
Identifiers: LCCN 2019036701 (print) | LCCN 2019036702 (ebook) |
ISBN 9780358299516 (hardcover) | ISBN 9780358299523 (trade paperback) |
ISBN 9780358296935 (ebook)
Subjects: LCSH: Graphic novels. | CYAC: Graphic novels. | Middle schools—Fiction. |
Schools—Fiction. | Fathers and daughters—Fiction. | Zeus (Greek deity)—Fiction. |
Gods, Greek—Fiction. | Mythology, Greek—Fiction.
Classification: LCC PZ7.7.C6664 Oh 2021 (print) | LCC PZ7.7.C6664 (ebook) | DDC
741.5/973—dc23
LC record available at https://lccn.loc.gov/2019036701
LC ebook record available at https://lccn.loc.gov/2019036702

Manufactured in China
SCP 10 9 8 7 6 5 4 3 2 1
4500805629

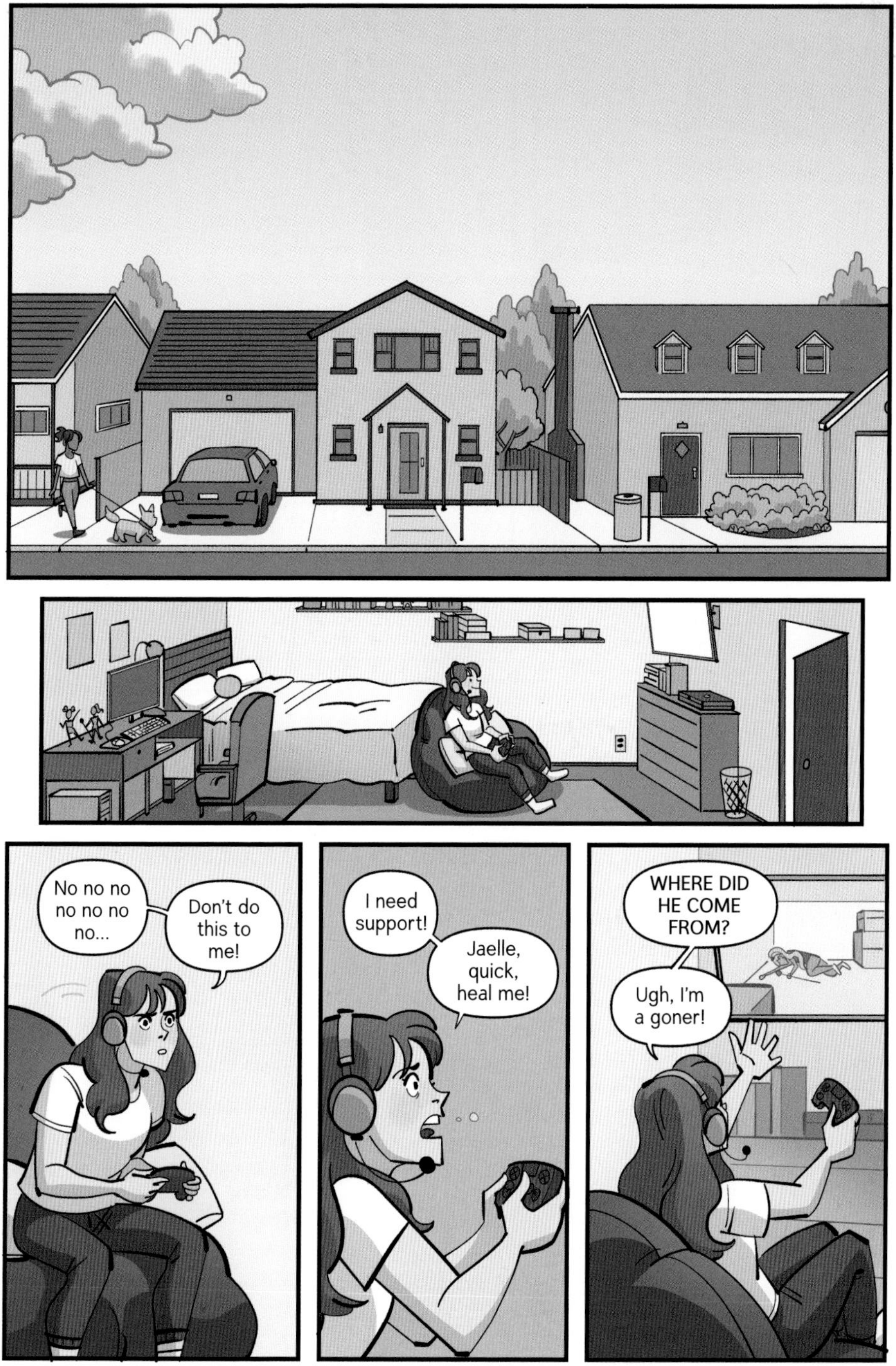
No no no no no no no...
Don't do this to me!
I need support!
Jaelle, quick, heal me!
WHERE DID HE COME FROM?
Ugh, I'm a goner!

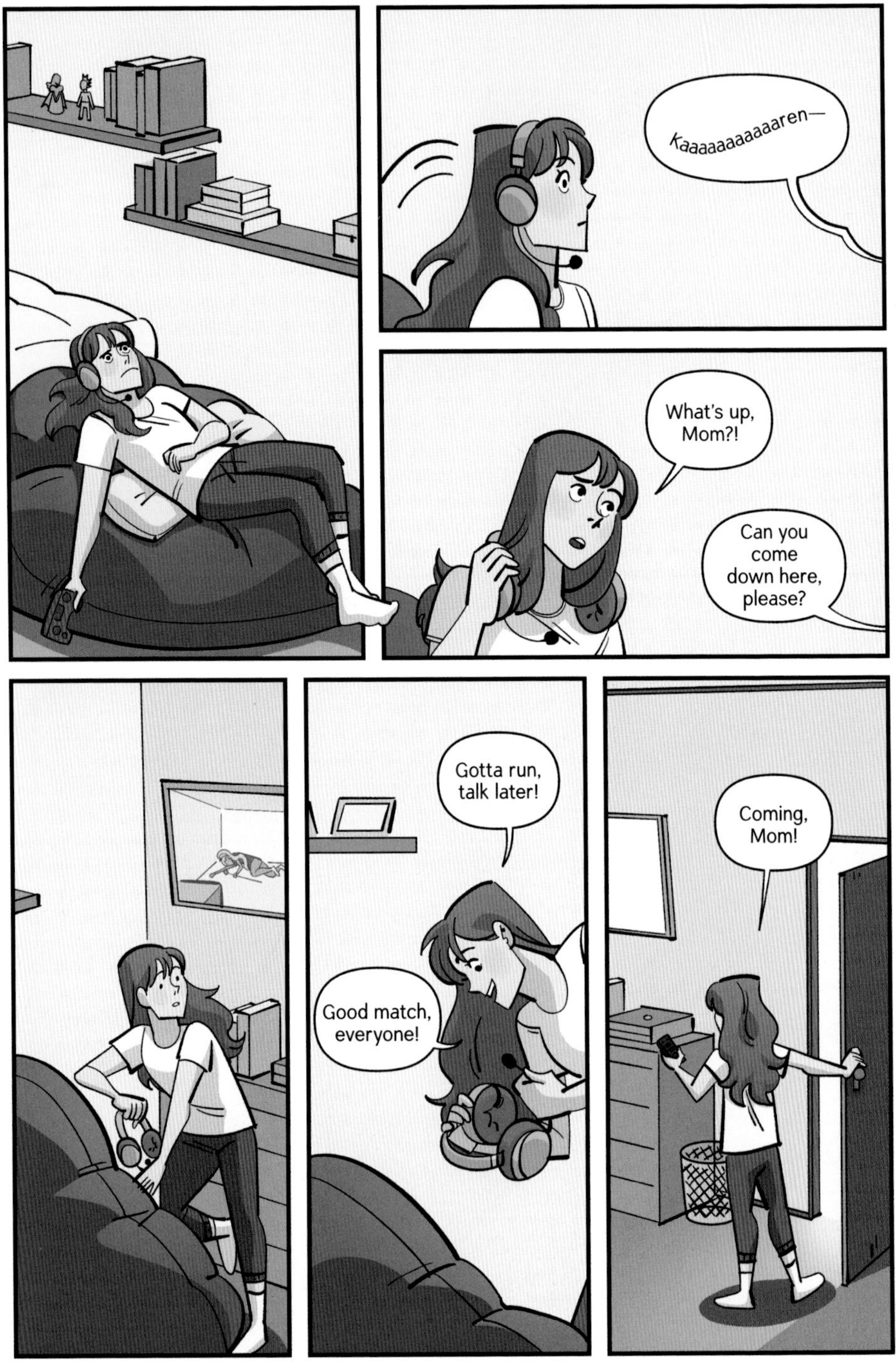
Kaaaaaaaaaaaren—
What's up, Mom?!
Can you come down here, please?
Gotta run, talk later!
Good match, everyone!
Coming, Mom!

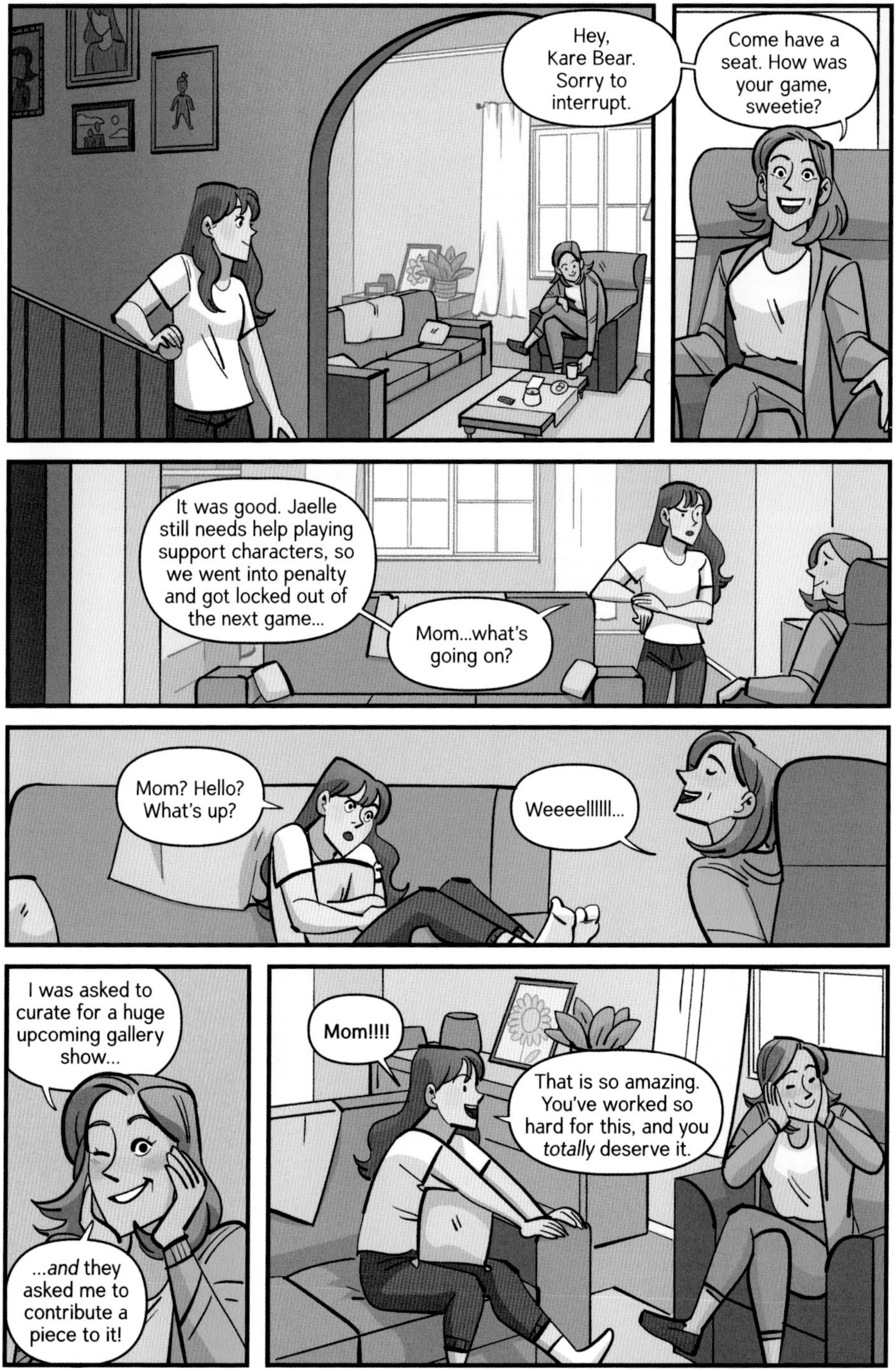
Hey, Kare Bear. Sorry to interrupt.
Come have a seat. How was your game, sweetie?
It was good. Jaelle still needs help playing support characters, so we went into penalty and got locked out of the next game...
Mom...what's going on?
Mom? Hello? What's up?
Weeeellllll...
I was asked to curate for a huge upcoming gallery show...
...*and* they asked me to contribute a piece to it!
Mom!!!!
That is so amazing. You've worked so hard for this, and you *totally* deserve it.

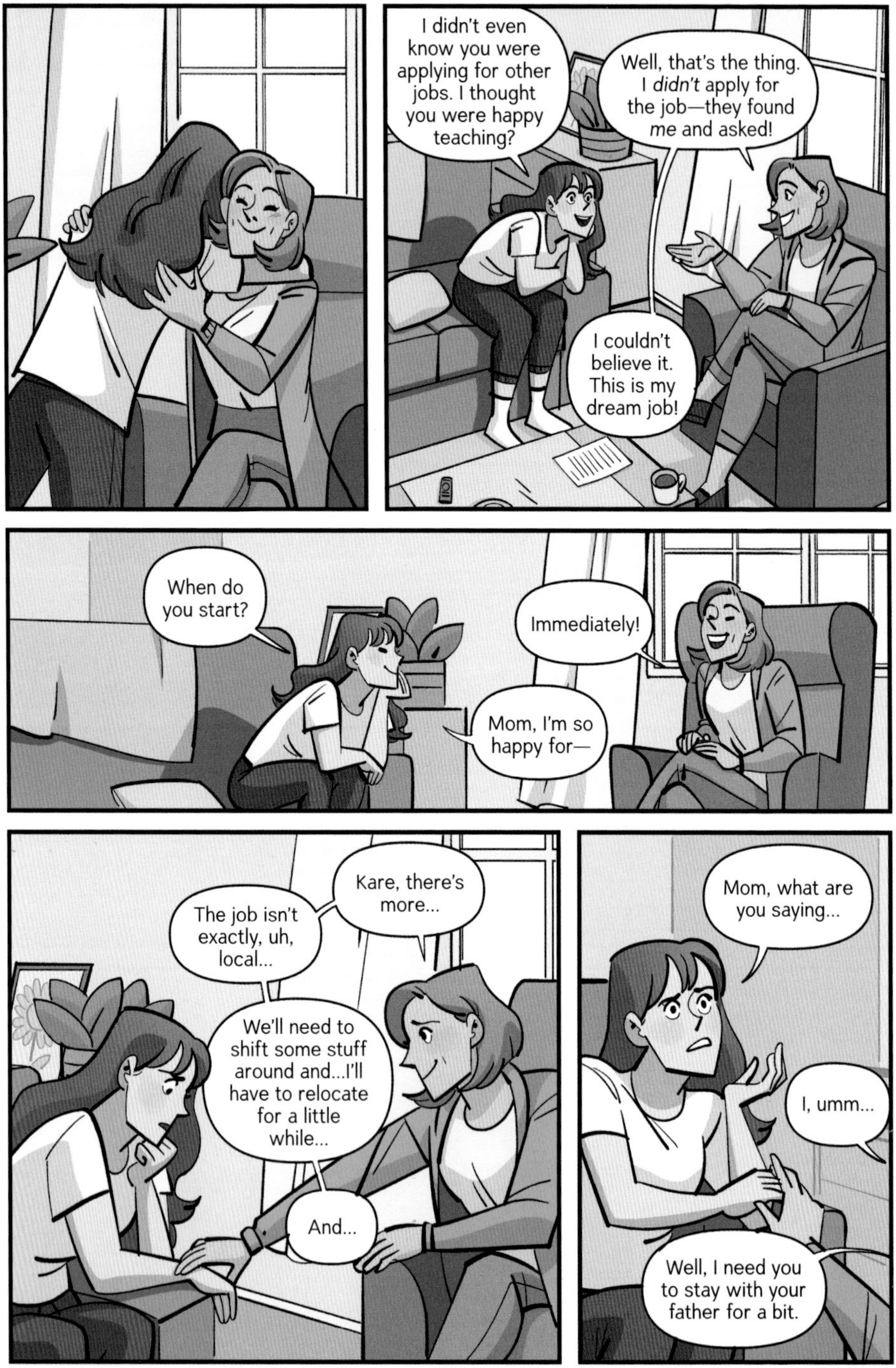
I didn't even know you were applying for other jobs. I thought you were happy teaching?
Well, that's the thing. I *didn't* apply for the job—they found *me* and asked!
I couldn't believe it. This is my dream job!
When do you start?
Immediately!
Mom, I'm so happy for—
Kare, there's more...
The job isn't exactly, uh, local...
We'll need to shift some stuff around and...I'll have to relocate for a little while...
And...
Mom, what are you saying...
I, umm...
Well, I need you to stay with your father for a bit.

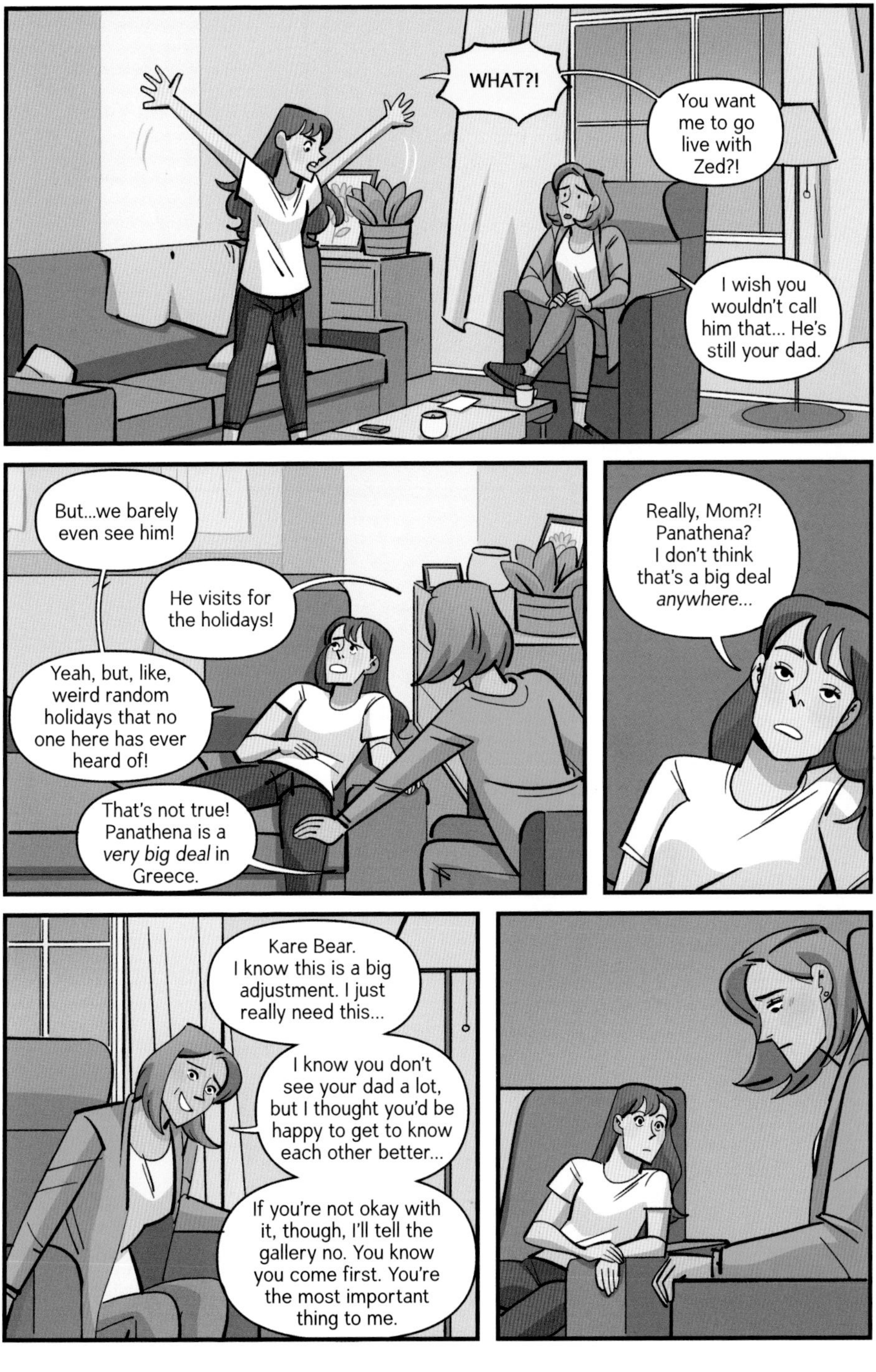
WHAT?!
You want me to go live with Zed?!
I wish you wouldn't call him that... He's still your dad.
But...we barely even see him!
He visits for the holidays!
Yeah, but, like, weird random holidays that no one here has ever heard of!
That's not true! Panathena is a *very big deal* in Greece.
Really, Mom?! Panathena? I don't think that's a big deal *anywhere*...
Kare Bear. I know this is a big adjustment. I just really need this...
I know you don't see your dad a lot, but I thought you'd be happy to get to know each other better...
If you're not okay with it, though, I'll tell the gallery no. You know you come first. You're the most important thing to me.

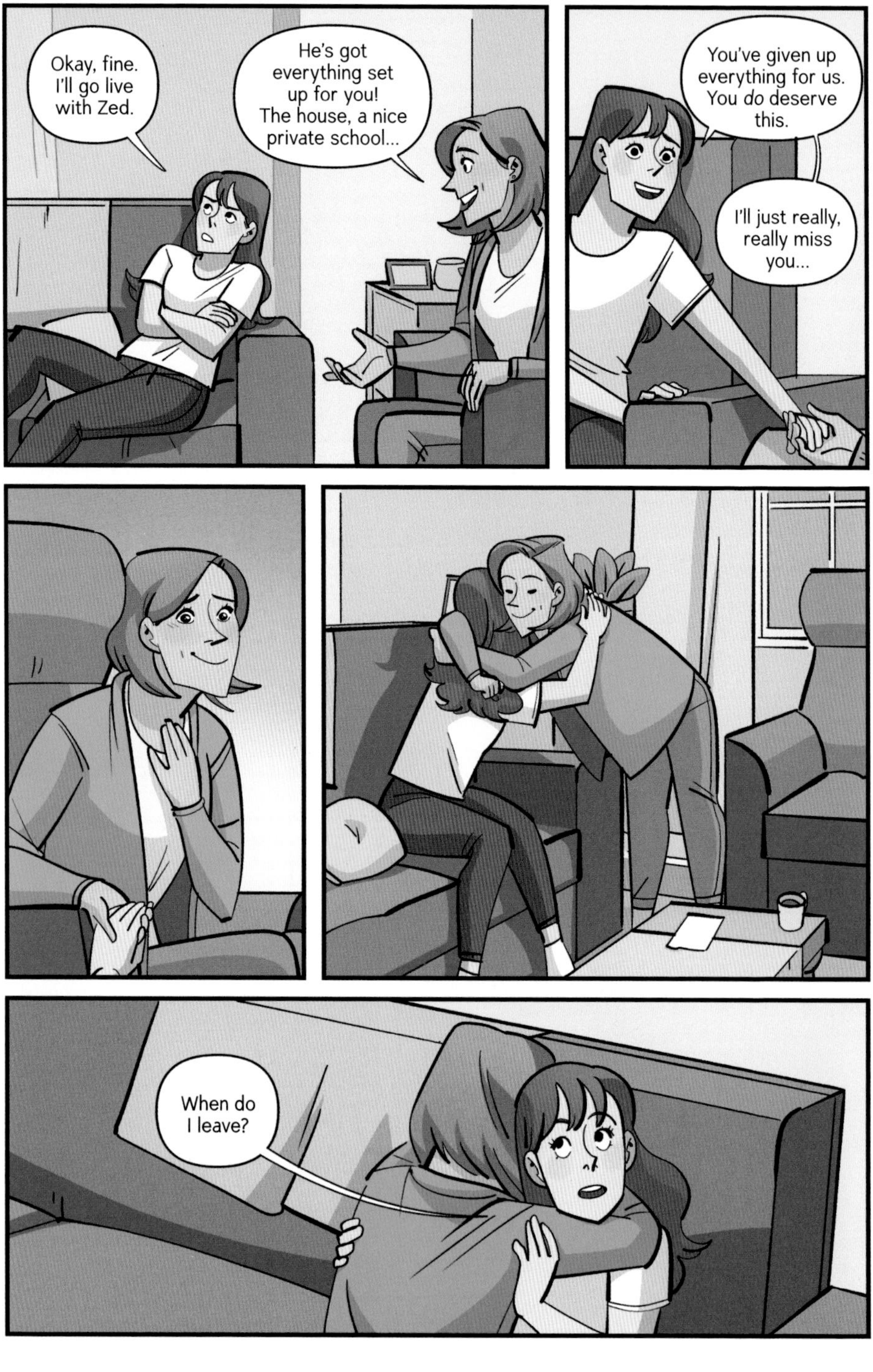
Okay, fine. I'll go live with Zed.
He's got everything set up for you! The house, a nice private school...
You've given up everything for us. You *do* deserve this.
I'll just really, really miss you...
When do I leave?

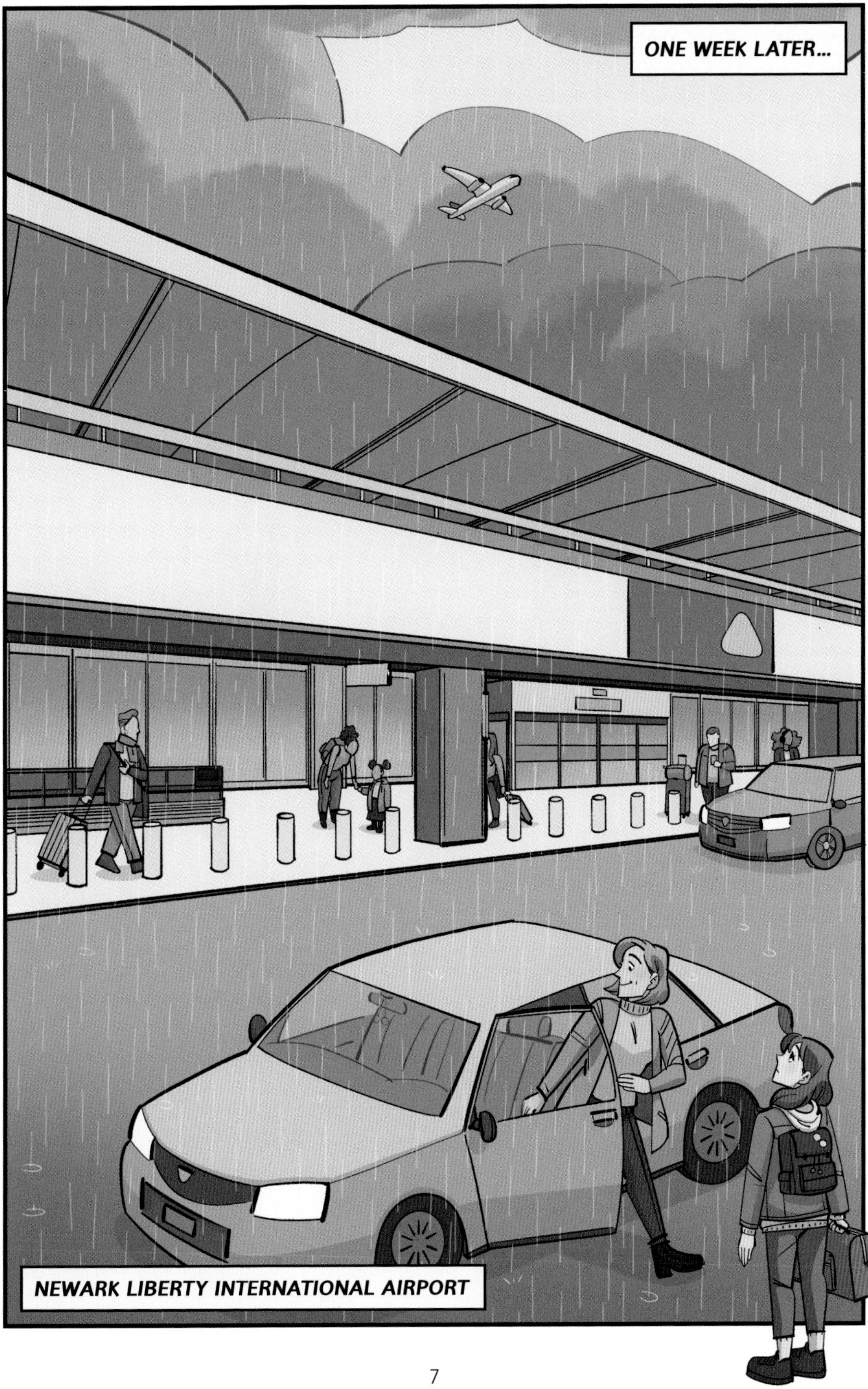

ONE WEEK LATER...
NEWARK LIBERTY INTERNATIONAL AIRPORT

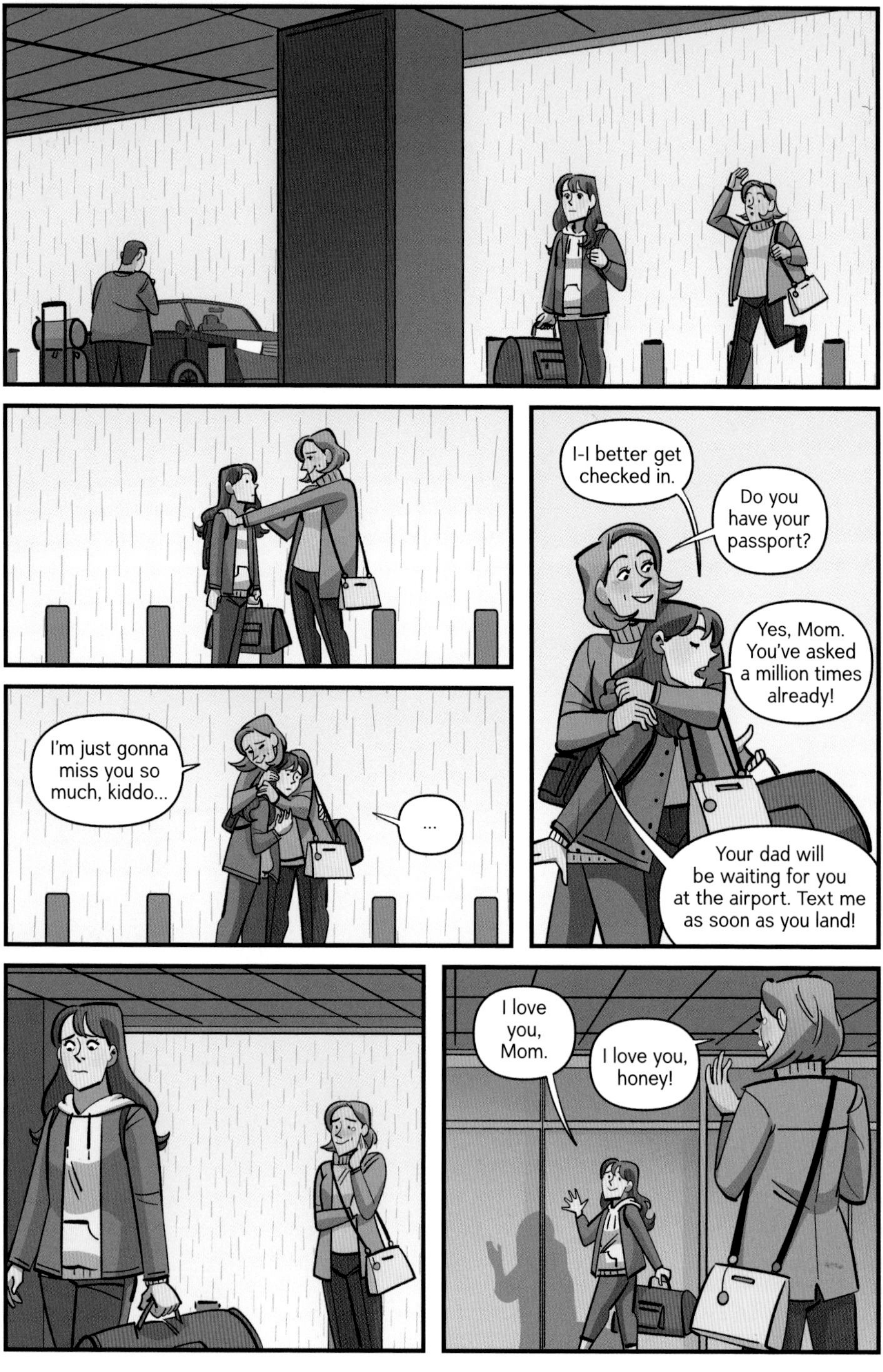
I-I better get checked in.
Do you have your passport?
Yes, Mom. You've asked a million times already!
Your dad will be waiting for you at the airport. Text me as soon as you land!
I'm just gonna miss you so much, kiddo...
...
I love you, Mom.
I love you, honey!

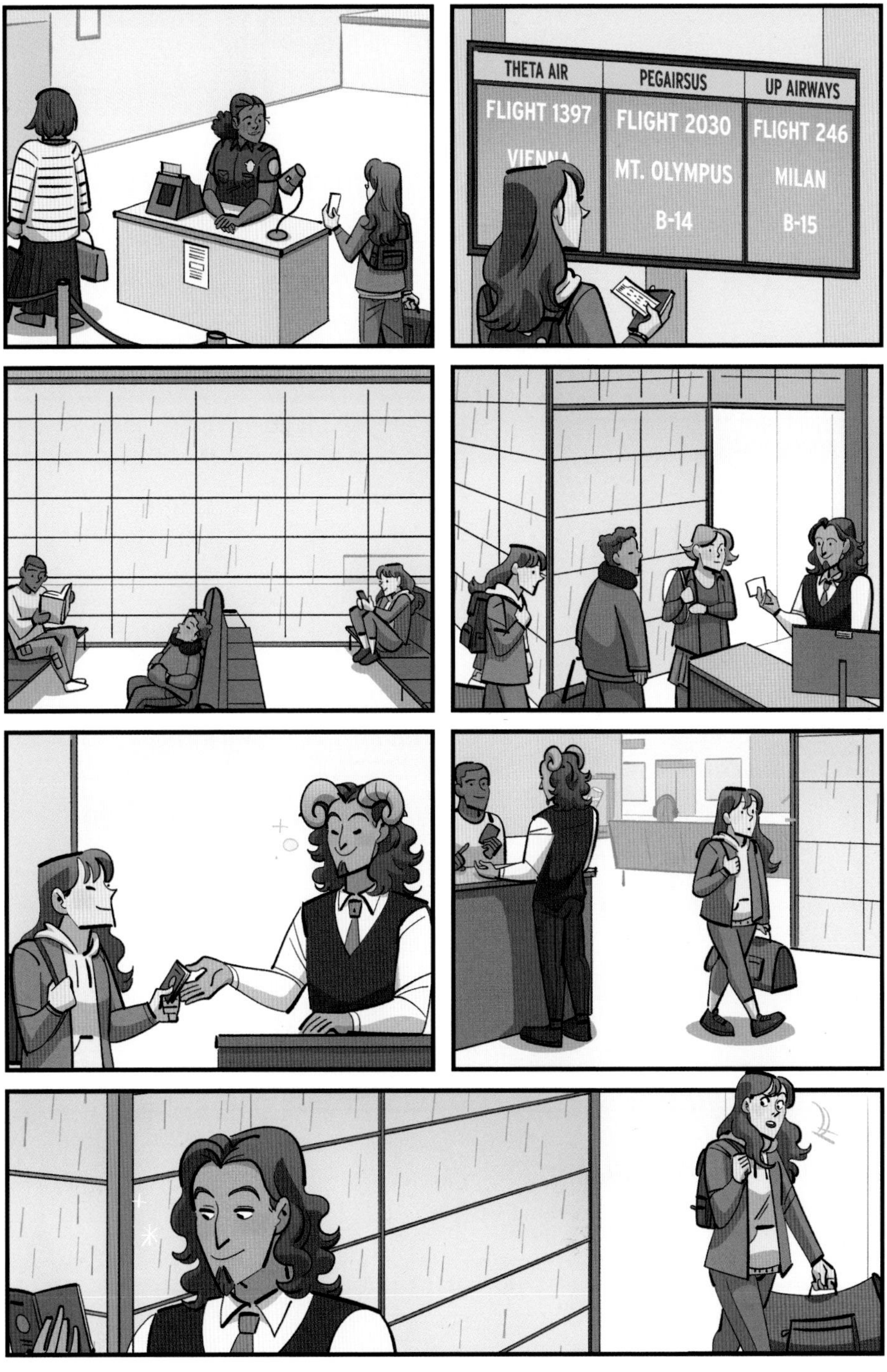
THETA AIR
FLIGHT 1397
VIENNA
PEGAIRSUS
FLIGHT 2030
MT. OLYMPUS
B-14
UP AIRWAYS
FLIGHT 246
MILAN
B-15

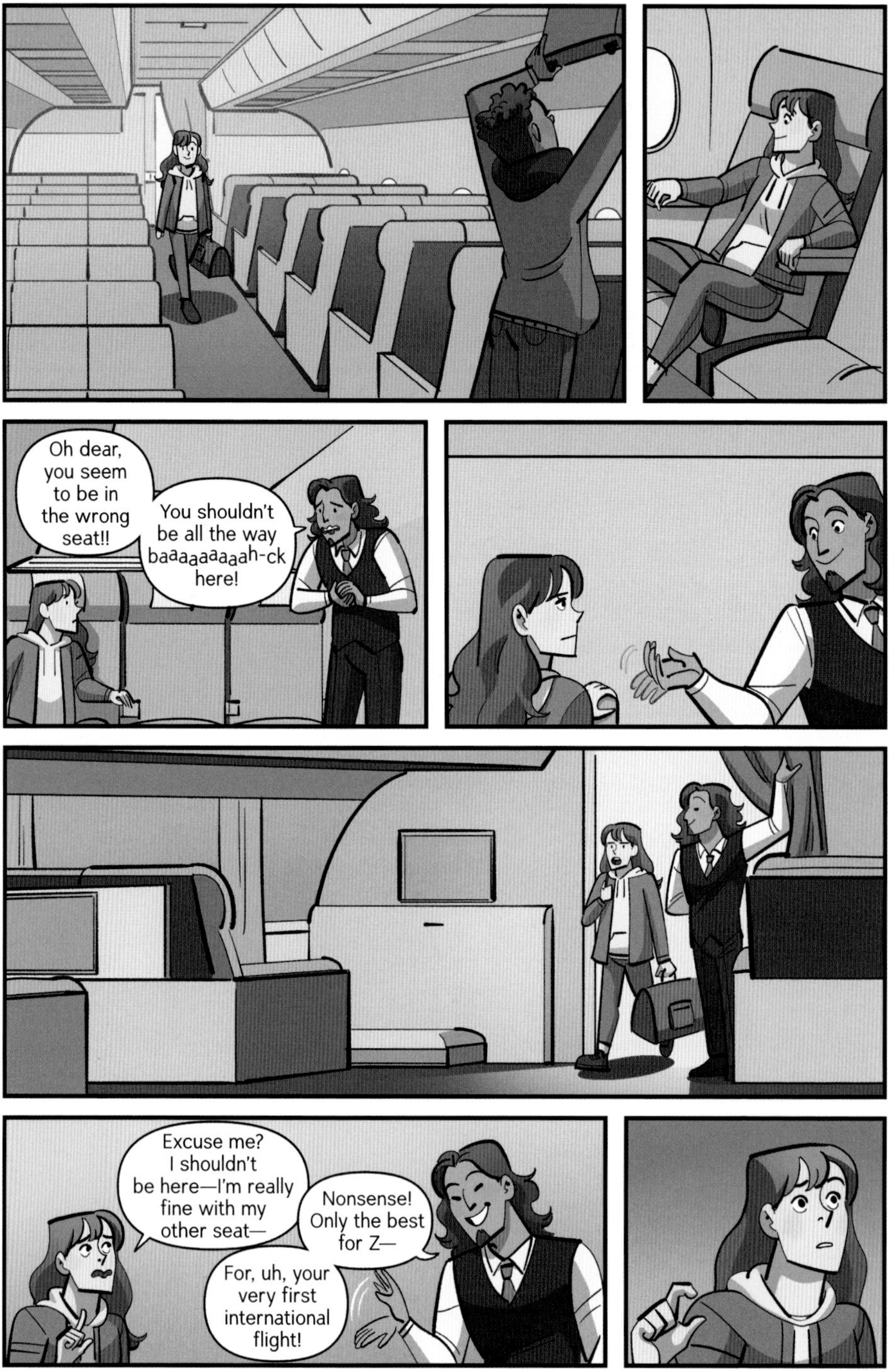
Oh dear, you seem to be in the wrong seat!!
You shouldn't be all the way baaaaaaaaah-ck here!
Excuse me? I shouldn't be here—I'm really fine with my other seat—
Nonsense! Only the best for Z—
For, uh, your very first international flight!

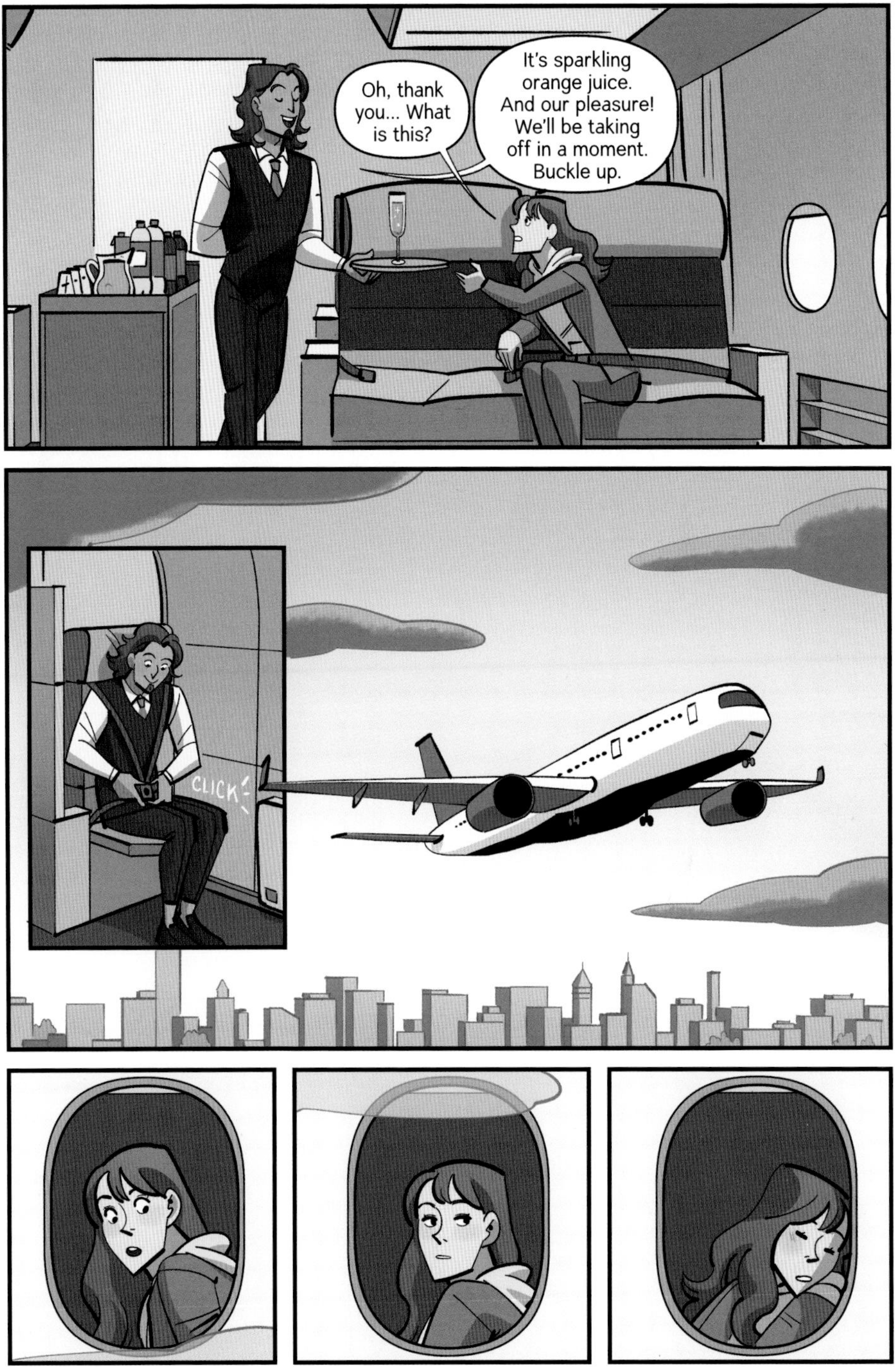

Oh, thank you... What is this?
It's sparkling orange juice. And our pleasure! We'll be taking off in a moment. Buckle up.
CLICK

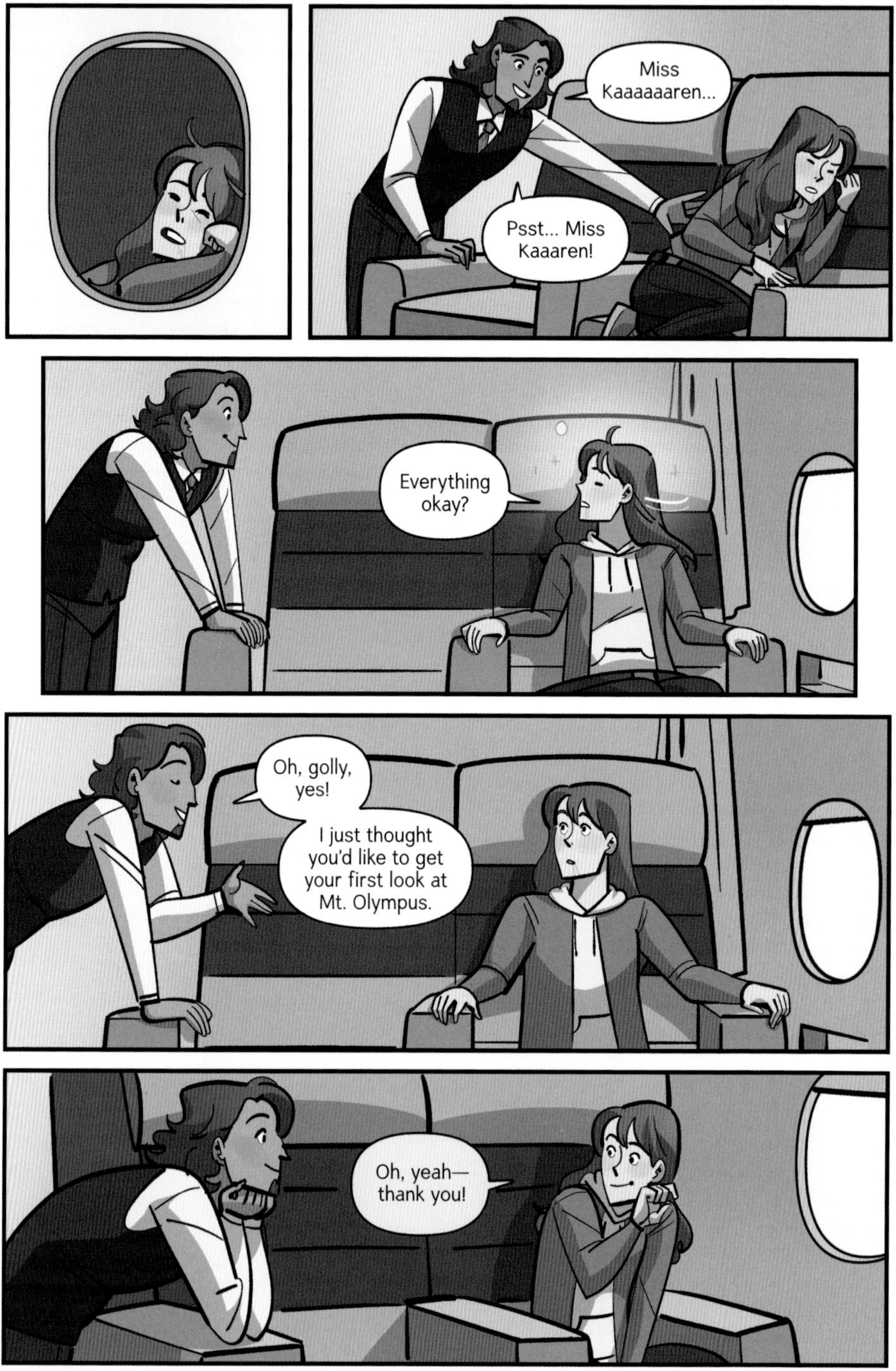
Miss Kaaaaaaren...
Psst... Miss Kaaaren!
Everything okay?
Oh, golly, yes!
I just thought you'd like to get your first look at Mt. Olympus.
Oh, yeah—thank you!

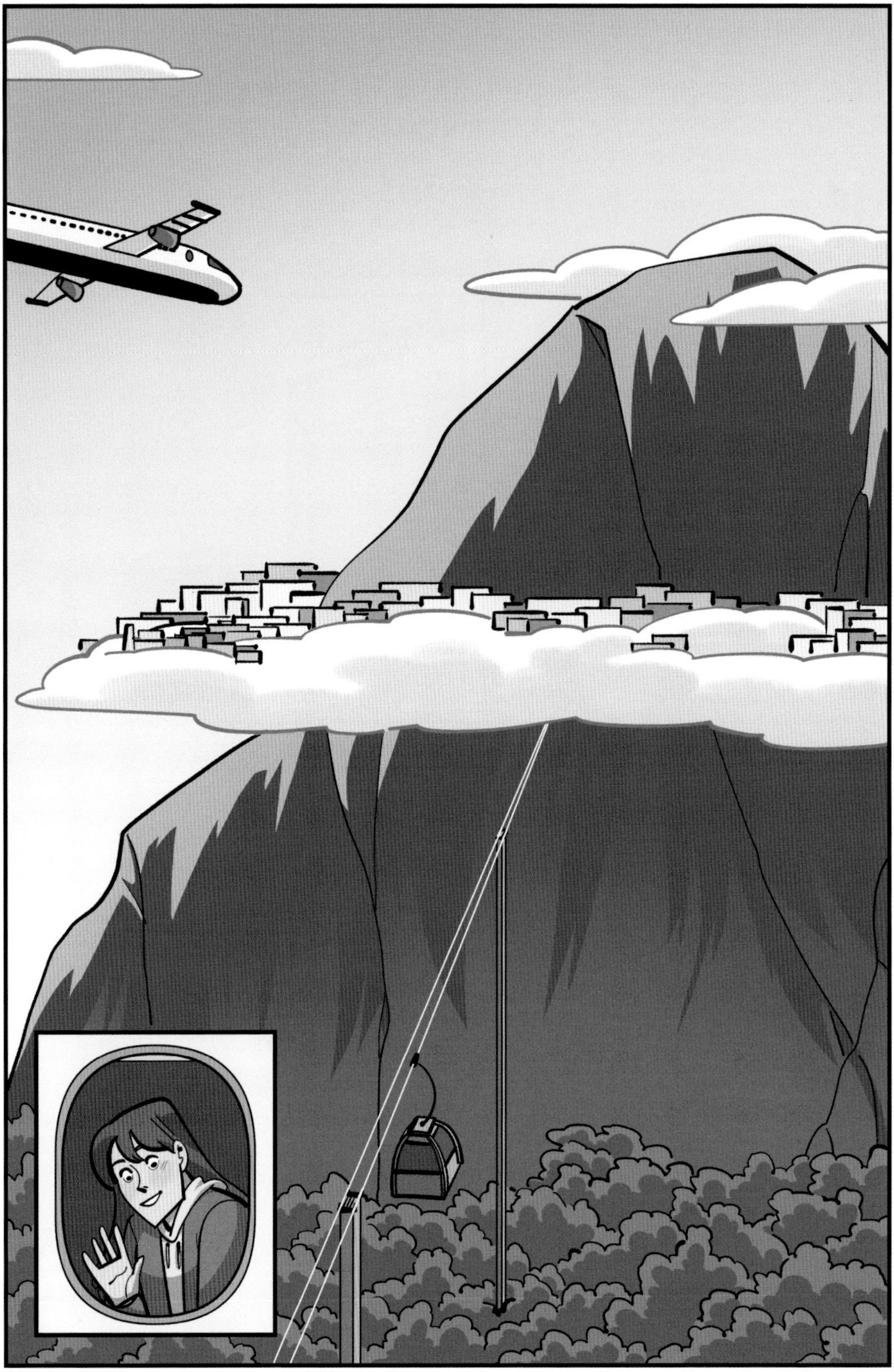

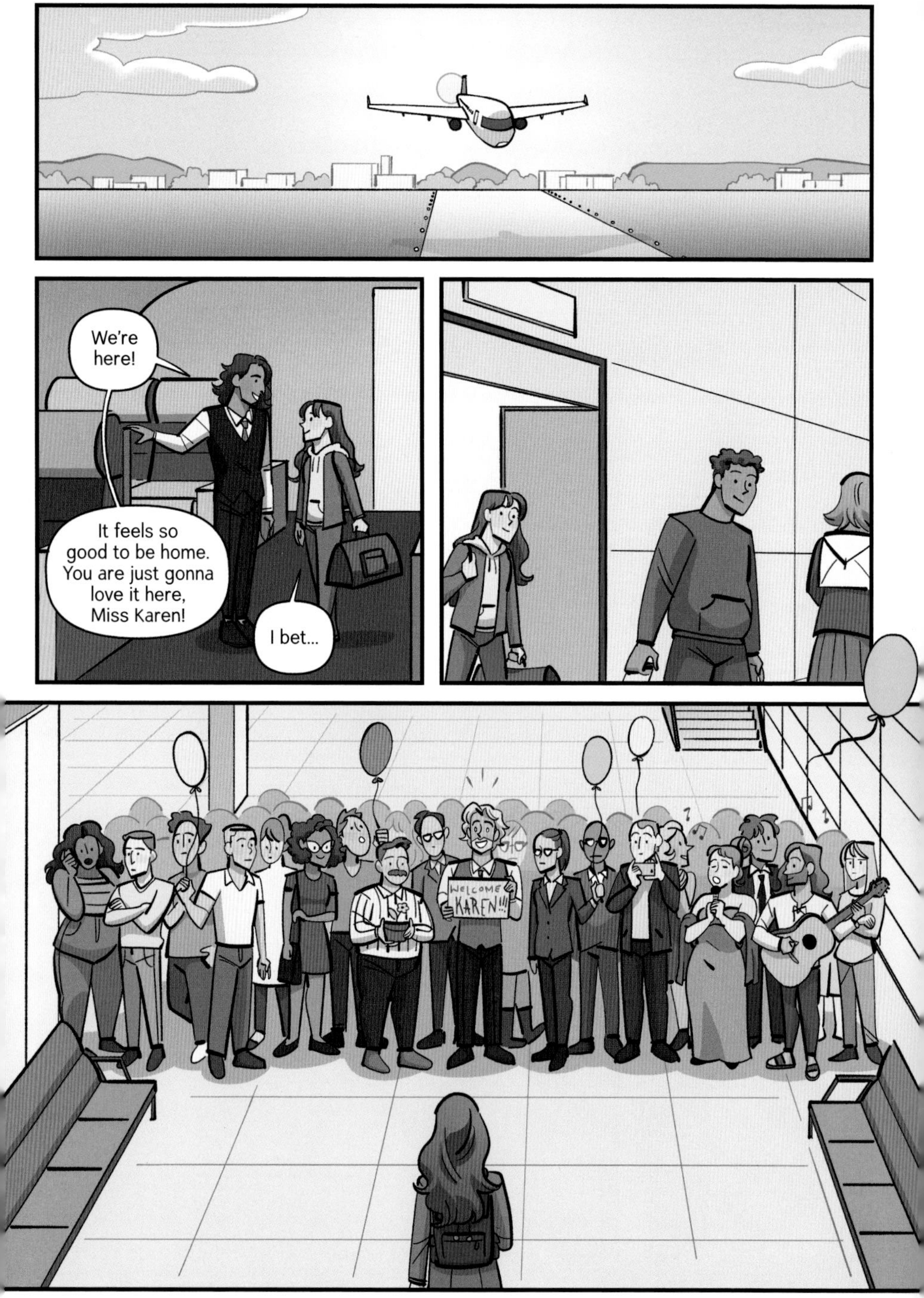
We're here!
It feels so good to be home. You are just gonna love it here, Miss Karen!
I bet...
WELCOME KAREN!!!

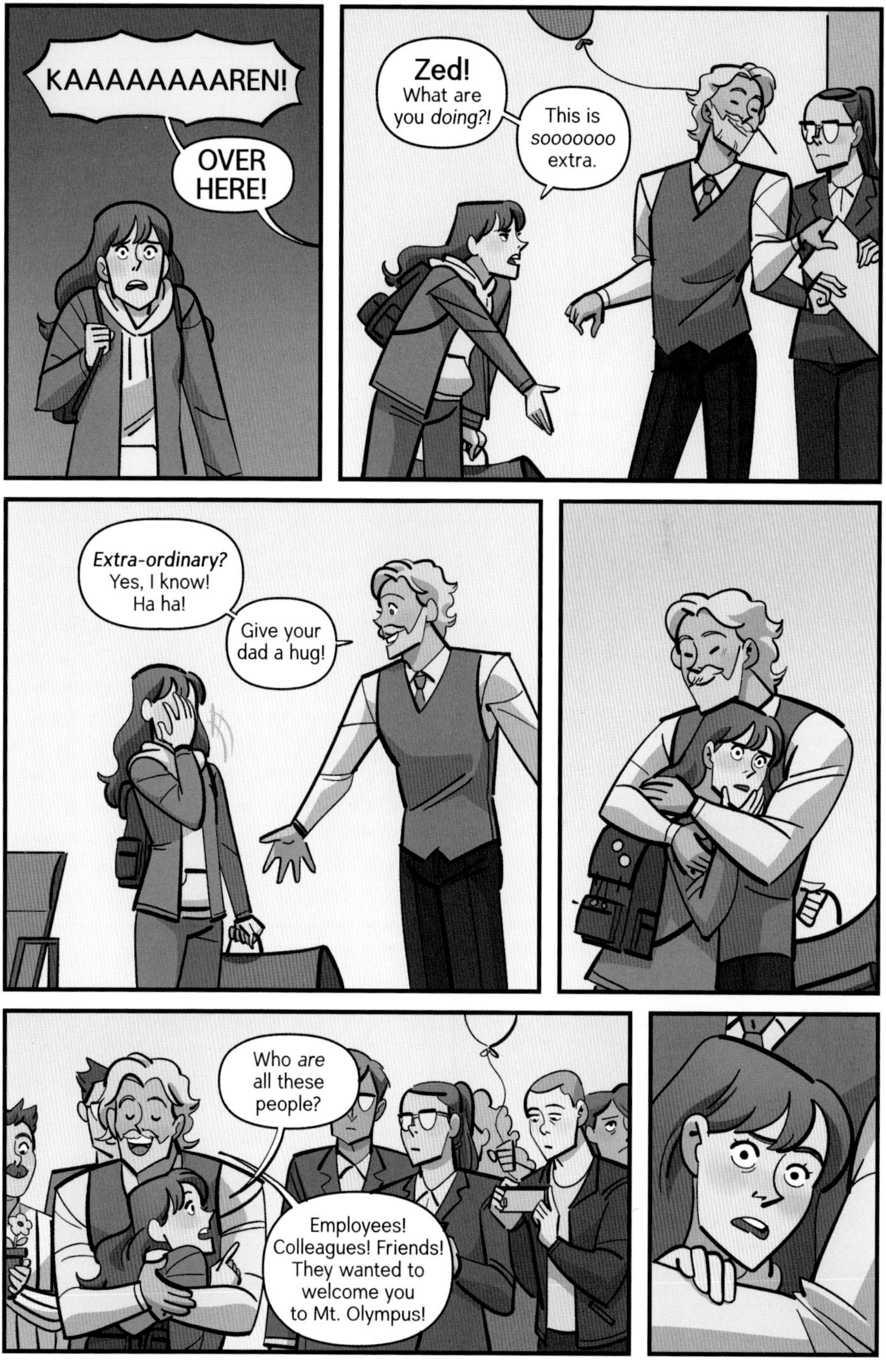
KAAAAAAAAREN!
OVER HERE!
Zed! What are you *doing?!*
This is *sooooooo* extra.
Extra-ordinary? Yes, I know! Ha ha!
Give your dad a hug!
Who *are* all these people?
Employees! Colleagues! Friends! They wanted to welcome you to Mt. Olympus!

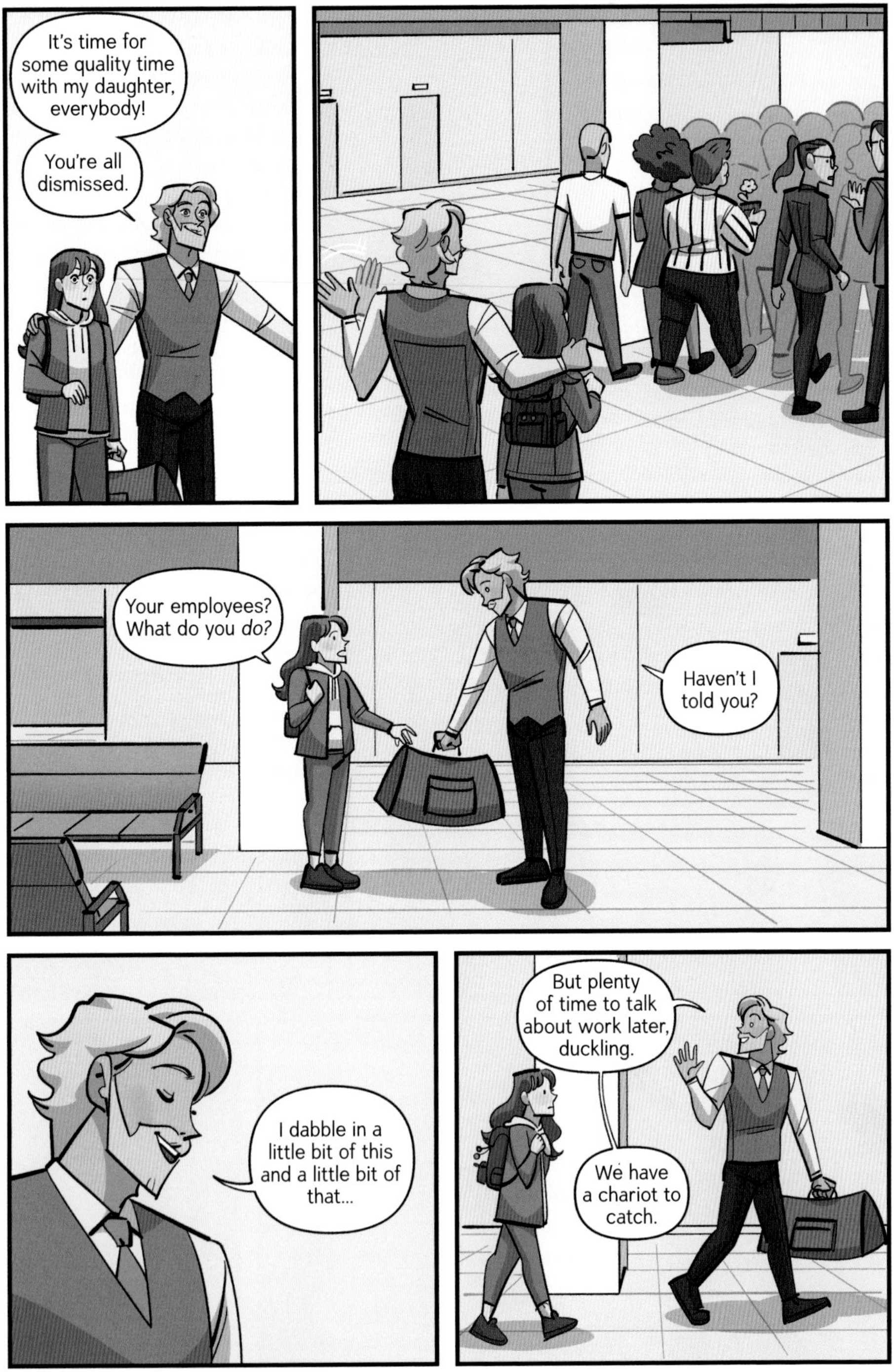
It's time for some quality time with my daughter, everybody!
You're all dismissed.
Your employees? What do you *do?*
Haven't I told you?
I dabble in a little bit of this and a little bit of that...
But plenty of time to talk about work later, duckling.
We have a chariot to catch.

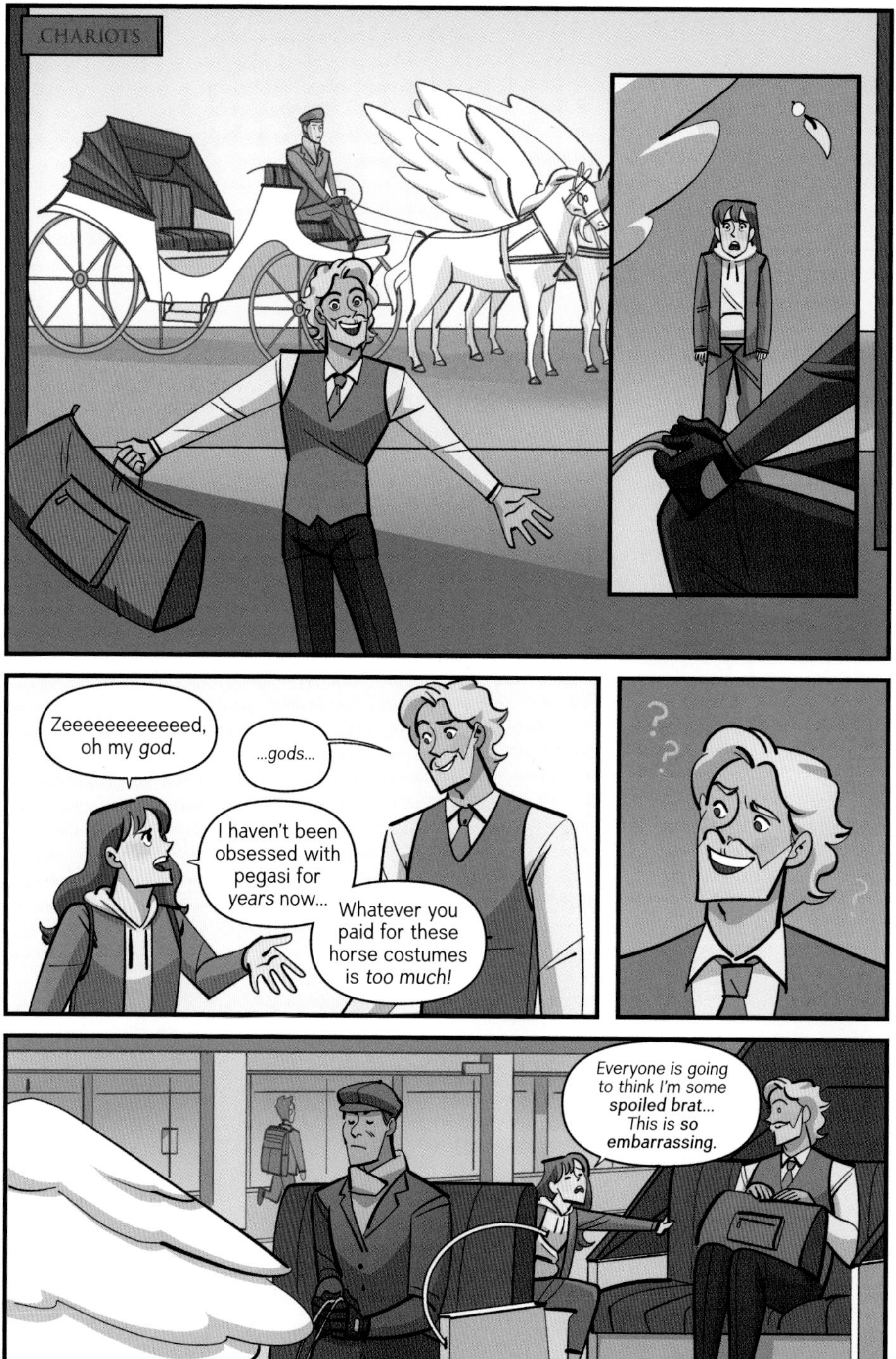
CHARIOTS
Zeeeeeeeeeeeed, oh my *god*.
...*gods*...
I haven't been obsessed with pegasi for *years* now...
Whatever you paid for these horse costumes is *too much!*
?
??
?
Everyone is going to think I'm some **spoiled brat...** *This is so* **embarrassing.**

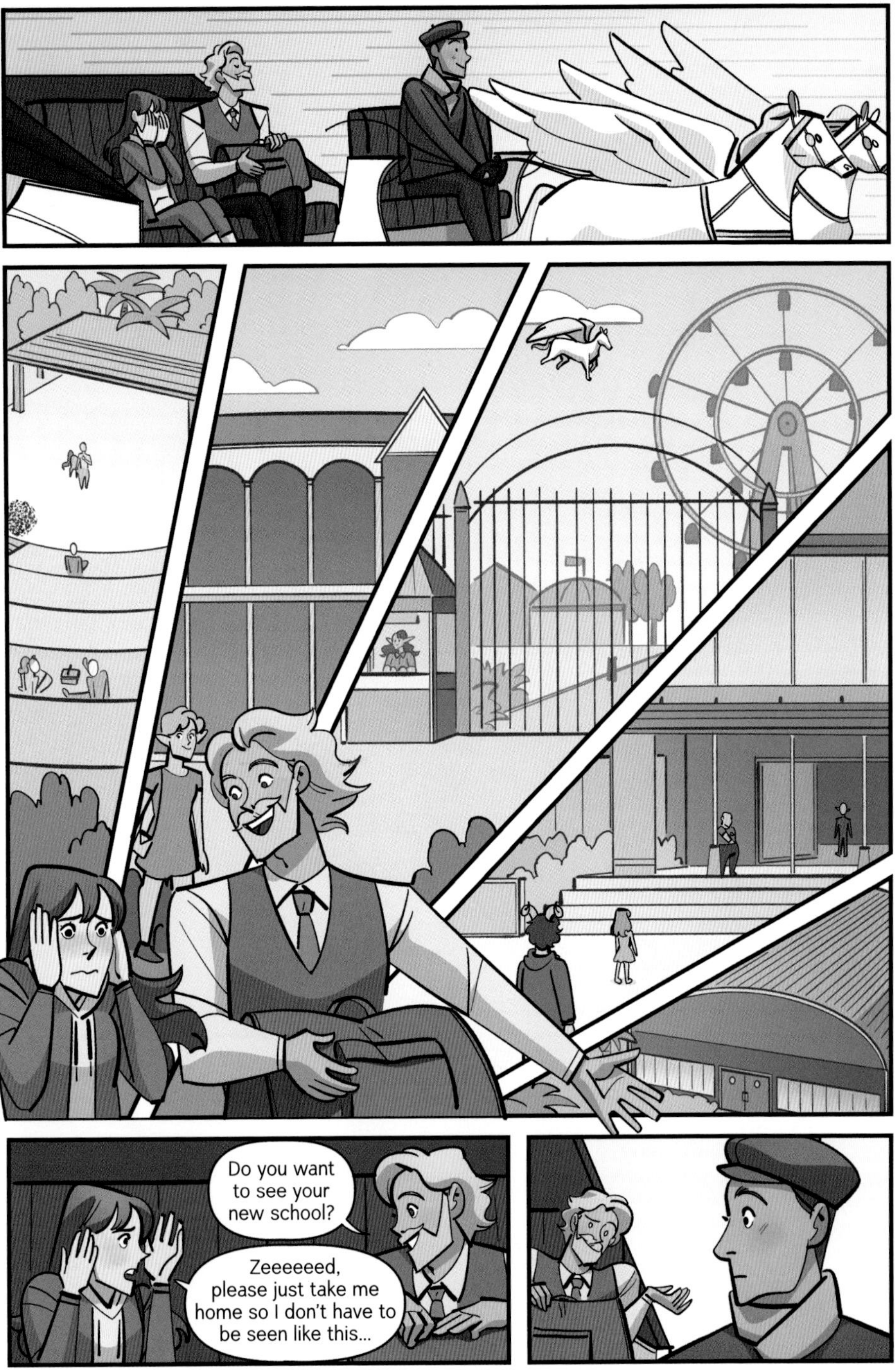
Do you want to see your new school?
Zeeeeeed, please just take me home so I don't have to be seen like this...

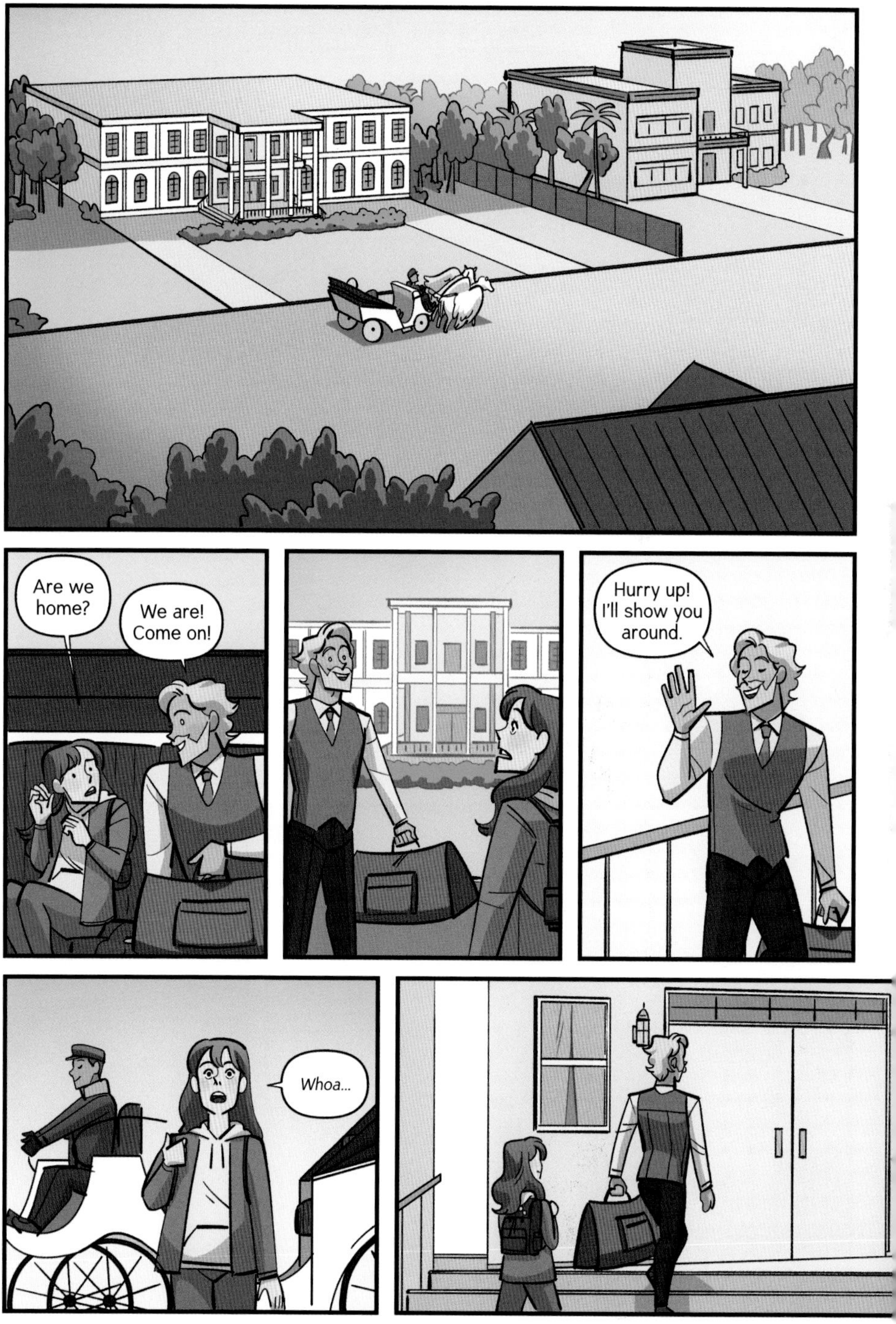
Are we home?
We are! Come on!
Hurry up! I'll show you around.
Whoa...

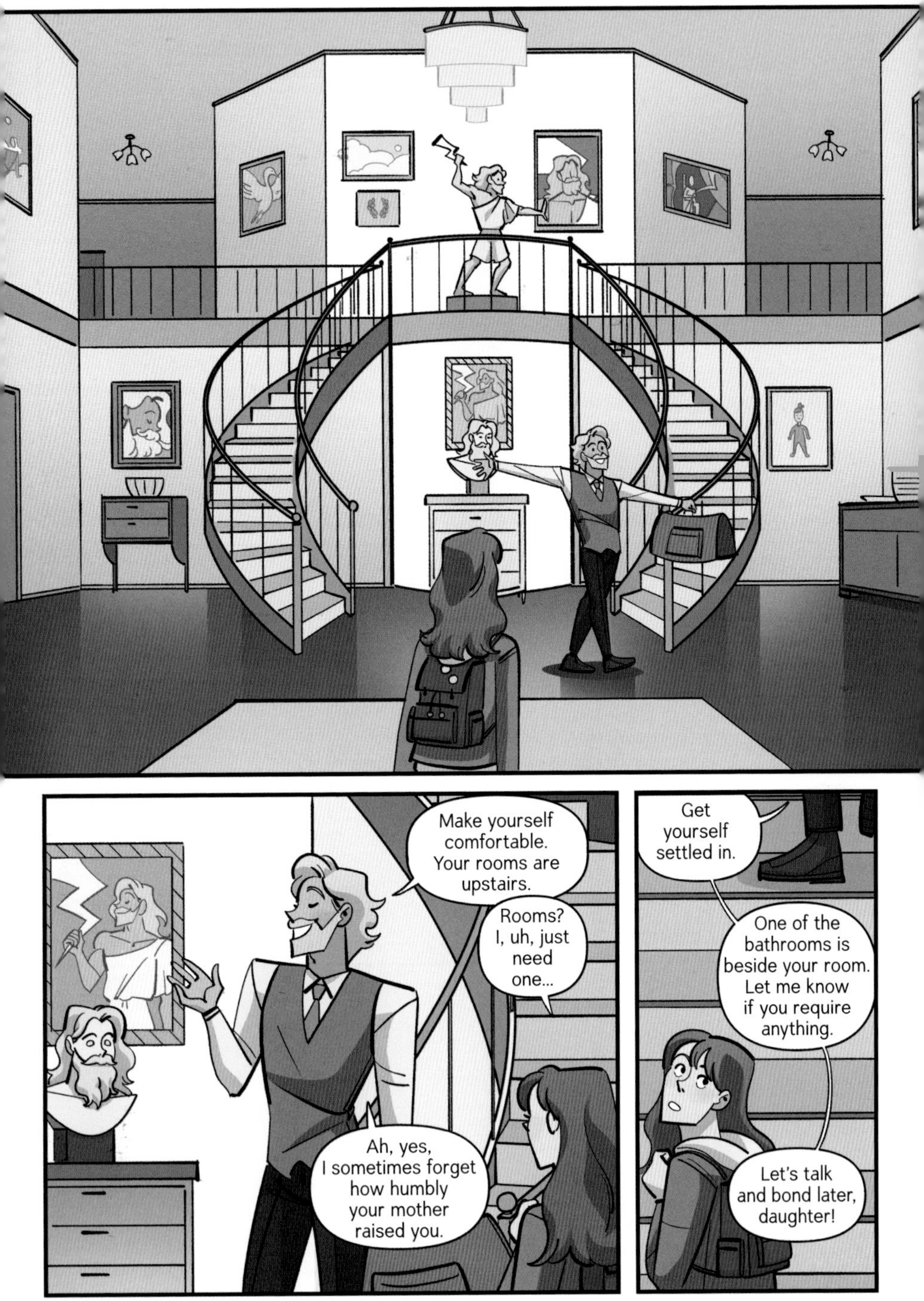
Make yourself comfortable. Your rooms are upstairs.
Rooms? I, uh, just need one...
Ah, yes, I sometimes forget how humbly your mother raised you.
Get yourself settled in.
One of the bathrooms is beside your room. Let me know if you require anything.
Let's talk and bond later, daughter!

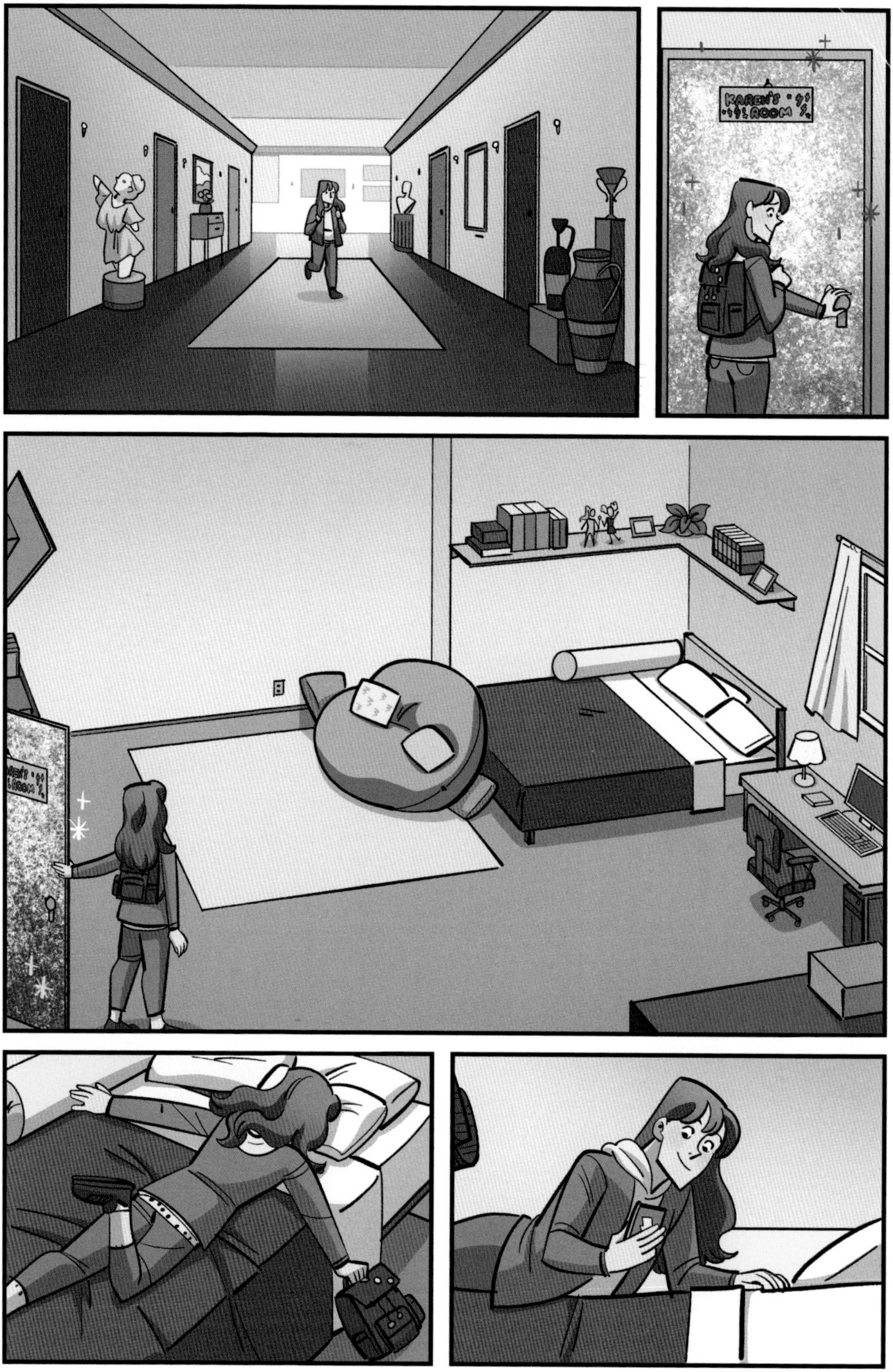
KAREN'S ROOM

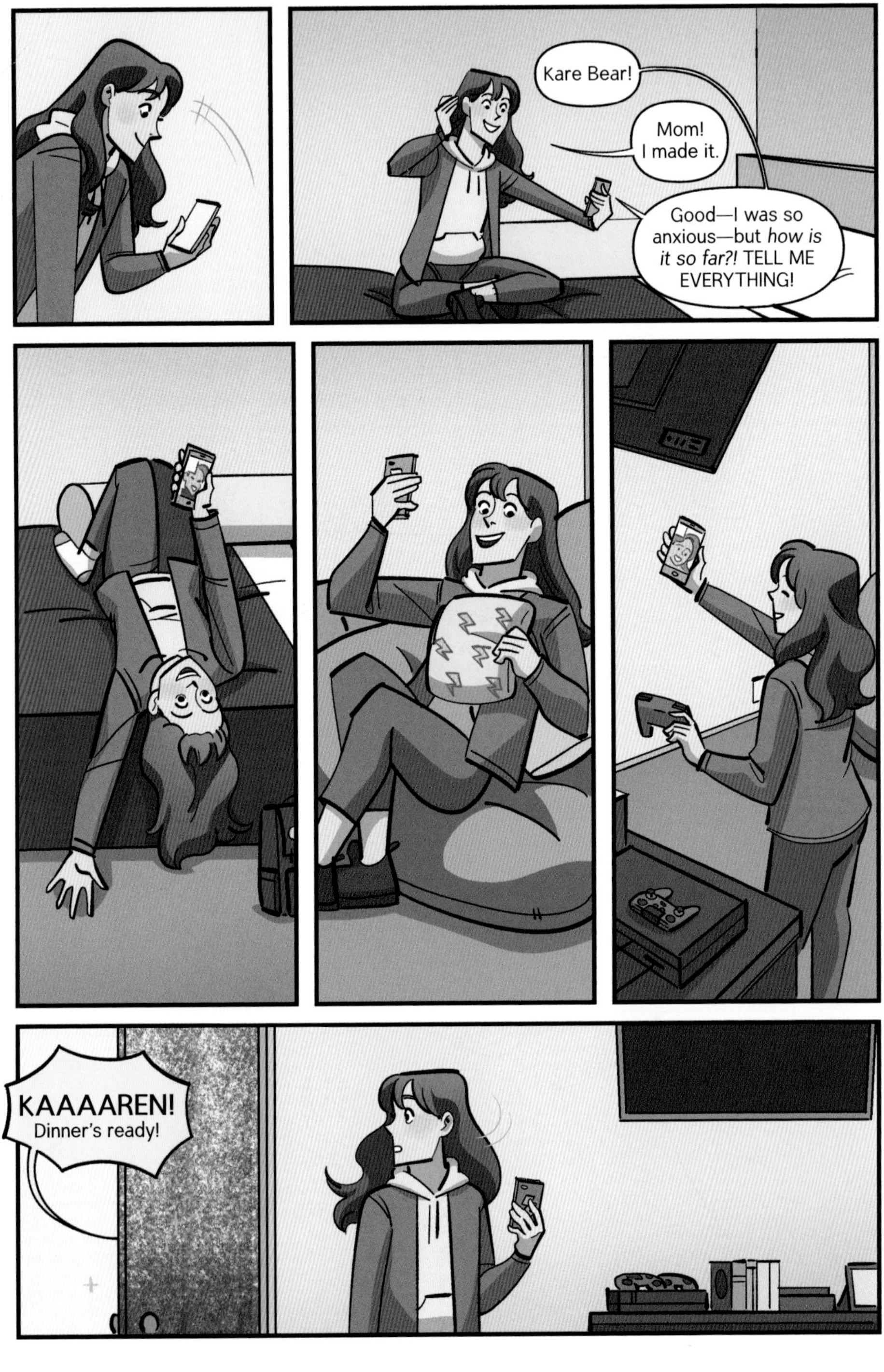
Kare Bear!
Mom! I made it.
Good—I was so anxious—but *how is it so far?!* TELL ME EVERYTHING!
KAAAAREN!
Dinner's ready!

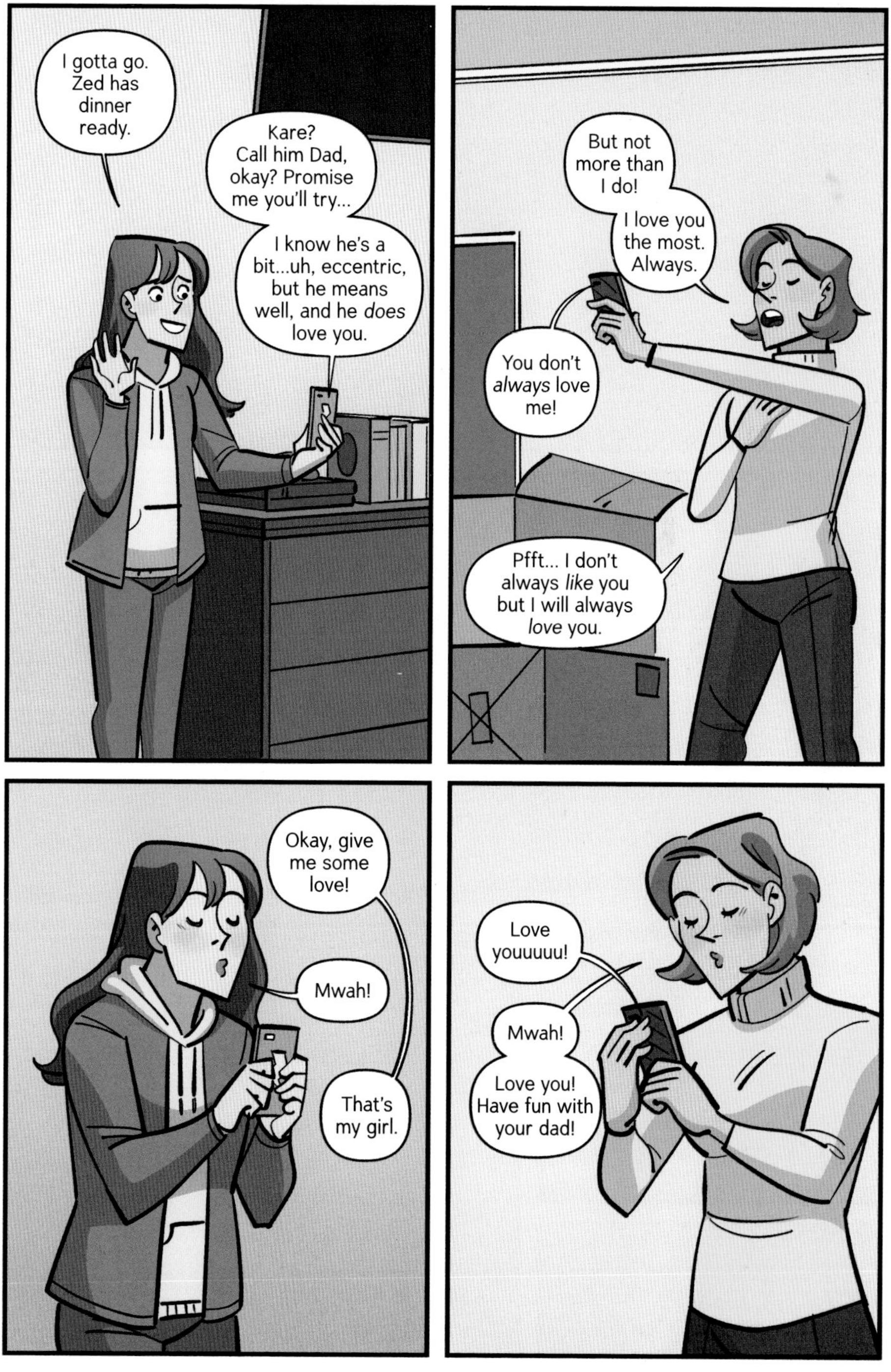
I gotta go. Zed has dinner ready.
Kare? Call him Dad, okay? Promise me you'll try...
I know he's a bit...uh, eccentric, but he means well, and he *does* love you.
But not more than I do!
I love you the most. Always.
You don't *always* love me!
Pfft... I don't always *like* you but I will always *love* you.
Okay, give me some love!
Mwah!
That's my girl.
Love youuuuu!
Mwah!
Love you! Have fun with your dad!

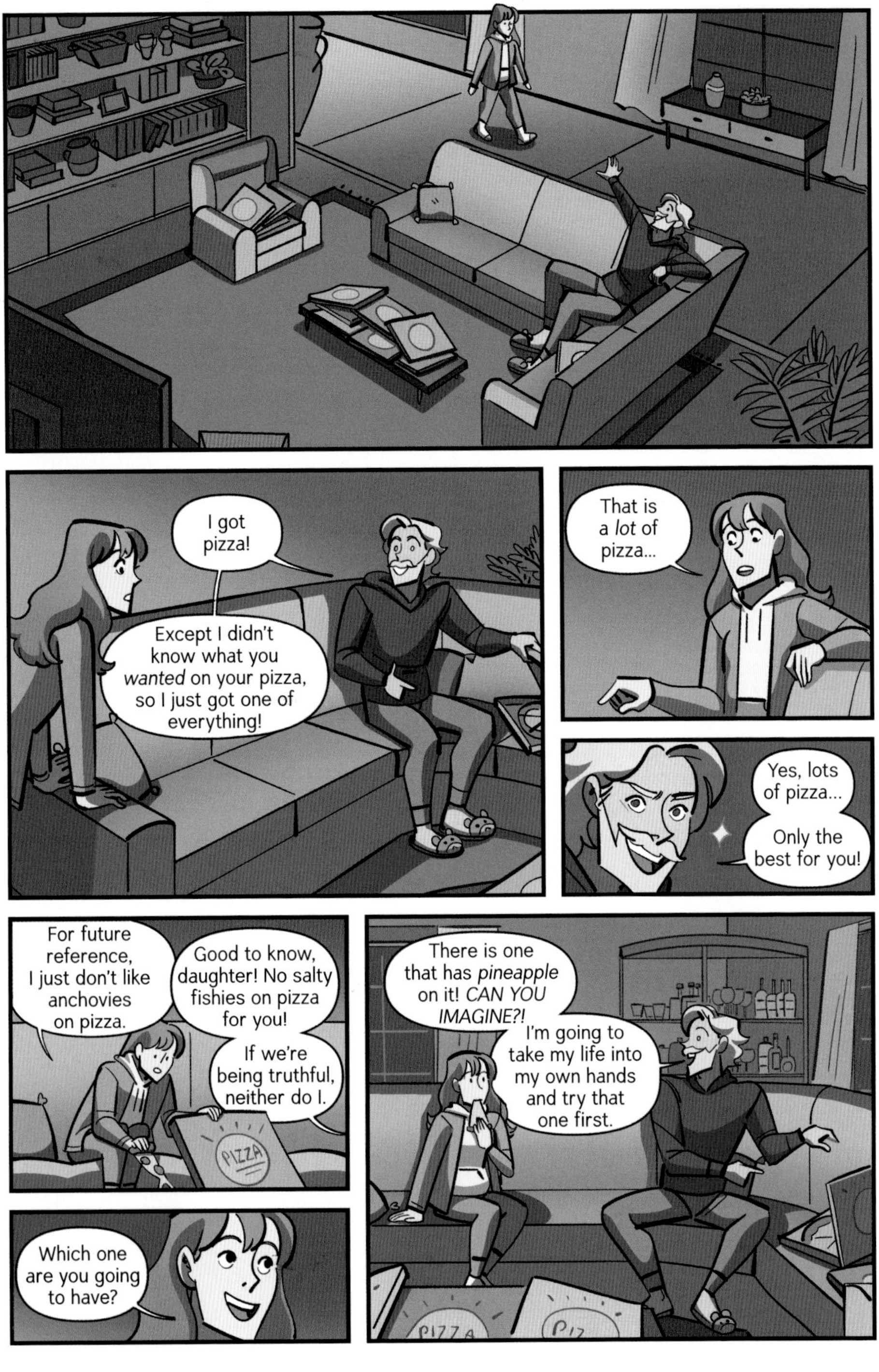

I got pizza!
Except I didn't know what you *wanted* on your pizza, so I just got one of everything!
That is a *lot* of pizza...
Yes, lots of pizza...
Only the best for you!
For future reference, I just don't like anchovies on pizza.
Good to know, daughter! No salty fishies on pizza for you!
If we're being truthful, neither do I.
PIZZA
Which one are you going to have?
There is one that has *pineapple* on it! *CAN YOU IMAGINE?!*
I'm going to take my life into my own hands and try that one first.

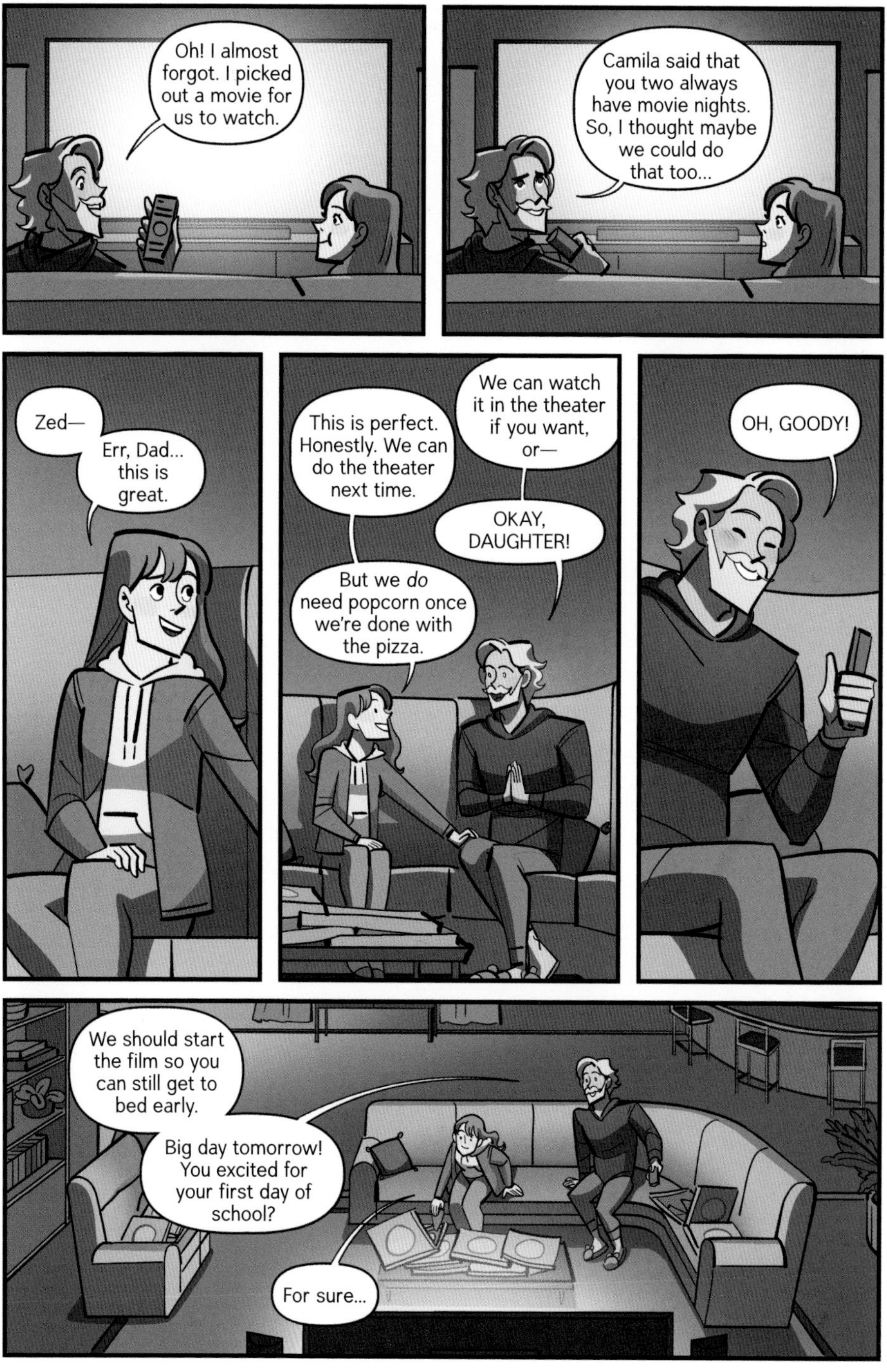
Oh! I almost forgot. I picked out a movie for us to watch.
Camila said that you two always have movie nights. So, I thought maybe we could do that too...
Zed—
Err, Dad... this is great.
This is perfect. Honestly. We can do the theater next time.
We can watch it in the theater if you want, or—
OKAY, DAUGHTER!
But we *do* need popcorn once we're done with the pizza.
OH, GOODY!
We should start the film so you can still get to bed early.
Big day tomorrow! You excited for your first day of school?
For sure...

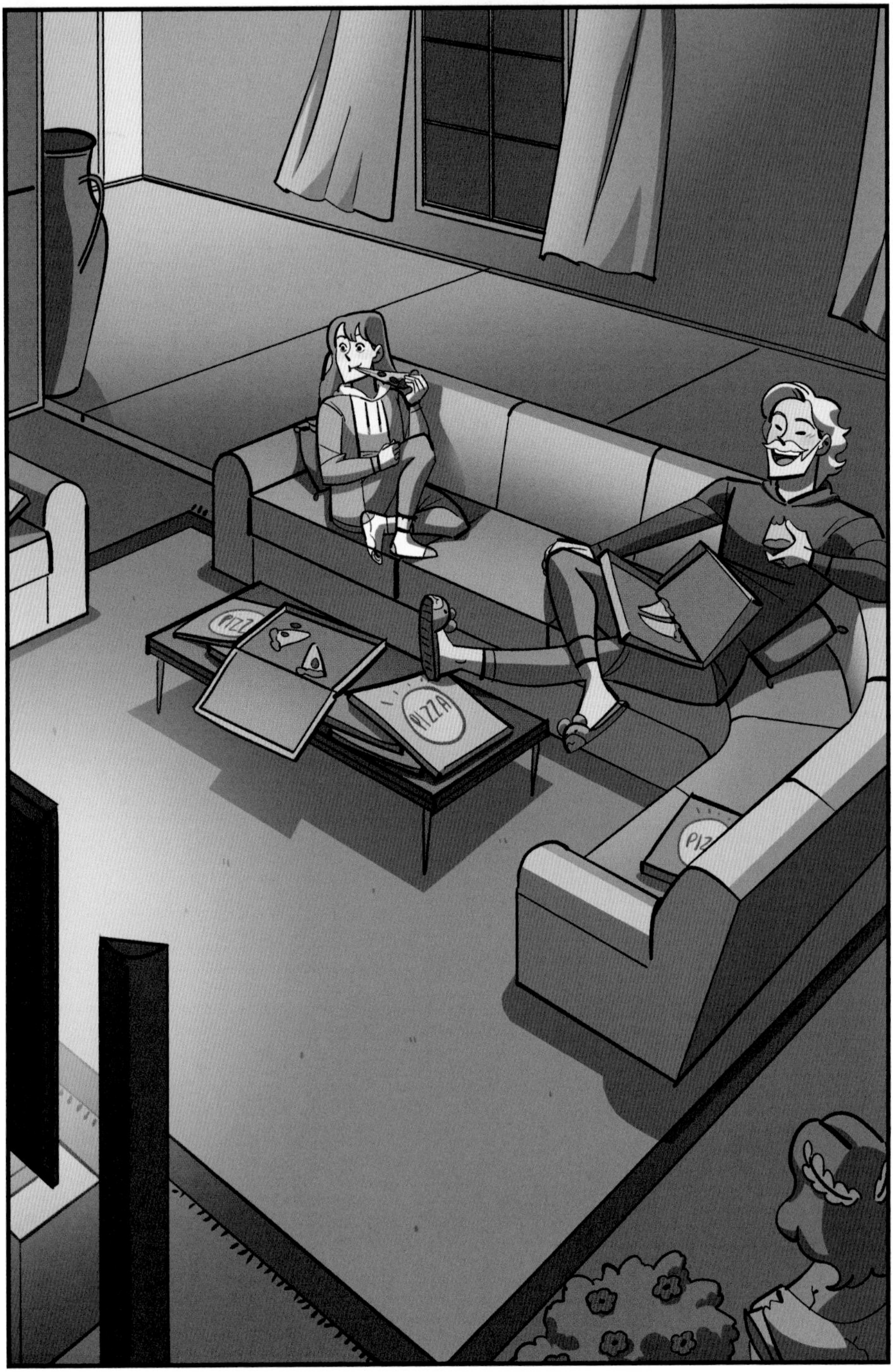
PIZZA

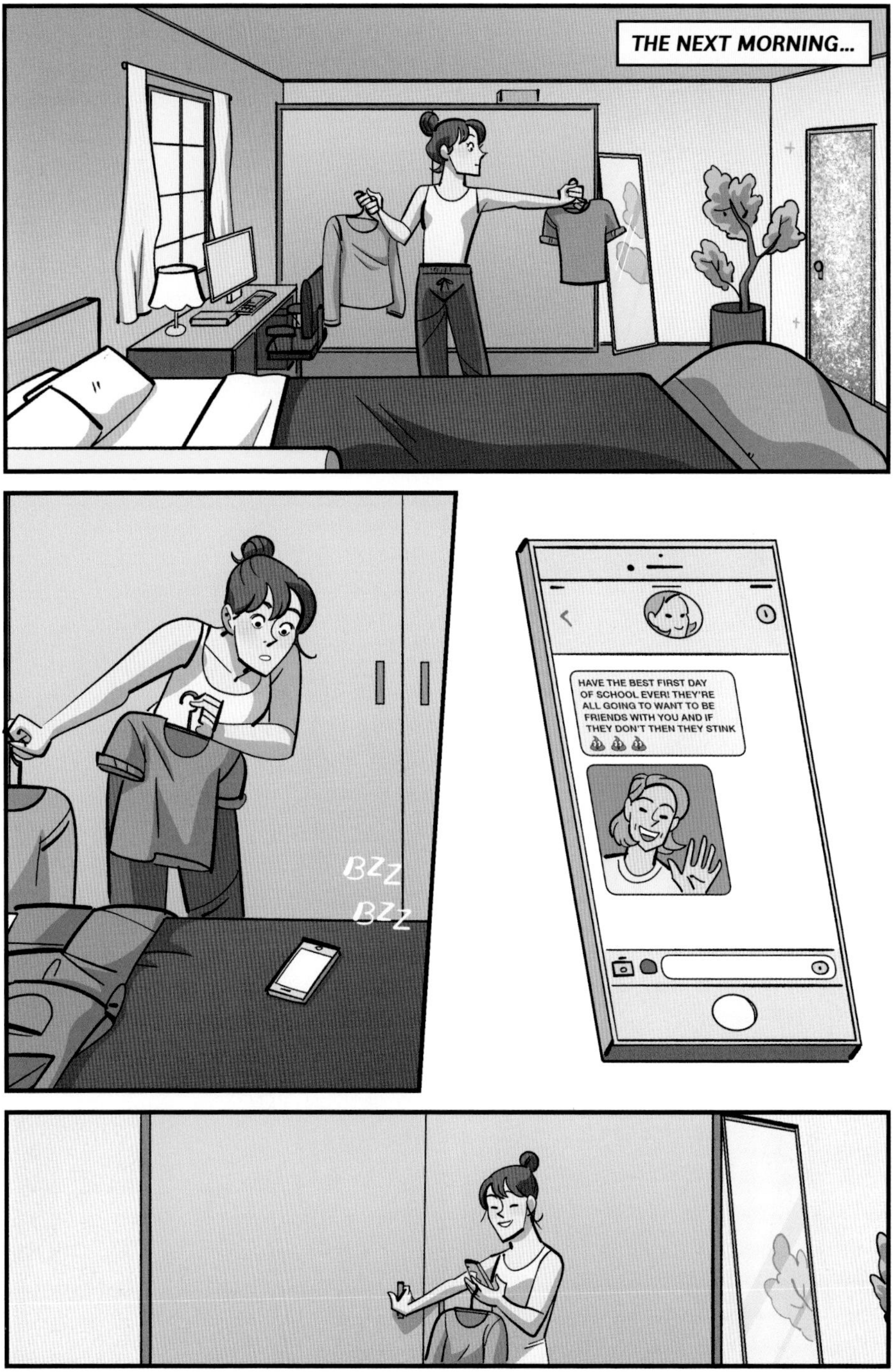
THE NEXT MORNING...
BZZ
BZZ
HAVE THE BEST FIRST DAY OF SCHOOL EVER! THEY'RE ALL GOING TO WANT TO BE FRIENDS WITH YOU AND IF THEY DON'T THEN THEY STINK

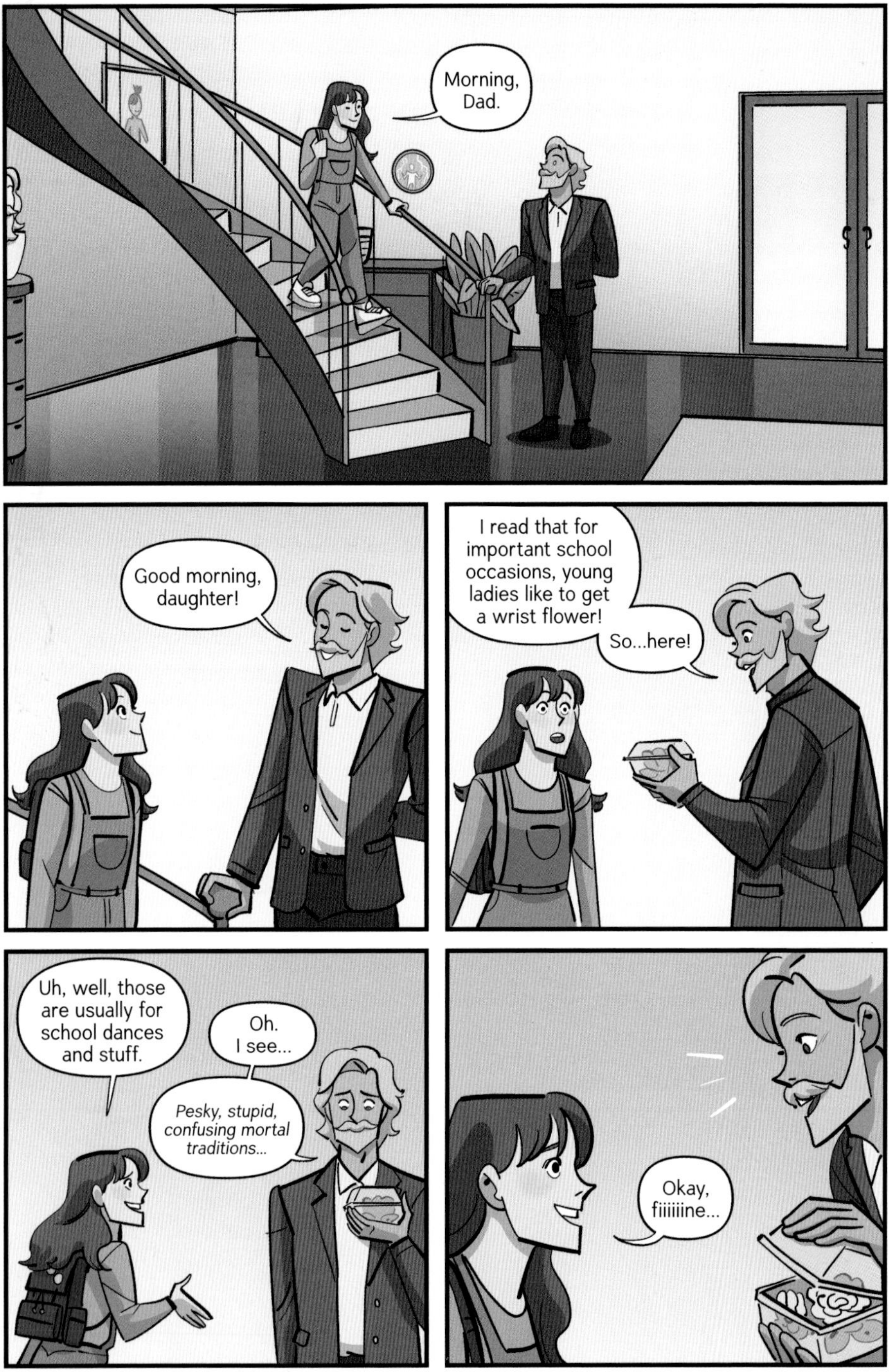
Morning, Dad.
Good morning, daughter!
I read that for important school occasions, young ladies like to get a wrist flower!
So...here!
Uh, well, those are usually for school dances and stuff.
Oh. I see...
Pesky, stupid, confusing mortal traditions...
Okay, fiiiiiine...

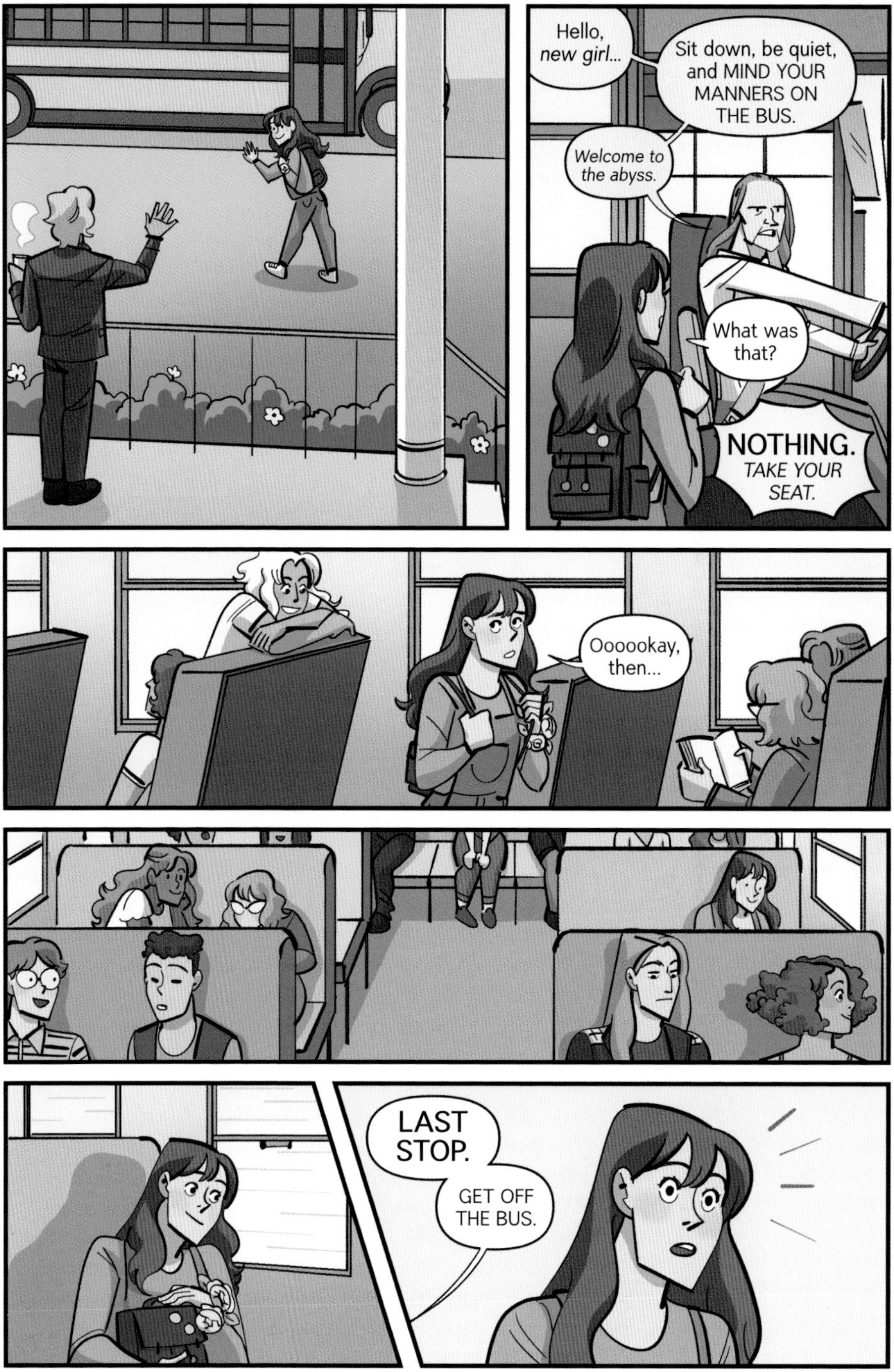
Hello, *new girl*...
Sit down, be quiet, and MIND YOUR MANNERS ON THE BUS.
Welcome to the abyss.
What was that?
NOTHING. *TAKE YOUR SEAT.*
Ooookay, then...
LAST STOP.
GET OFF THE BUS.

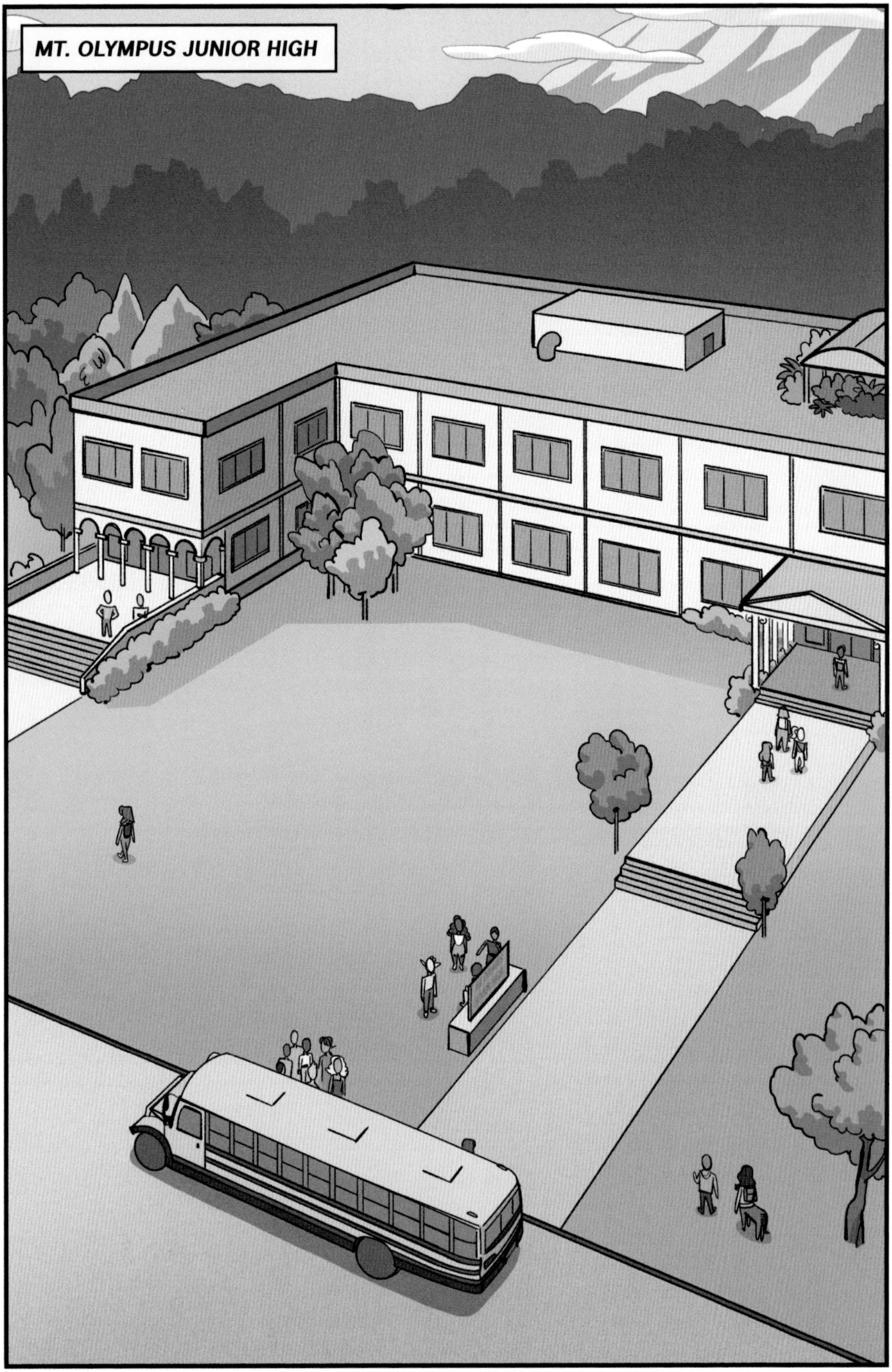
MT. OLYMPUS JUNIOR HIGH

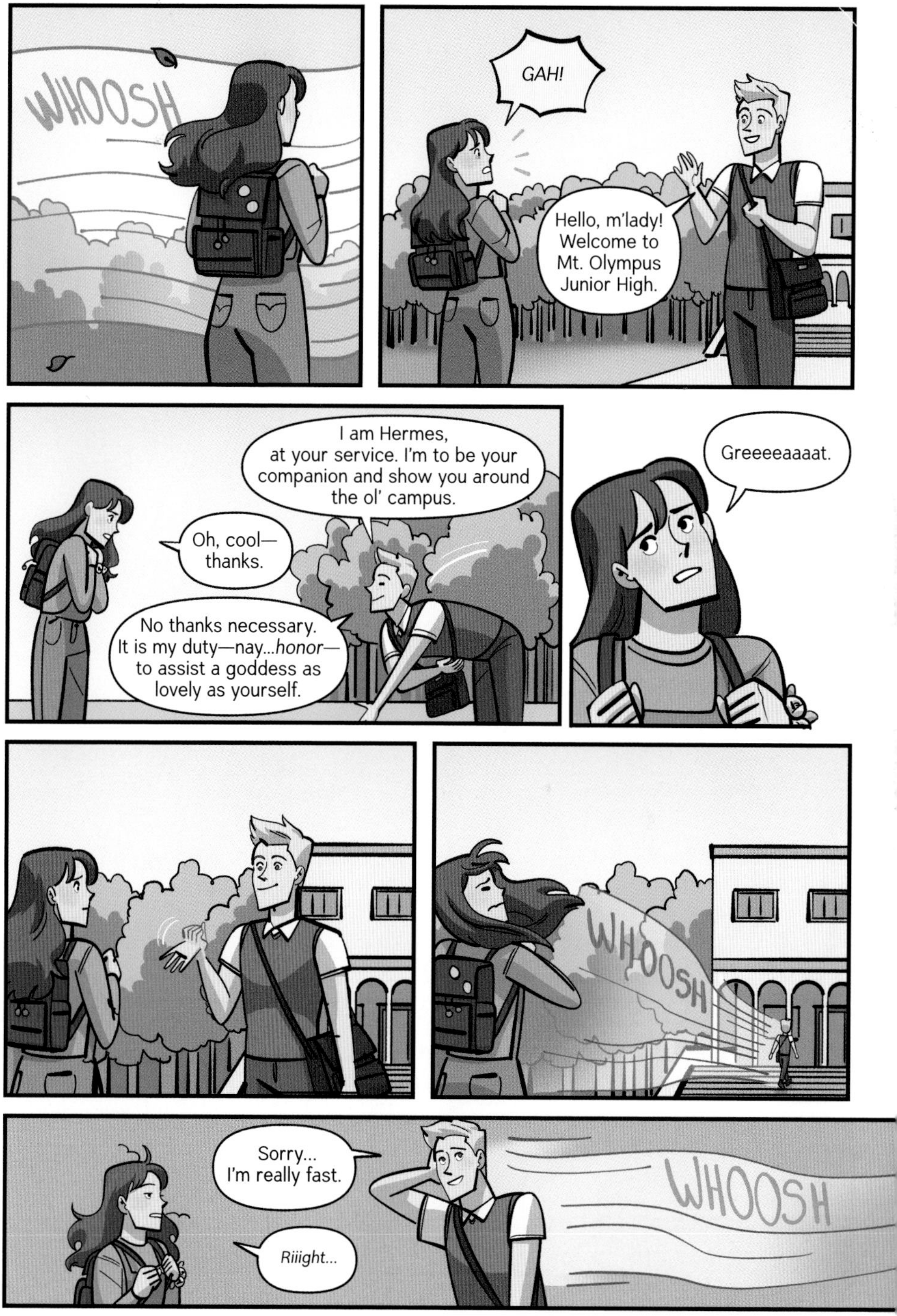
WHOOSH
GAH!
Hello, m'lady! Welcome to Mt. Olympus Junior High.
I am Hermes, at your service. I'm to be your companion and show you around the ol' campus.
Oh, cool— thanks.
No thanks necessary. It is my duty—nay...*honor*— to assist a goddess as lovely as yourself.
Greeeeaaaat.
WHOOSH
Sorry... I'm really fast.
Riiight...
WHOOSH

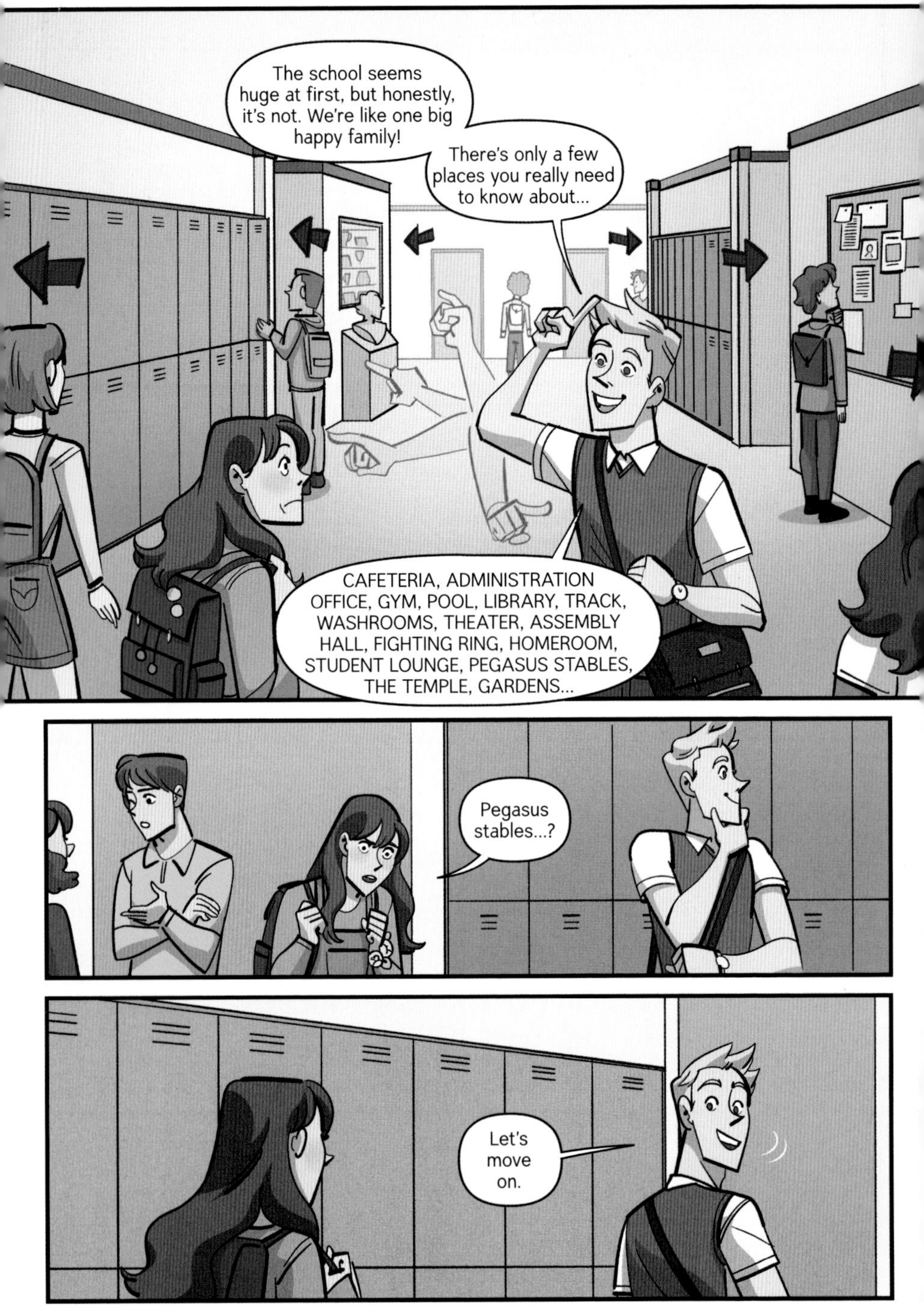
The school seems huge at first, but honestly, it's not. We're like one big happy family!
There's only a few places you really need to know about...
CAFETERIA, ADMINISTRATION OFFICE, GYM, POOL, LIBRARY, TRACK, WASHROOMS, THEATER, ASSEMBLY HALL, FIGHTING RING, HOMEROOM, STUDENT LOUNGE, PEGASUS STABLES, THE TEMPLE, GARDENS...
Pegasus stables...?
Let's move on.

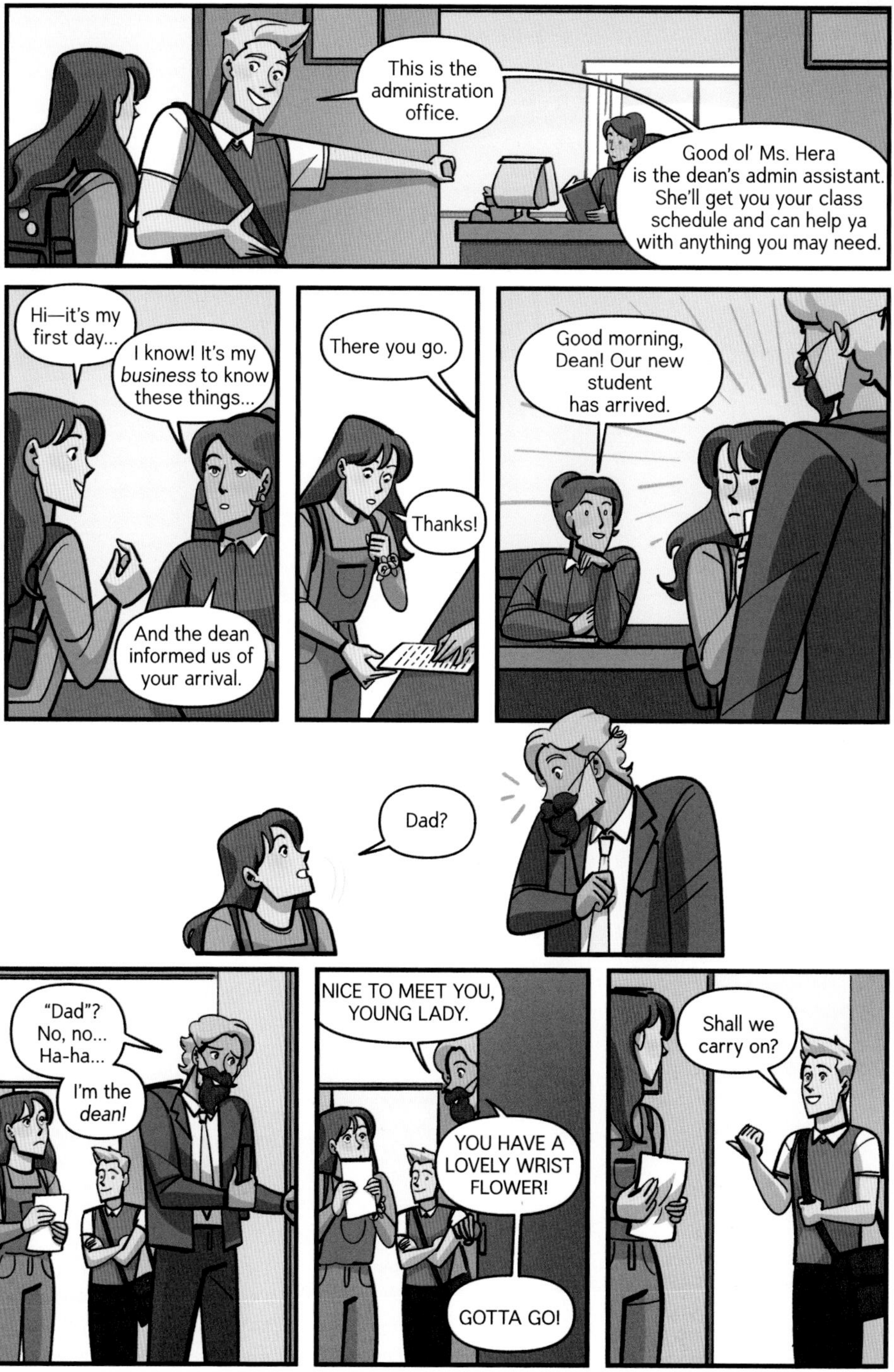
This is the administration office.
Good ol' Ms. Hera is the dean's admin assistant. She'll get you your class schedule and can help ya with anything you may need.
Hi—it's my first day...
I know! It's my *business* to know these things...
And the dean informed us of your arrival.
There you go.
Thanks!
Good morning, Dean! Our new student has arrived.
Dad?
"Dad"? No, no... Ha-ha...
I'm the *dean!*
NICE TO MEET YOU, YOUNG LADY.
YOU HAVE A LOVELY WRIST FLOWER!
GOTTA GO!
Shall we carry on?

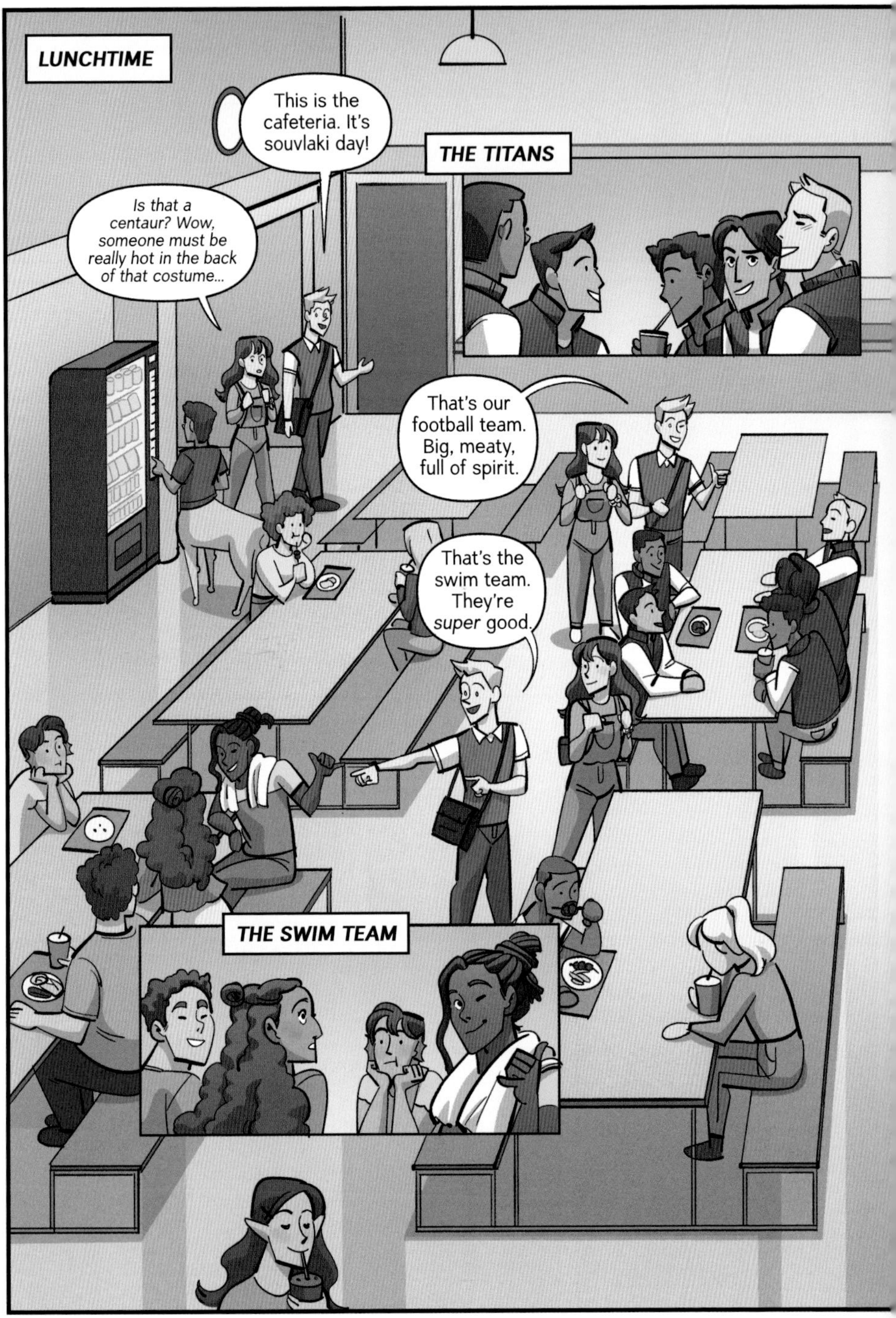
LUNCHTIME
This is the cafeteria. It's souvlaki day!
Is that a centaur? Wow, someone must be really hot in the back of that costume...
THE TITANS
That's our football team. Big, meaty, full of spirit.
That's the swim team. They're *super* good.
THE SWIM TEAM

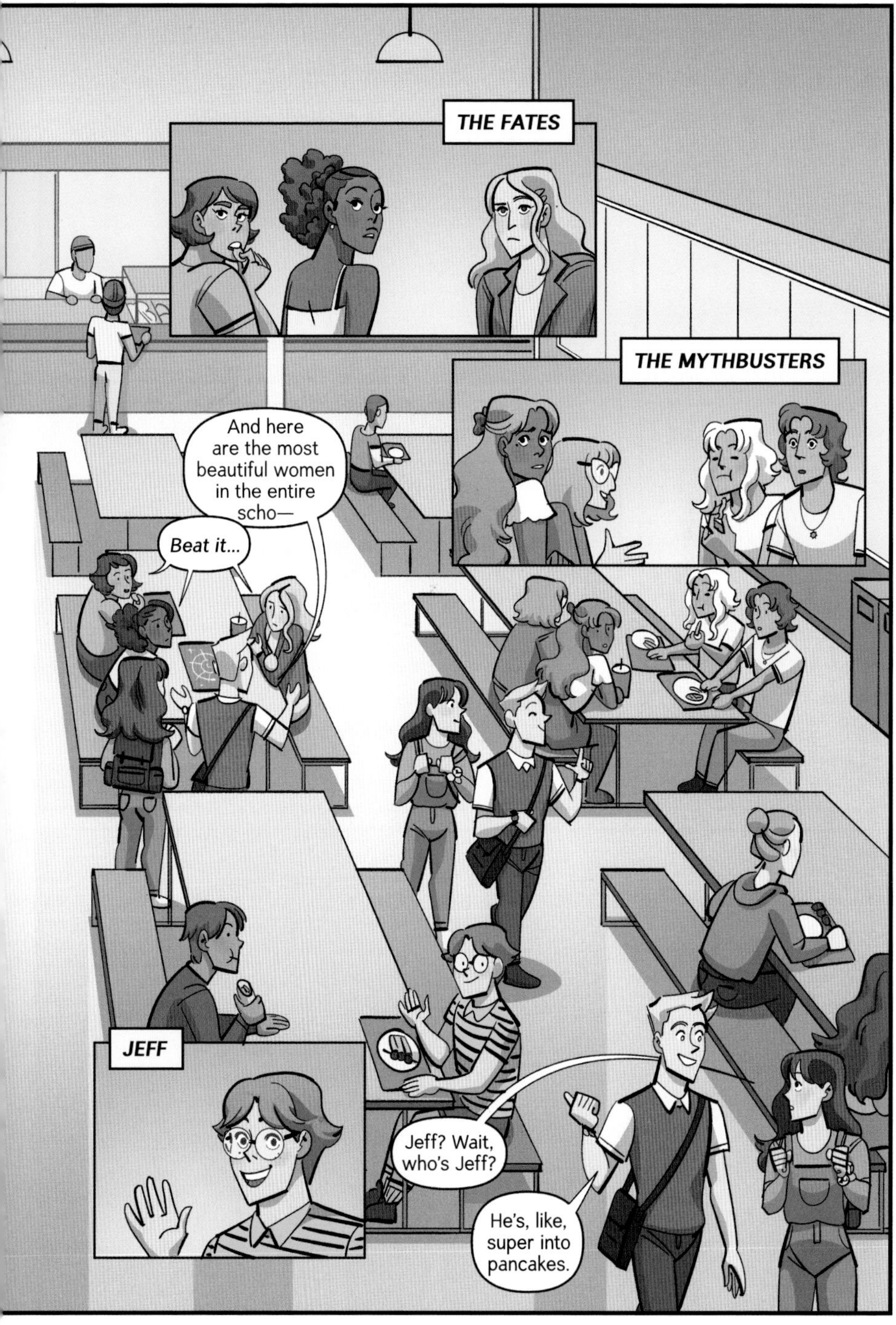
THE FATES
THE MYTHBUSTERS
And here are the most beautiful women in the entire scho—
Beat it...
JEFF
Jeff? Wait, who's Jeff?
He's, like, super into pancakes.

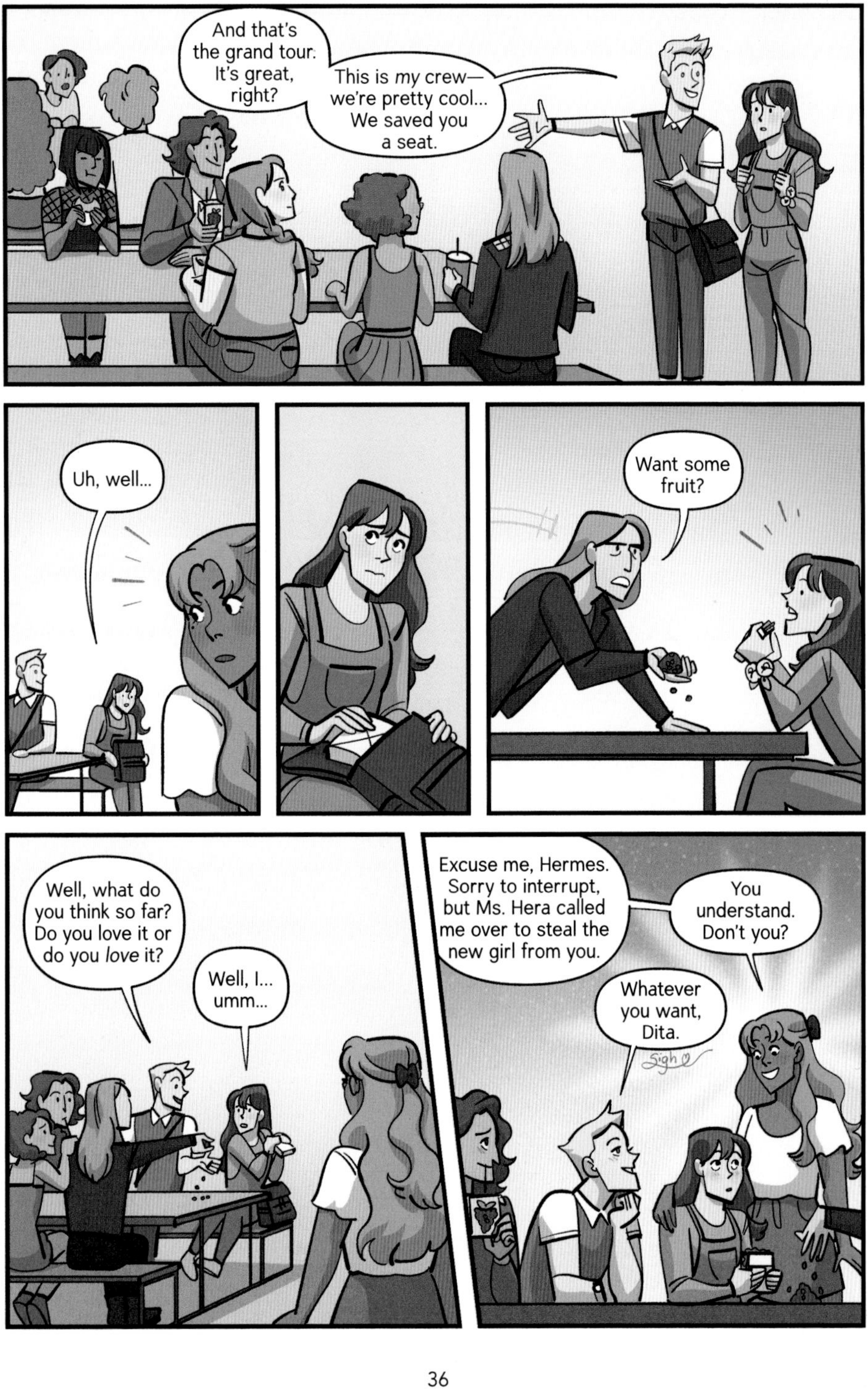
And that's the grand tour. It's great, right?
This is my crew— we're pretty cool... We saved you a seat.
Uh, well...
Want some fruit?
Well, what do you think so far? Do you love it or do you love it?
Well, I... umm...
Excuse me, Hermes. Sorry to interrupt, but Ms. Hera called me over to steal the new girl from you.
You understand. Don't you?
Whatever you want, Dita.
Sigh

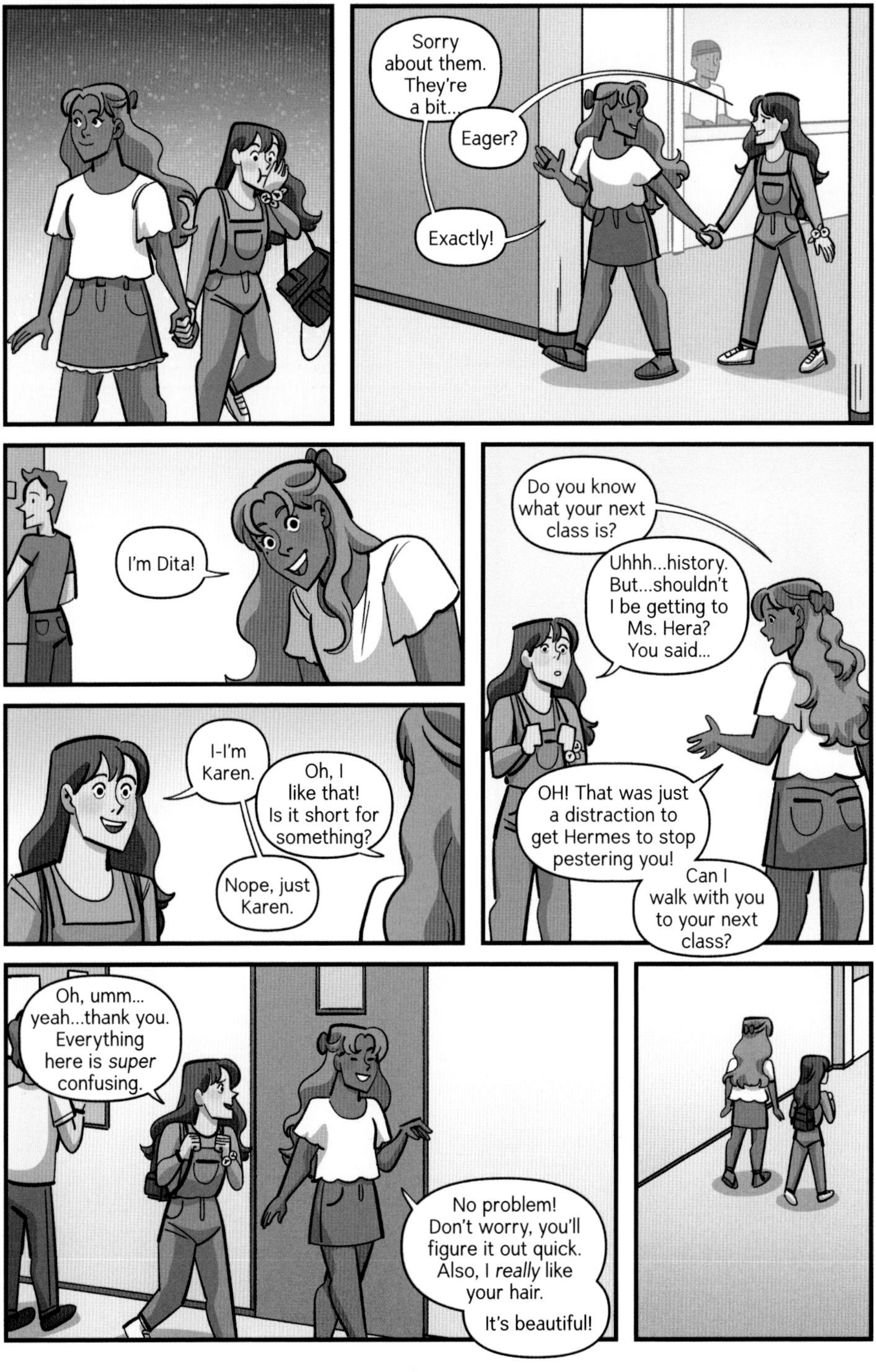
Sorry about them. They're a bit...
Eager?
Exactly!
I'm Dita!
Do you know what your next class is?
Uhhh...history. But...shouldn't I be getting to Ms. Hera? You said...
OH! That was just a distraction to get Hermes to stop pestering you!
Can I walk with you to your next class?
I-I'm Karen.
Oh, I like that! Is it short for something?
Nope, just Karen.
Oh, umm... yeah...thank you. Everything here is *super* confusing.
No problem! Don't worry, you'll figure it out quick. Also, I *really* like your hair.
It's beautiful!

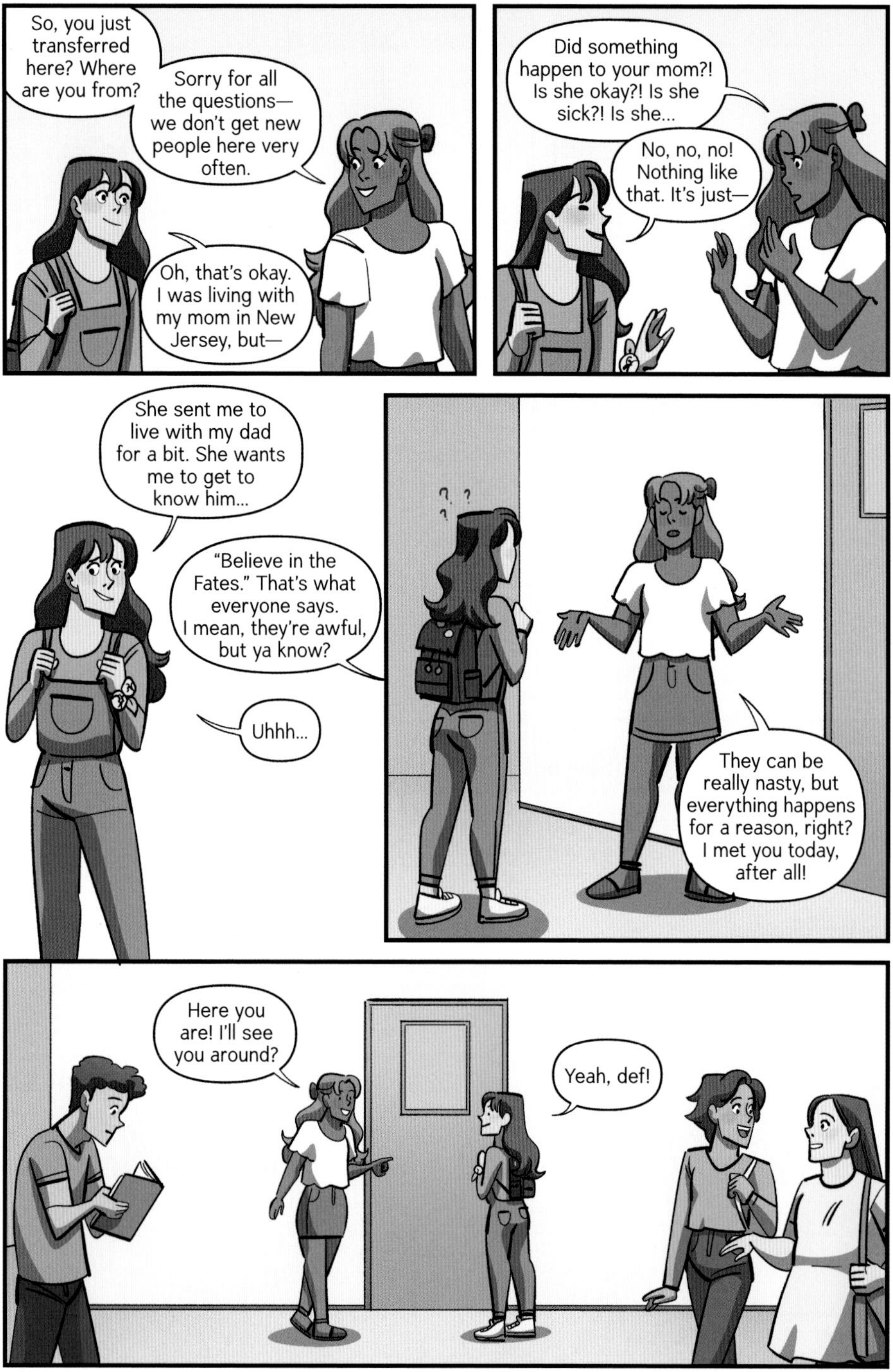

So, you just transferred here? Where are you from?
Sorry for all the questions—we don't get new people here very often.
Oh, that's okay. I was living with my mom in New Jersey, but—
Did something happen to your mom?! Is she okay?! Is she sick?! Is she...
No, no, no! Nothing like that. It's just—
She sent me to live with my dad for a bit. She wants me to get to know him...
"Believe in the Fates." That's what everyone says. I mean, they're awful, but ya know?
Uhhh...
They can be really nasty, but everything happens for a reason, right? I met you today, after all!
Here you are! I'll see you around?
Yeah, def!

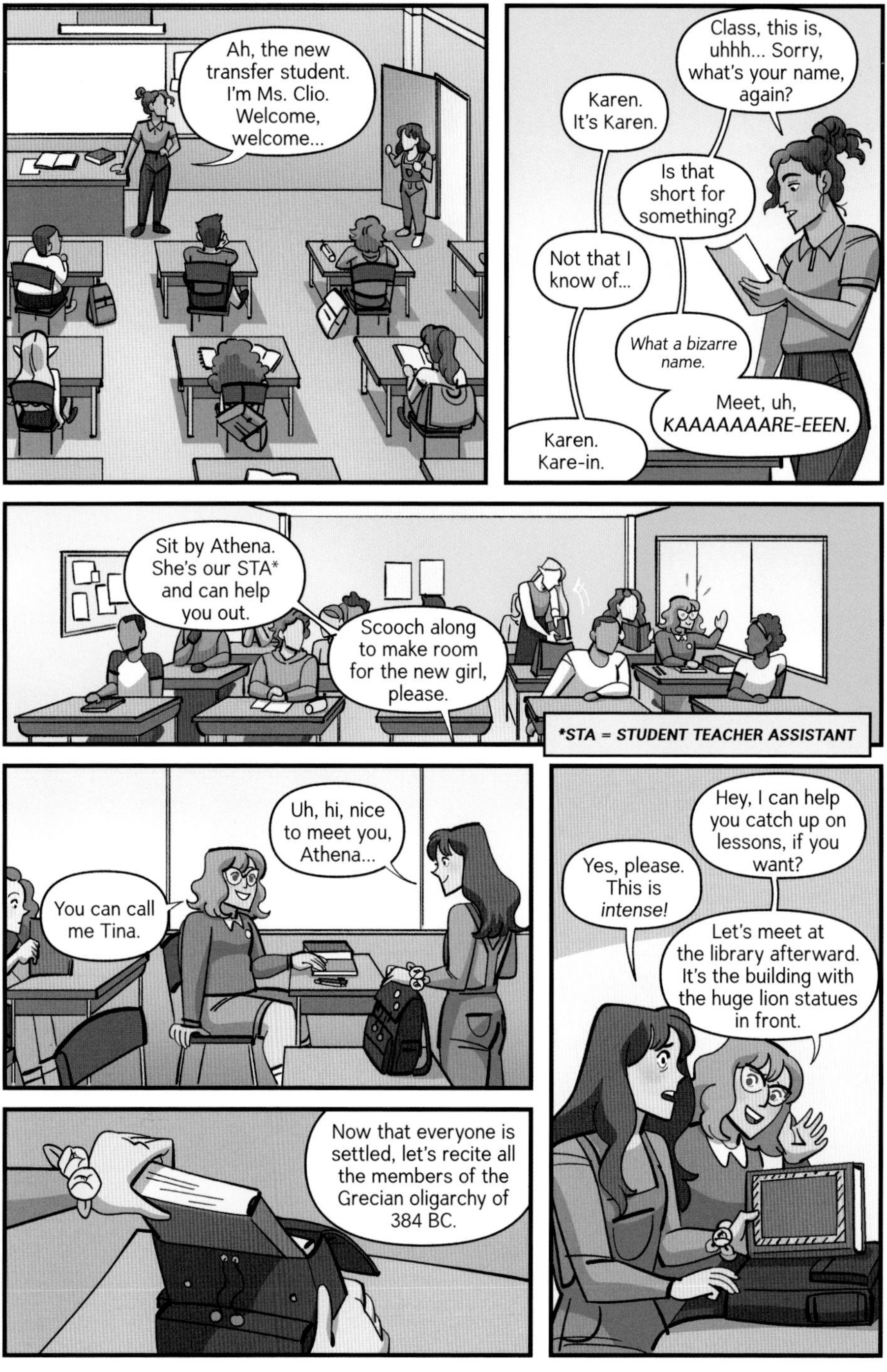
Ah, the new transfer student. I'm Ms. Clio. Welcome, welcome...
Class, this is, uhhh... Sorry, what's your name, again?
Karen. It's Karen.
Is that short for something?
Not that I know of...
What a bizarre name.
Meet, uh, *KAAAAAAARE-EEEN.*
Karen. Kare-in.
Sit by Athena. She's our STA* and can help you out.
Scooch along to make room for the new girl, please.
*STA = STUDENT TEACHER ASSISTANT
Uh, hi, nice to meet you, Athena...
You can call me Tina.
Hey, I can help you catch up on lessons, if you want?
Yes, please. This is *intense!*
Let's meet at the library afterward. It's the building with the huge lion statues in front.
Now that everyone is settled, let's recite all the members of the Grecian oligarchy of 384 BC.

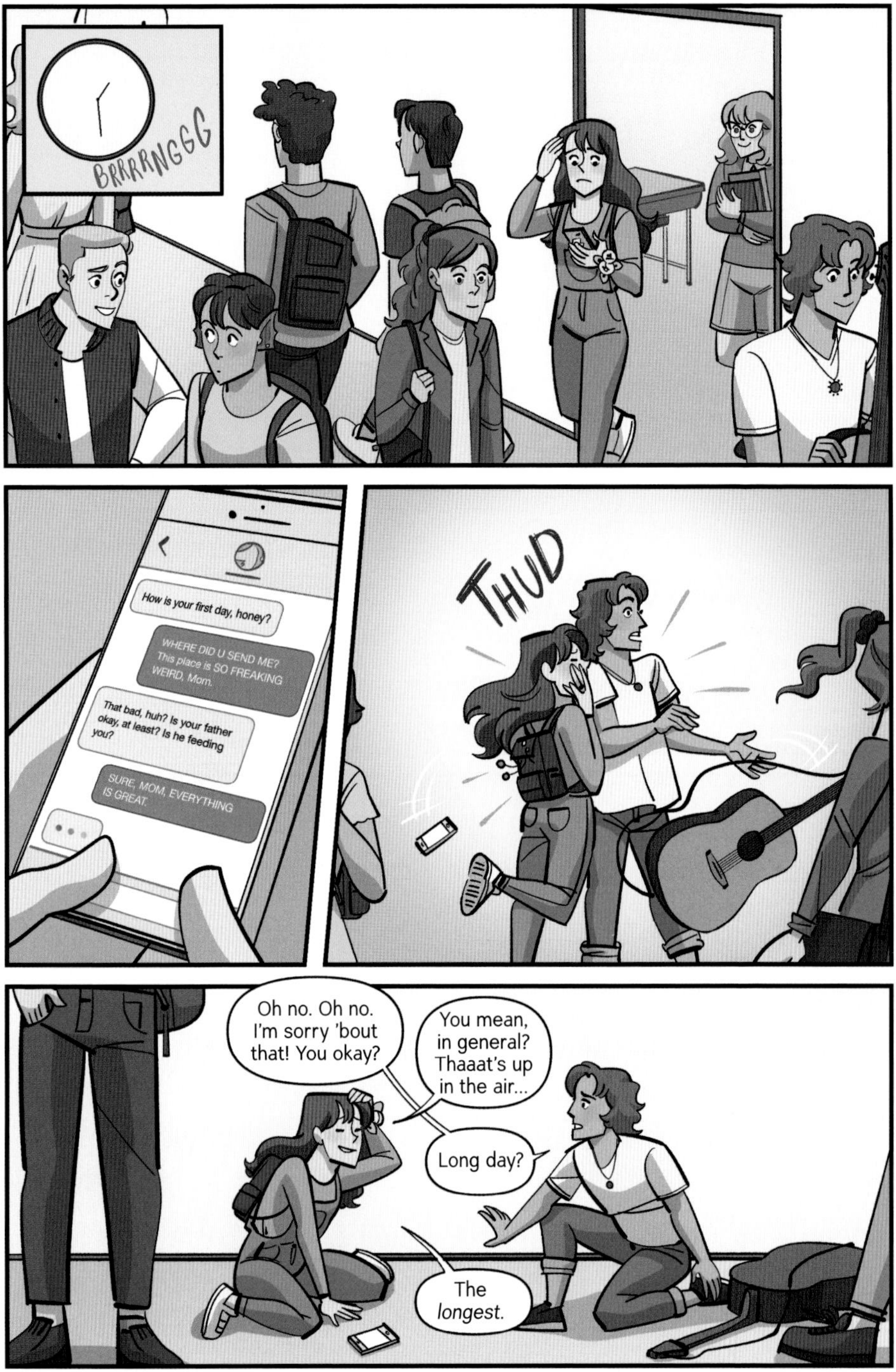
BRRRRNGGG
How is your first day, honey?
WHERE DID U SEND ME? This place is SO FREAKING WEIRD, Mom.
That bad, huh? Is your father okay, at least? Is he feeding you?
SURE, MOM, EVERYTHING IS GREAT.
THUD
Oh no. Oh no. I'm sorry 'bout that! You okay?
You mean, in general? Thaaat's up in the air...
Long day?
The *longest*.

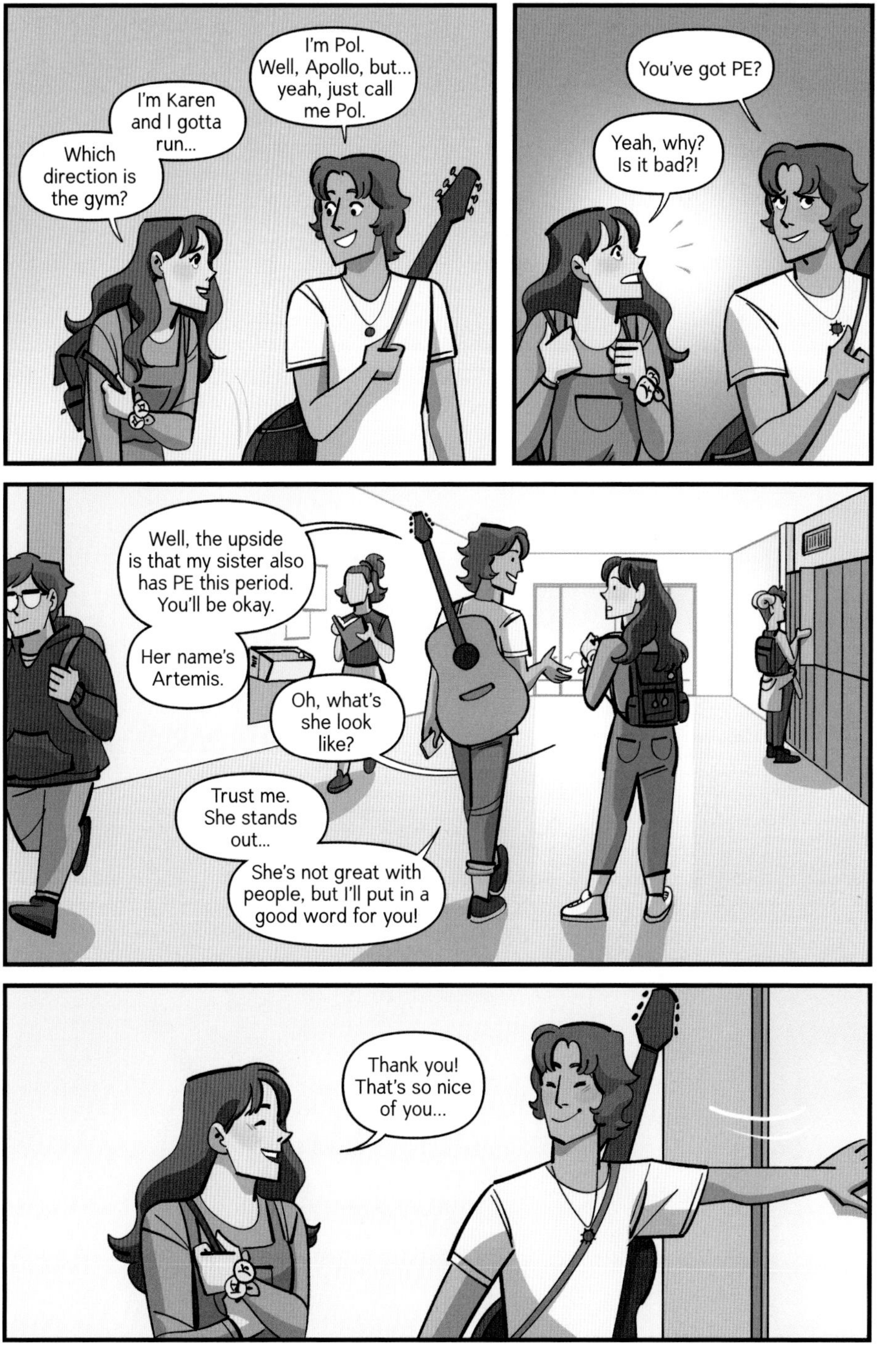
I'm Karen and I gotta run...
Which direction is the gym?
I'm Pol. Well, Apollo, but... yeah, just call me Pol.
You've got PE?
Yeah, why? Is it bad?!
Well, the upside is that my sister also has PE this period. You'll be okay.
Her name's Artemis.
Oh, what's she look like?
Trust me. She stands out...
She's not great with people, but I'll put in a good word for you!
Thank you! That's so nice of you...

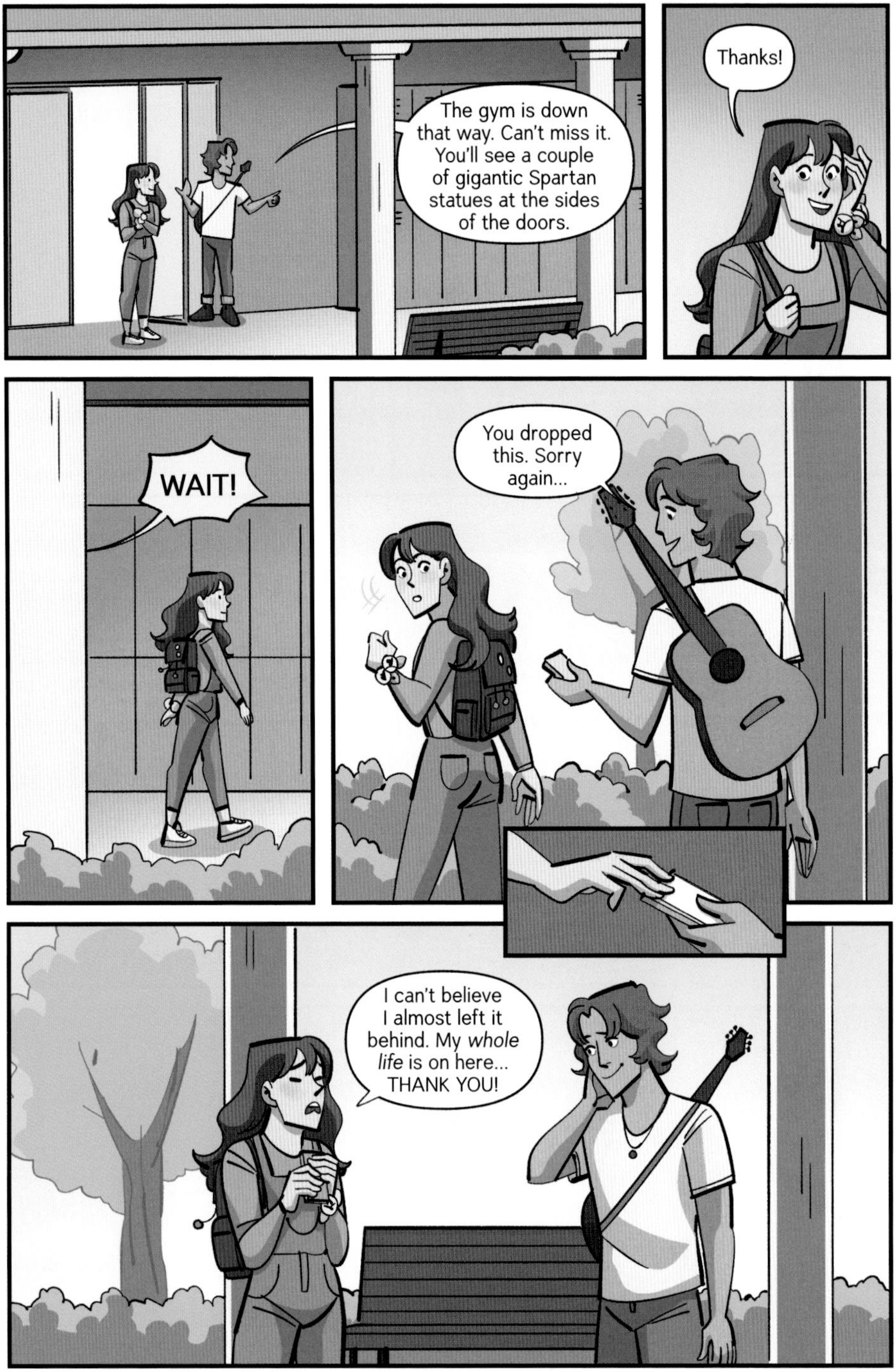
The gym is down that way. Can't miss it. You'll see a couple of gigantic Spartan statues at the sides of the doors.
Thanks!
WAIT!
You dropped this. Sorry again...
I can't believe I almost left it behind. My *whole life* is on here... THANK YOU!

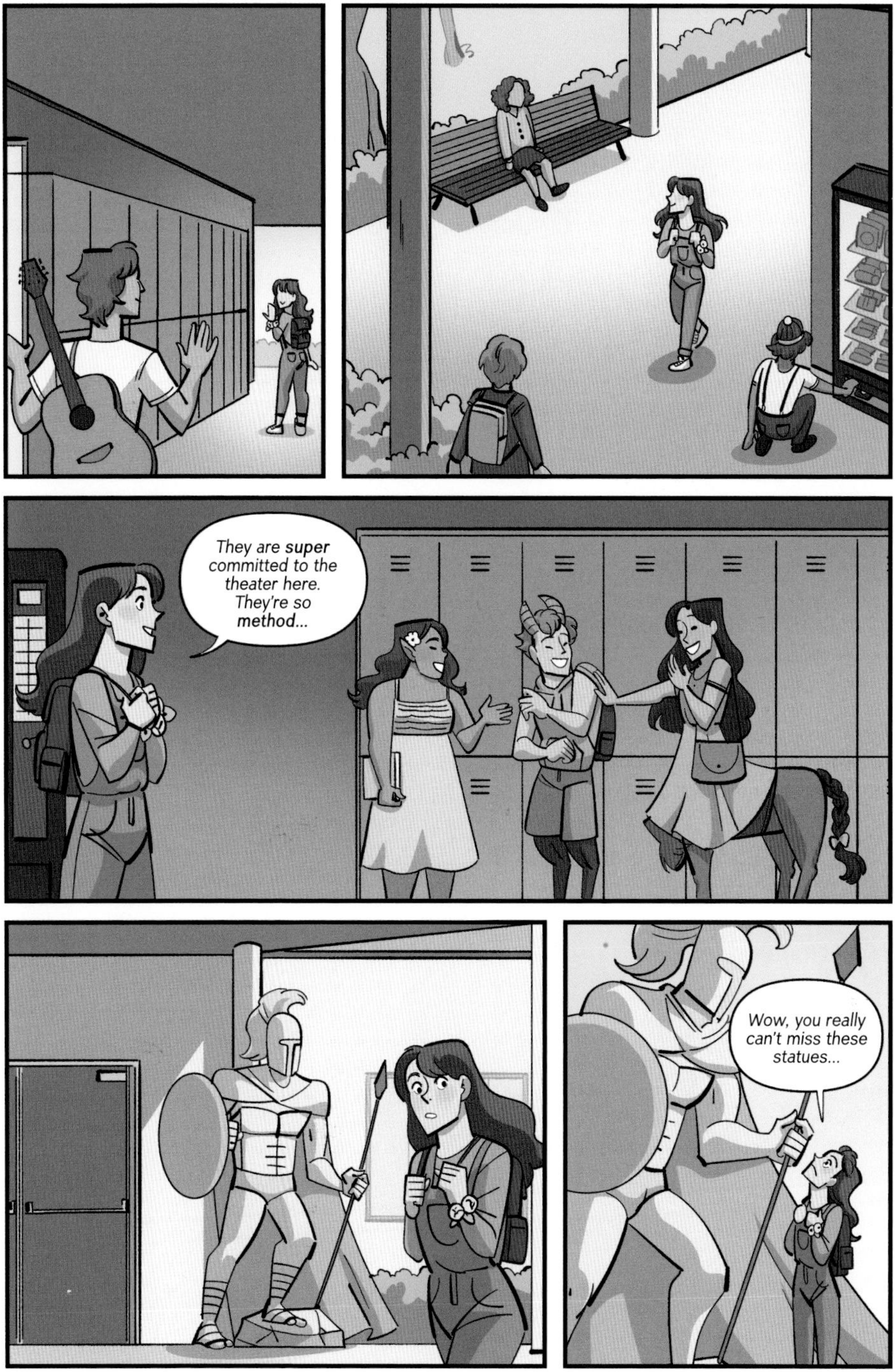
They are **super** committed to the theater here. They're so **method**...
Wow, you really can't miss these statues...

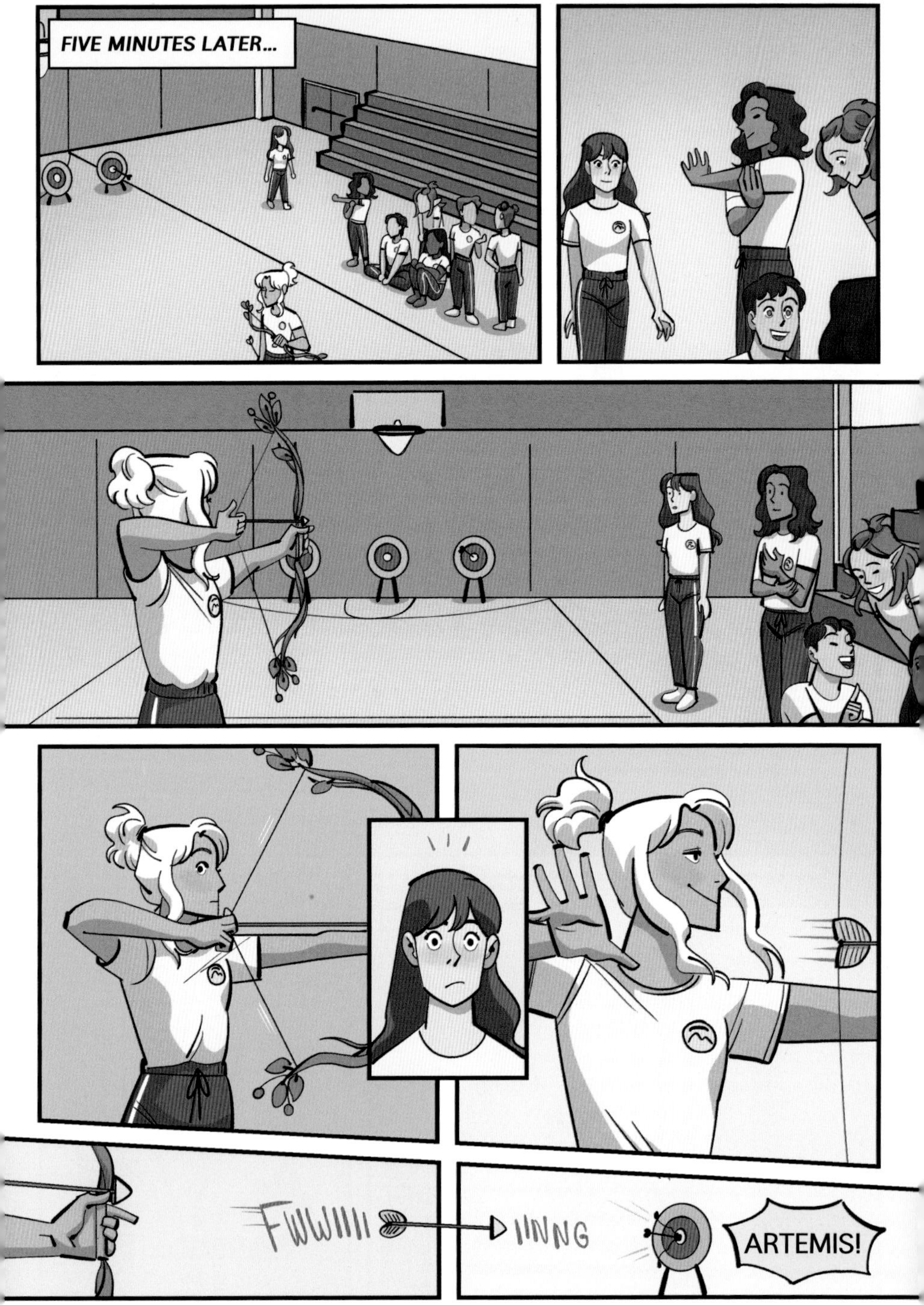
FIVE MINUTES LATER...
FWWIIII
IINNG
ARTEMIS!

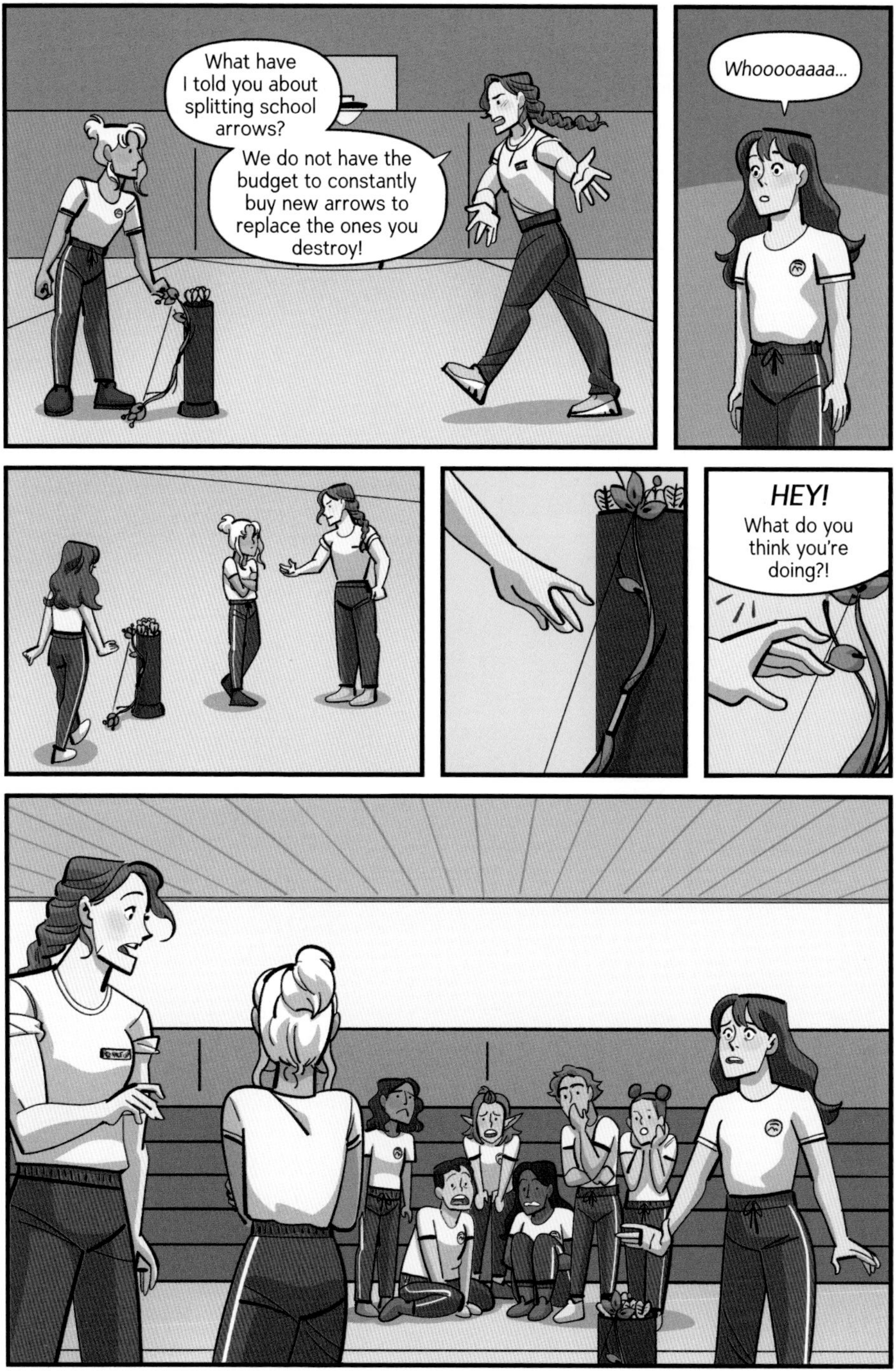
What have I told you about splitting school arrows?
We do not have the budget to constantly buy new arrows to replace the ones you destroy!
Whoooaaaa...
HEY!
What do you think you're doing?!

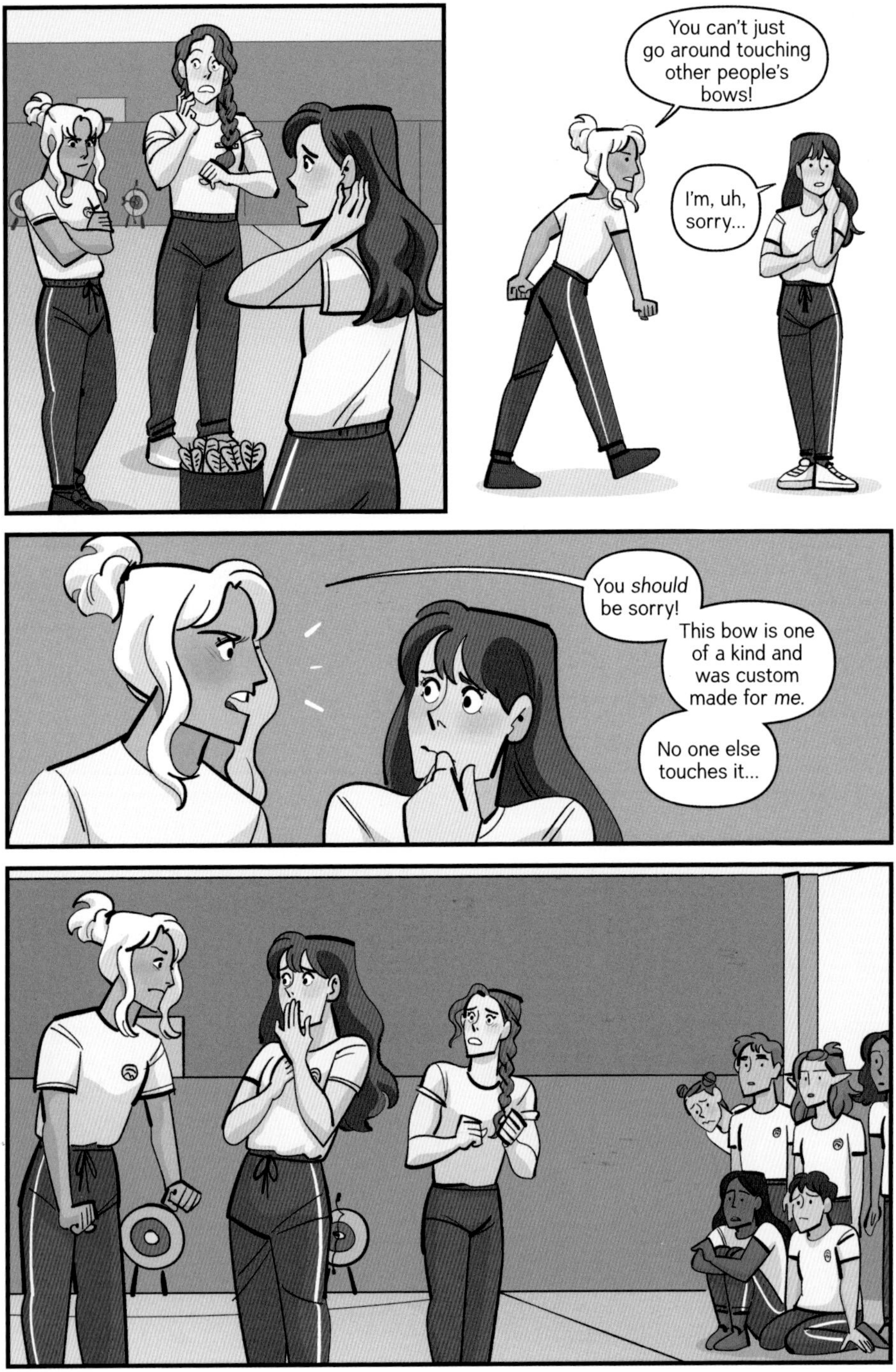
You can't just go around touching other people's bows!
I'm, uh, sorry...
You *should* be sorry!
This bow is one of a kind and was custom made for *me*.
No one else touches it...

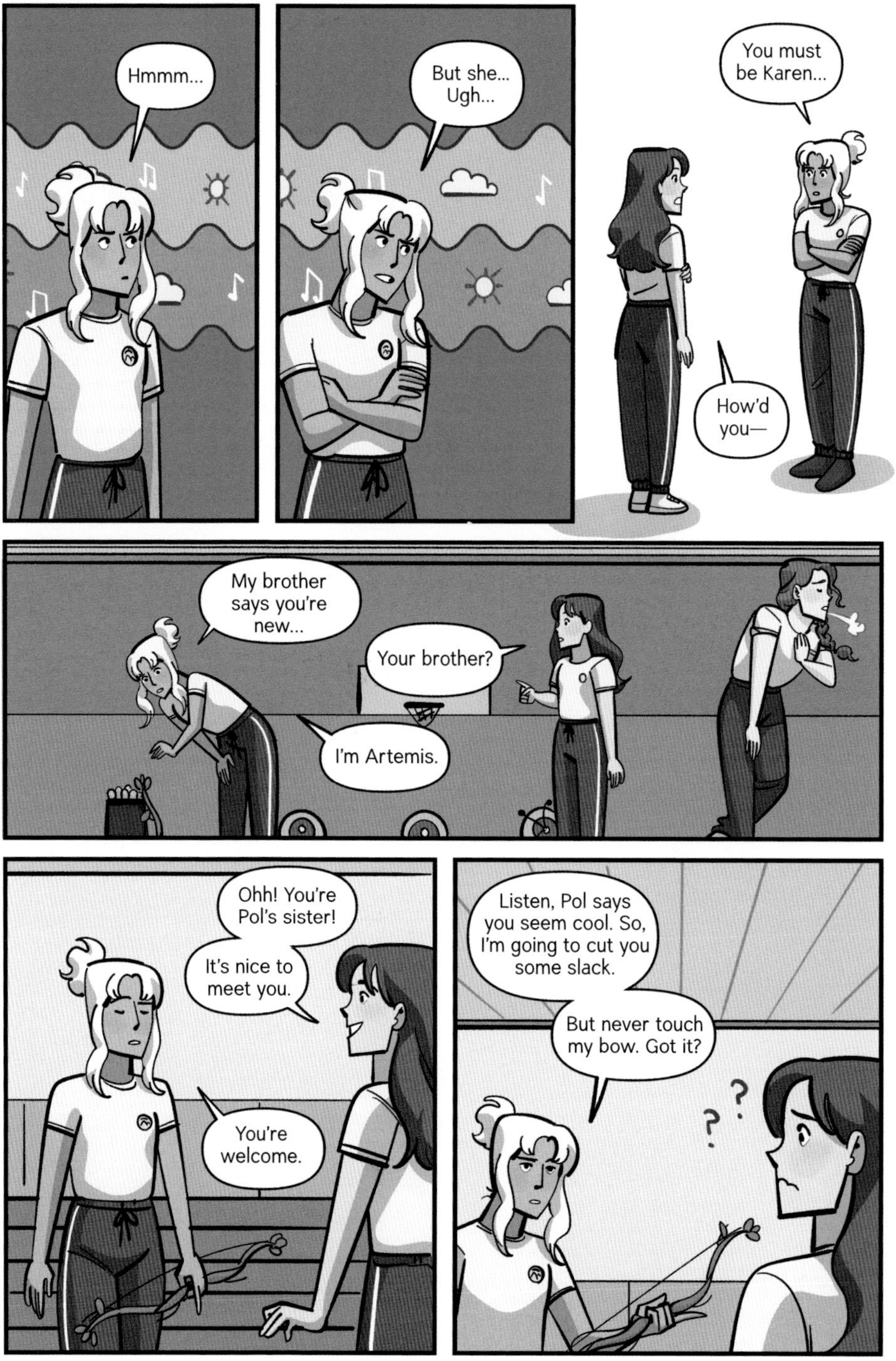

Hmmm...
But she...
Ugh...
You must be Karen...
How'd you—
My brother says you're new...
Your brother?
I'm Artemis.
Ohh! You're Pol's sister!
It's nice to meet you.
You're welcome.
Listen, Pol says you seem cool. So, I'm going to cut you some slack.
But never touch my bow. Got it?
? ?

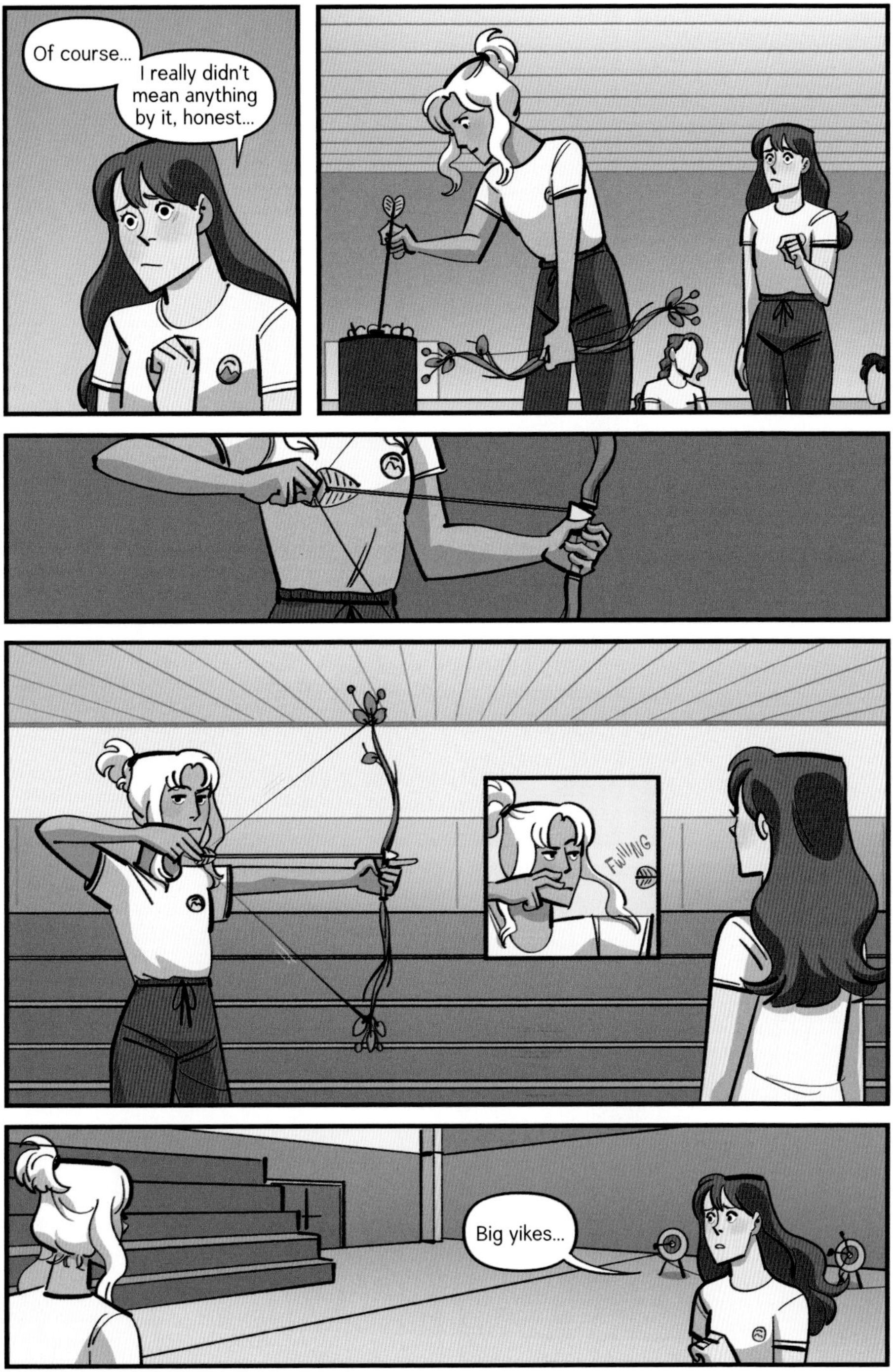
Of course...
I really didn't mean anything by it, honest...
FWIING
Big yikes...

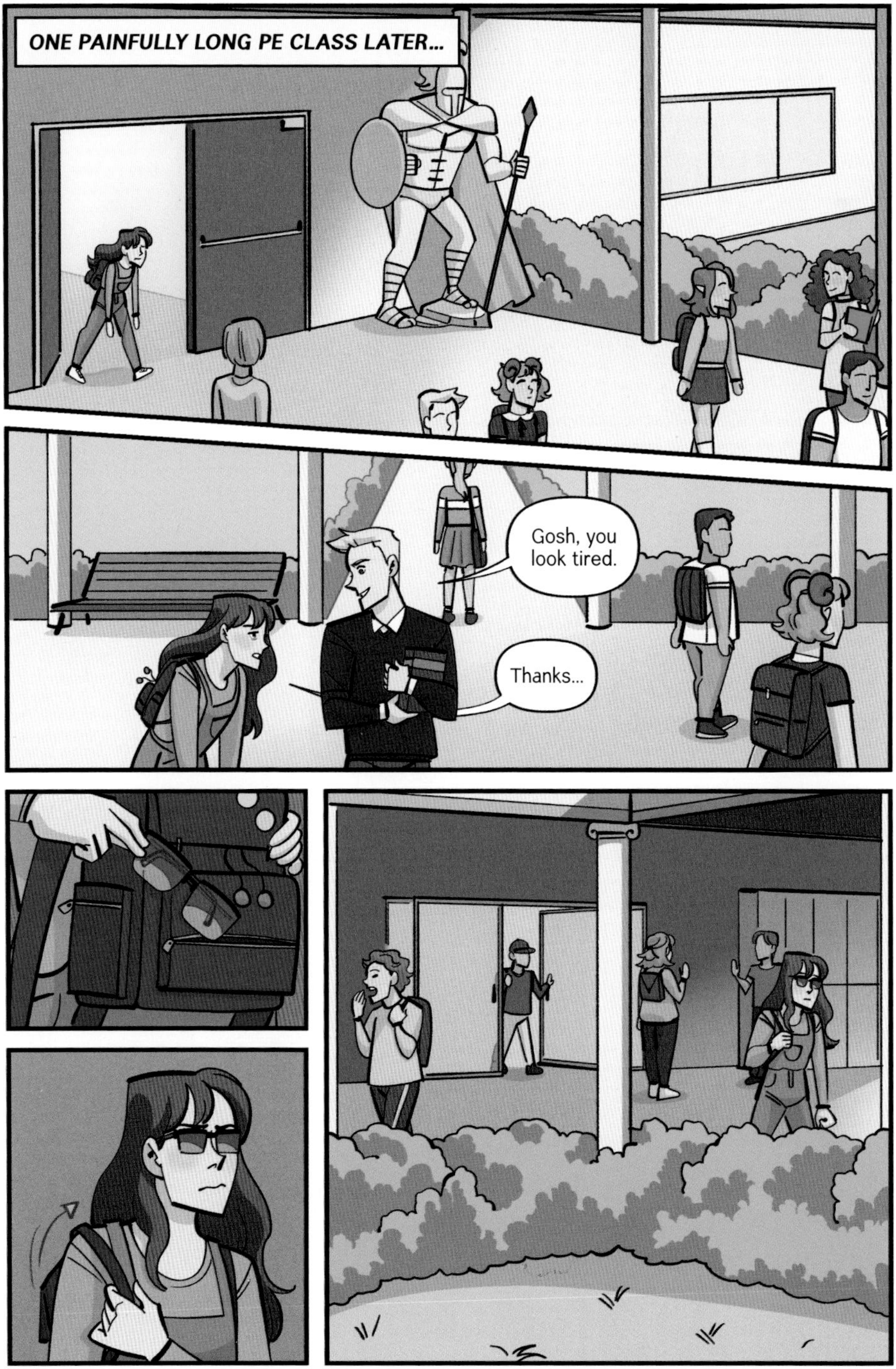
ONE PAINFULLY LONG PE CLASS LATER...
Gosh, you look tired.
Thanks...

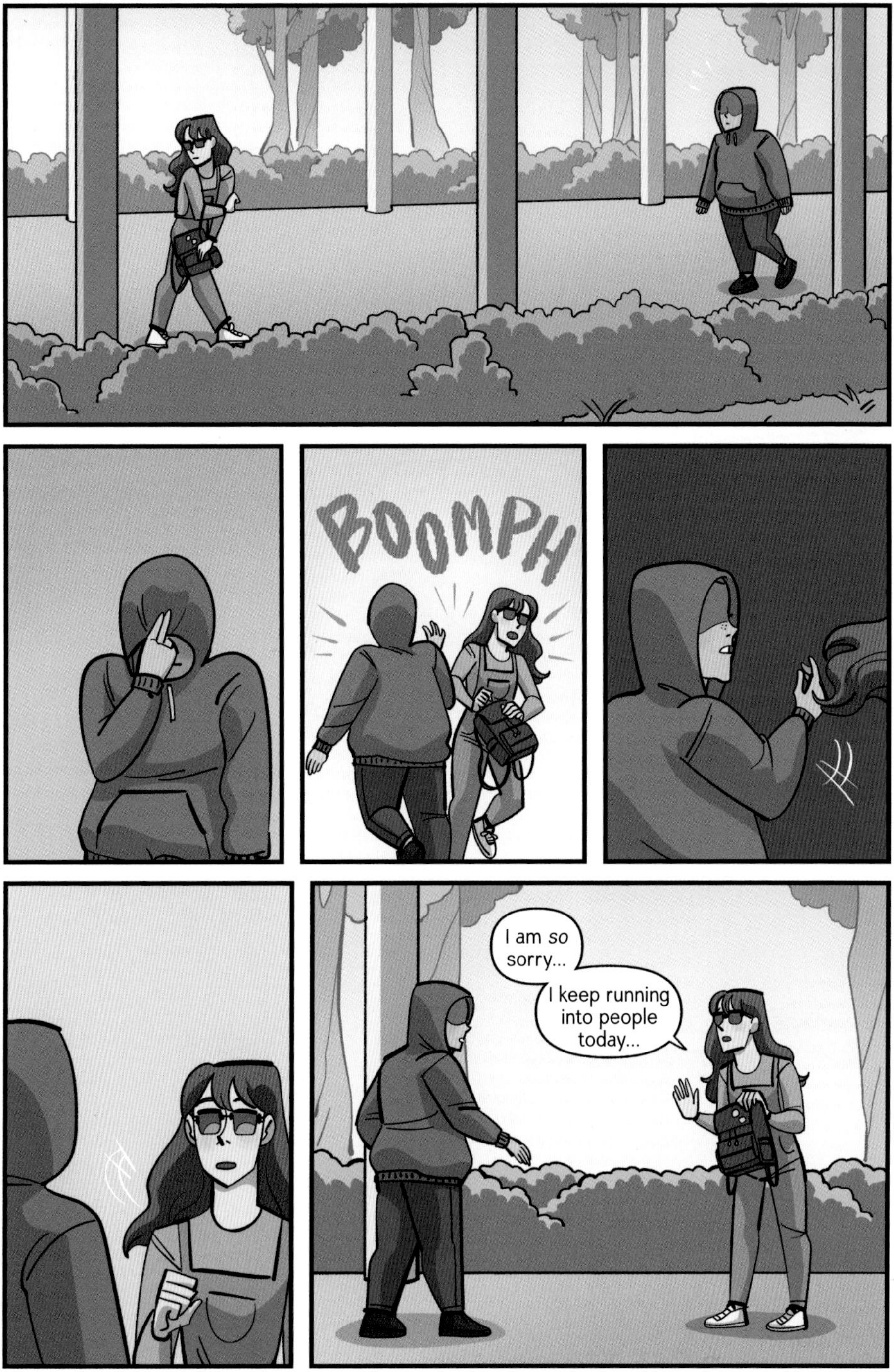
BOOMPH
I am *so* sorry...
I keep running into people today...

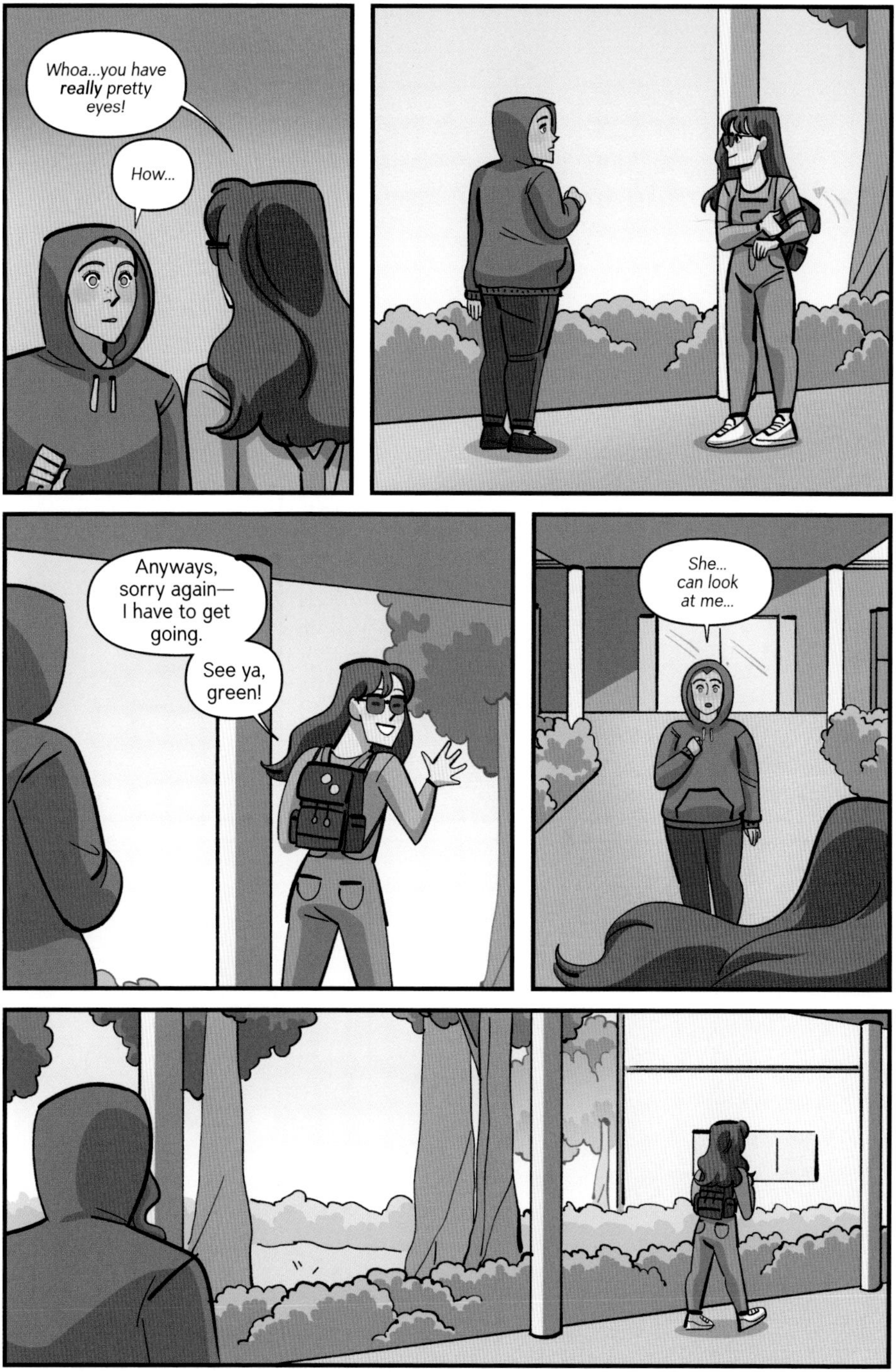
Whoa...you have **really** pretty eyes!
How...
Anyways, sorry again— I have to get going.
See ya, green!
She... can look at me...

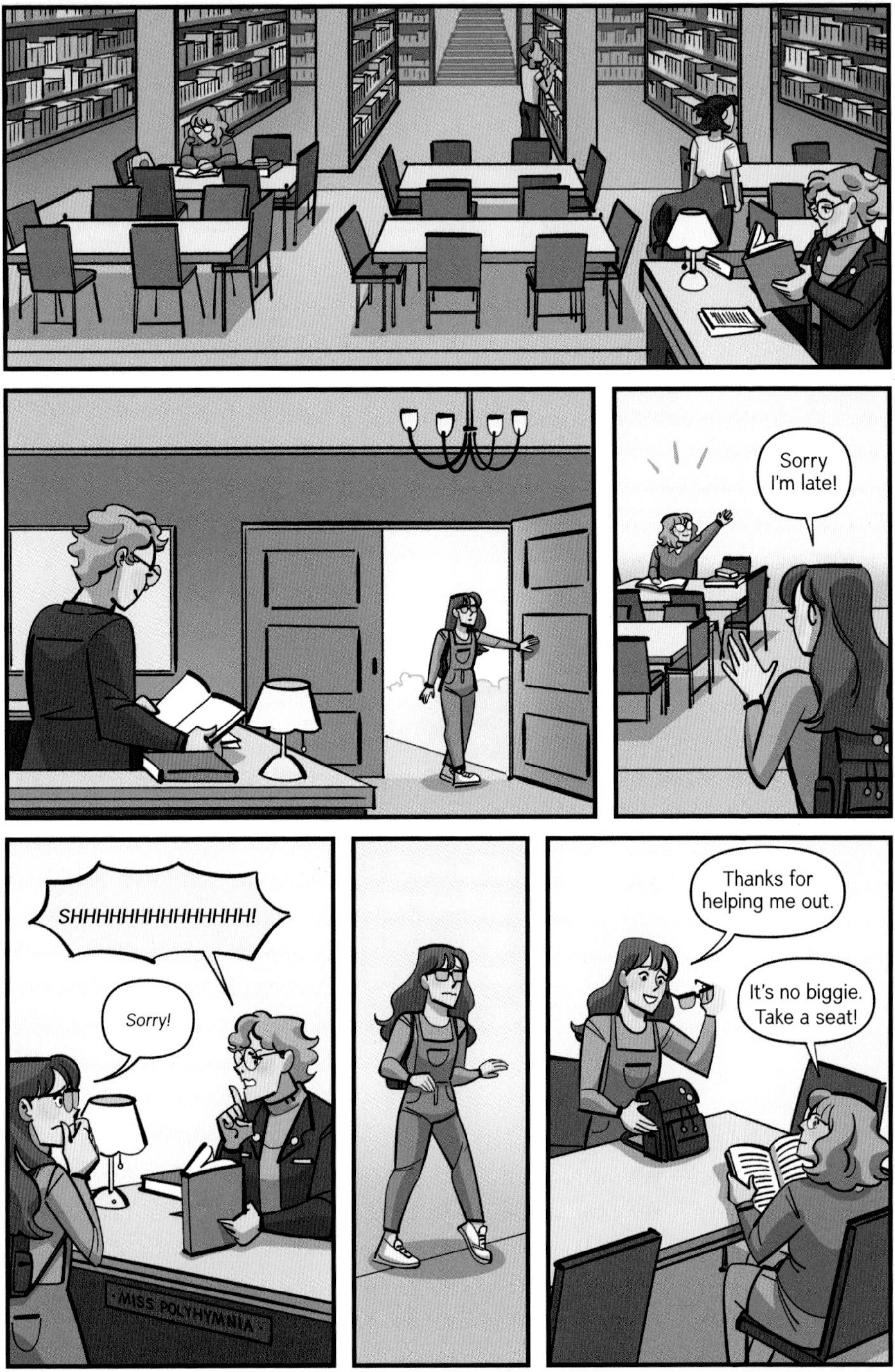
Sorry I'm late!
SHHHHHHHHHHHHHH!
Sorry!
MISS POLYHYMNIA
Thanks for helping me out.
It's no biggie. Take a seat!

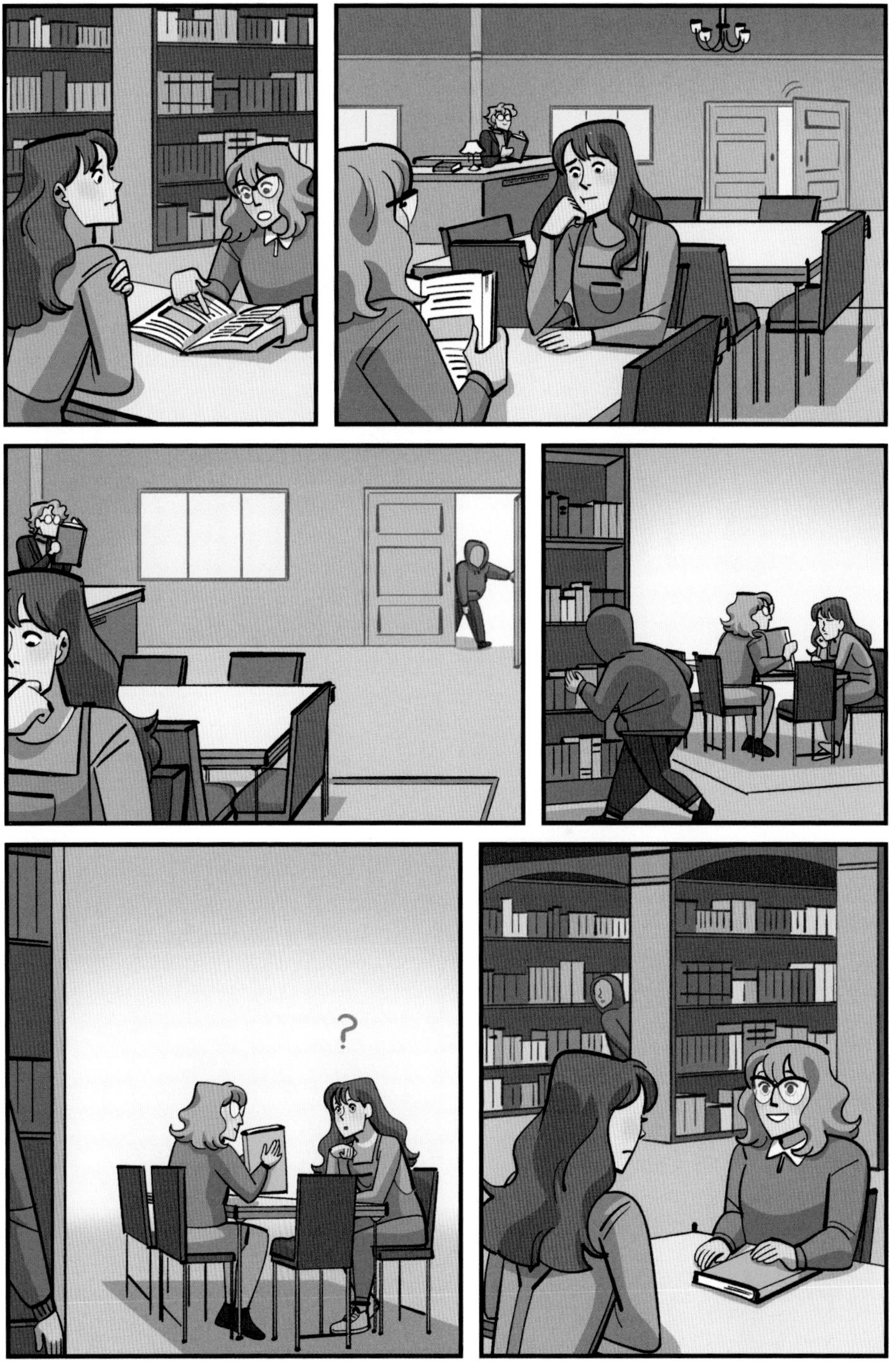
?

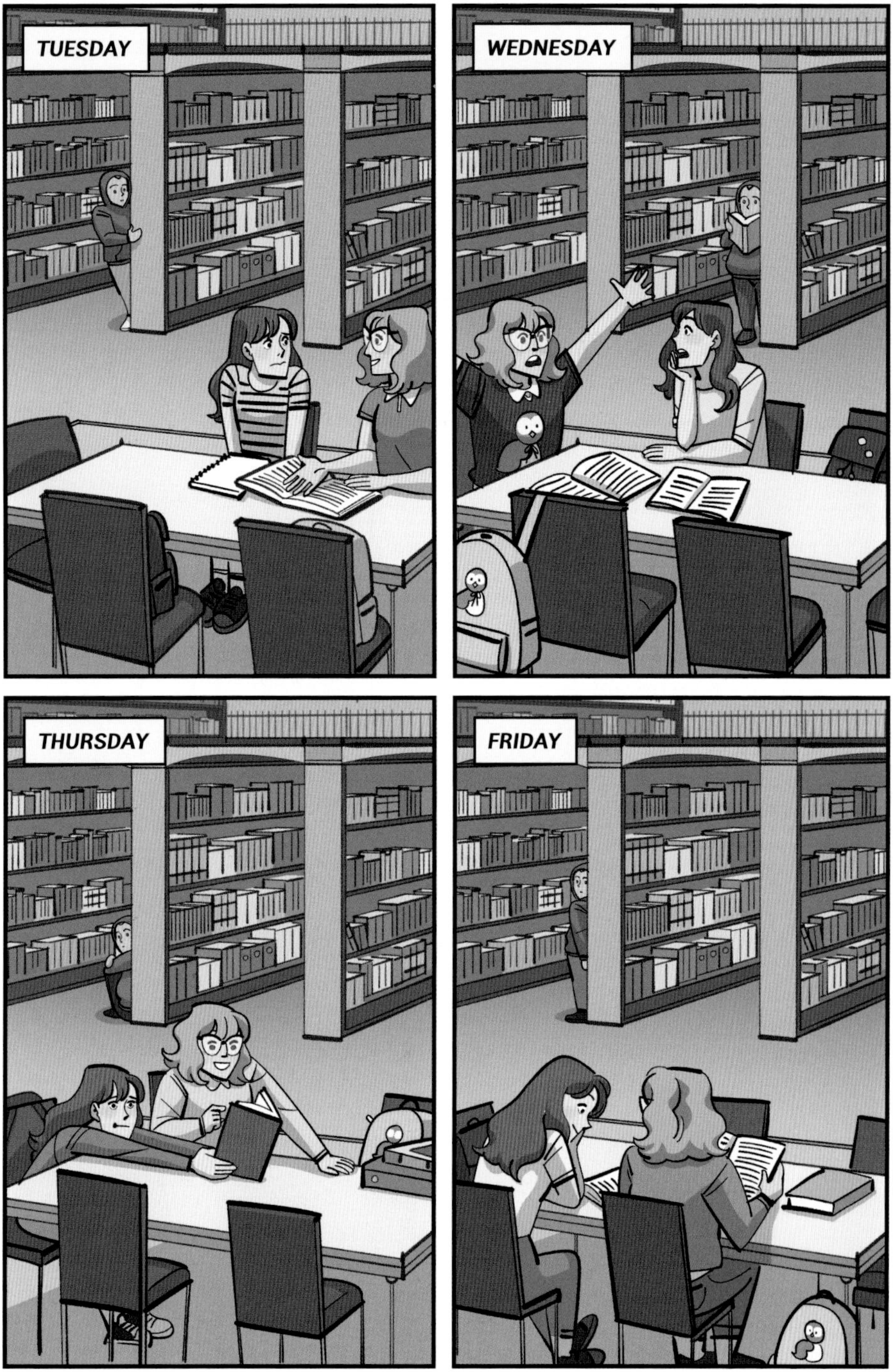
TUESDAY
WEDNESDAY
THURSDAY
FRIDAY

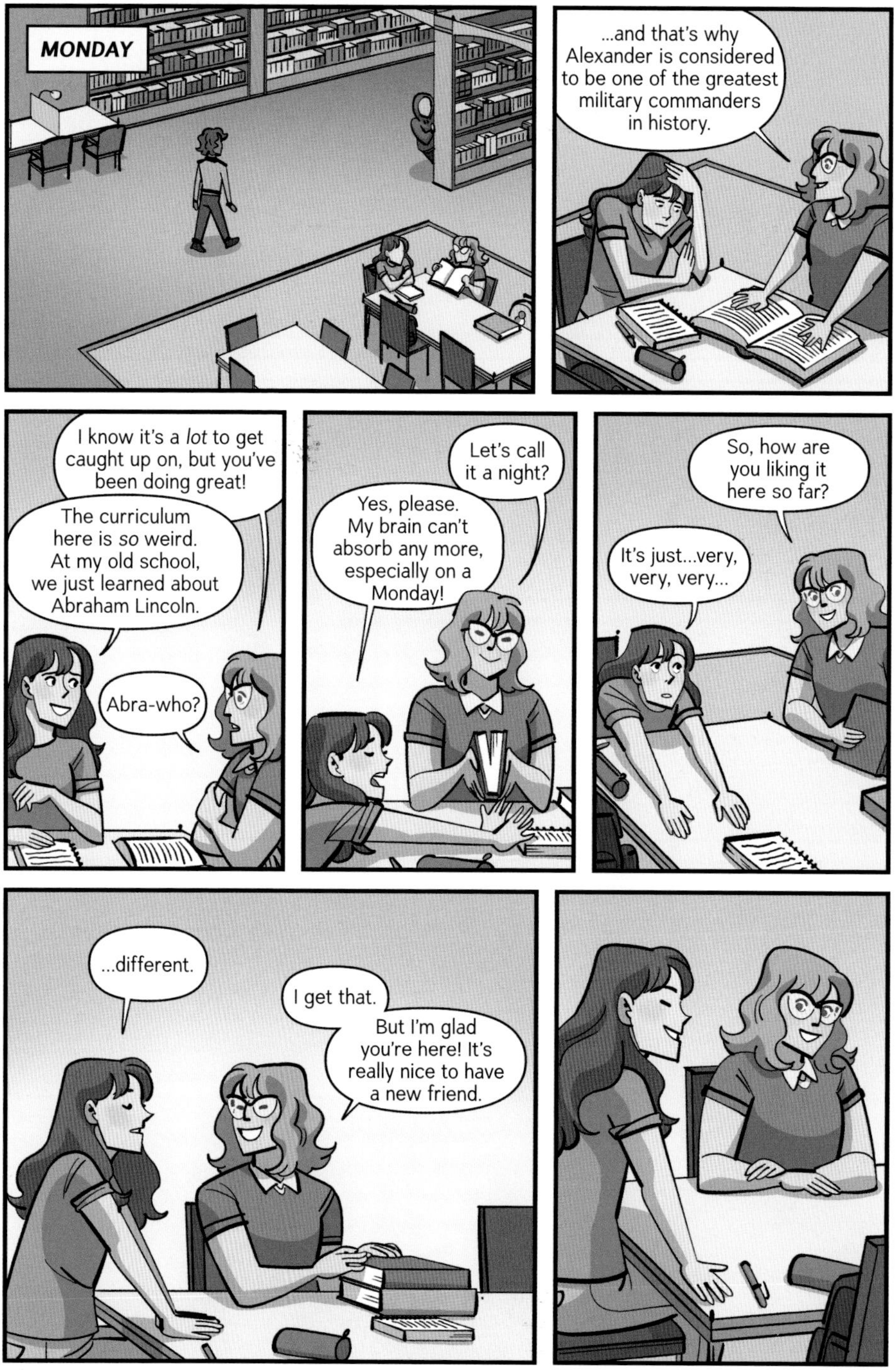
MONDAY
...and that's why Alexander is considered to be one of the greatest military commanders in history.
I know it's a *lot* to get caught up on, but you've been doing great!
The curriculum here is *so* weird. At my old school, we just learned about Abraham Lincoln.
Abra-who?
Let's call it a night?
Yes, please. My brain can't absorb any more, especially on a Monday!
So, how are you liking it here so far?
It's just...very, very, very...
...different.
I get that.
But I'm glad you're here! It's really nice to have a new friend.

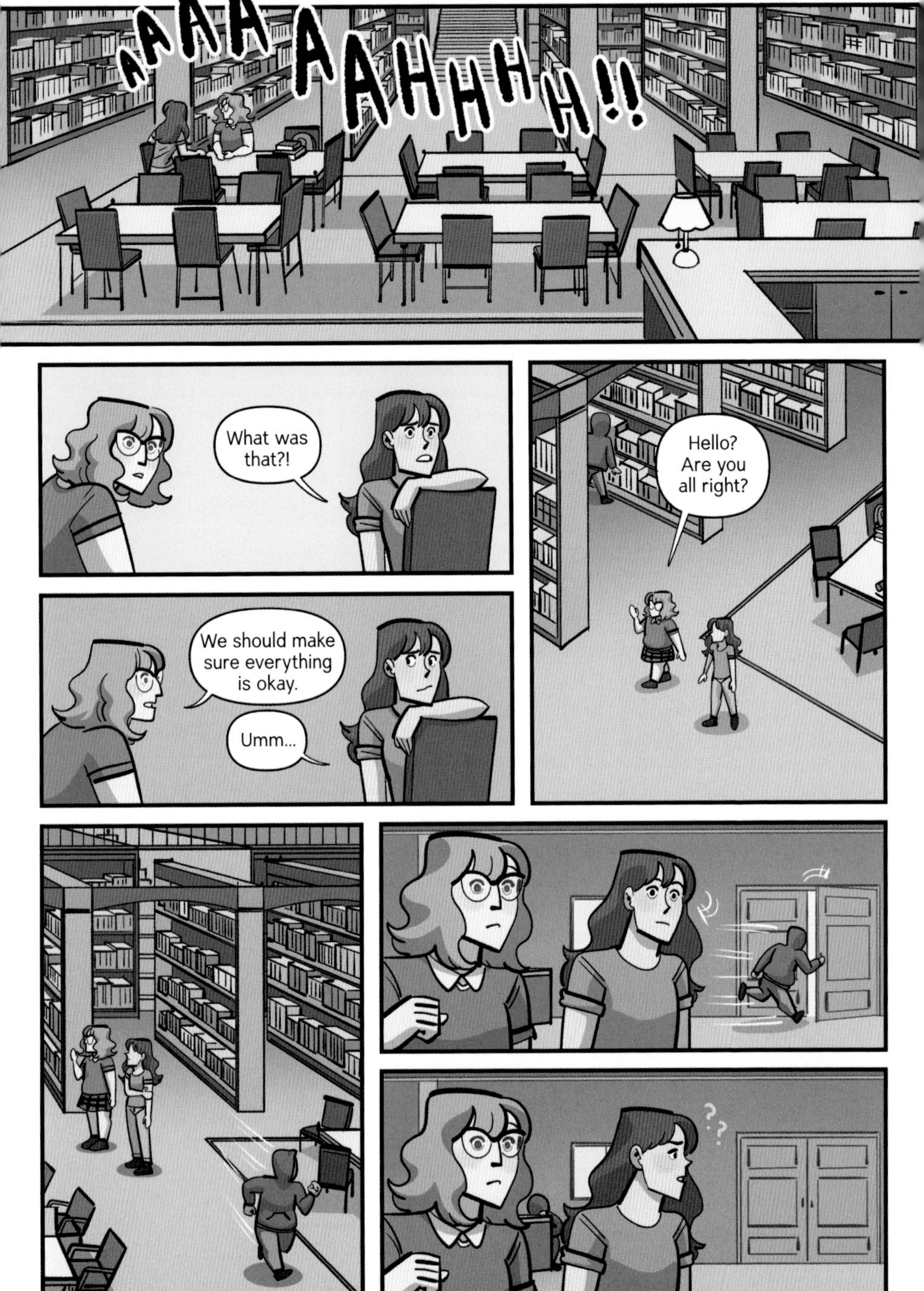

AAAAAAHHHHH!!
What was that?!
Hello? Are you all right?
We should make sure everything is okay.
Umm...

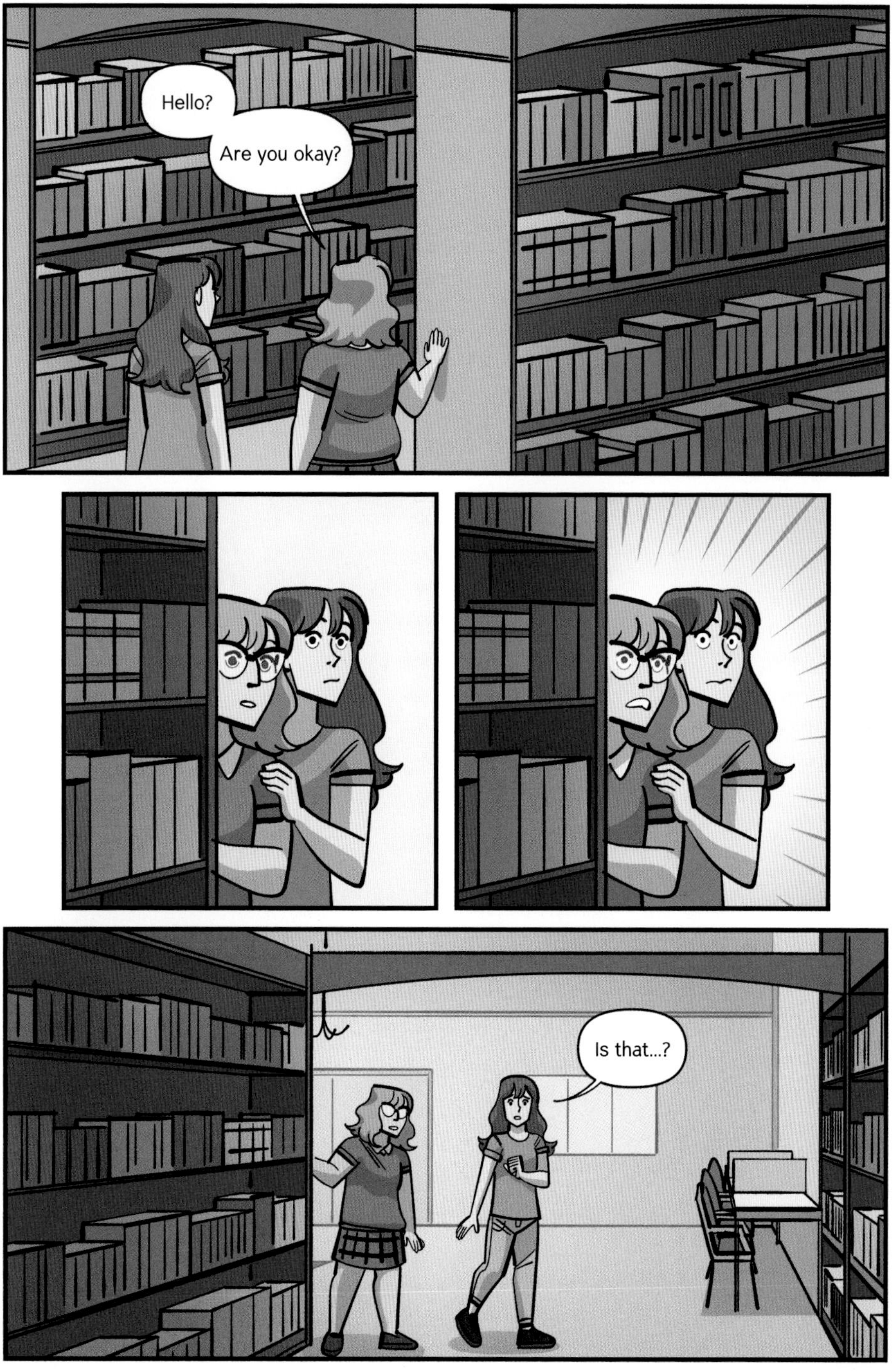
Hello?
Are you okay?
Is that...?

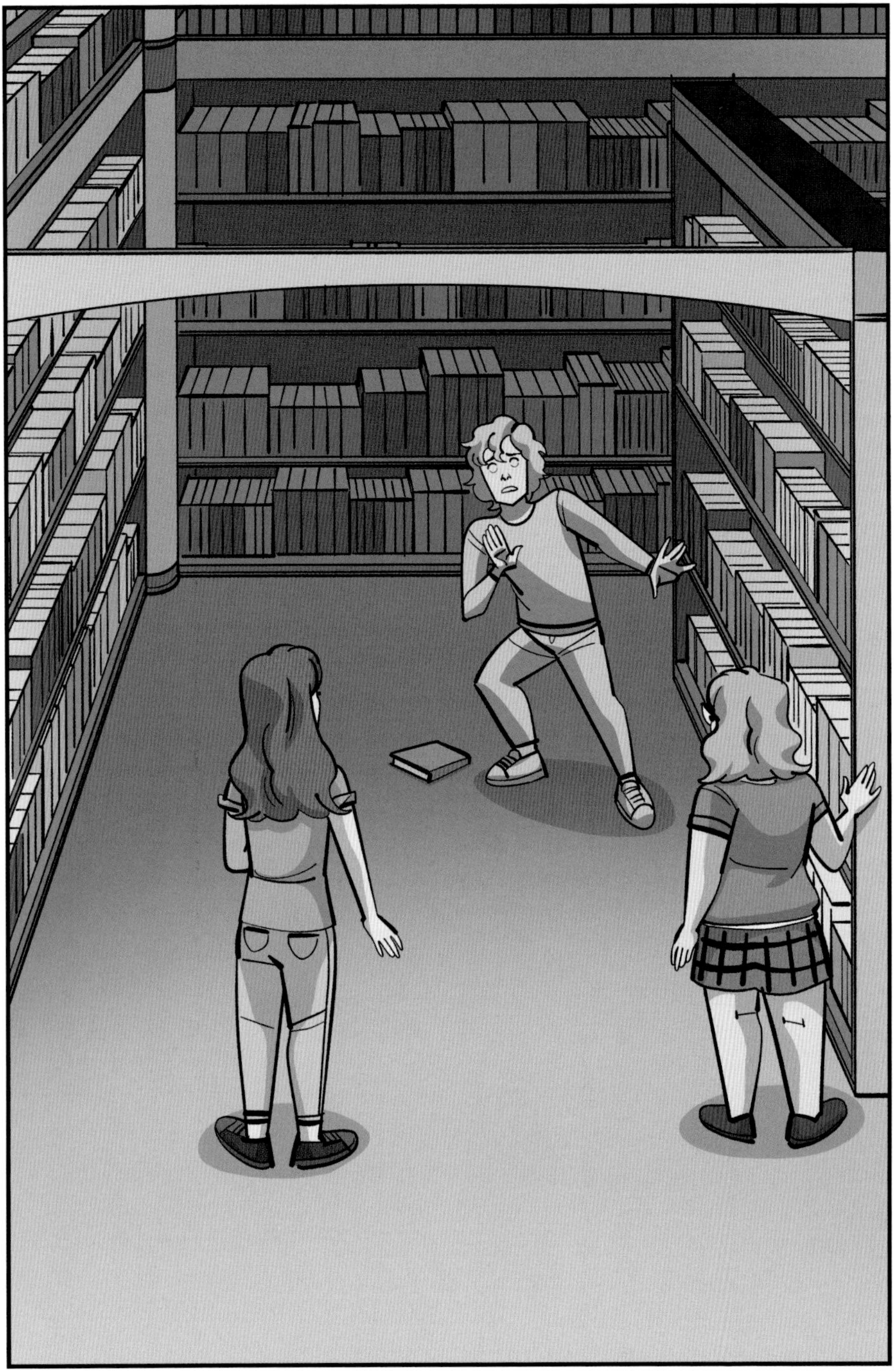

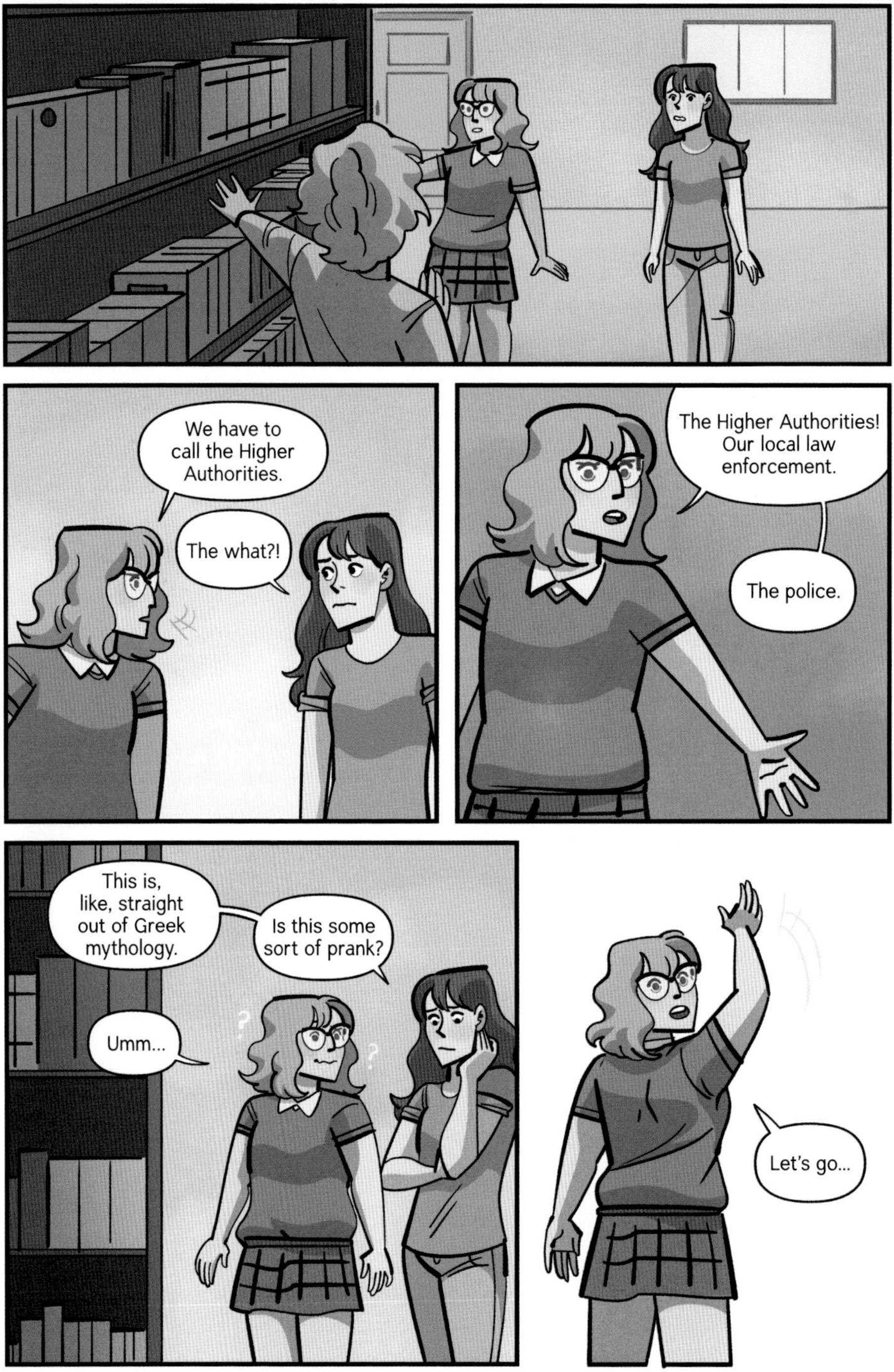
We have to call the Higher Authorities.
The what?!
The Higher Authorities! Our local law enforcement.
The police.
This is, like, straight out of Greek mythology.
Is this some sort of prank?
Umm...
Let's go...

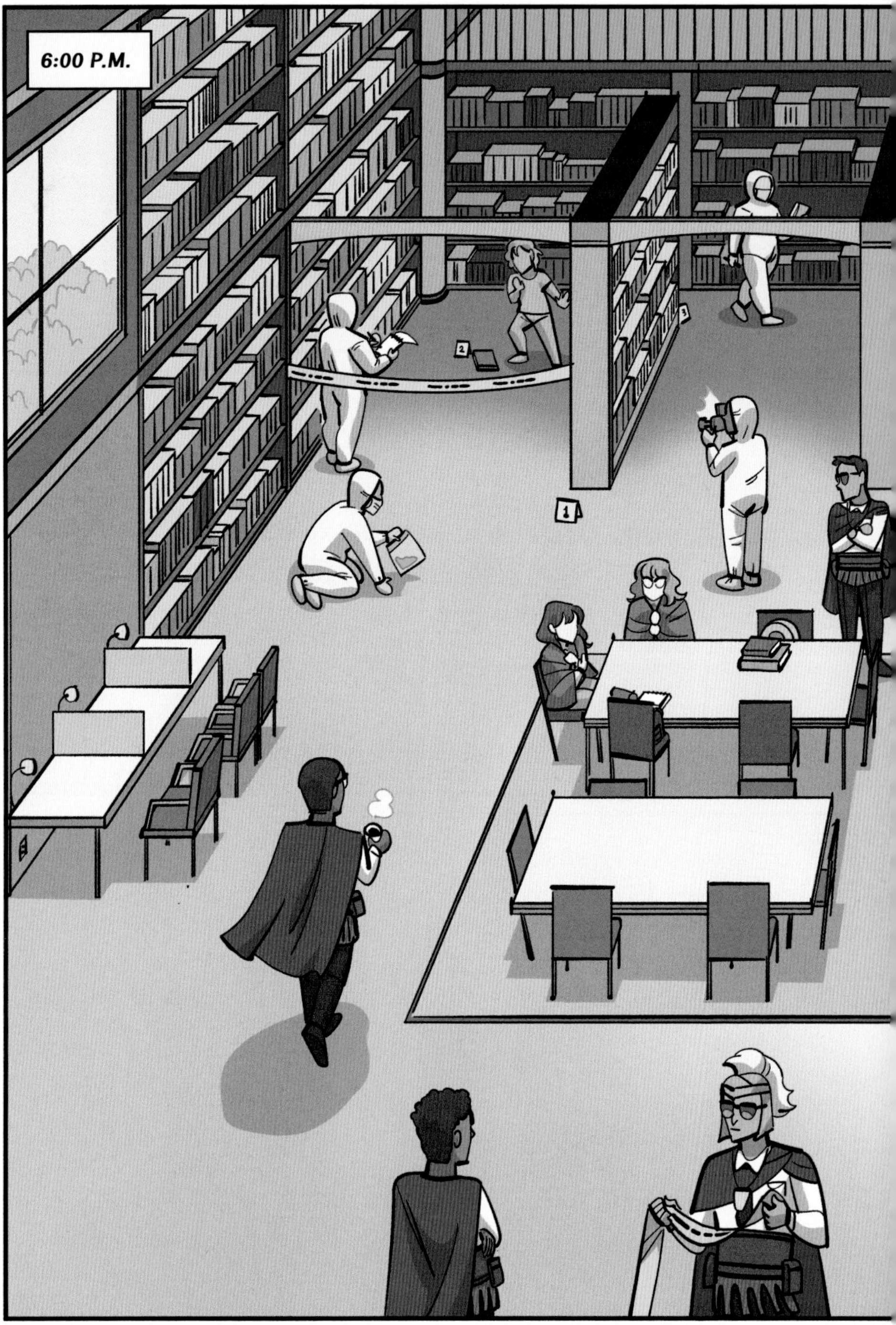
6:00 P.M.

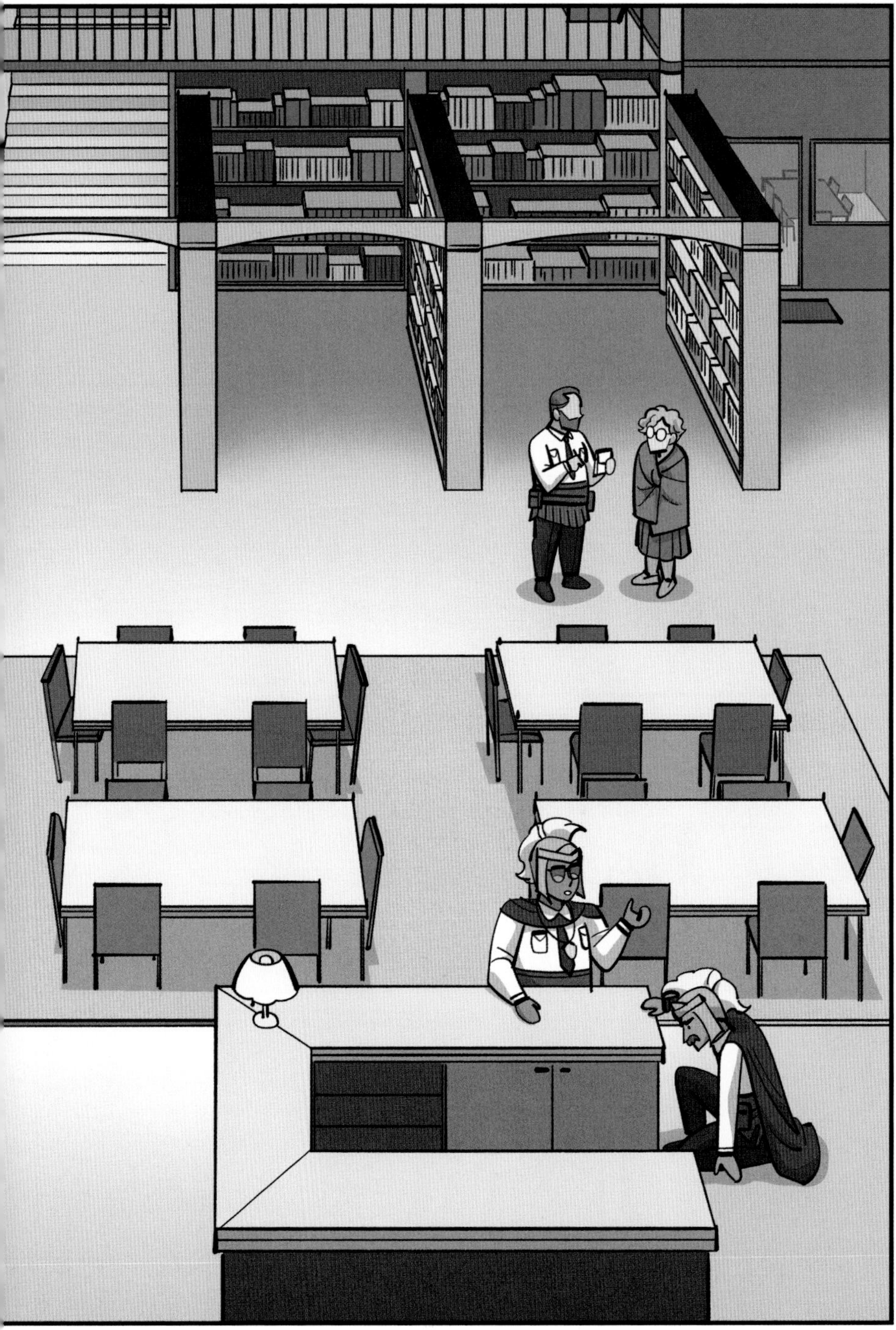

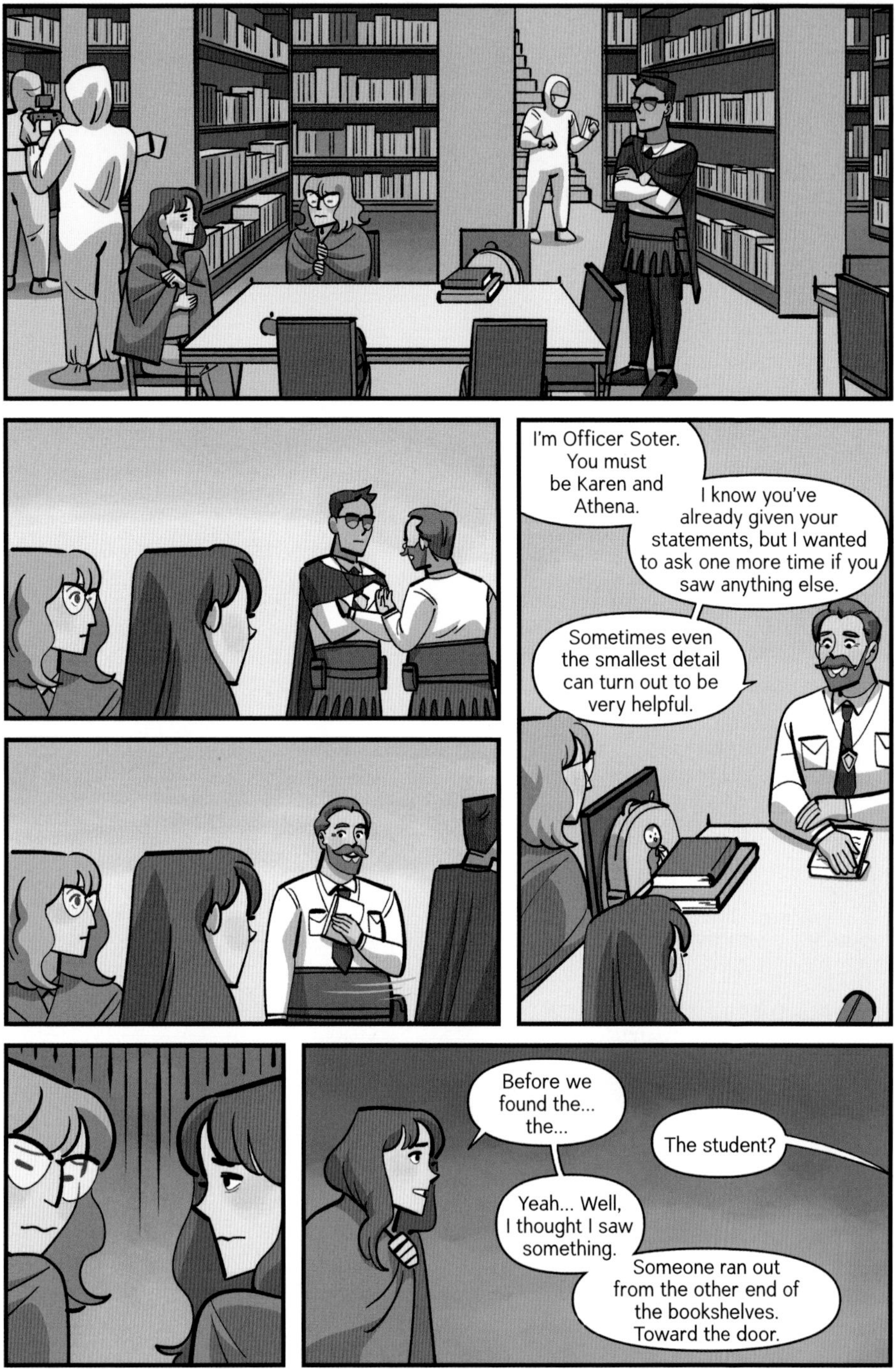
I'm Officer Soter. You must be Karen and Athena.
I know you've already given your statements, but I wanted to ask one more time if you saw anything else.
Sometimes even the smallest detail can turn out to be very helpful.
Before we found the... the...
The student?
Yeah... Well, I thought I saw something.
Someone ran out from the other end of the bookshelves. Toward the door.

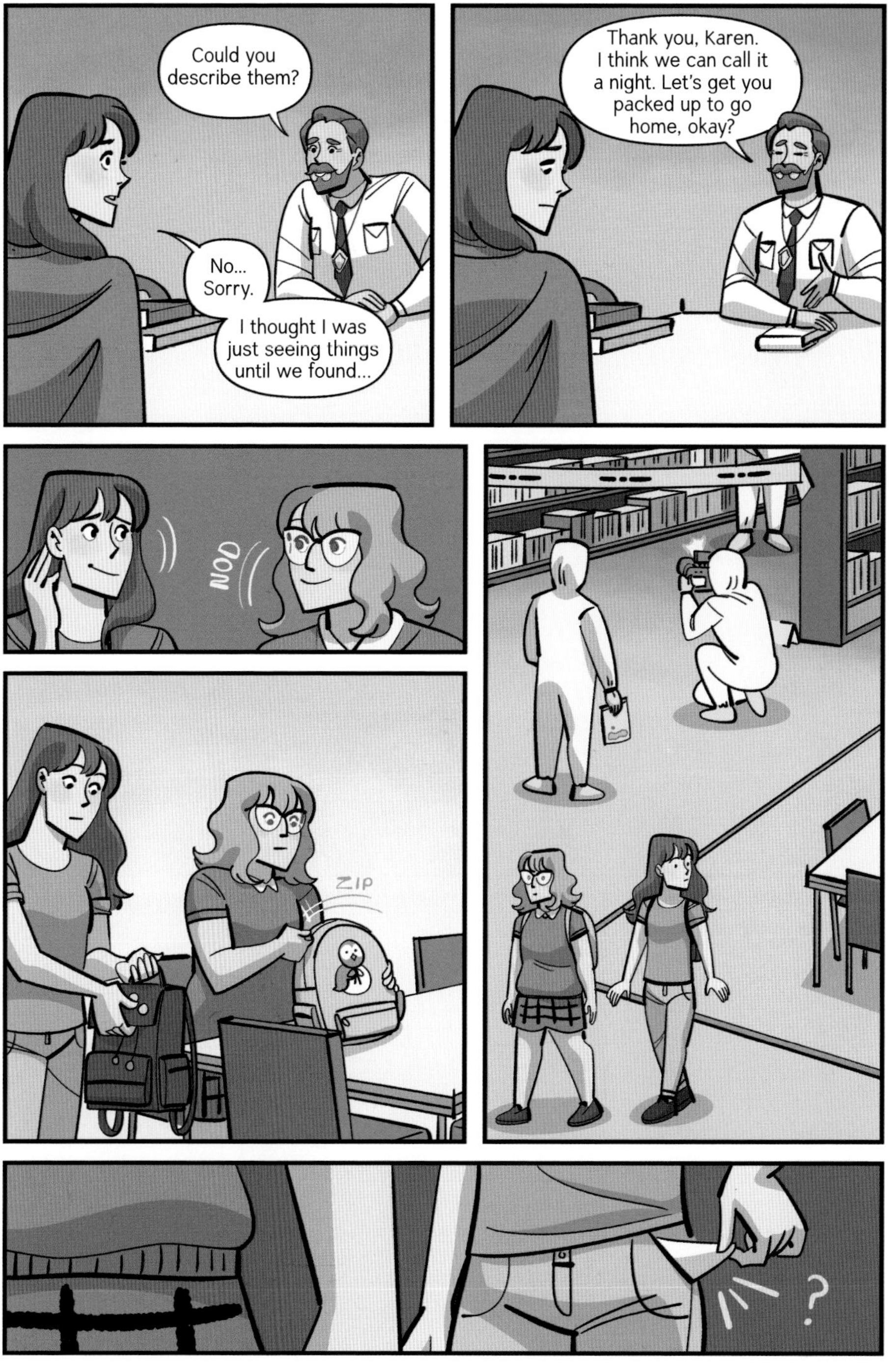

Could you describe them?
No... Sorry.
I thought I was just seeing things until we found...
Thank you, Karen. I think we can call it a night. Let's get you packed up to go home, okay?
NOD
ZIP
?

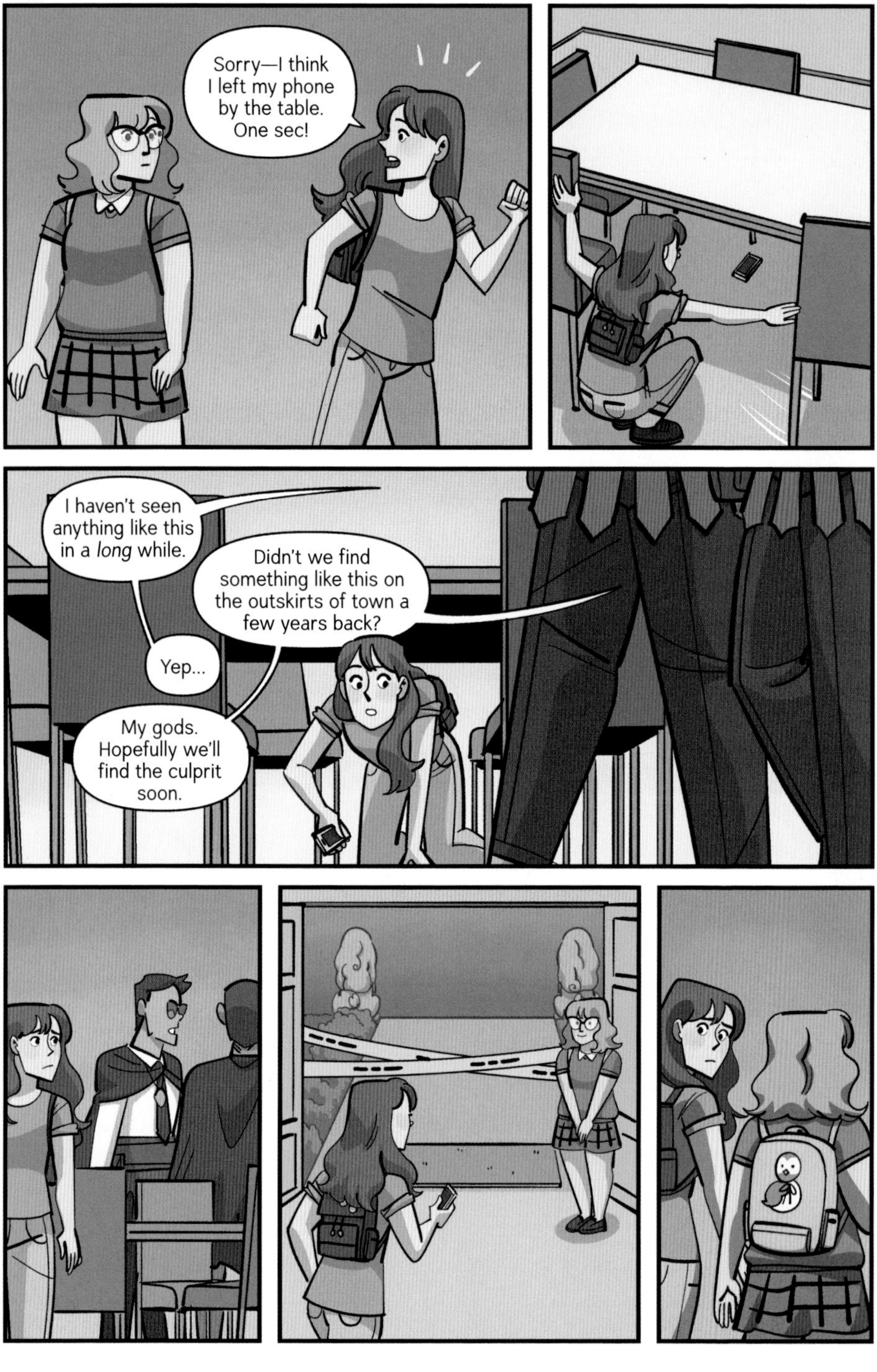
Sorry—I think I left my phone by the table. One sec!
I haven't seen anything like this in a *long* while.
Didn't we find something like this on the outskirts of town a few years back?
Yep...
My gods. Hopefully we'll find the culprit soon.

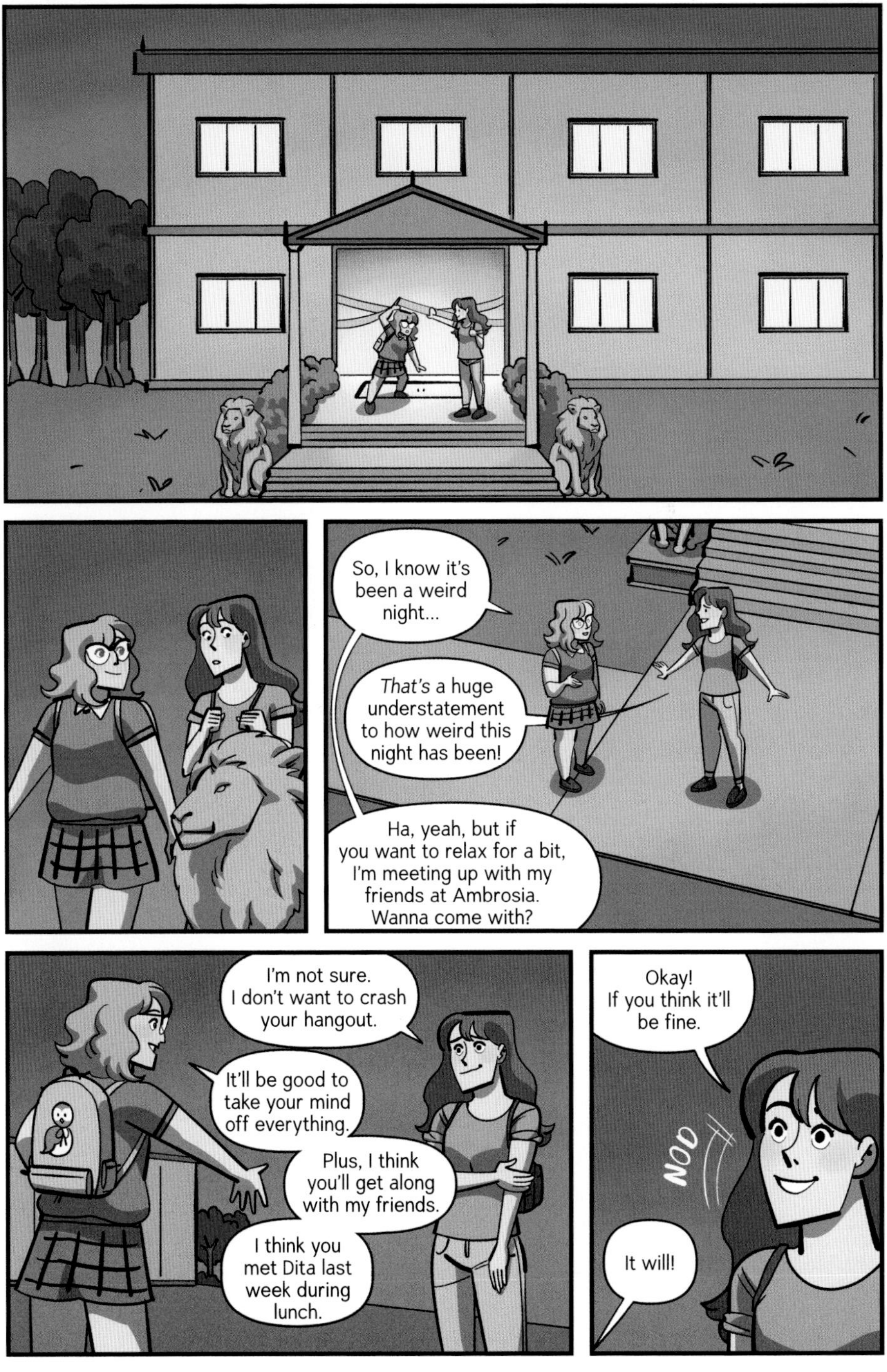
So, I know it's been a weird night...
That's a huge understatement to how weird this night has been!
Ha, yeah, but if you want to relax for a bit, I'm meeting up with my friends at Ambrosia. Wanna come with?
I'm not sure. I don't want to crash your hangout.
It'll be good to take your mind off everything.
Plus, I think you'll get along with my friends.
I think you met Dita last week during lunch.
Okay! If you think it'll be fine.
NOD
It will!

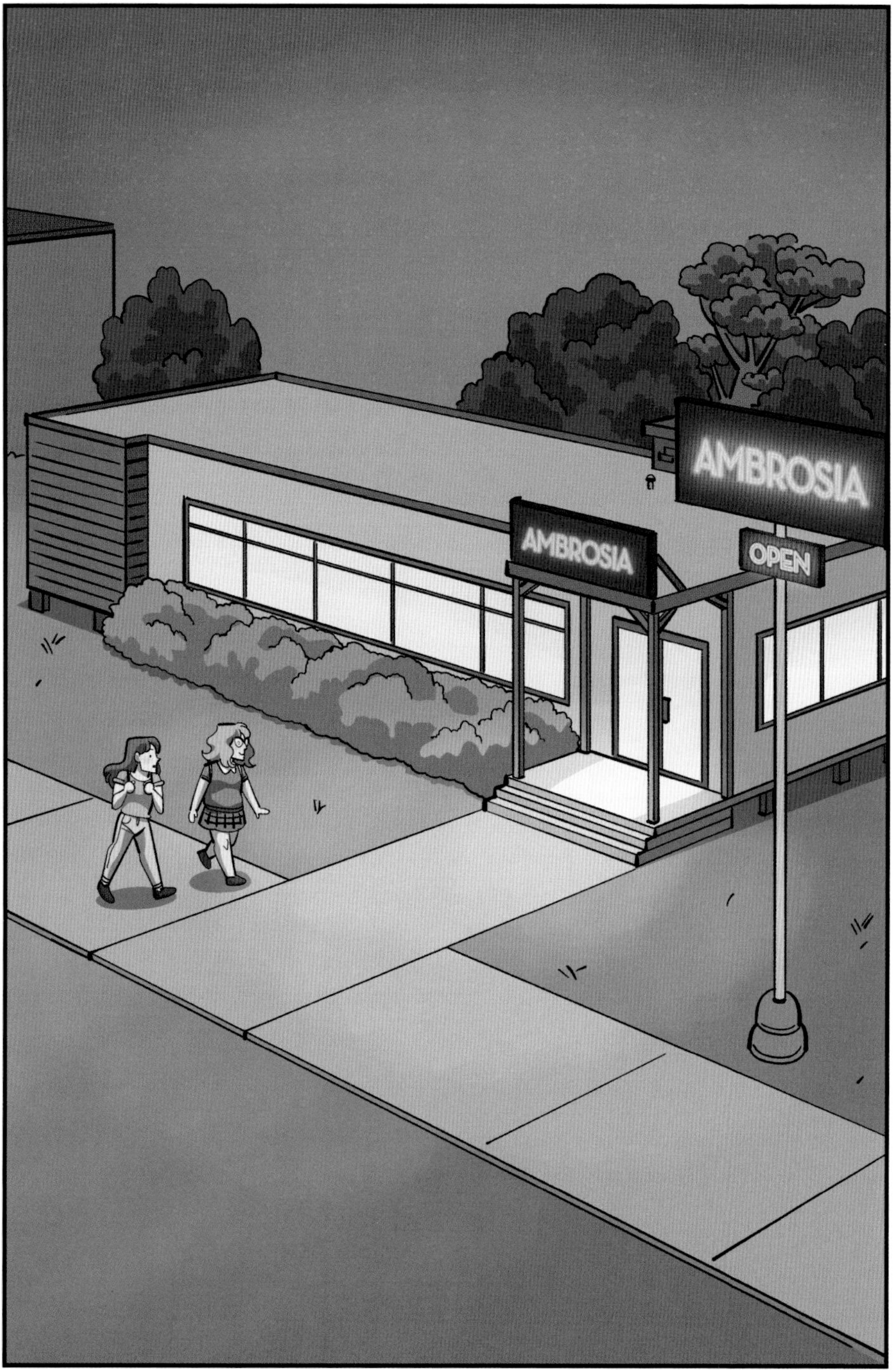
AMBROSIA
AMBROSIA
OPEN

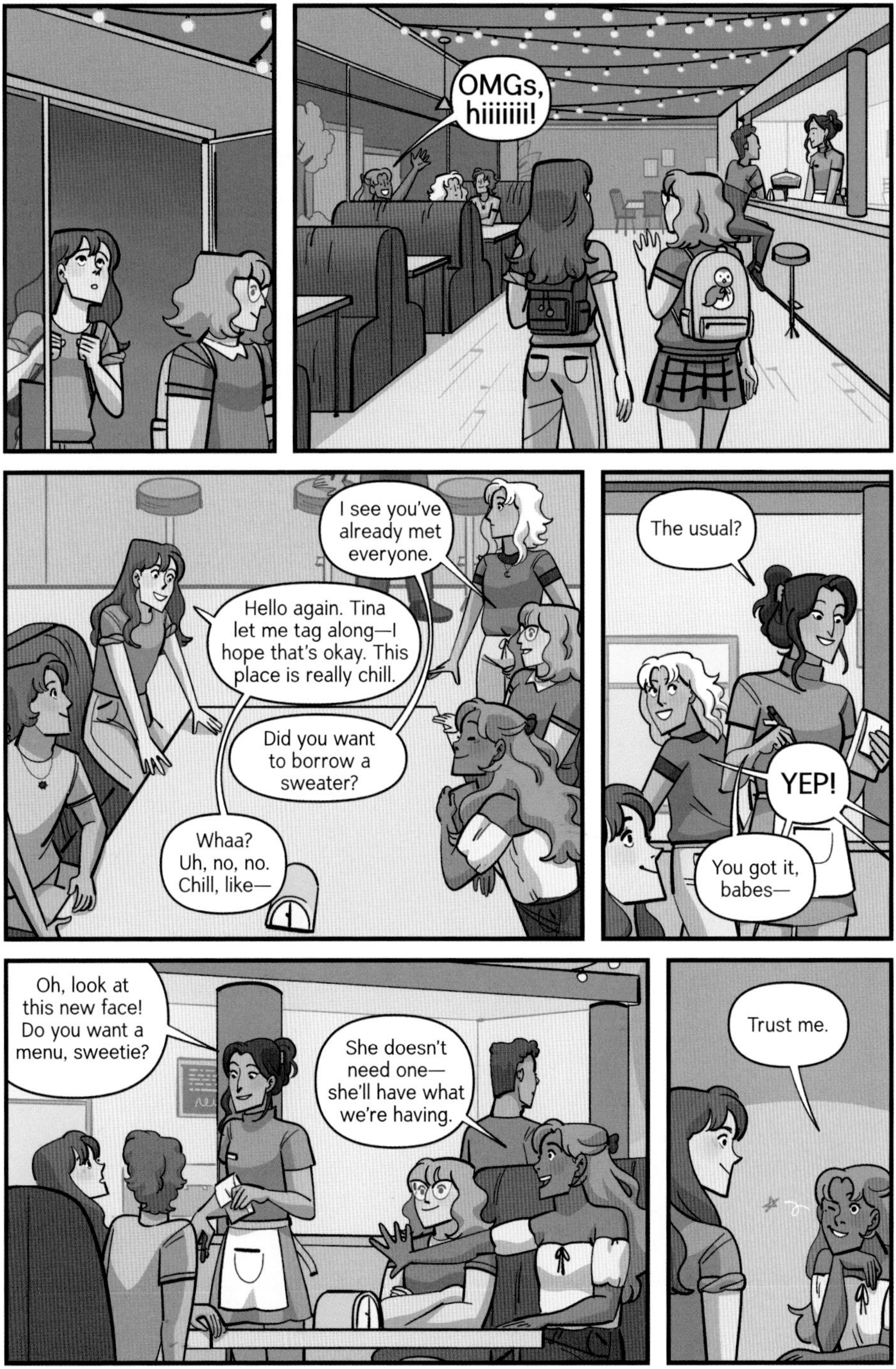
OMGs, hiiiiiii!
Hello again. Tina let me tag along—I hope that's okay. This place is really chill.
I see you've already met everyone.
Did you want to borrow a sweater?
Whaa? Uh, no, no. Chill, like—
The usual?
YEP!
You got it, babes—
Oh, look at this new face! Do you want a menu, sweetie?
She doesn't need one—she'll have what we're having.
Trust me.

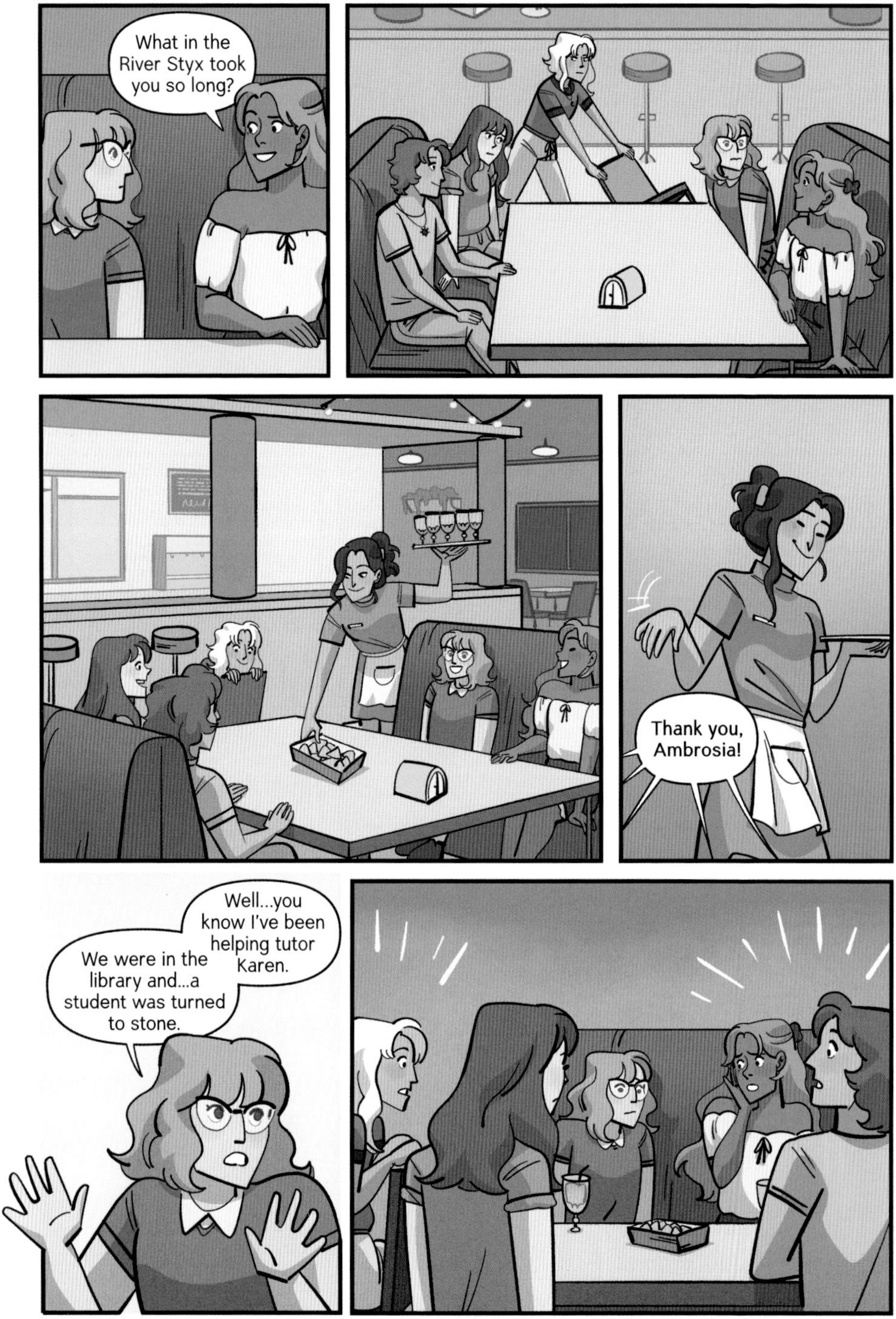
What in the River Styx took you so long?
Thank you, Ambrosia!
Well...you know I've been helping tutor Karen.
We were in the library and...a student was turned to stone.

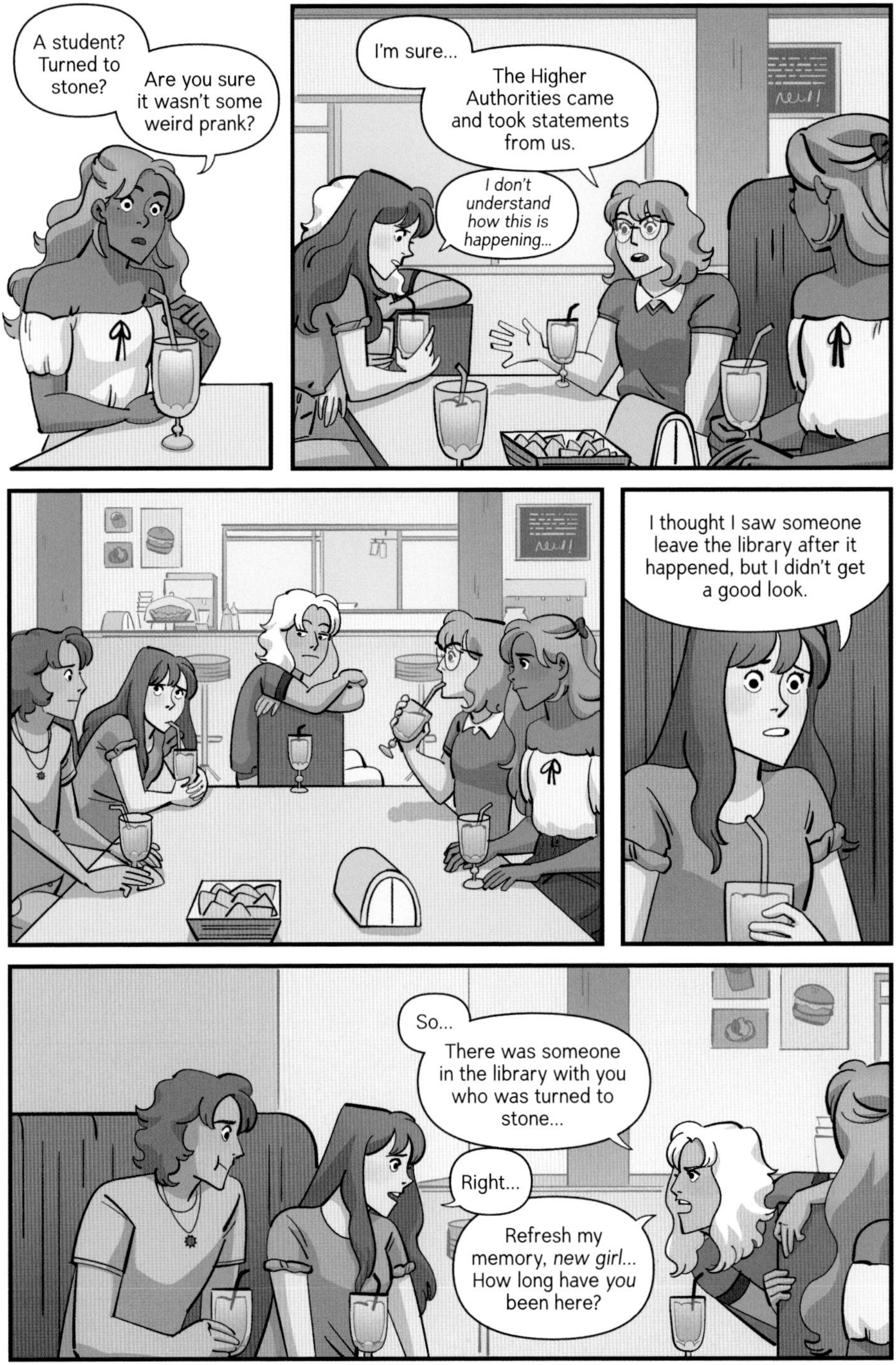
A student? Turned to stone?
Are you sure it wasn't some weird prank?
I'm sure...
The Higher Authorities came and took statements from us.
I don't understand how this is happening...
I thought I saw someone leave the library after it happened, but I didn't get a good look.
So...
There was someone in the library with you who was turned to stone...
Right...
Refresh my memory, *new girl*... How long have *you* been here?

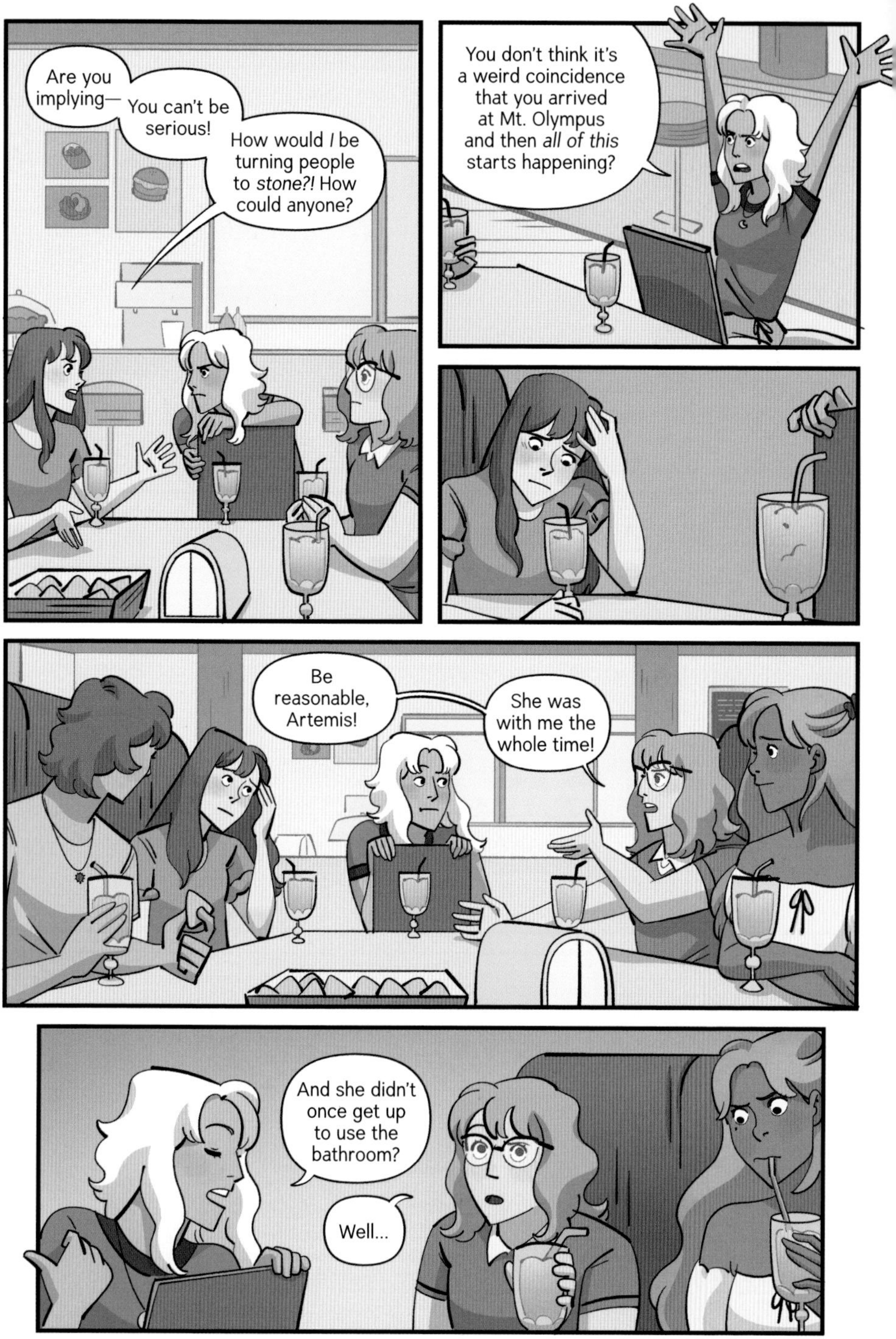
Are you implying—
You can't be serious!
How would *I* be turning people to *stone?!* How could anyone?
You don't think it's a weird coincidence that you arrived at Mt. Olympus and then *all of this* starts happening?
Be reasonable, Artemis!
She was with me the whole time!
And she didn't once get up to use the bathroom?
Well...

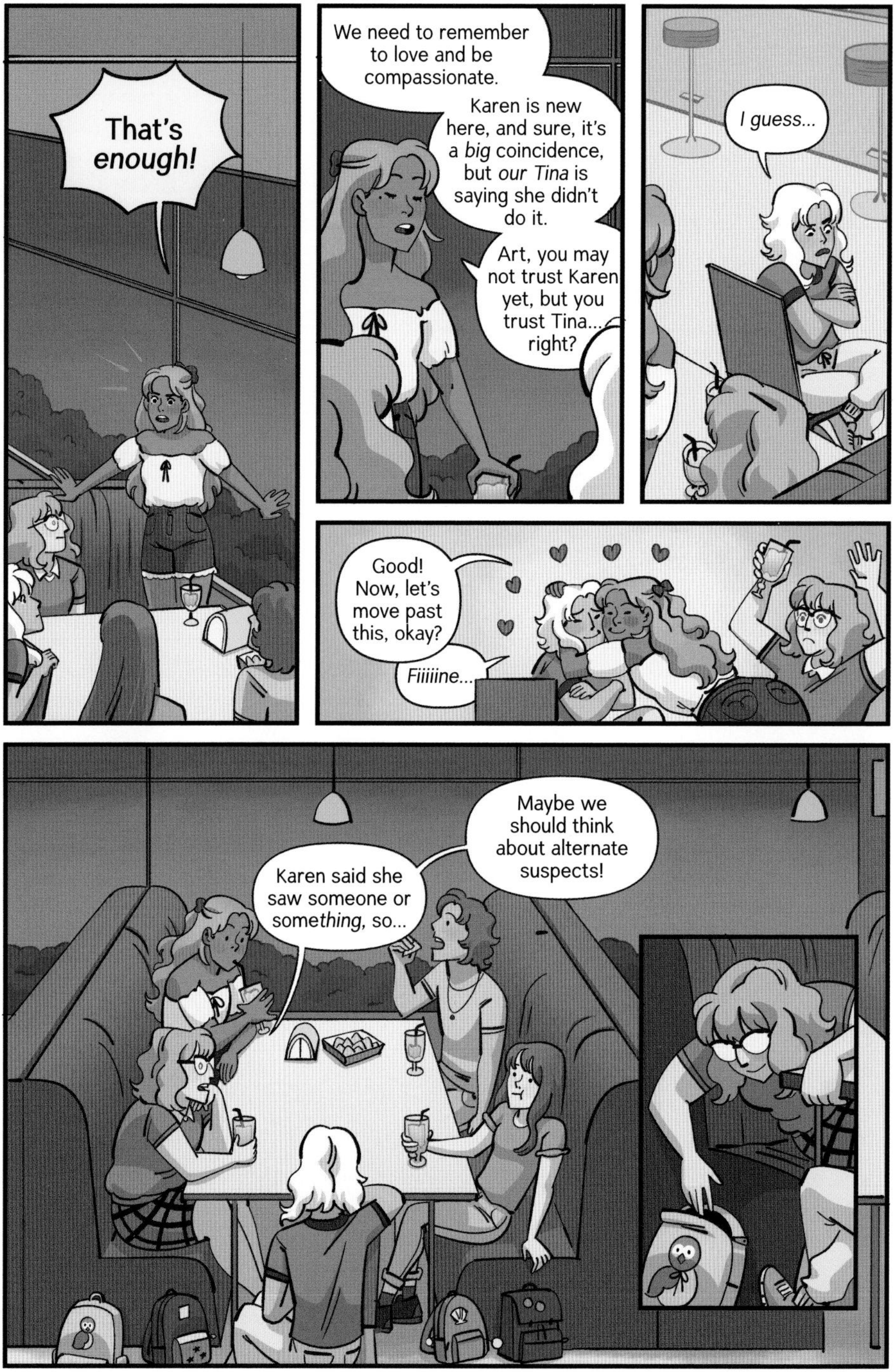
That's *enough!*
We need to remember to love and be compassionate.
Karen is new here, and sure, it's a *big* coincidence, but *our Tina* is saying she didn't do it.
Art, you may not trust Karen yet, but you trust Tina... right?
I guess...
Good! Now, let's move past this, okay?
Fiiiiine...
Maybe we should think about alternate suspects!
Karen said she saw someone or some*thing,* so...

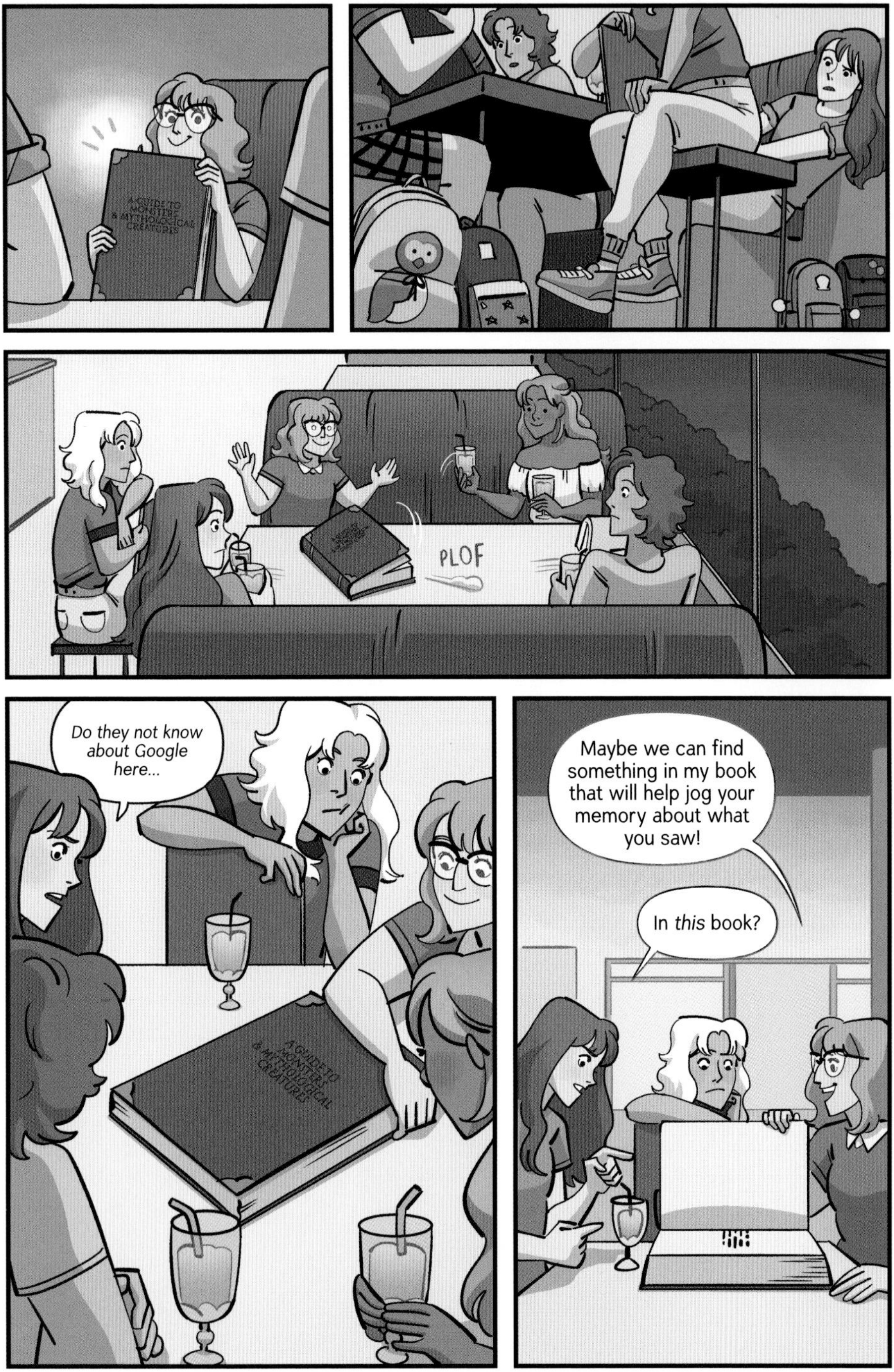
A GUIDE TO MONSTERS & MYTHOLOGICAL CREATURES
PLOF
Do they not know about Google here...
A GUIDE TO MONSTERS & MYTHOLOGICAL CREATURES
Maybe we can find something in my book that will help jog your memory about what you saw!
In *this* book?

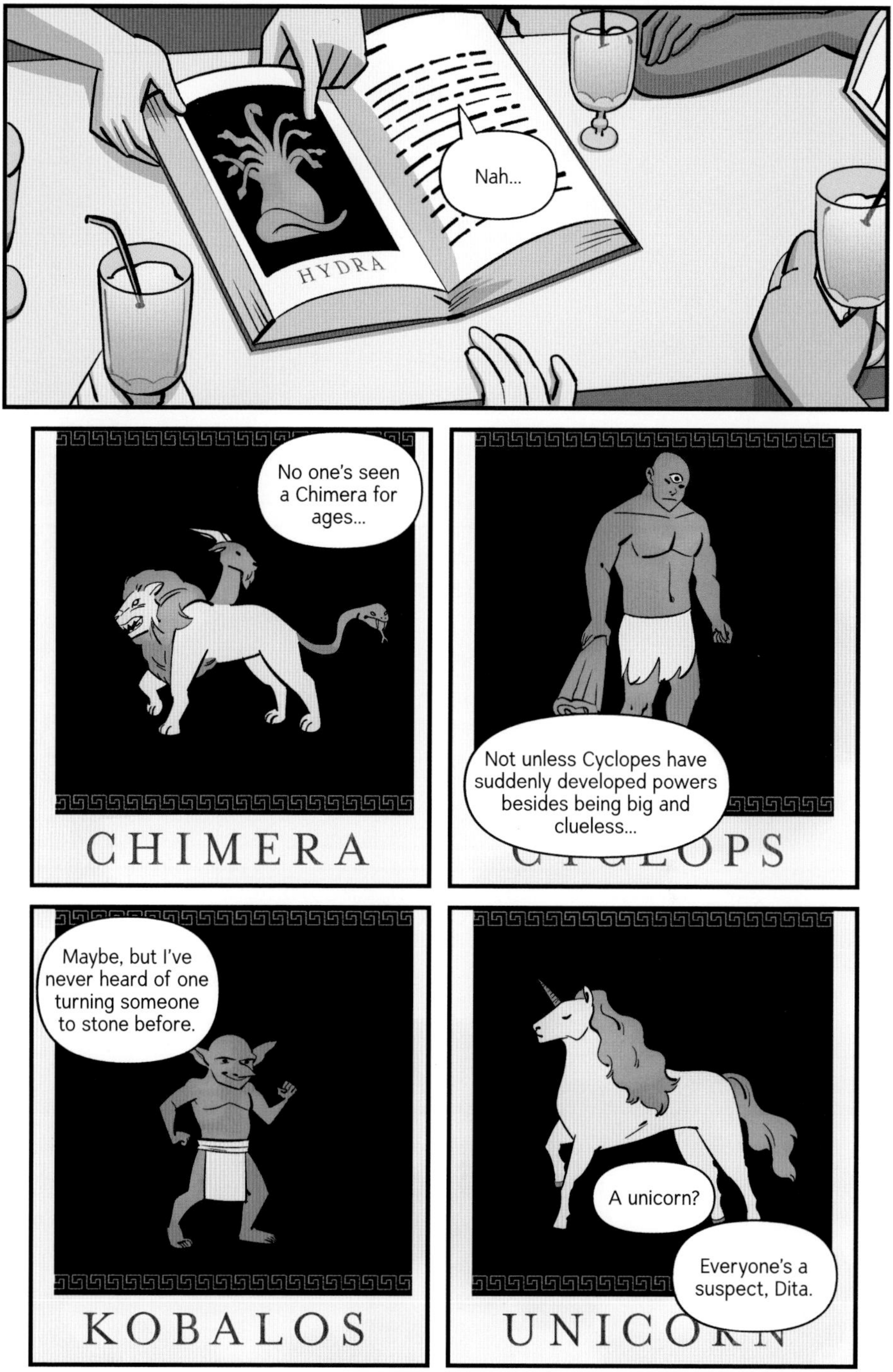
HYDRA
Nah...
No one's seen a Chimera for ages...
CHIMERA
Not unless Cyclopes have suddenly developed powers besides being big and clueless...
Maybe, but I've never heard of one turning someone to stone before.
KOBALOS
A unicorn?
Everyone's a suspect, Dita.

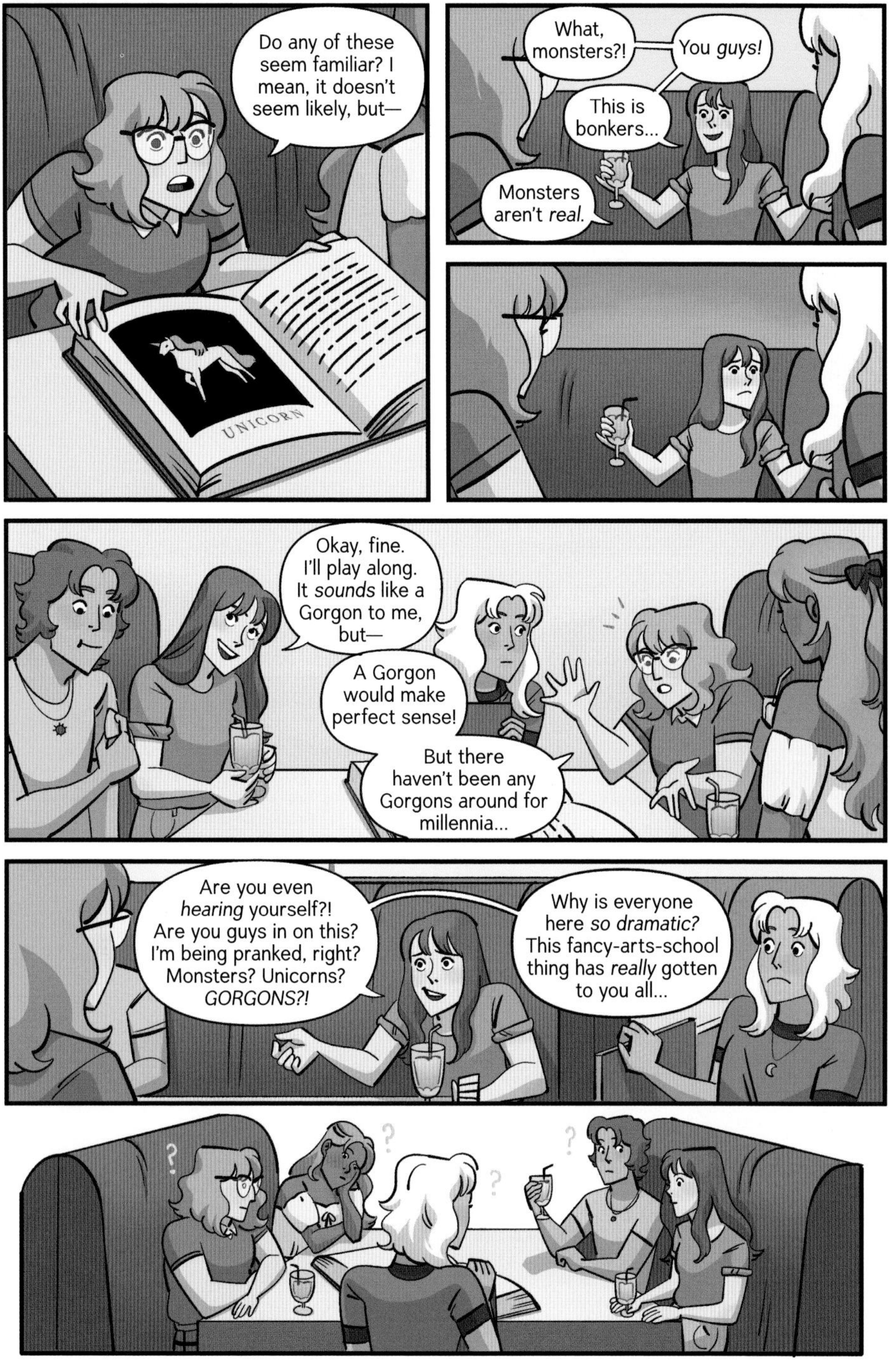
Do any of these seem familiar? I mean, it doesn't seem likely, but—
UNICORN
What, monsters?!
You *guys!*
This is bonkers...
Monsters aren't *real.*
Okay, fine. I'll play along. It *sounds* like a Gorgon to me, but—
A Gorgon would make perfect sense!
But there haven't been any Gorgons around for millennia...
Are you even *hearing* yourself?! Are you guys in on this? I'm being pranked, right? Monsters? Unicorns? *GORGONS?!*
Why is everyone here *so dramatic?* This fancy-arts-school thing has *really* gotten to you all...
?
?
?
?

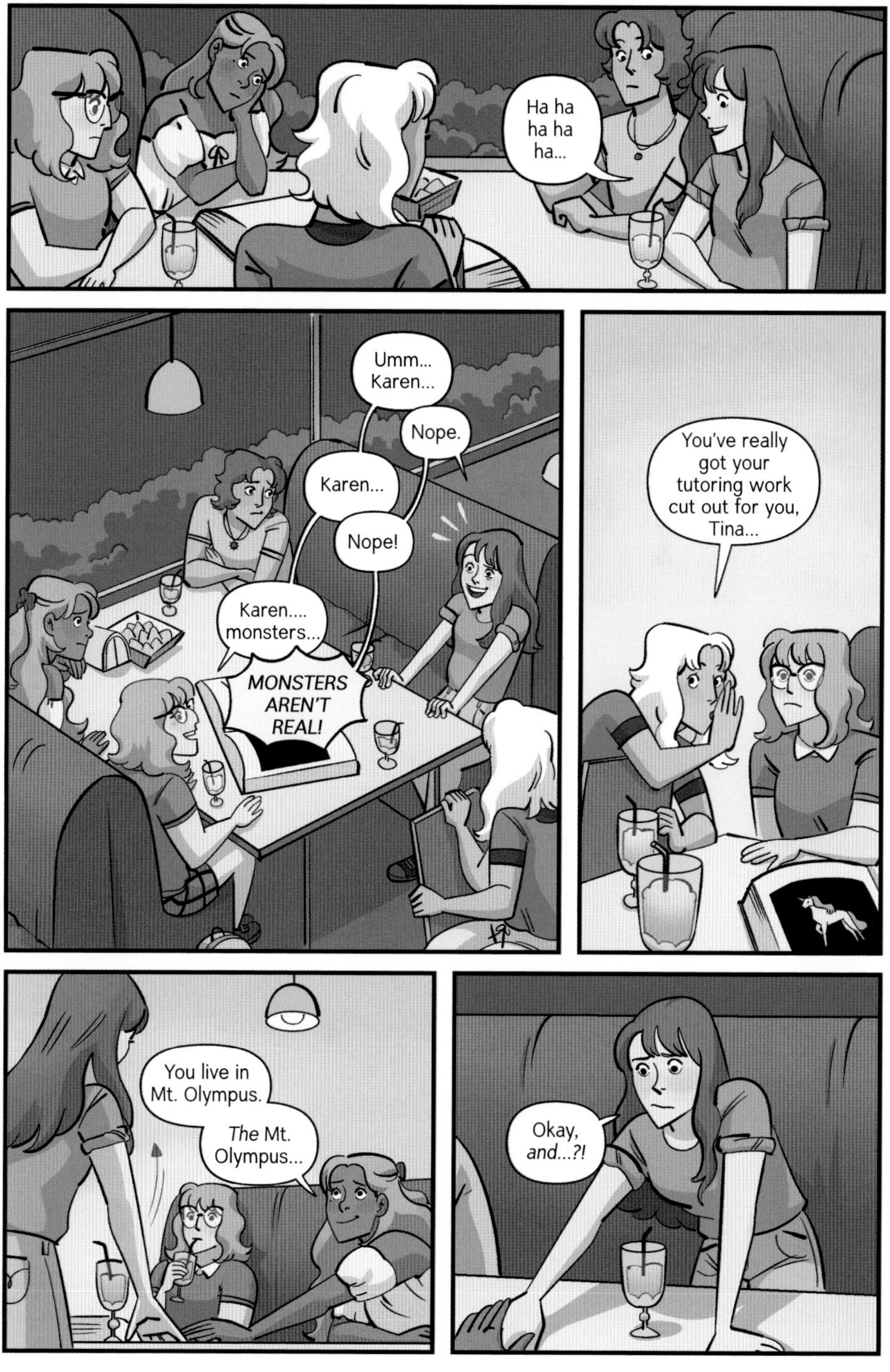

Ha ha ha ha ha...
Umm... Karen...
Nope.
Karen...
Nope!
Karen.... monsters...
MONSTERS AREN'T REAL!
You've really got your tutoring work cut out for you, Tina...
You live in Mt. Olympus.
The Mt. Olympus...
Okay, *and...?!*

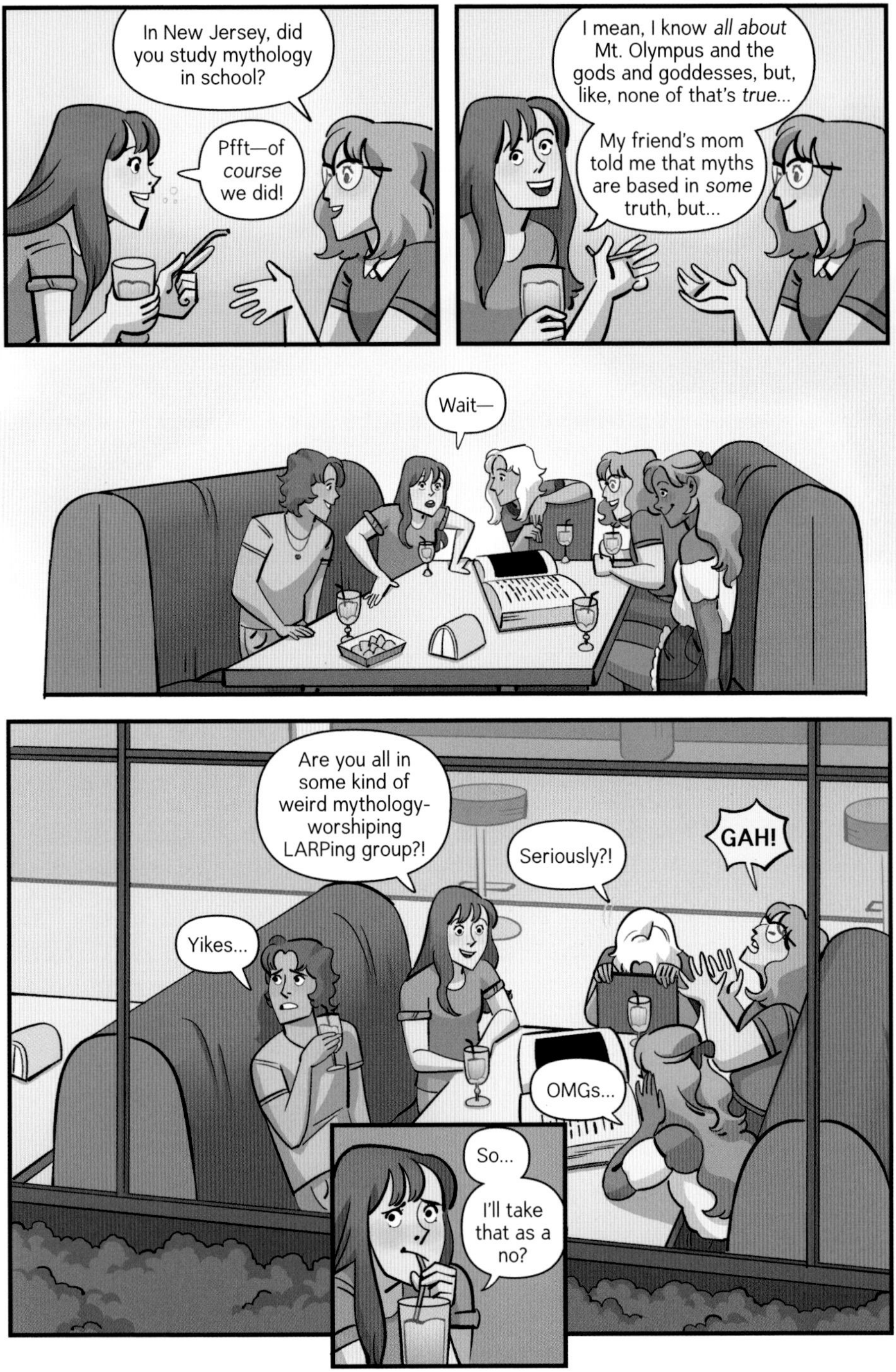
In New Jersey, did you study mythology in school?
Pfft—of *course* we did!
I mean, I know *all about* Mt. Olympus and the gods and goddesses, but, like, none of that's *true*...
My friend's mom told me that myths are based in *some* truth, but...
Wait—
Are you all in some kind of weird mythology-worshiping LARPing group?!
Seriously?!
GAH!
Yikes...
OMGs...
So...
I'll take that as a no?

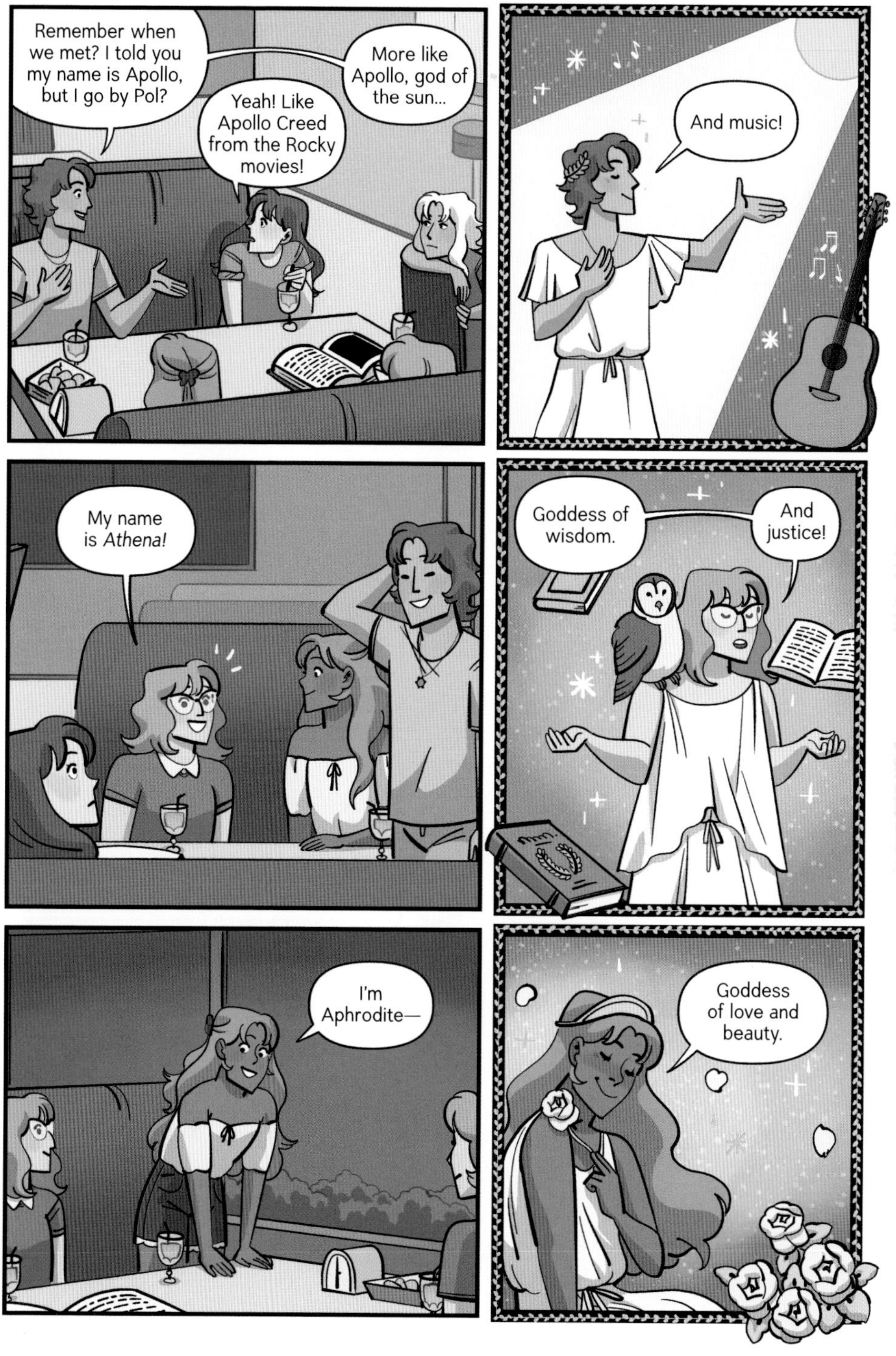

Remember when we met? I told you my name is Apollo, but I go by Pol?
Yeah! Like Apollo Creed from the Rocky movies!
More like Apollo, god of the sun...
And music!
My name is *Athena!*
Goddess of wisdom.
And justice!
I'm Aphrodite—
Goddess of love and beauty.

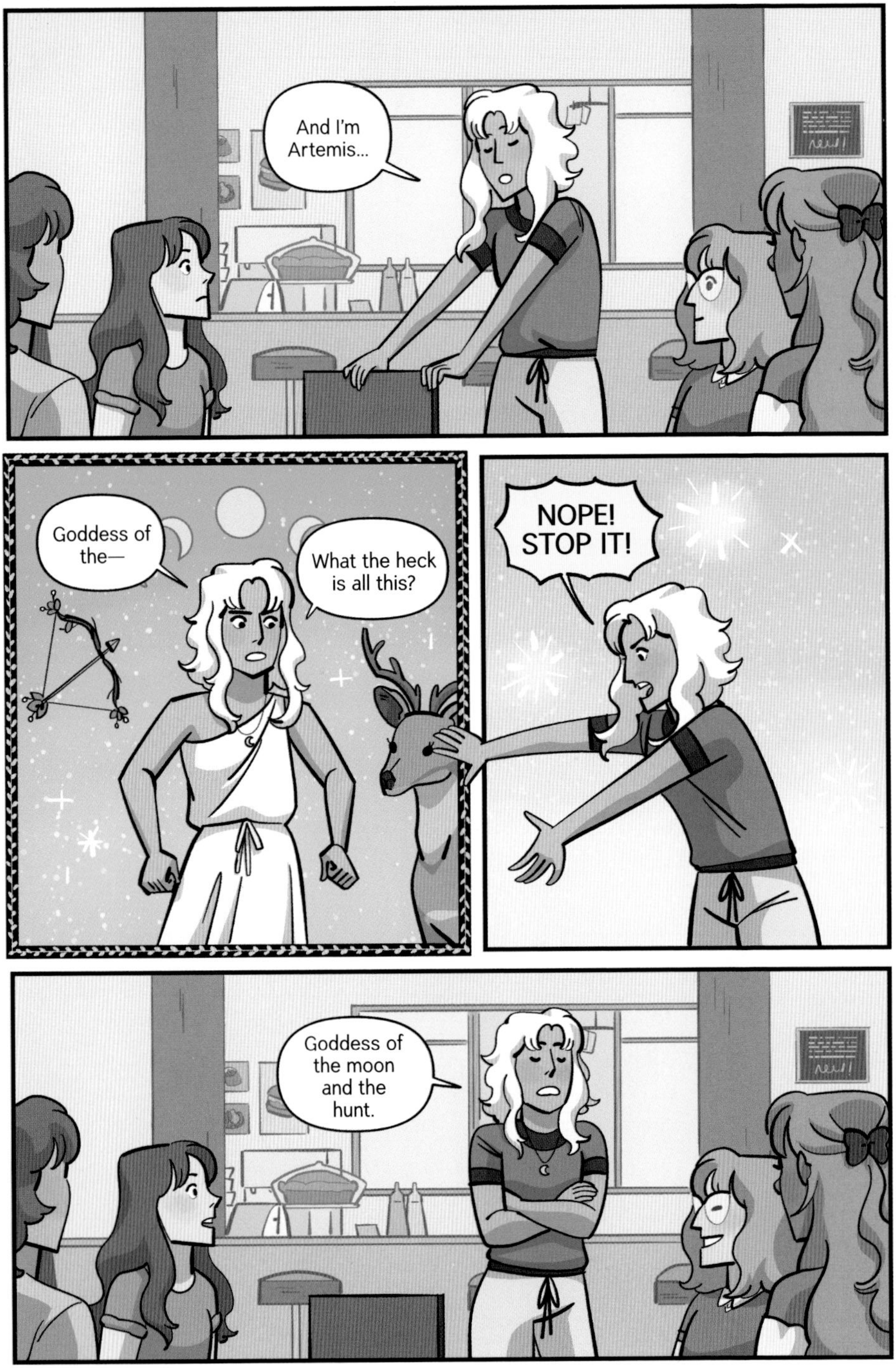
And I'm Artemis...
Goddess of the—
What the heck is all this?
NOPE! STOP IT!
Goddess of the moon and the hunt.

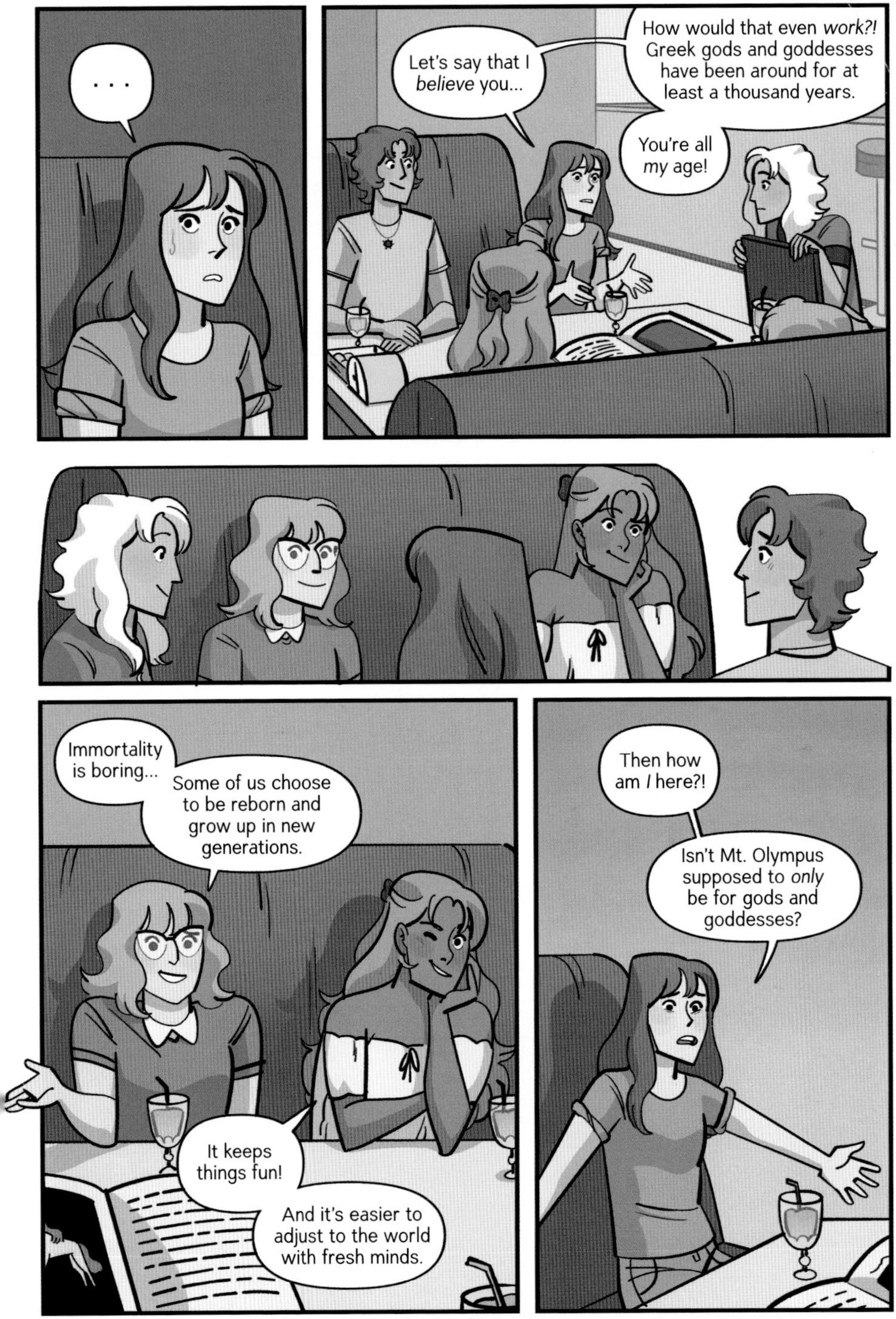
. . .
Let's say that I *believe* you...
How would that even *work?!* Greek gods and goddesses have been around for at least a thousand years.
You're all *my* age!
Immortality is boring...
Some of us choose to be reborn and grow up in new generations.
It keeps things fun!
And it's easier to adjust to the world with fresh minds.
Then how am *I* here?!
Isn't Mt. Olympus supposed to *only* be for gods and goddesses?

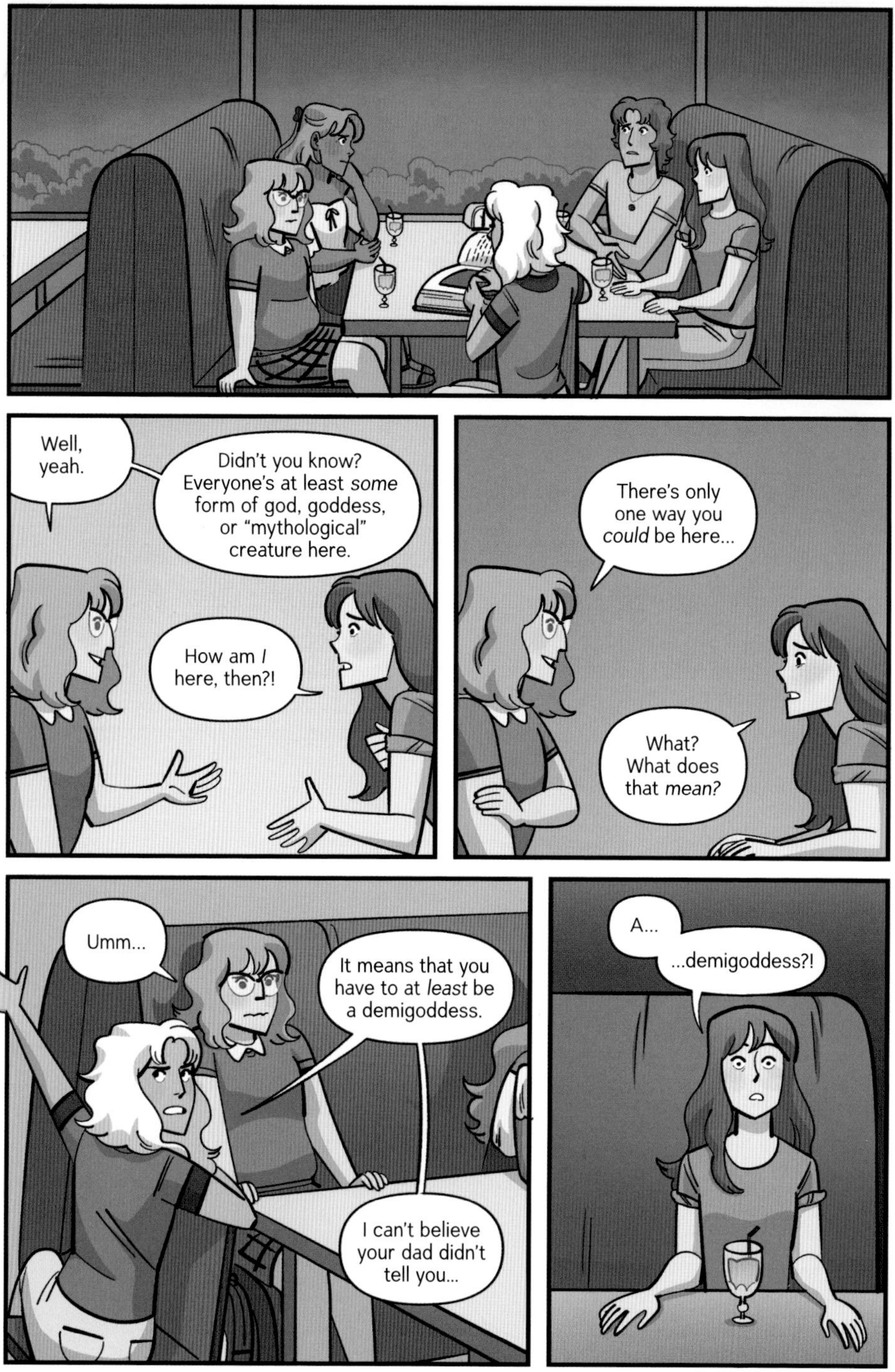
Well, yeah.
Didn't you know? Everyone's at least *some* form of god, goddess, or "mythological" creature here.
How am *I* here, then?!
There's only one way you *could* be here...
What? What does that *mean?*
Umm...
It means that you have to at *least* be a demigoddess.
I can't believe your dad didn't tell you...
A...
...demigoddess?!

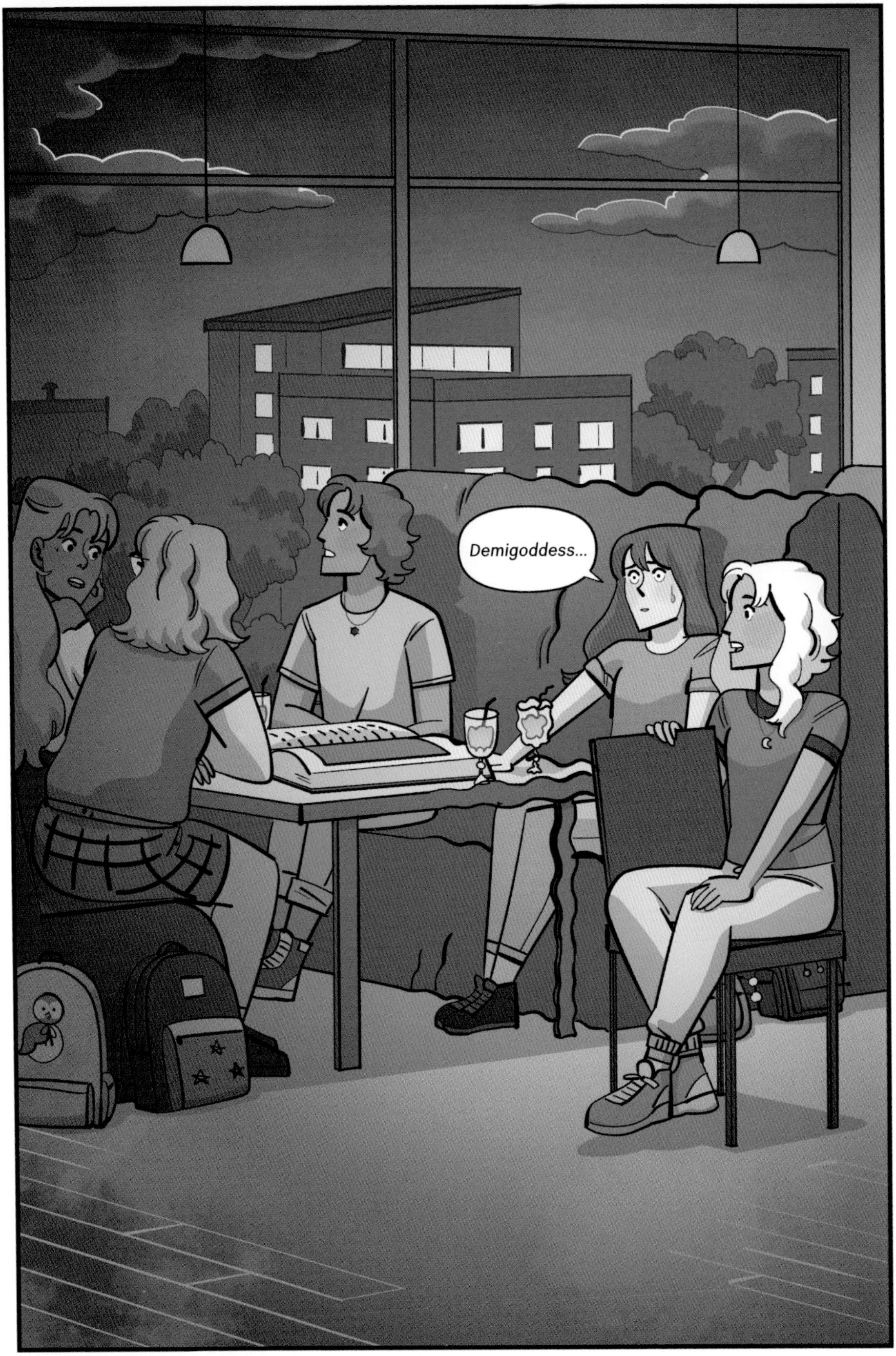
Demigoddess...

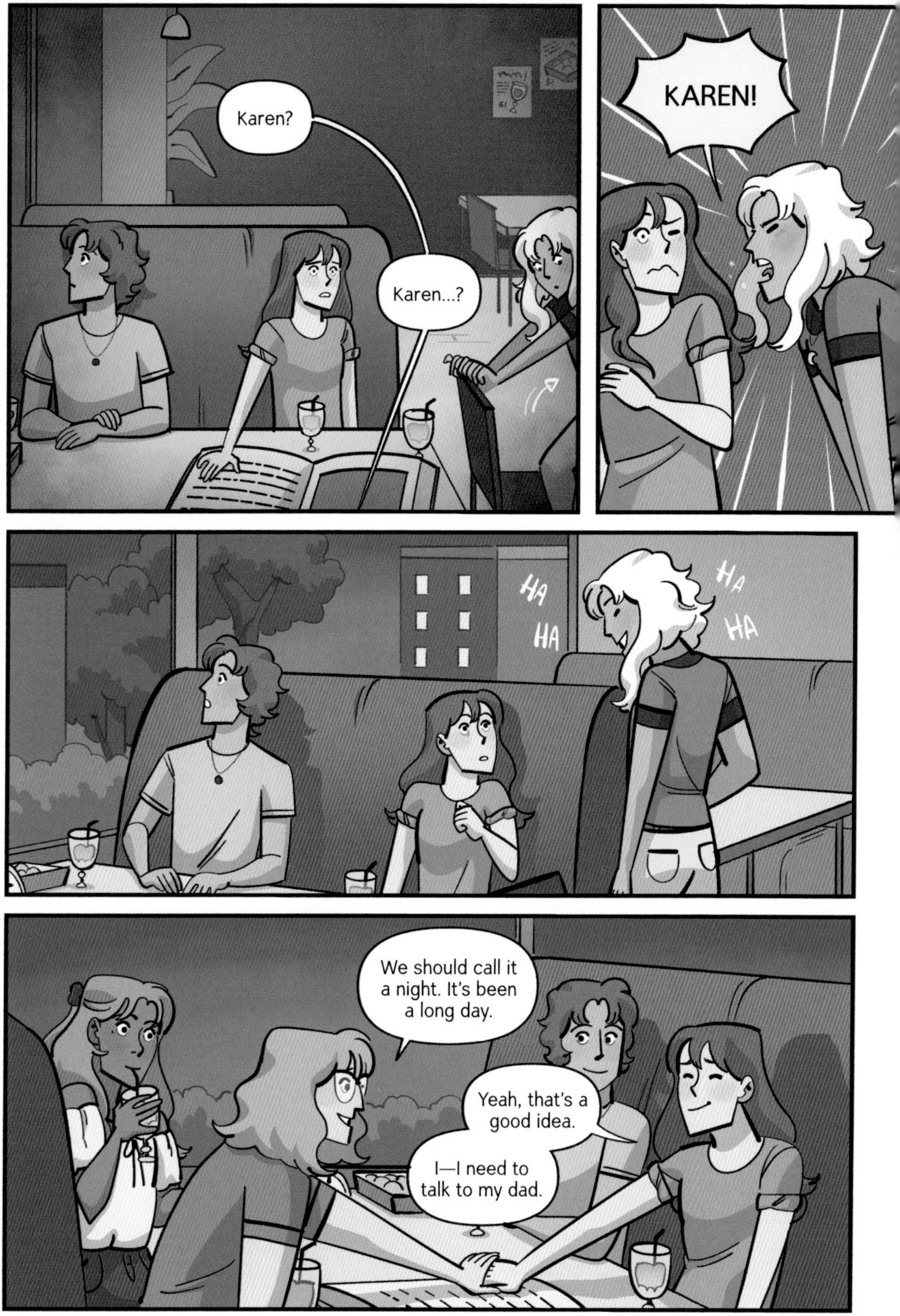
Karen?
Karen...?
KAREN!
HA
HA
HA
HA
We should call it a night. It's been a long day.
Yeah, that's a good idea.
I—I need to talk to my dad.

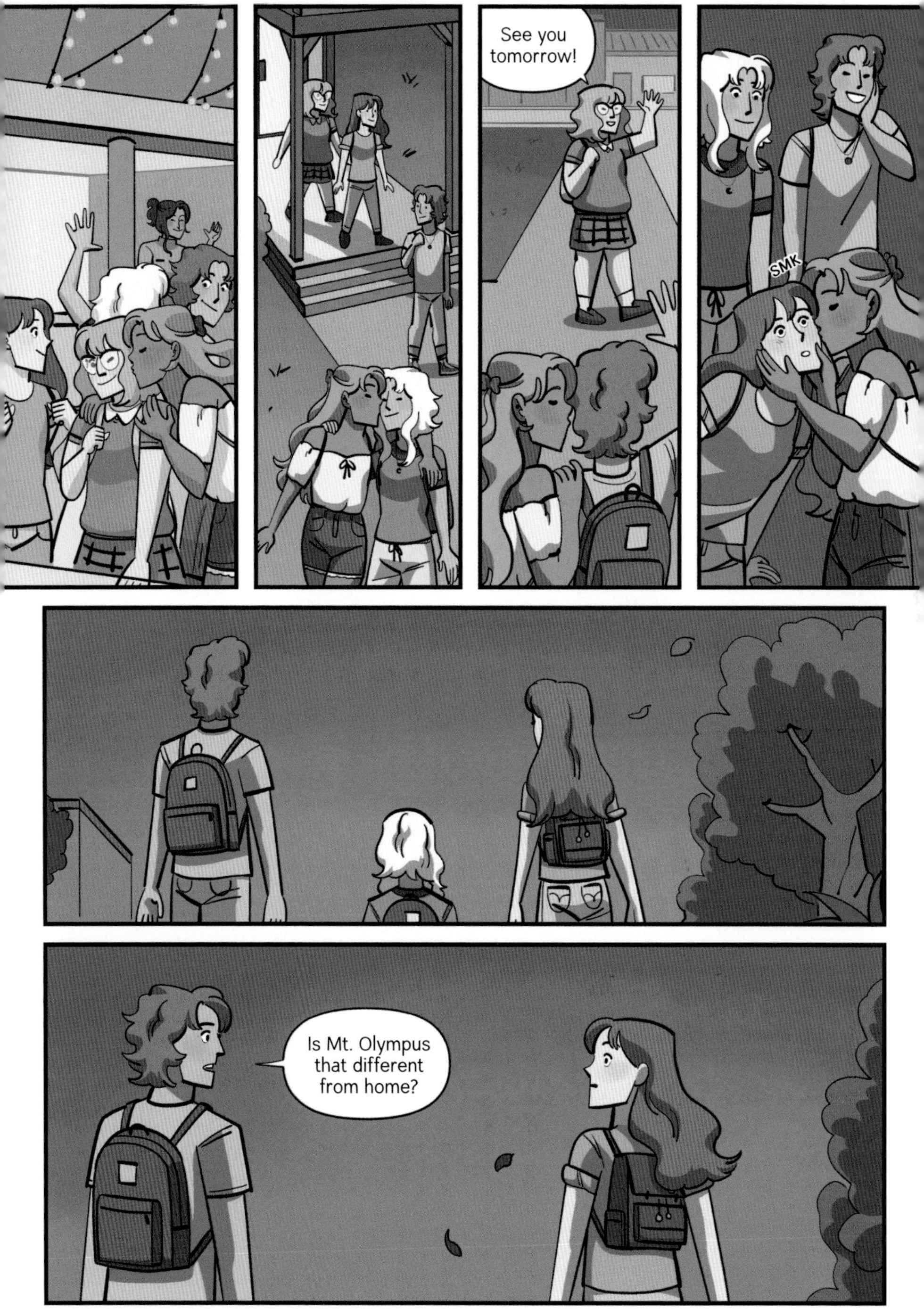
See you tomorrow!
SMK
Is Mt. Olympus that different from home?

84

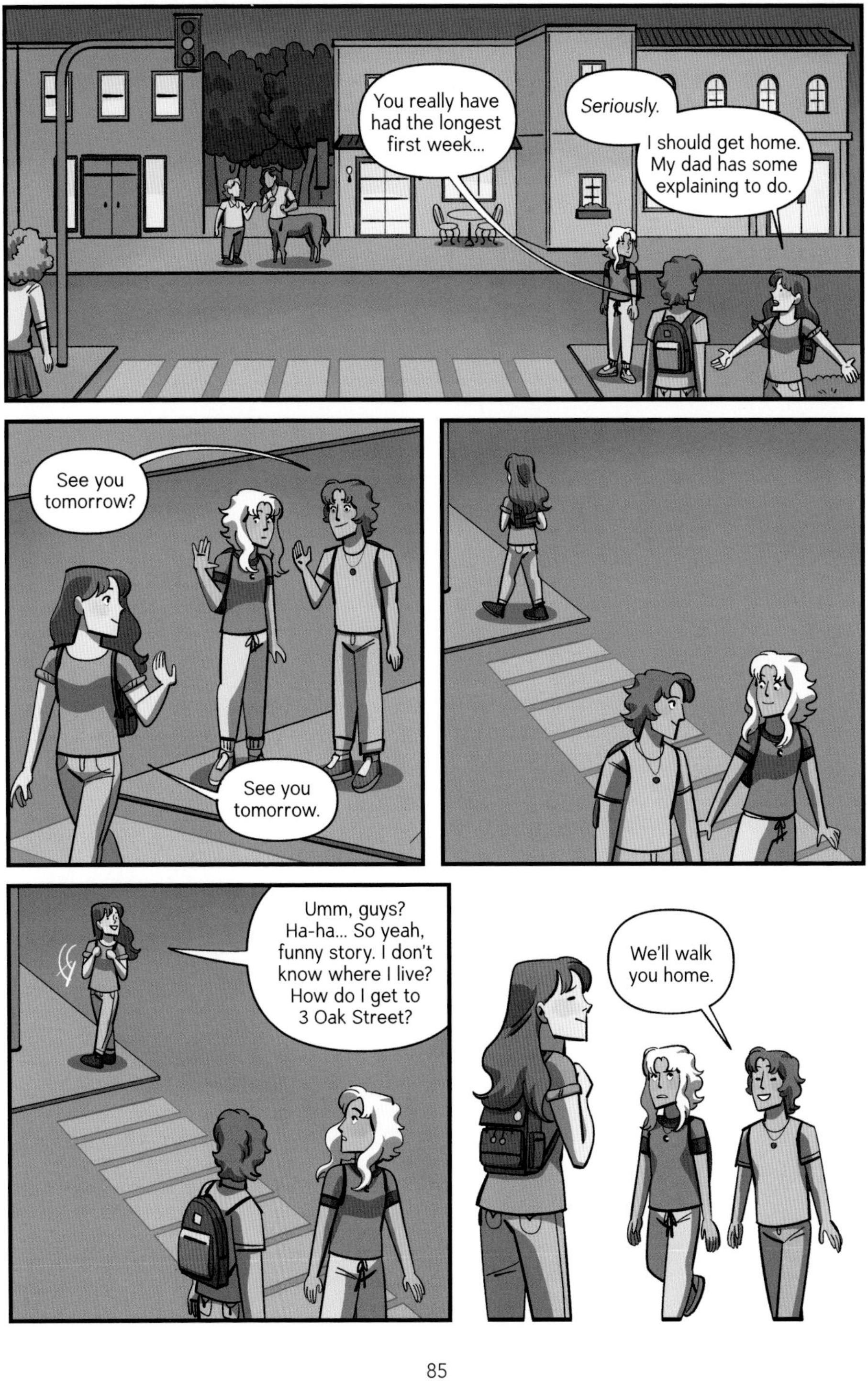
You really have had the longest first week...
Seriously.
I should get home. My dad has some explaining to do.
See you tomorrow?
See you tomorrow.
Umm, guys? Ha-ha... So yeah, funny story. I don't know where I live? How do I get to 3 Oak Street?
We'll walk you home.

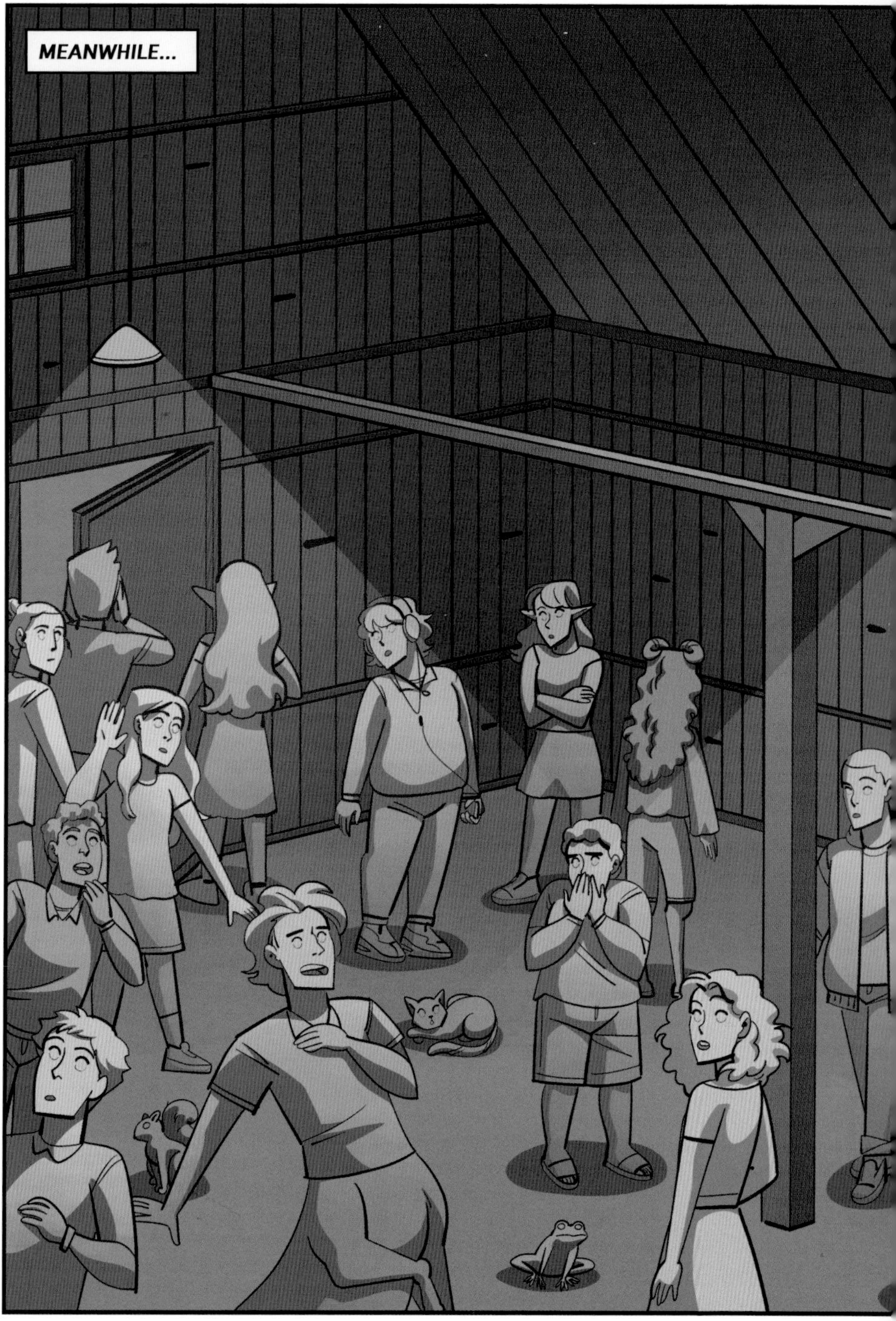
MEANWHILE...

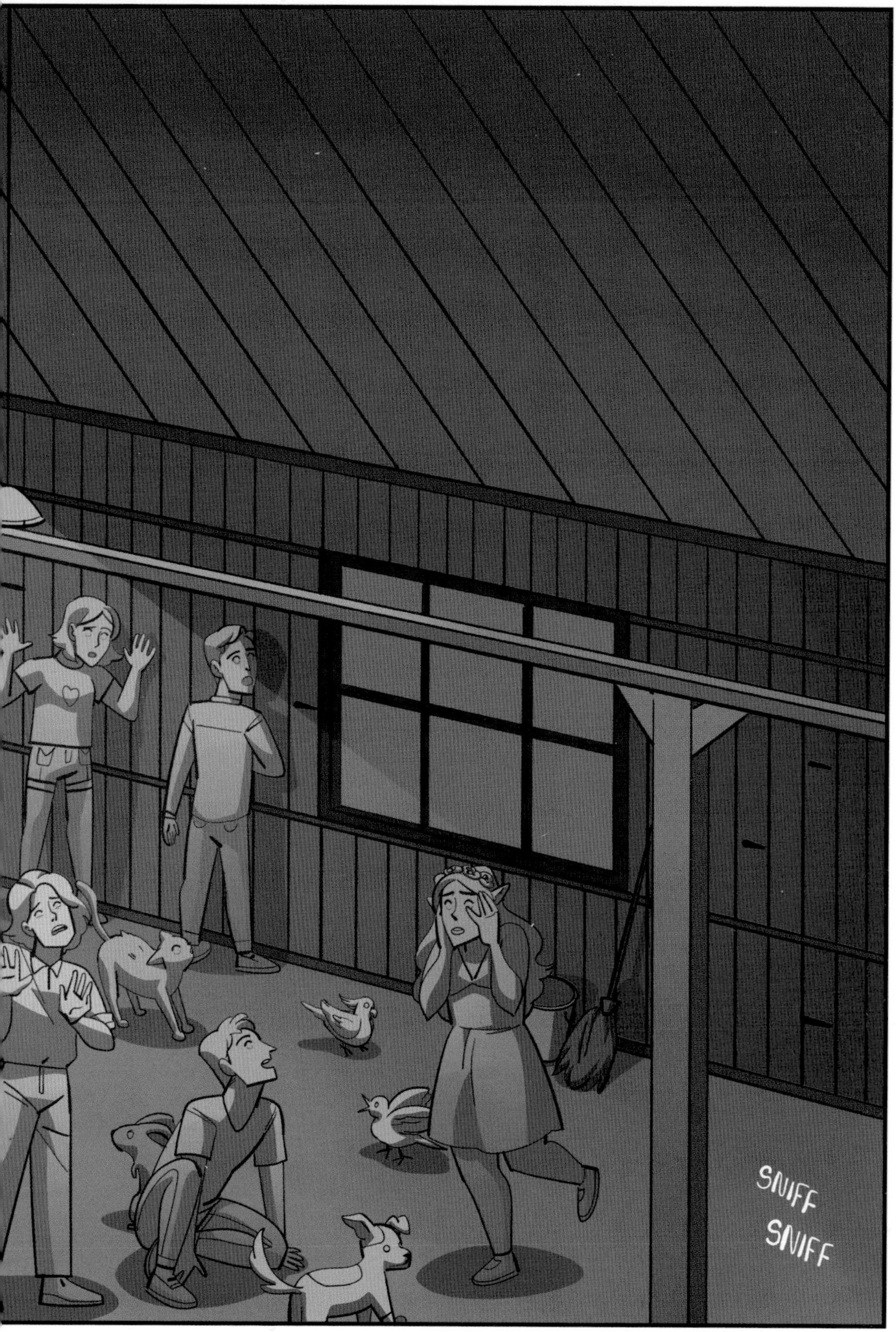
SNIFF
SNIFF

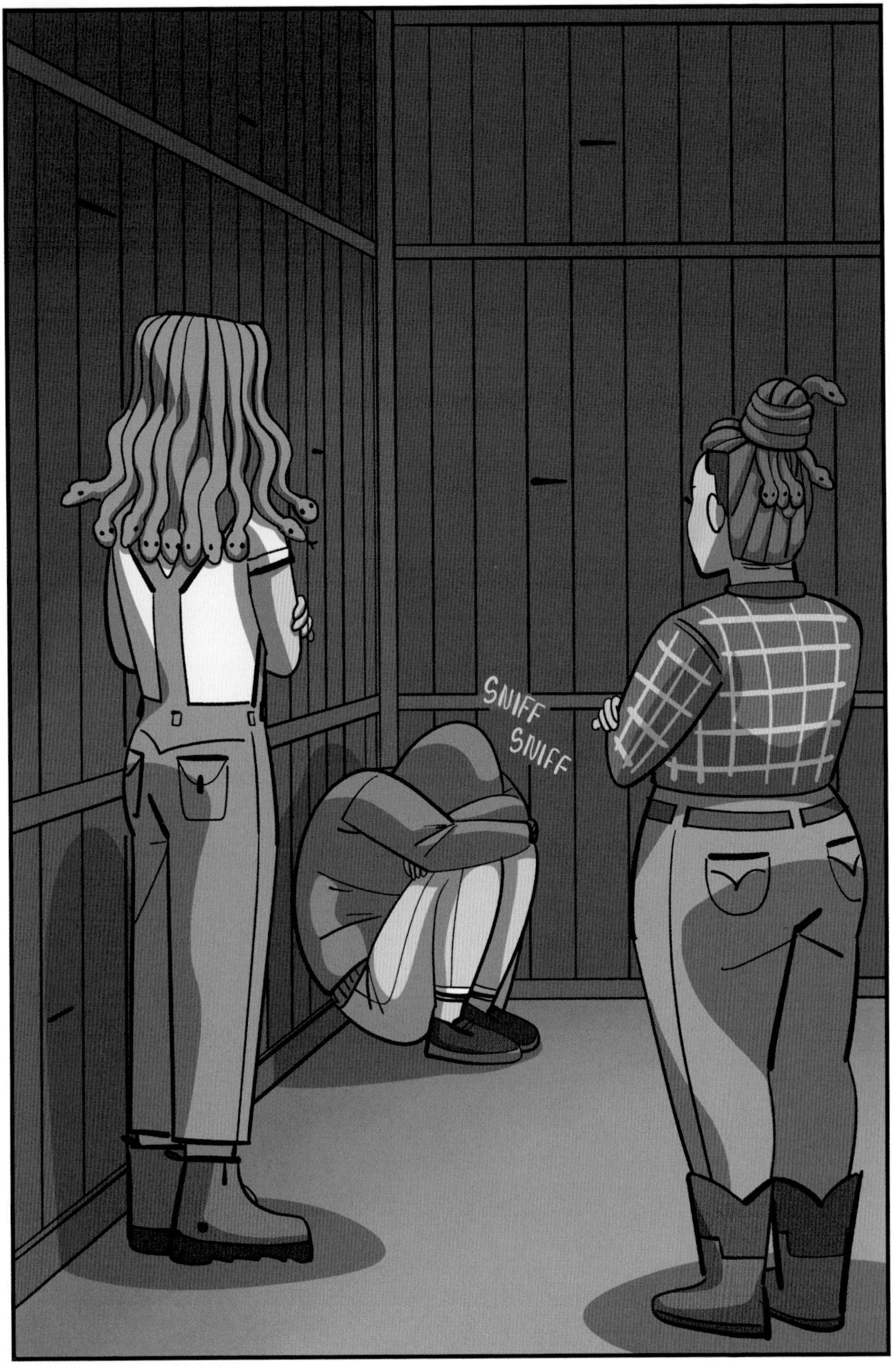
SNIFF
SNIFF

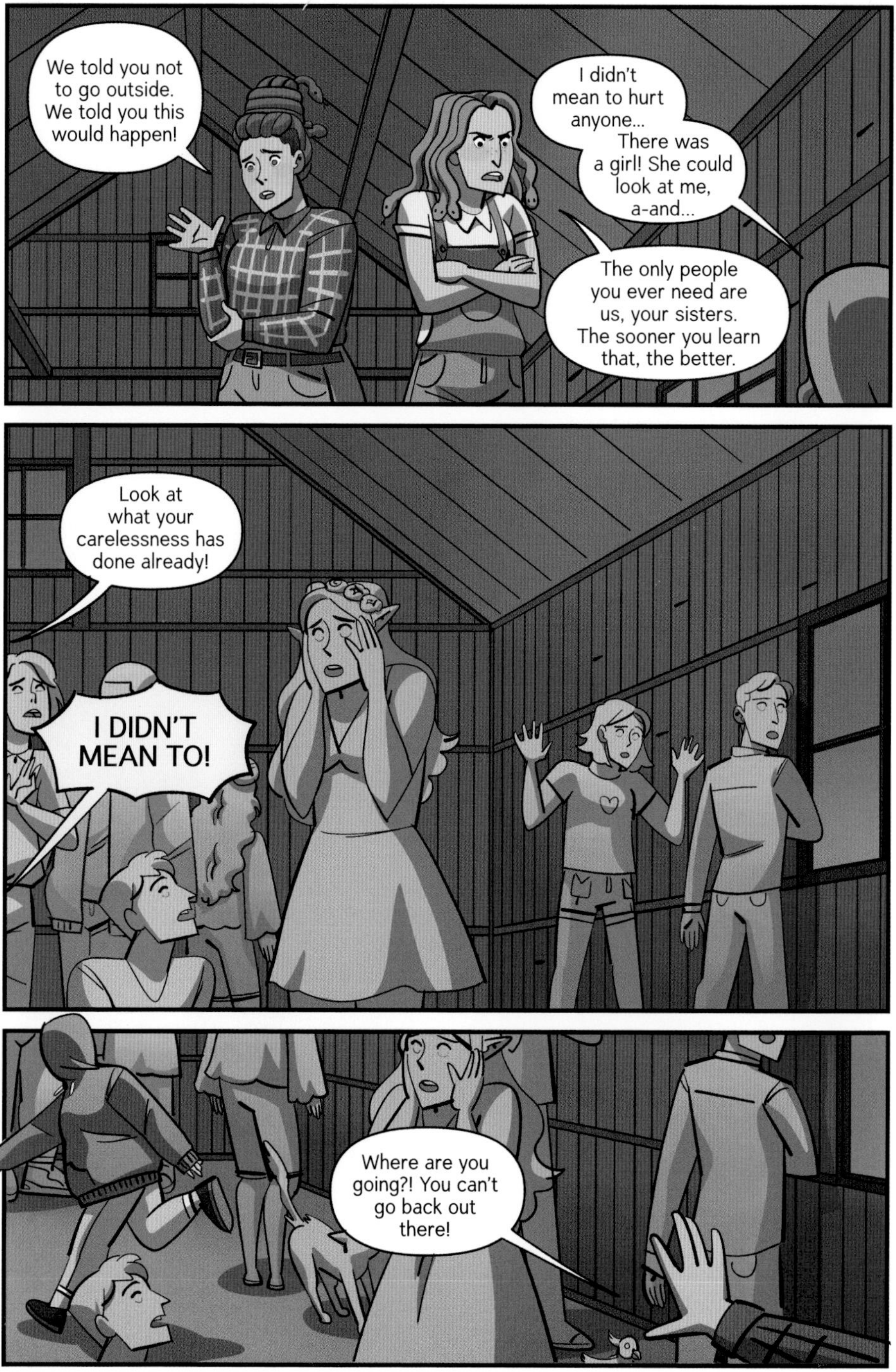
We told you not to go outside. We told you this would happen!
I didn't mean to hurt anyone... There was a girl! She could look at me, a-and...
The only people you ever need are us, your sisters. The sooner you learn that, the better.
Look at what your carelessness has done already!
I DIDN'T MEAN TO!
Where are you going?! You can't go back out there!

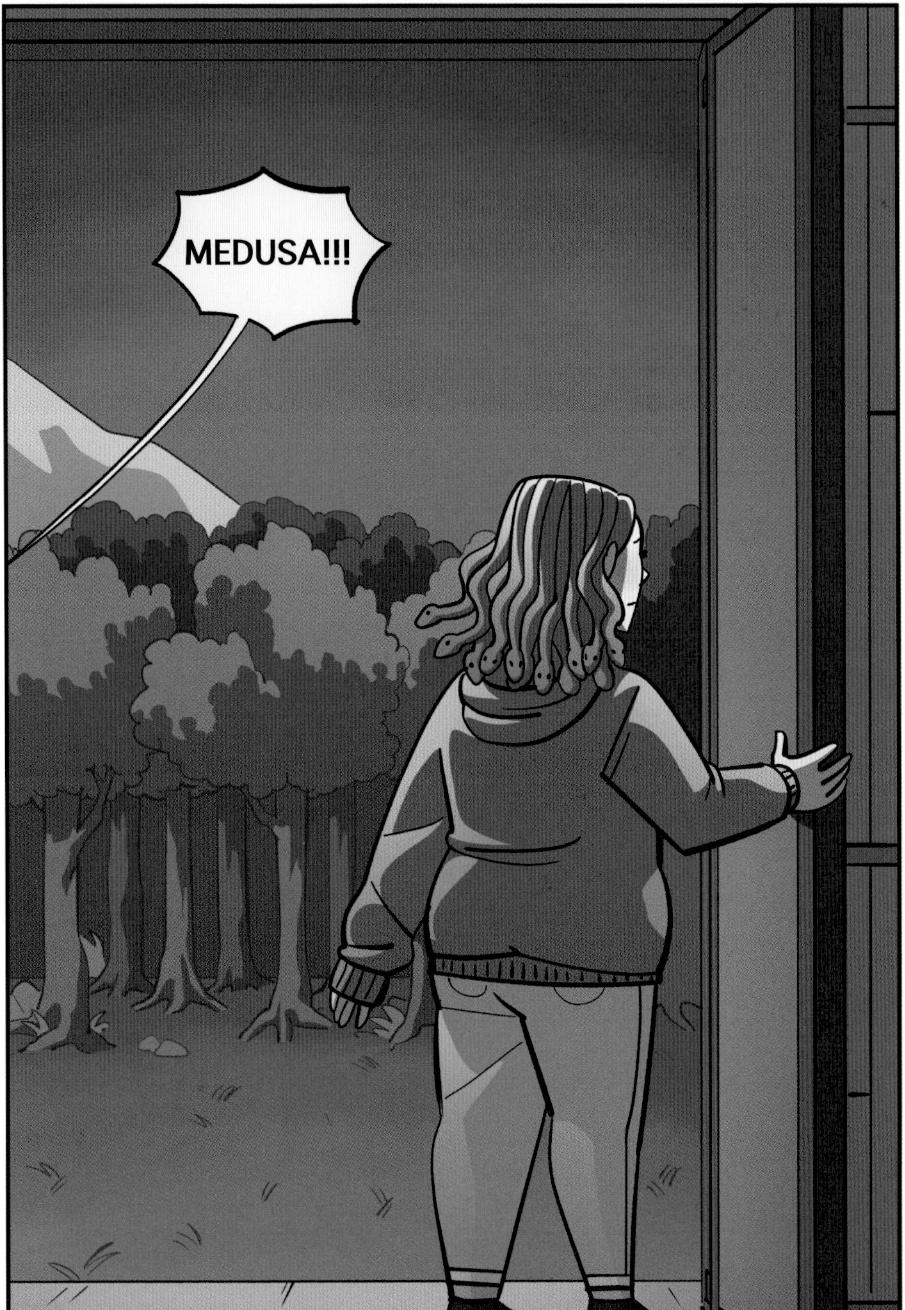
MEDUSA!!!

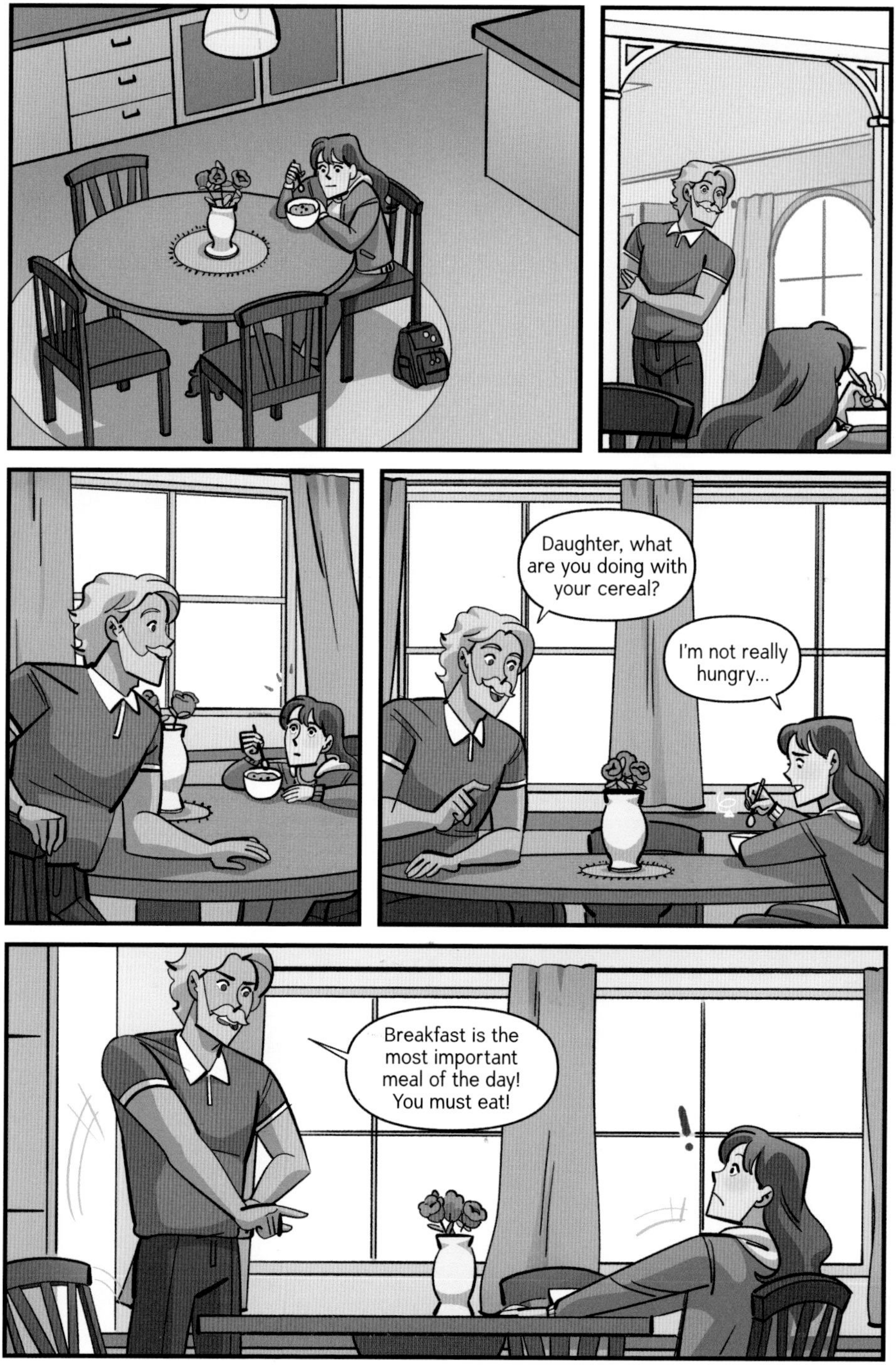
Daughter, what are you doing with your cereal?
I'm not really hungry...
Breakfast is the most important meal of the day! You must eat!

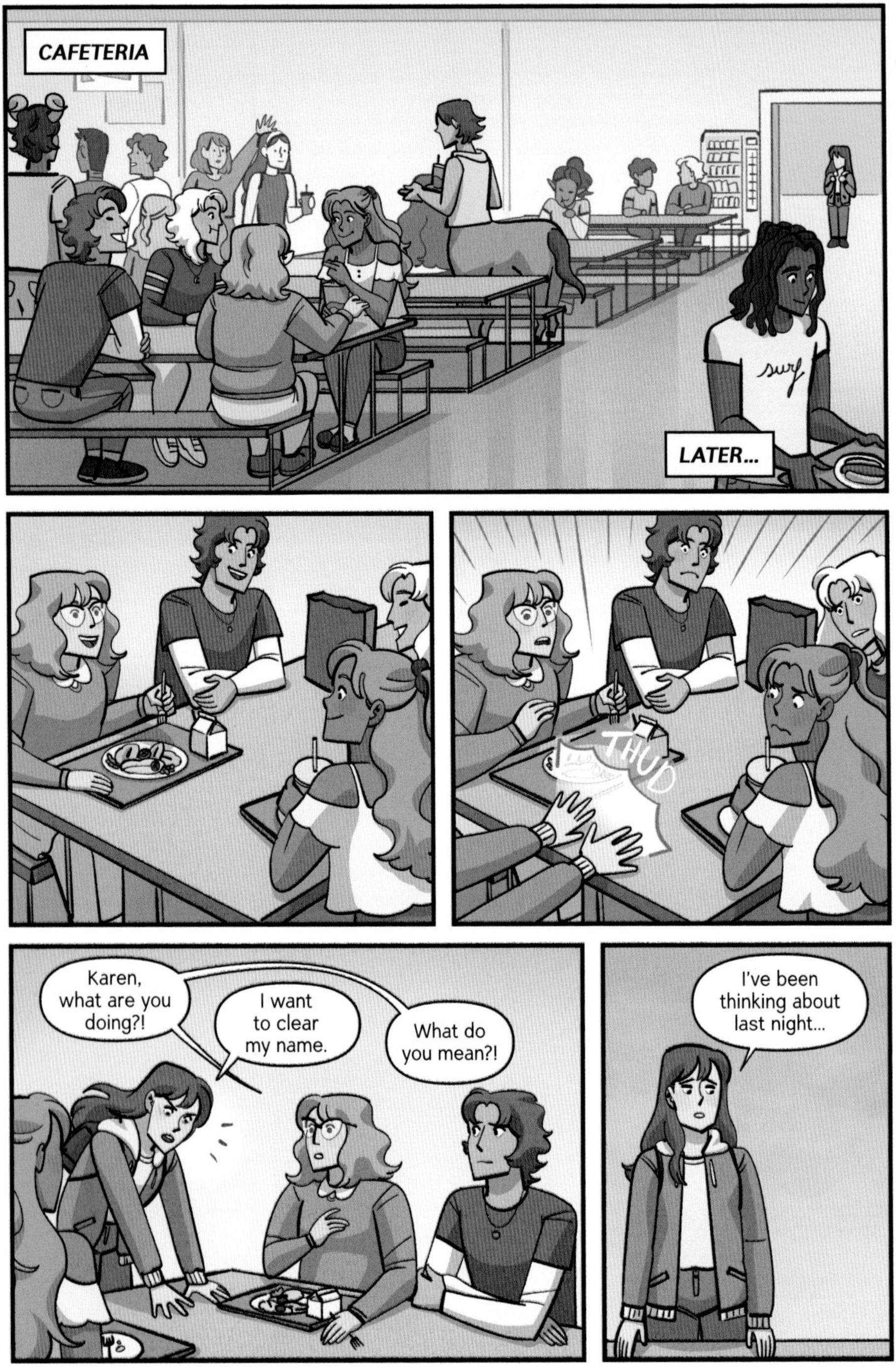
CAFETERIA
surf
LATER...
THUD
Karen, what are you doing?!
I want to clear my name.
What do you mean?!
I've been thinking about last night...

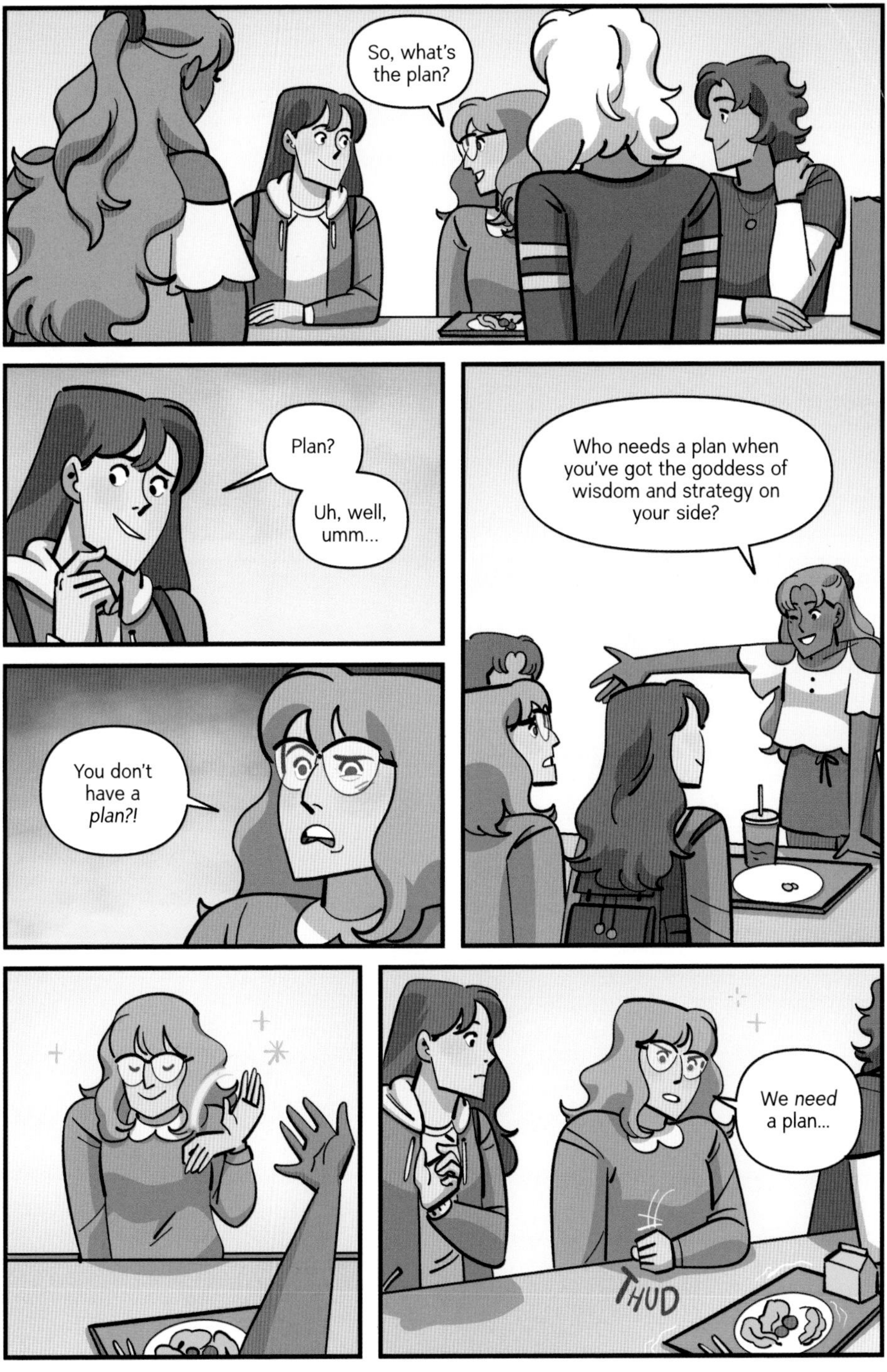
So, what's the plan?
Plan?
Uh, well, umm...
Who needs a plan when you've got the goddess of wisdom and strategy on your side?
You don't have a *plan?!*
THUD
We *need* a plan...

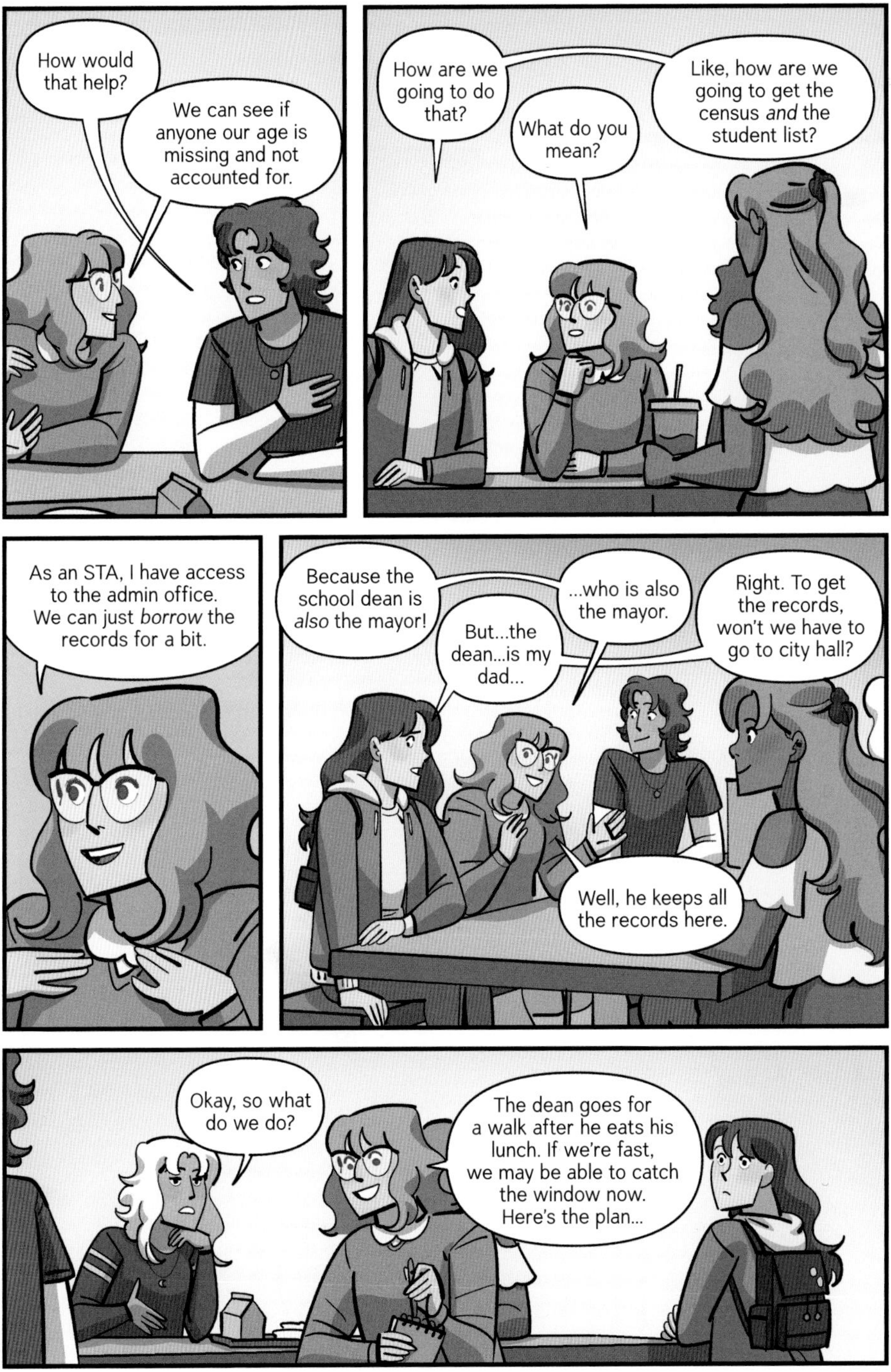
How would that help?
We can see if anyone our age is missing and not accounted for.
How are we going to do that?
What do you mean?
Like, how are we going to get the census *and* the student list?
As an STA, I have access to the admin office. We can just *borrow* the records for a bit.
Because the school dean is *also* the mayor!
...who is also the mayor.
But...the dean...is my dad...
Right. To get the records, won't we have to go to city hall?
Well, he keeps all the records here.
Okay, so what do we do?
The dean goes for a walk after he eats his lunch. If we're fast, we may be able to catch the window now. Here's the plan...

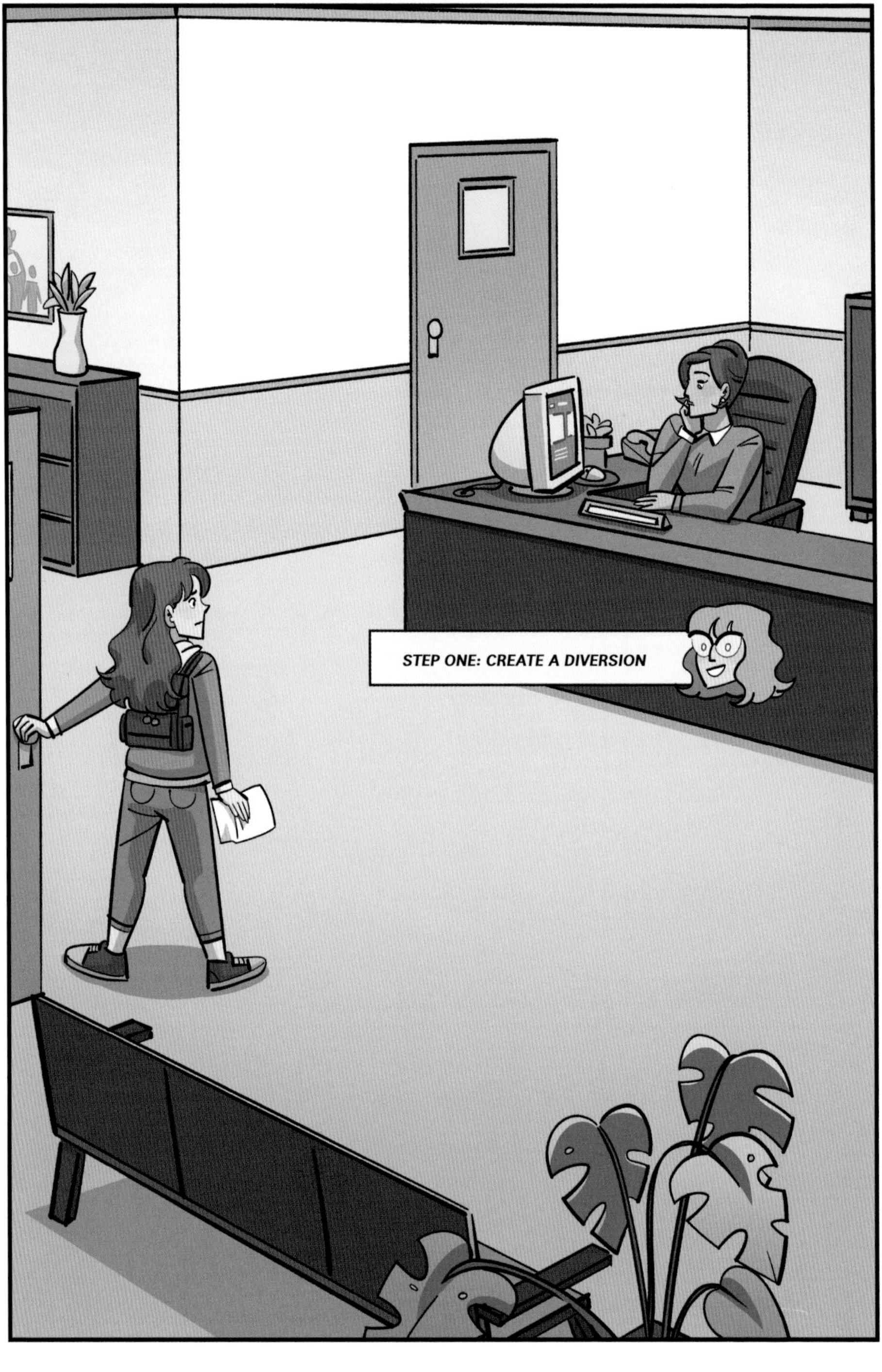
STEP ONE: CREATE A DIVERSION

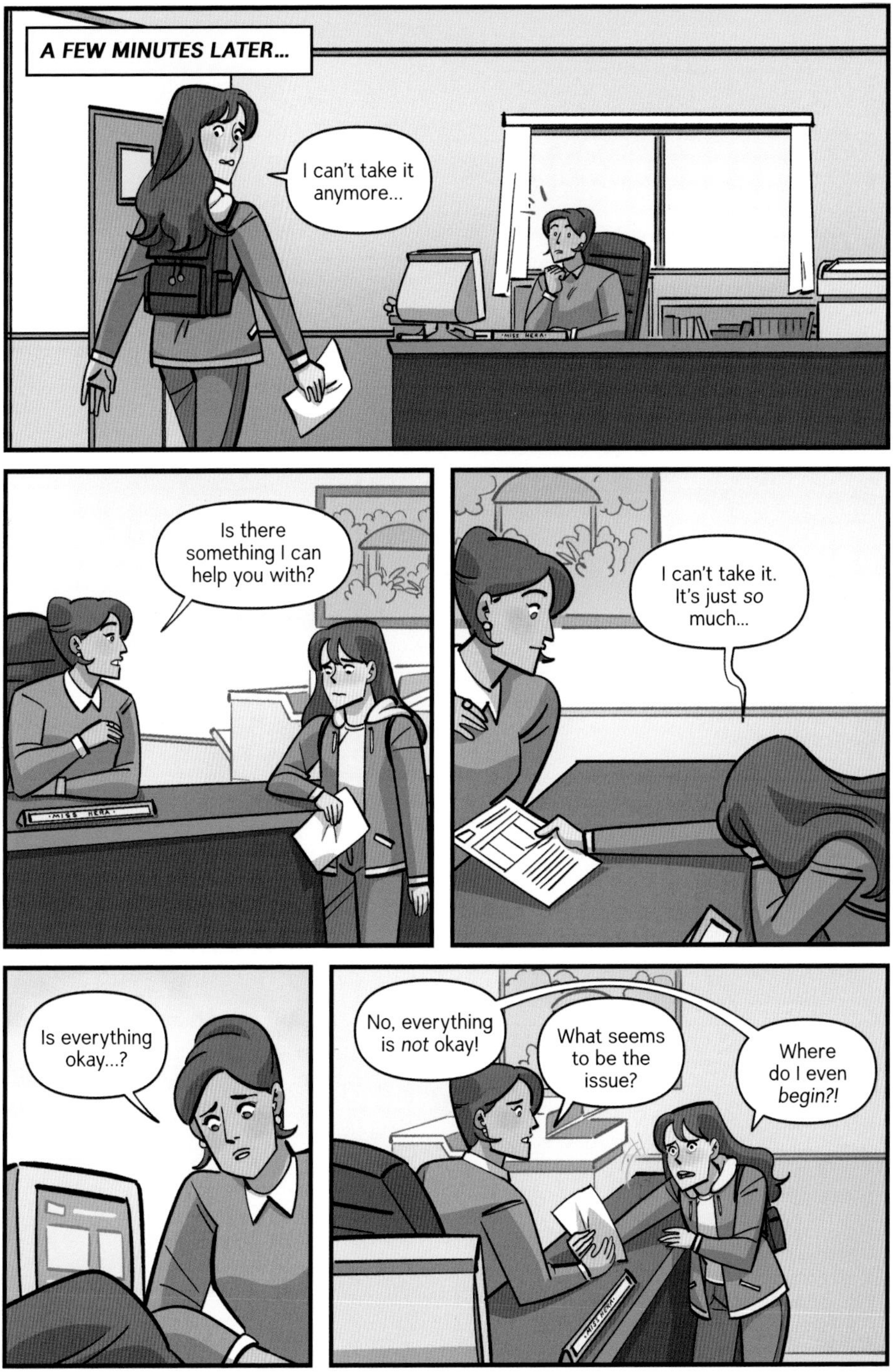
A FEW MINUTES LATER...
I can't take it anymore...
MISS HERA
Is there something I can help you with?
MISS HERA
I can't take it. It's just *so* much...
Is everything okay...?
No, everything is *not* okay!
What seems to be the issue?
Where do I even *begin?!*
MISS HERA

STEP THREE: SNEAK INTO THE DEAN'S OFFICE

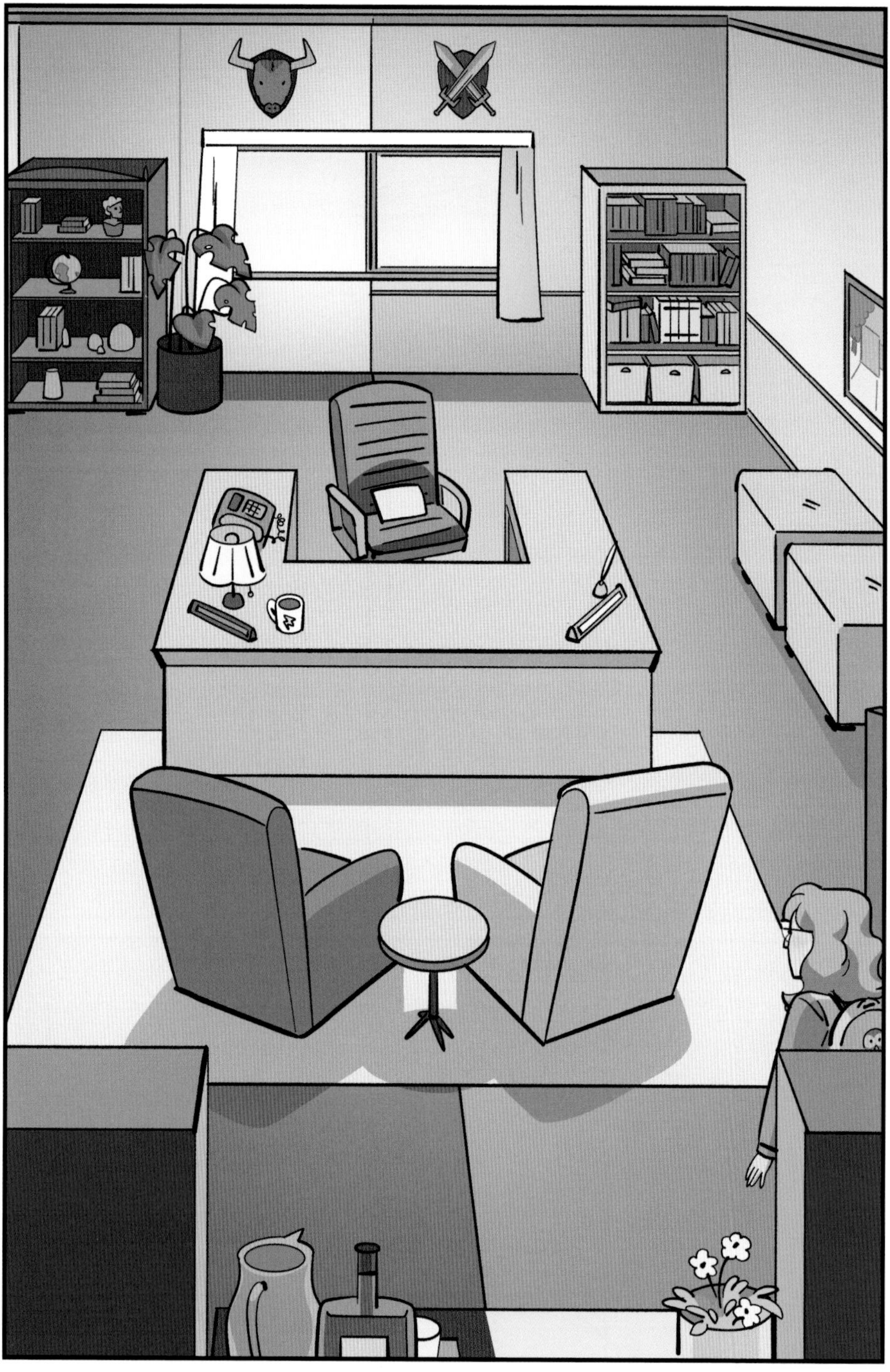

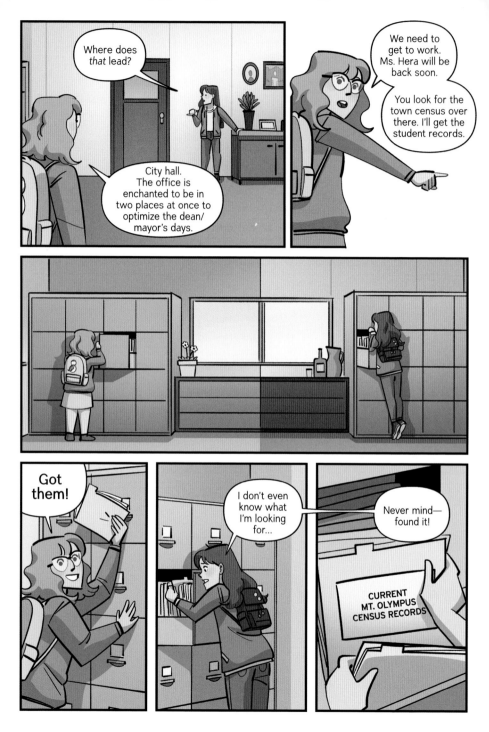

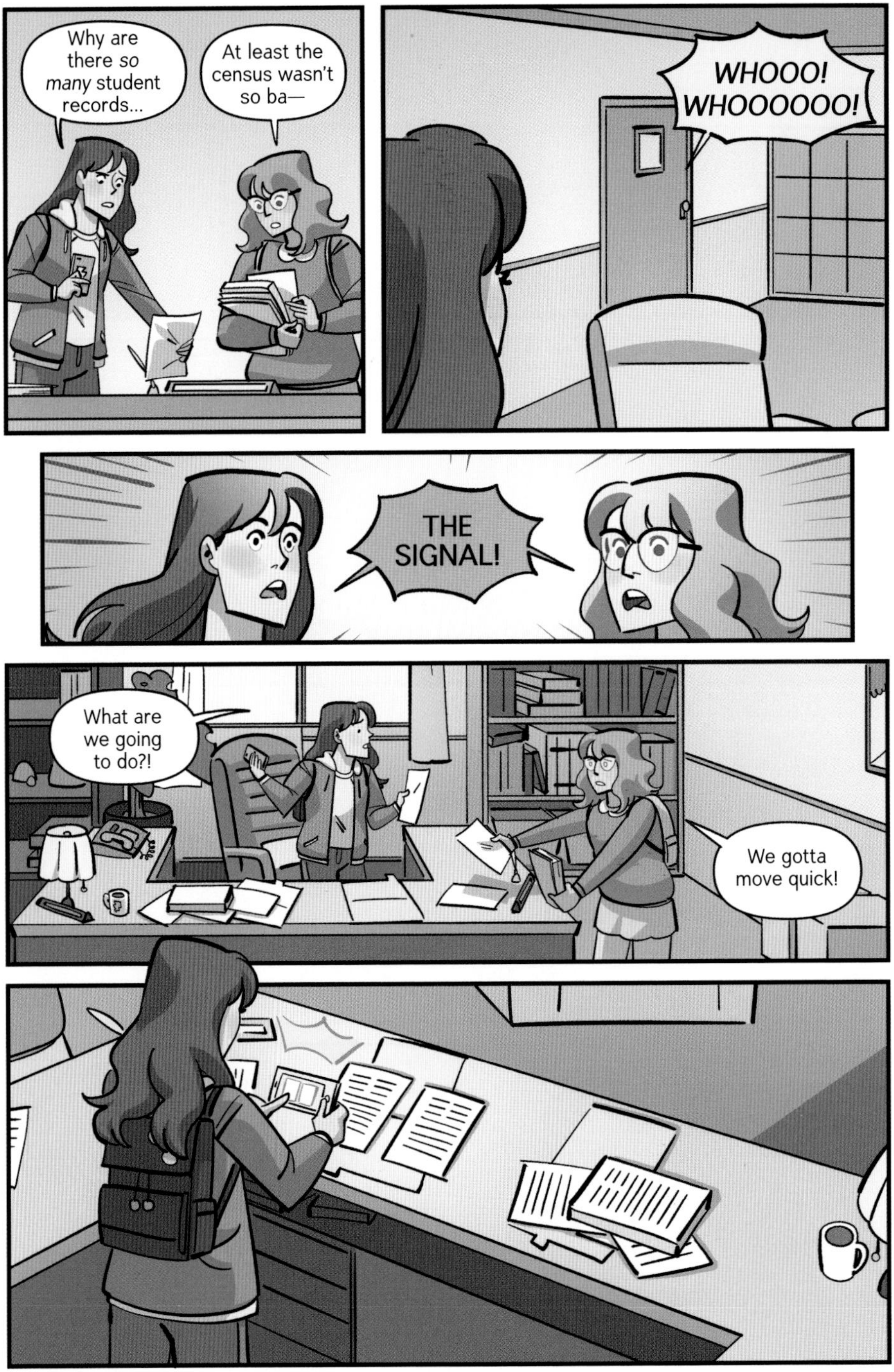
Why are there *so many* student records...
At least the census wasn't so ba—
WHOOO! WHOOOOOO!
THE SIGNAL!
What are we going to do?!
We gotta move quick!

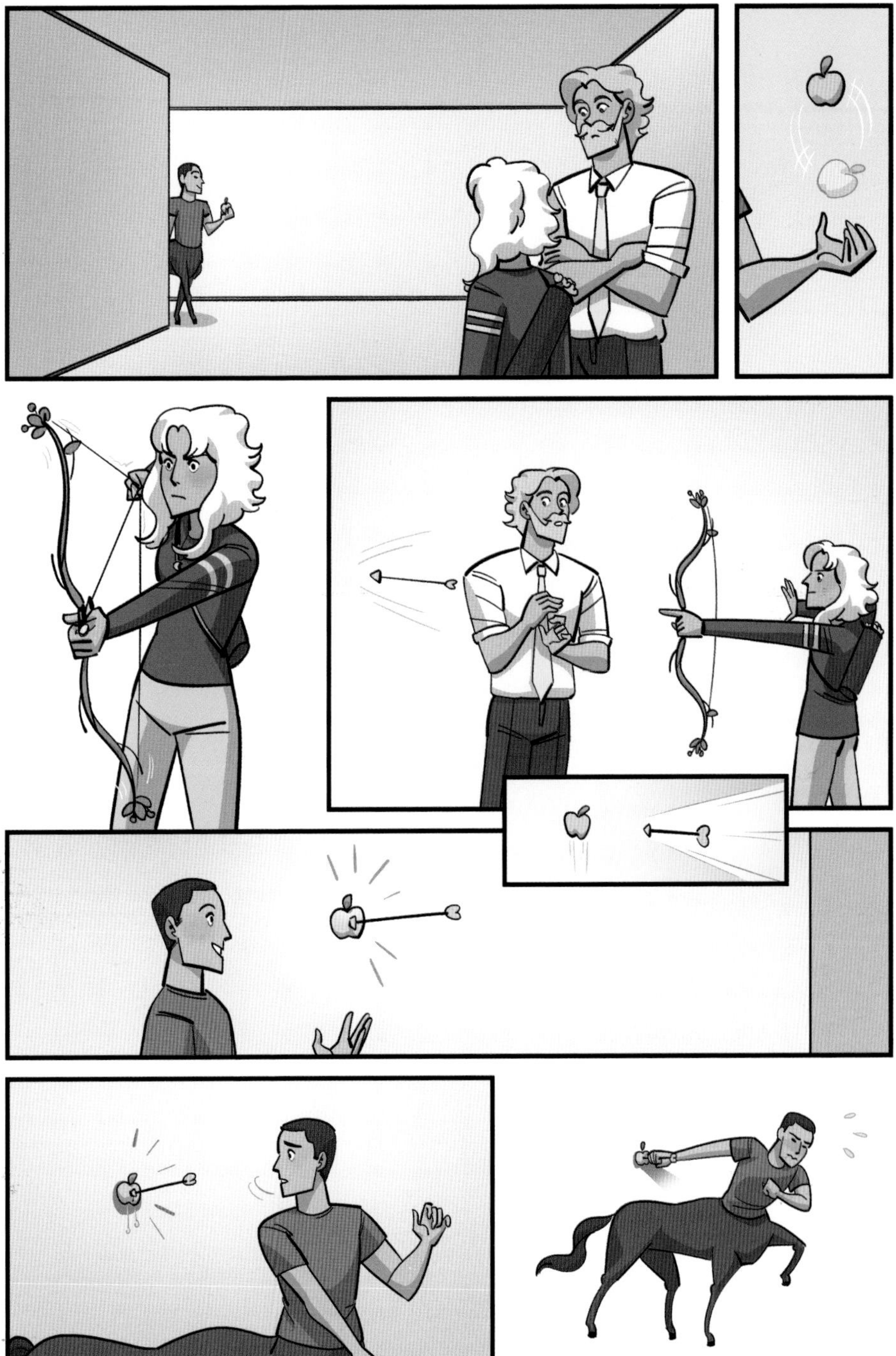

120

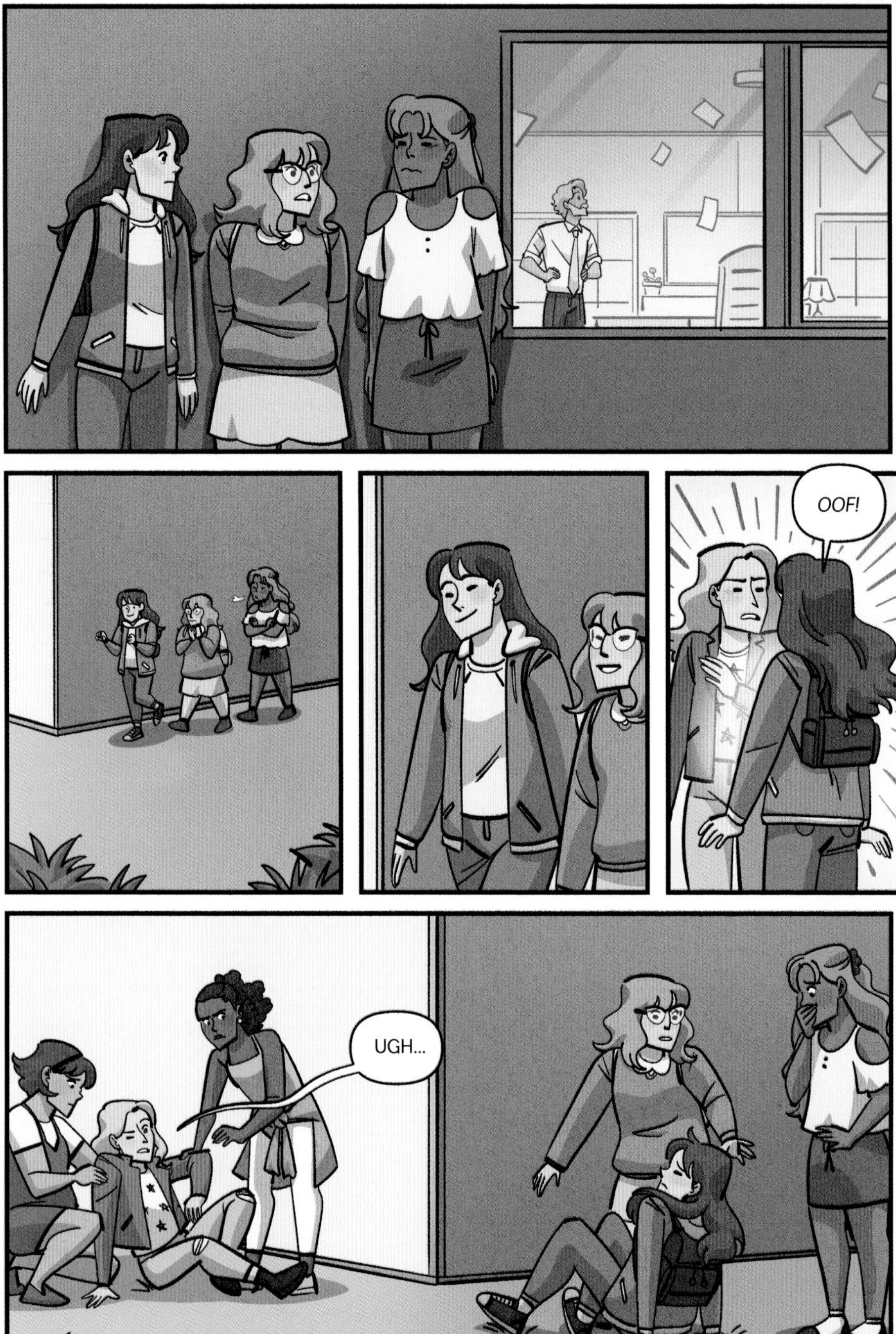
OOF!
UGH...

123

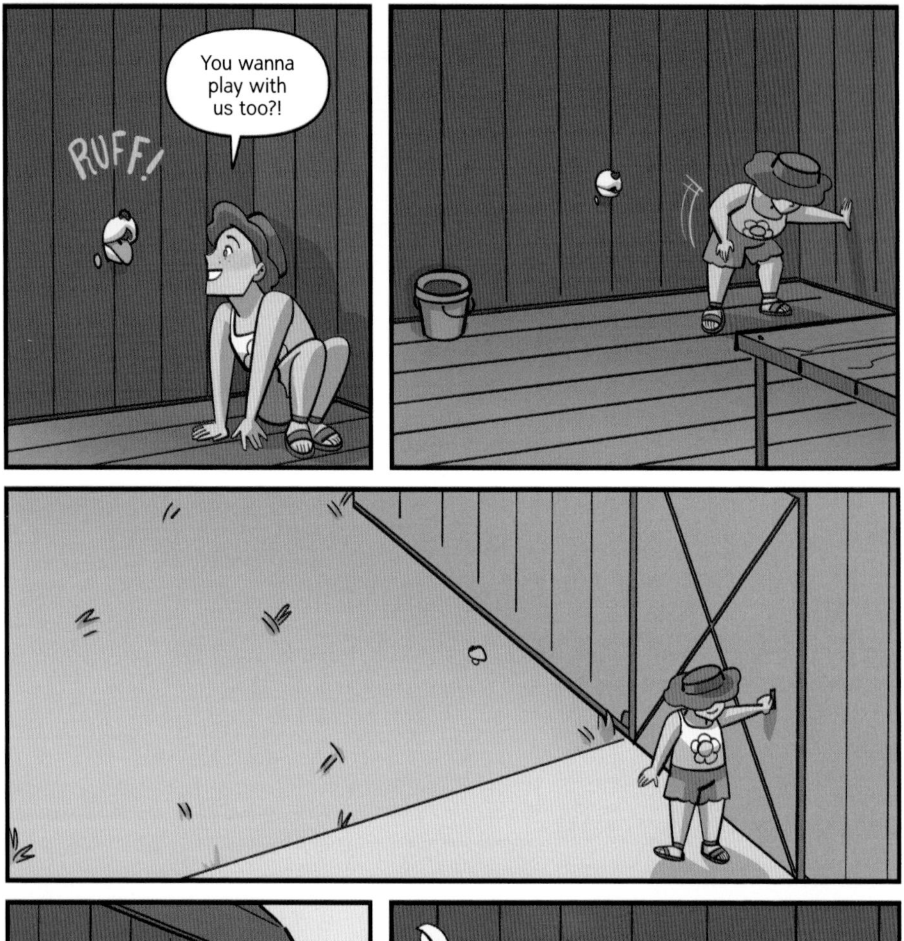
RUFF!
You wanna play with us too?!

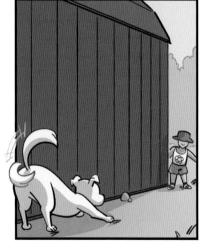

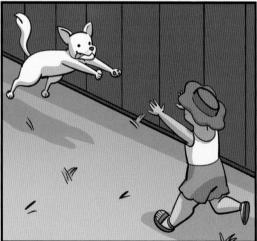

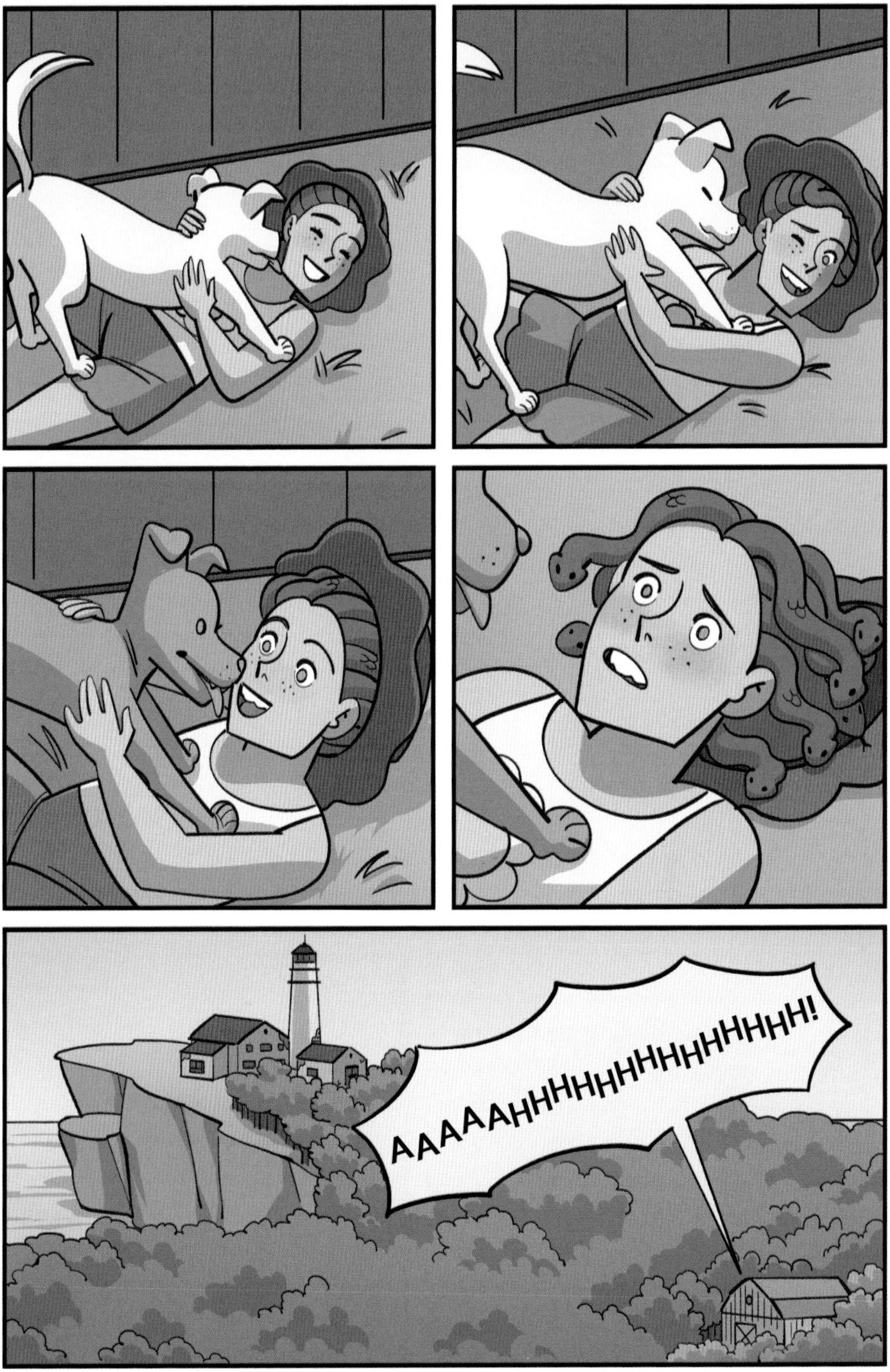
AAAAHHHHHHHHHHHHHHH!

133

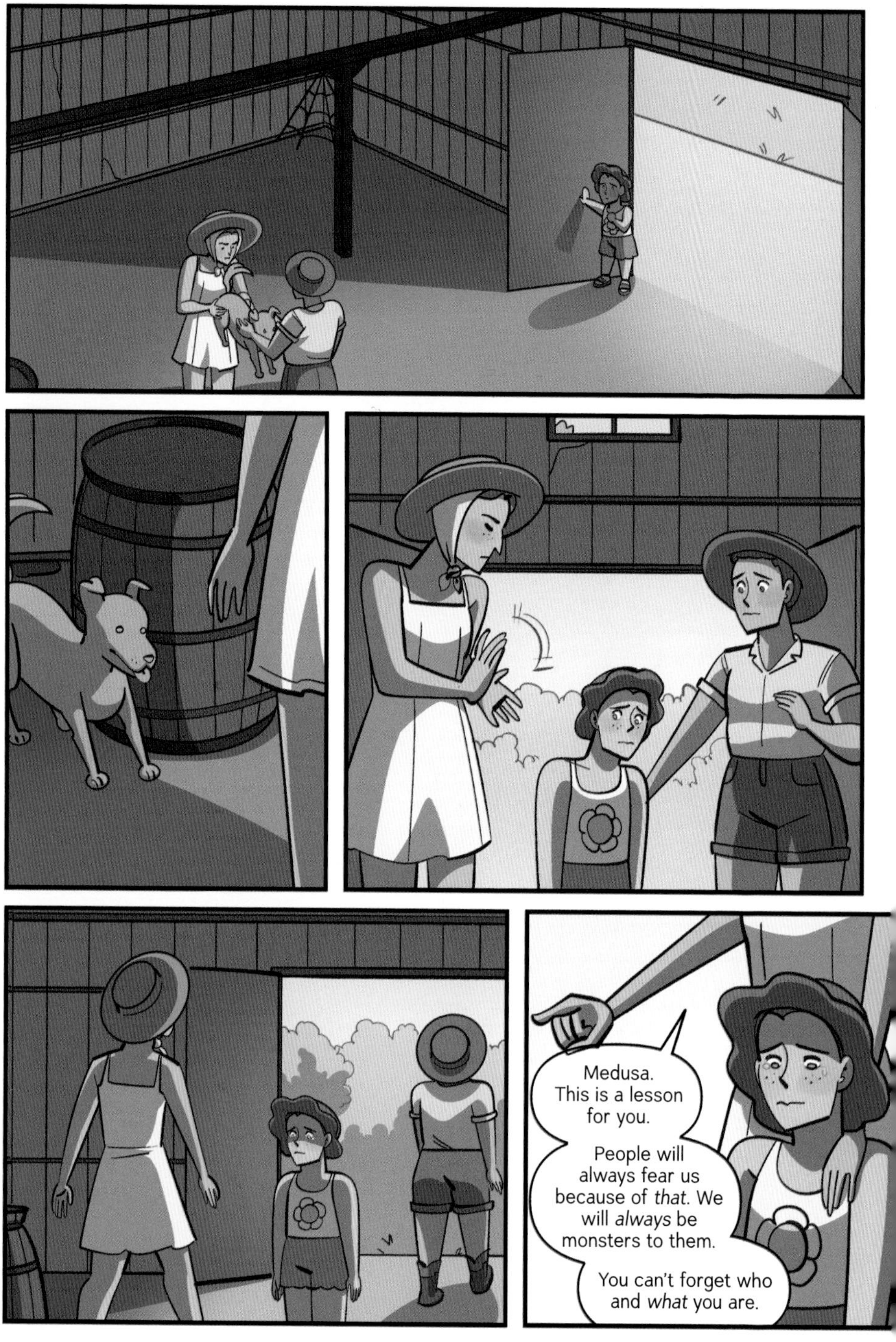
Medusa. This is a lesson for you.
People will always fear us because of *that*. We will *always* be monsters to them.
You can't forget who and *what* you are.

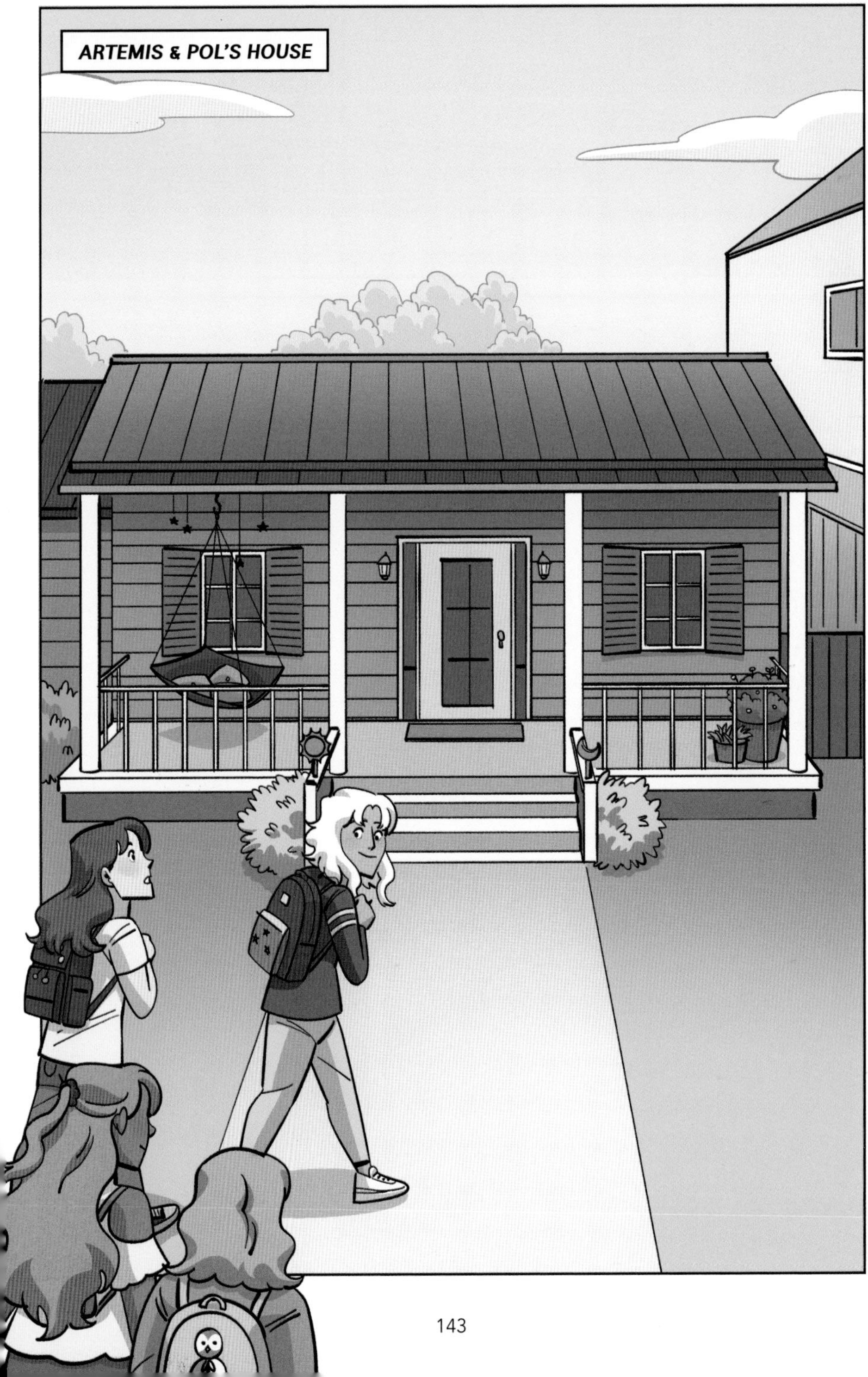
ARTEMIS & POL'S HOUSE

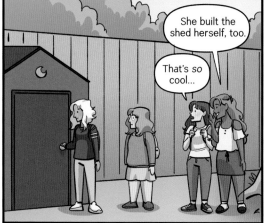

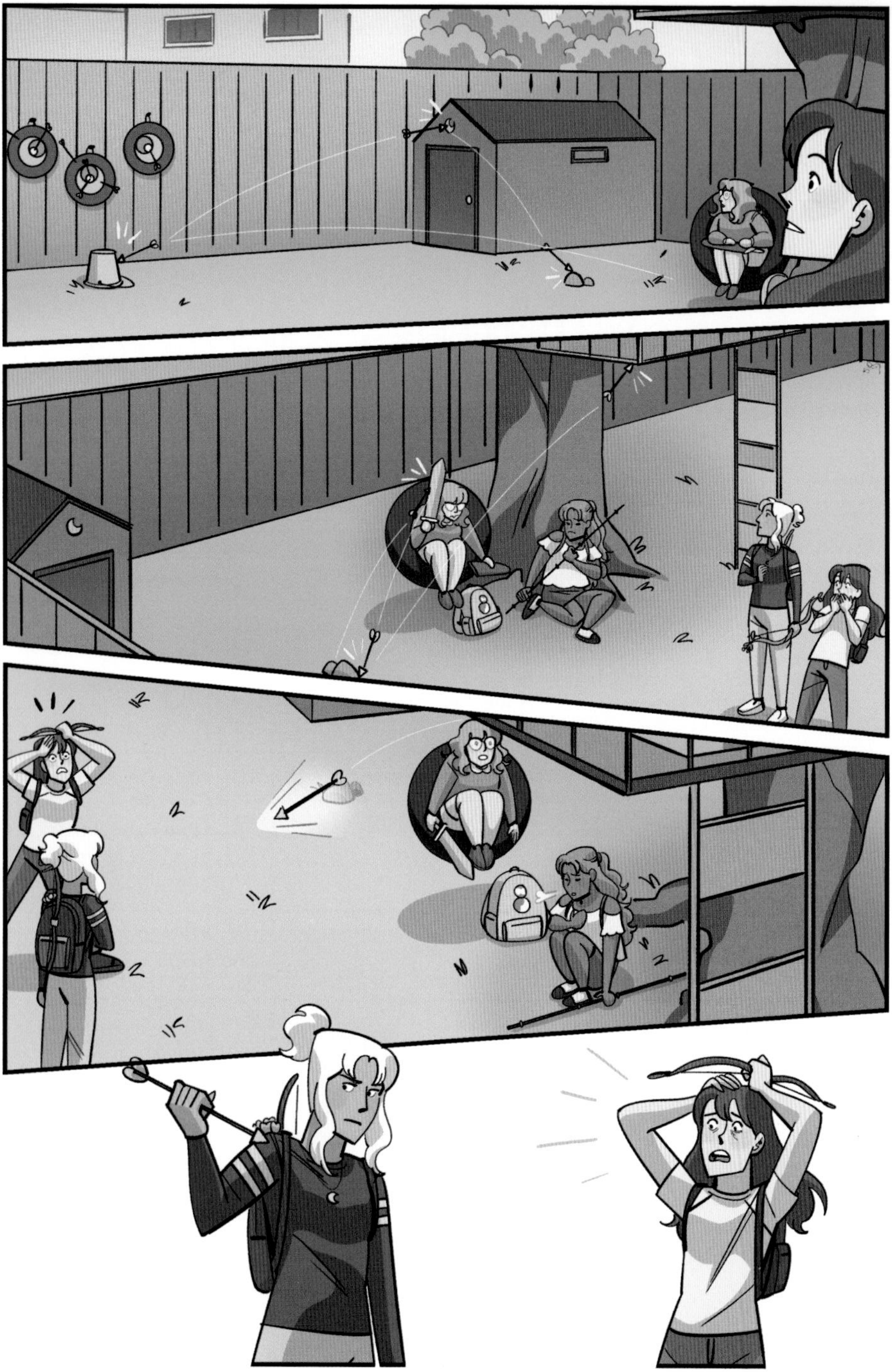

149

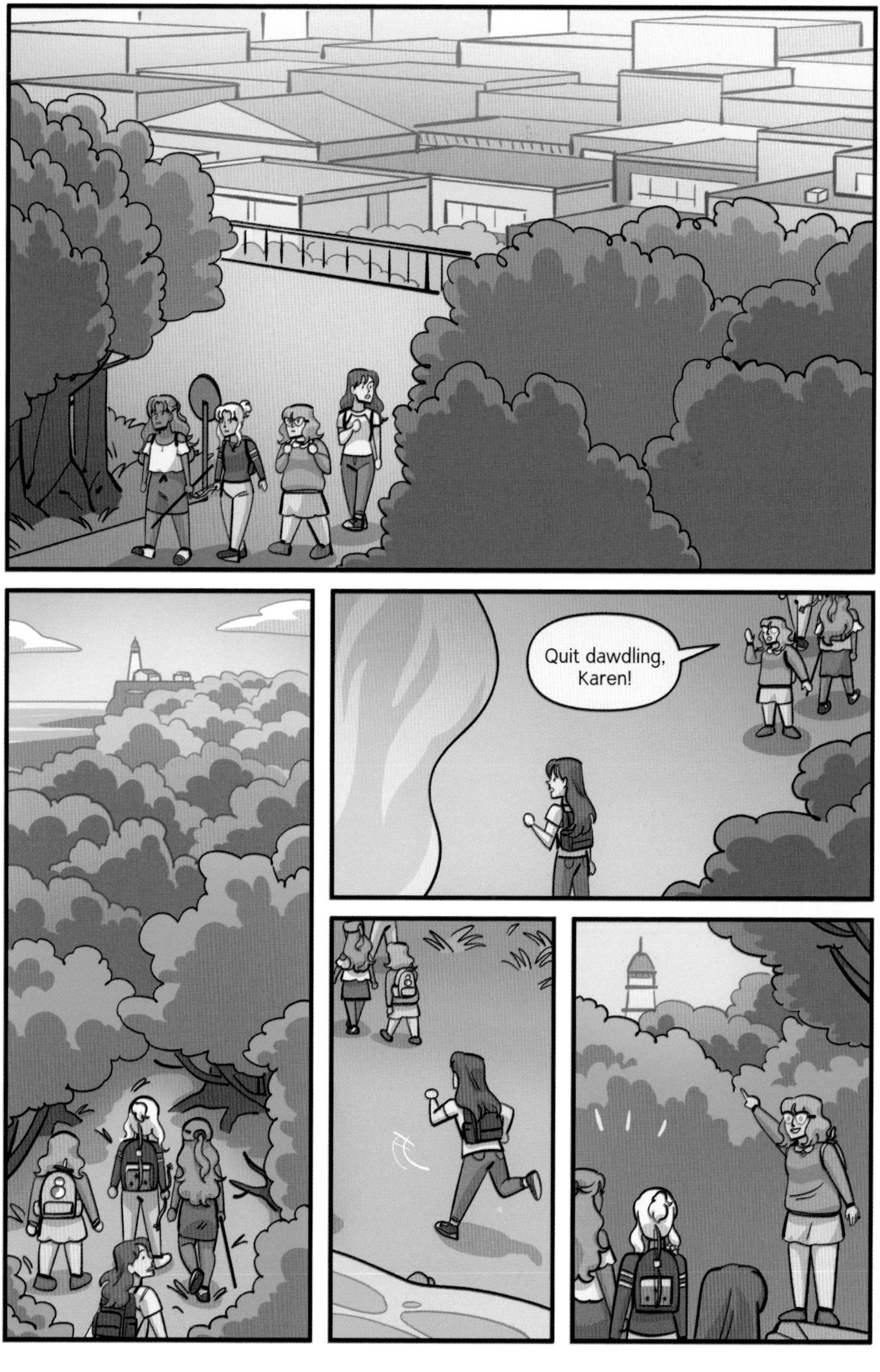
Quit dawdling, Karen!

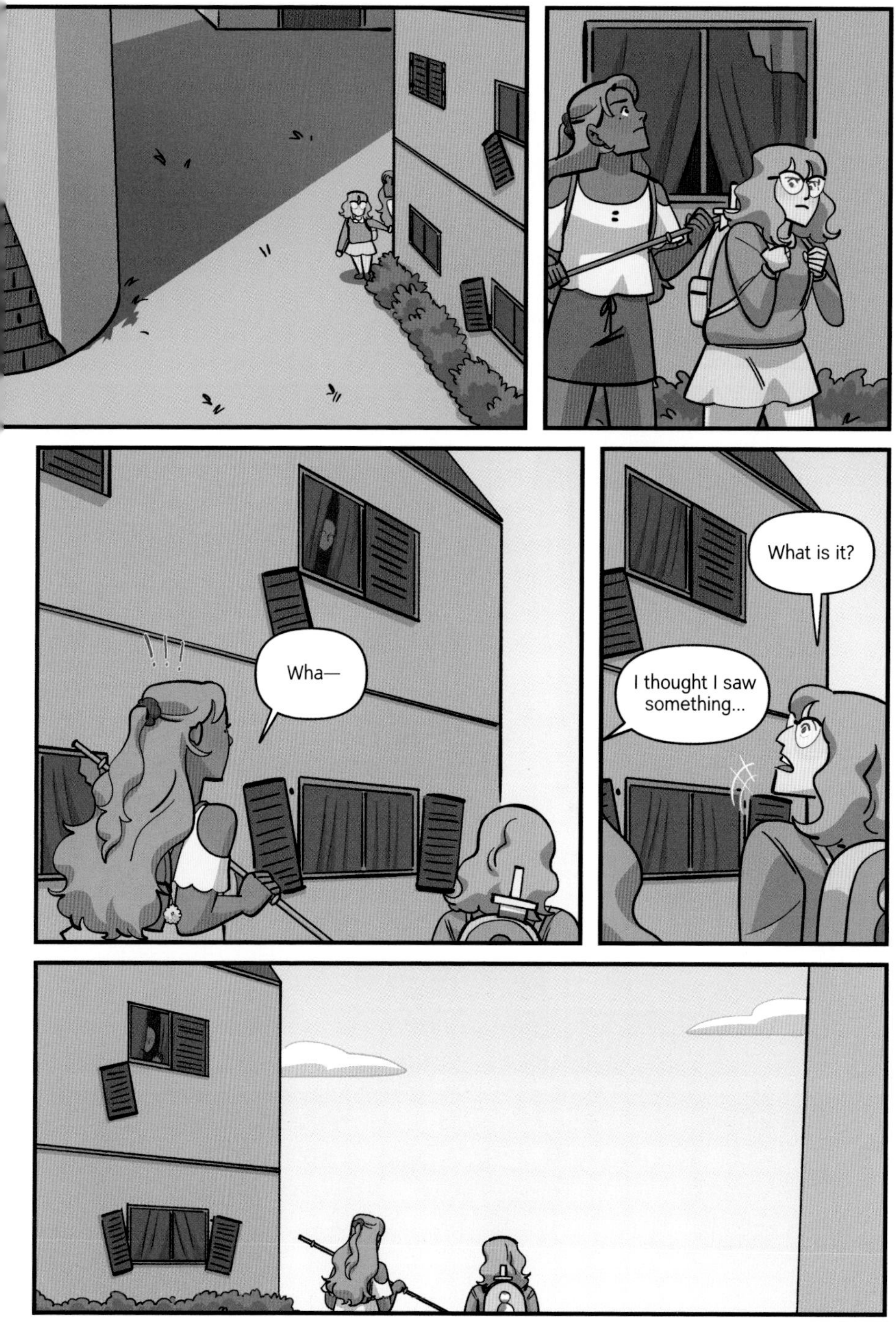
!!!
Wha—
What is it?
I thought I saw something...

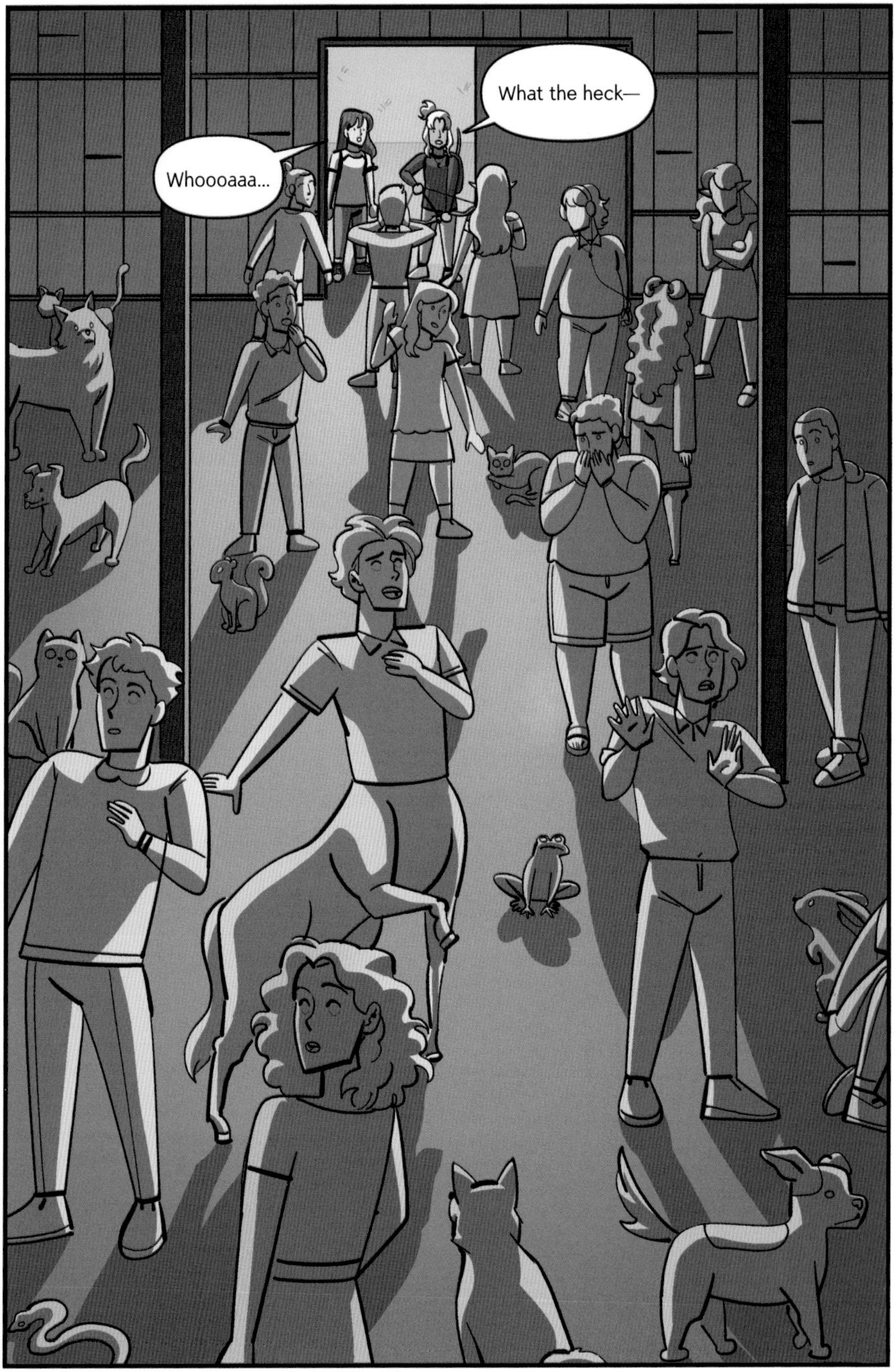
What the heck—
Whoooaaa...

157

161

163

164

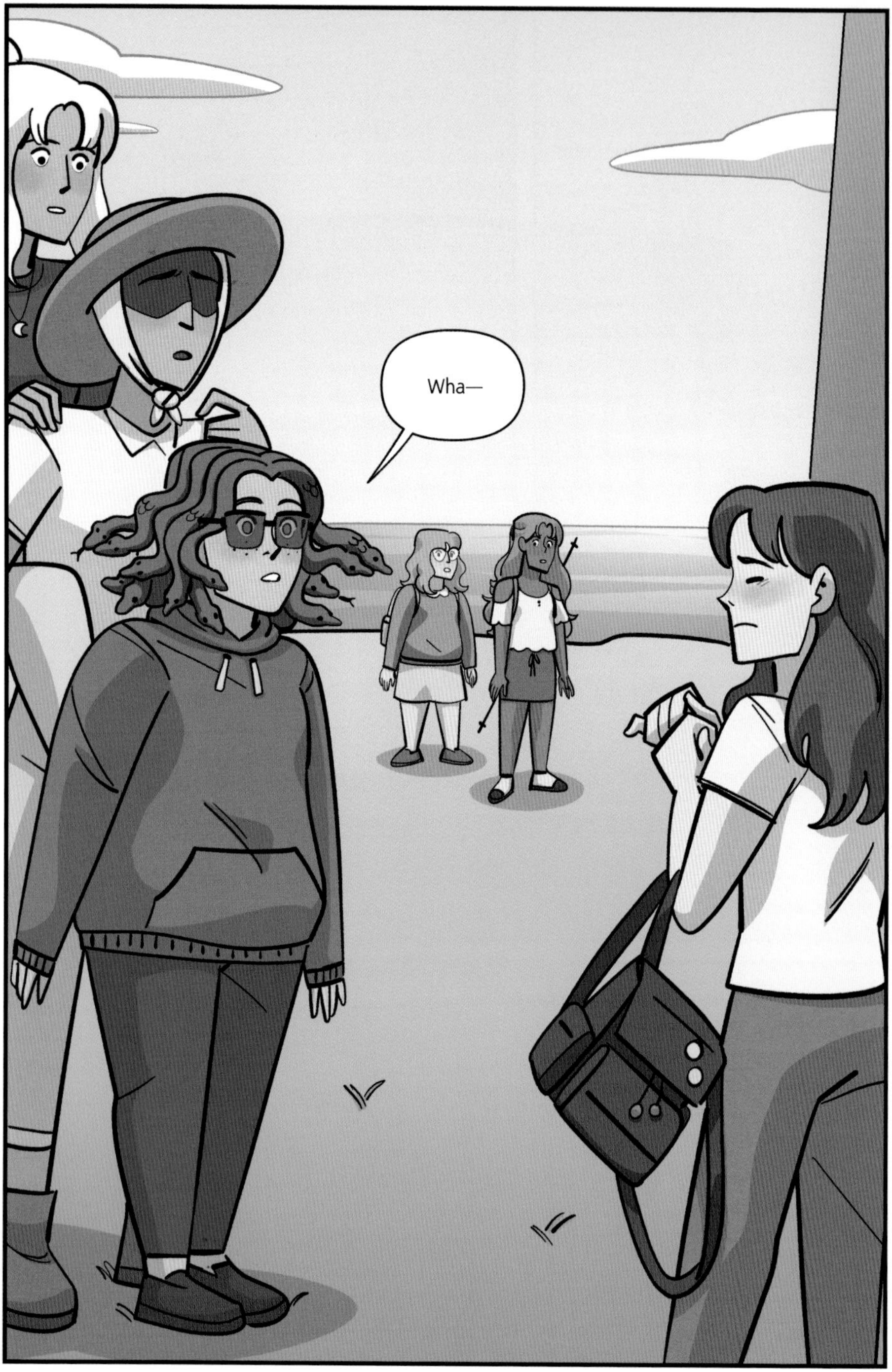
Wha—

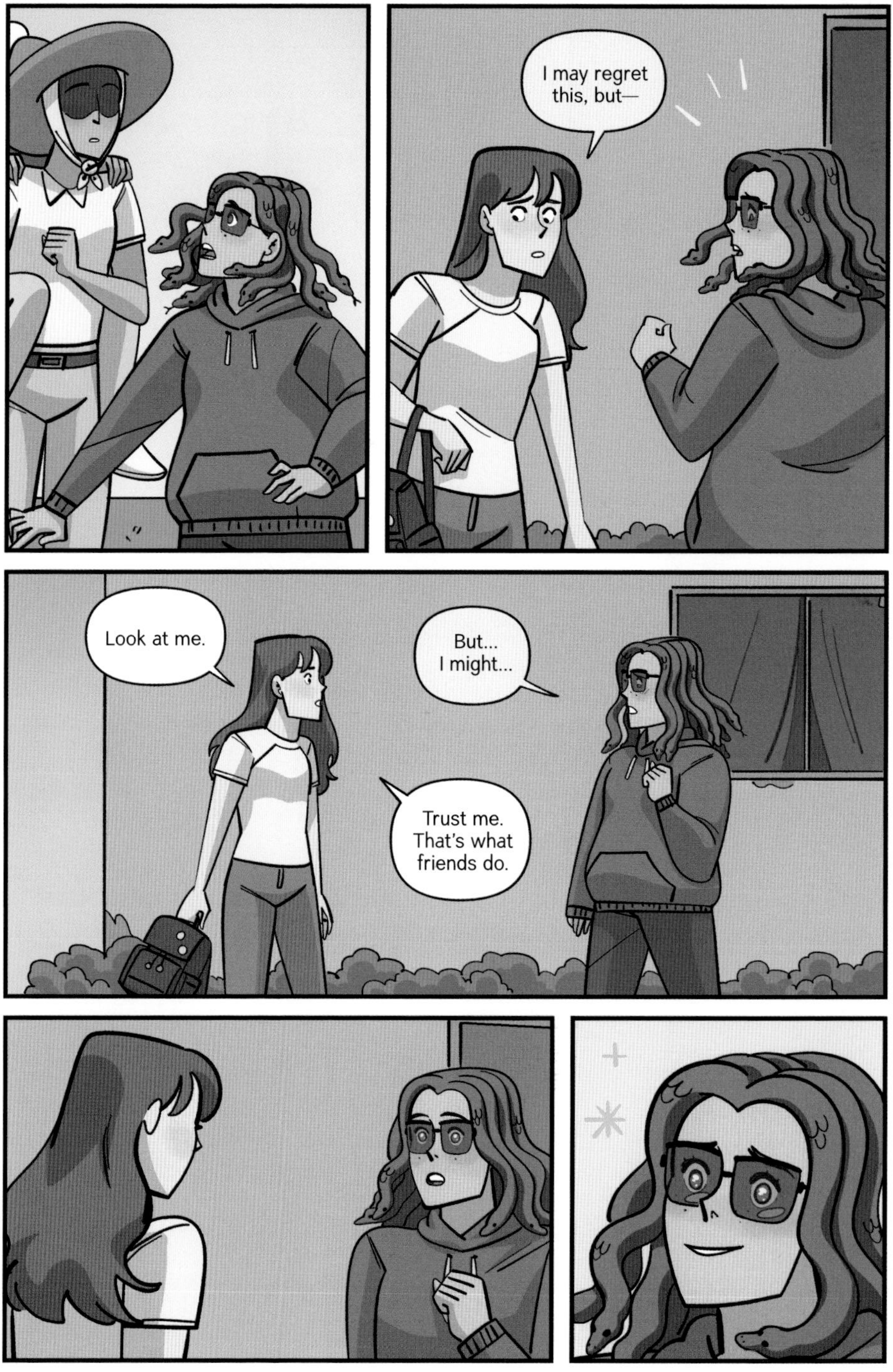
I may regret this, but—
Look at me.
But... I might...
Trust me. That's what friends do.

171

177

180

182

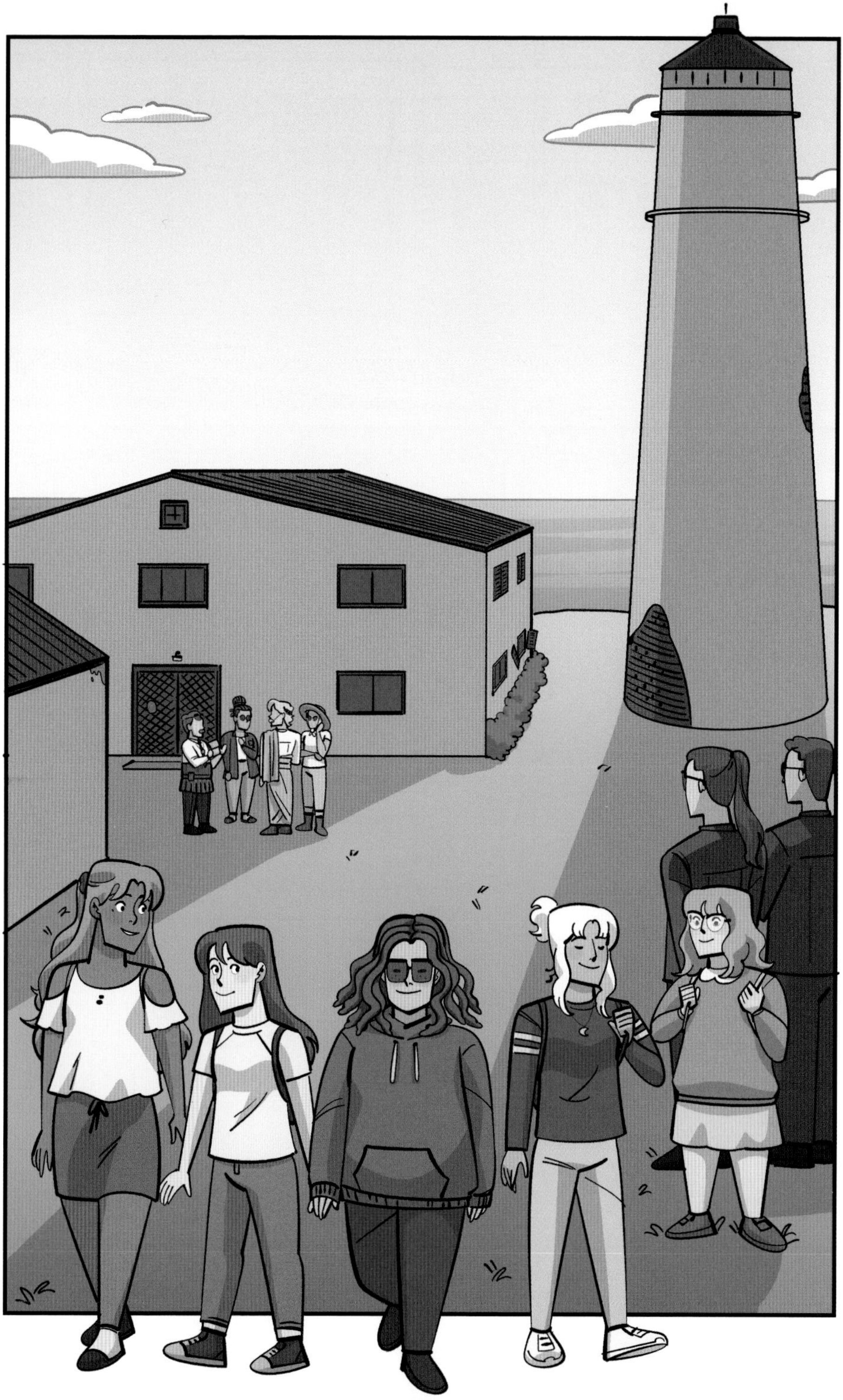

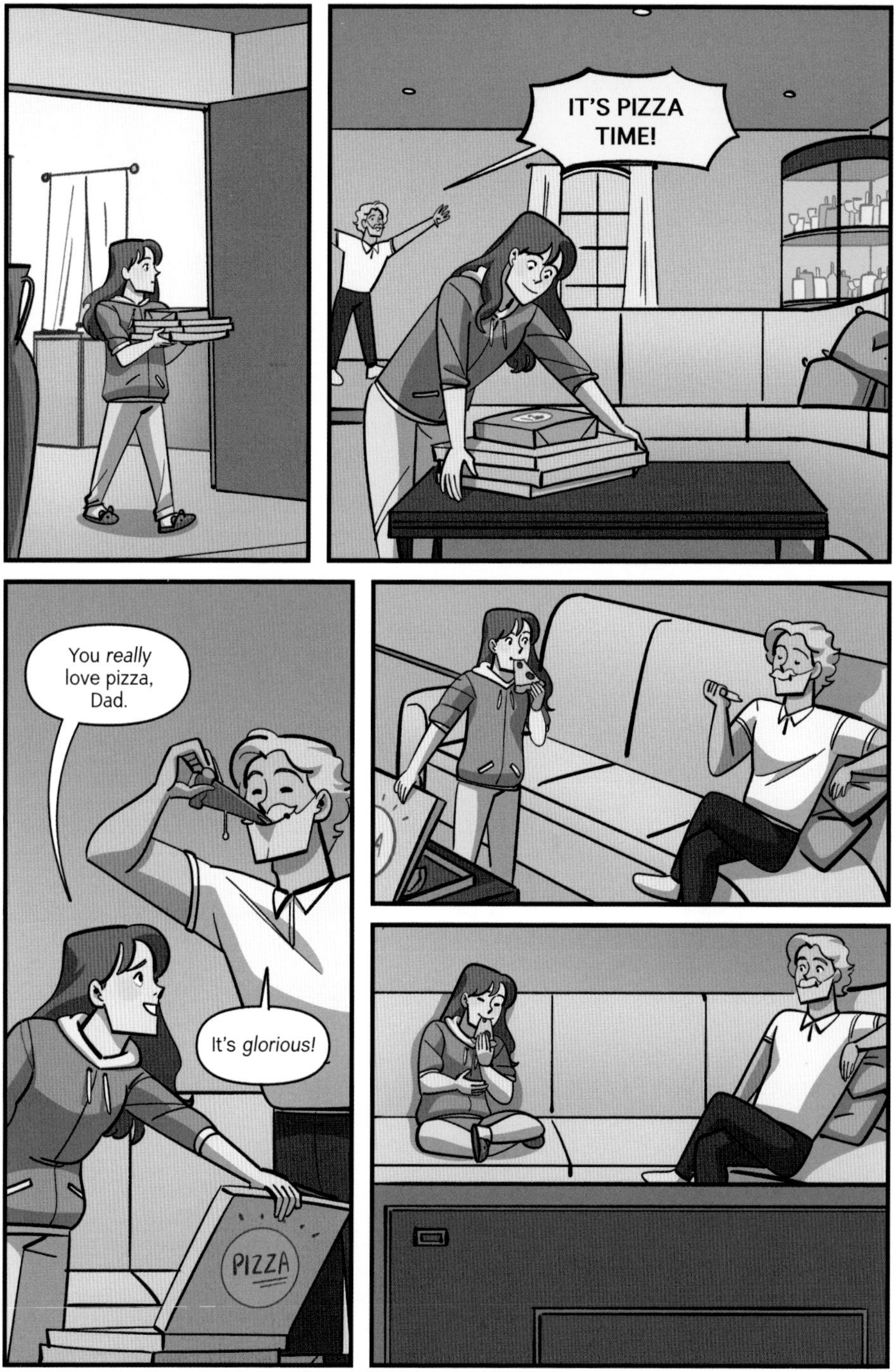
IT'S PIZZA TIME!
You *really* love pizza, Dad.
It's *glorious!*
PIZZA

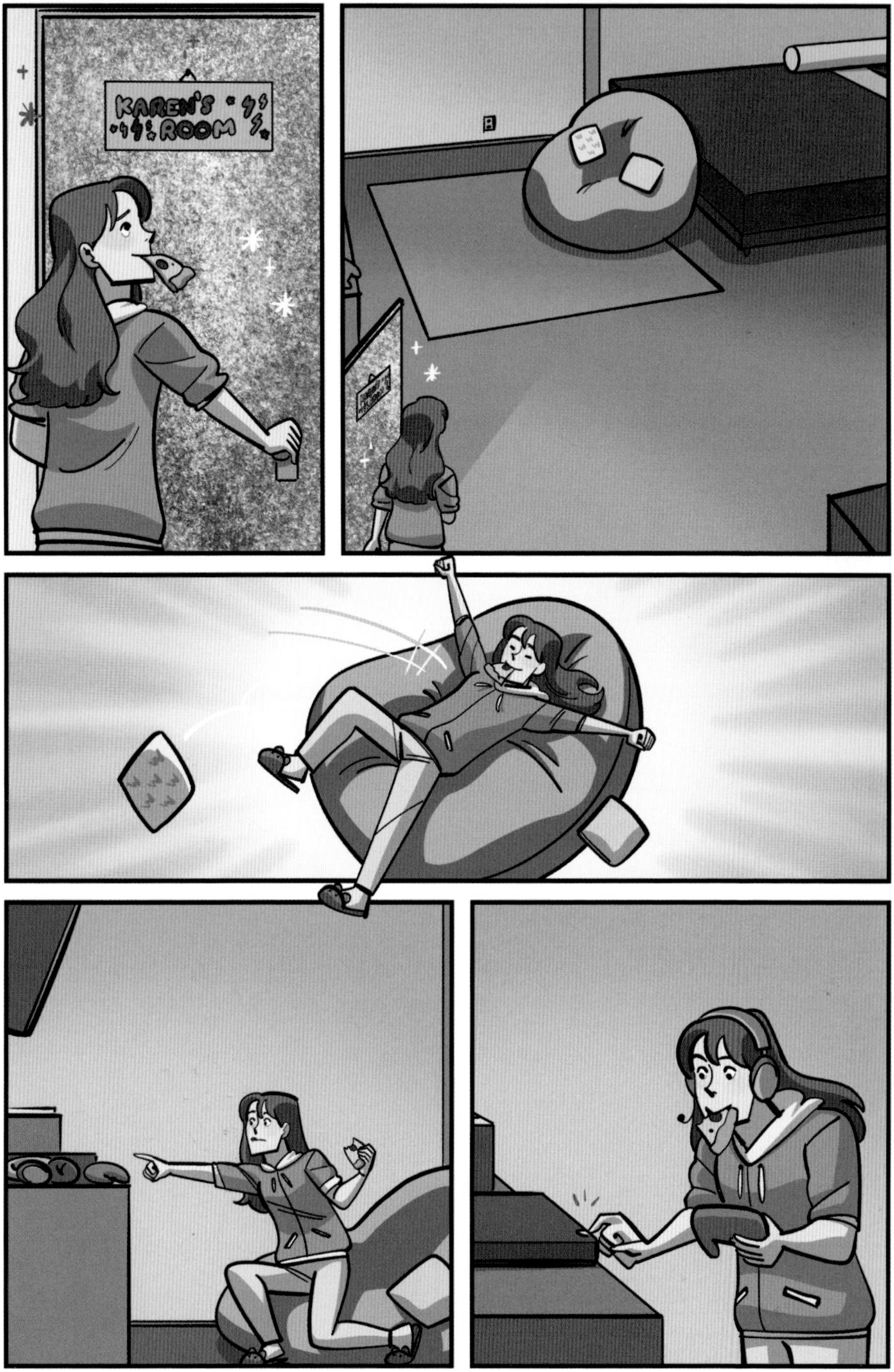
KAREN'S ROOM

195

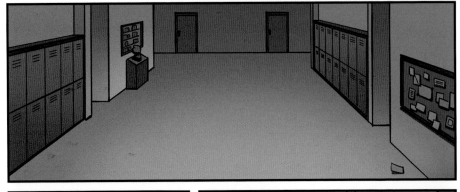

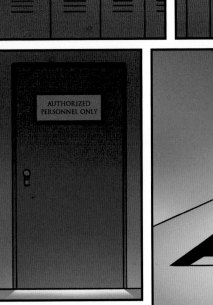

AUTHORIZED
PERSONNEL ONLY

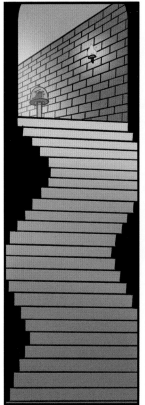

THE END...FOR NOW

KAREN'S MYTHOLOGY NOTES!!!

OMGs. "
Being HANDSOME? ~

Did Pol write this, because
LOL, I'M _never_ letting him live
this down. I guess it's not the
worst thing to be known for,
and it is true... @@

APOLLO

Apollo is the god of the sun, but also the god of music, poetry, light, enlightenment, healing, plague, and disease. He is the son of the Titaness Leto and the twin brother of Artemis, the goddess of the moon. Apollo is known for being handsome, helping mortals, and protecting them from evil. He participated in many musical contests with other gods, such as Pan, the god of shepherds and sheep, and a satyr named Marsyas.

Good at hunting.

Got it—remind me to _never_
get on Artemis's bad side...
again. I should talk to her
about helping me with my
archery, though. :·

> NOTE TO SELF: <
   Text Artemis later.

ARTEMIS

Goddess of the moon and goddess of the hunt, Artemis is well known for her hunting skills as well as her love of archery and wild animals. She is the daughter of the Titaness Leto and the twin sister of Apollo, the god of the sun. Artemis spends most of her time in the forest roaming around with animals and nymphs and is one of the most respected goddesses.

Everything here tracks!
Dita is an _actual_ treasure...
How can you meet her and
not immediately feel the love
that she radiates?!
   ♡ ″ ′ ″ ′ ♡ ♡
   ♡ Talk about girl crush...
      ♡   ♡

APHRODITE

Aphrodite is the goddess of love and beauty and was born from the foam of the sea on the island of Cyprus. She is the most beautiful among the goddesses, usually with long, flowing hair and sweet-smelling clothes. The goddess spreads love among women and men, gods and mortals.

ATHENA

Athena is the goddess of wisdom, courage, law, and justice. She's also the goddess of many other things, including strength, mathematics, crafts, war, and inspiration. Athena is known for using her wits in battle as well as her strength. In a famous tale, she fought Poseidon for Athens, which resulted in her growing the first olive tree and the city being named after her.

Wow. When they say strong women get things done, I'm pretty sure they were using Tina as a role model. What isn't she the goddess of?! My amazing friend, the overachiever! ♡ #SquadGoals

HERMES

The fastest god in all of Mt. Olympus, Hermes is the messenger of the gods, but also the god of thieves and travelers, and he's the official guide to the Underworld. Born to the nymph Maia, Hermes is also known as a trickster god. A surprising fact about the messenger god is how much he enjoys crafts. Hermes invented the lyre from a tortoise shell and gave it to Apollo as a peace offering for stealing his cattle.

CRAFTS?

I somehow can't picture Hermes doing anything besides, well, being Hermes. Now I have an image of Hermes knitting in my head. Can he just run really fast or can he knit really fast, too? Hmmm...

THE FATES

The Fates, or the Moirai, are three goddesses who determine the fates of mortals. The three goddesses measure a person's lifespan as well as their suffering. Clotho (the Spinner) spins the thread, Lachesis (the Allotter) measures the thread, and Atropos (the Inflexible) cuts the thread.

I know middle school is already scary to most people, but how could you not be terrified going to school with these girls?

AVOID WHENEVER POSSIBLE—YIKES.

Medusa gets a _real_ bad rap in the history books, but she's so nice? Who could blame her for being a little grumpy from time to time, though, when the gods turn your hair into snakes!!!! ICK! I wonder what kind of conditioner she uses...

MEDUSA

Daughter of Phorcys and Ceto, Medusa was once a mortal woman who was turned into a Gorgon by the gods as a punishment. And while Medusa was once mortal, her two sisters, Stheno and Euryale, were born immortal. Medusa is known for the snakes in her hair and the ability to turn anyone she stares at to stone.

WOW, THIS GUY HAD IT ROUGH... I mean, I know I have some parental things to work through, but WOW, this really takes the cake.

I bet his family dinners are reeeeeeeeal interesting, to say the least.

ZEUS

God of thunder and the sky, Zeus is the king of the gods (and men). He is the son of the Titans Cronus and Rhea. Cronus believed that one of his children would overthrow him, so he swallowed Zeus's siblings whole, but Rhea protected her son by hiding him in a cave. Zeus has always been seen as the peacemaker (or mediator) when the other gods are fighting with one another. One symbol that he's known for is his thunderbolt.

BIBLIOGRAPHY

- Greek Mythology: greekmythology.com.
- Hamilton, Edith. *Mythology: Timeless Tales of Gods and Heroes.* New York: Grand Central Publishing, 1999.
- Kershaw, Steve. *Mythologica.* Minneapolis: Wide Eyed Editions, 2019.
- Napoli, Donna Jo. *Treasury of Greek Mythology: Classic Stories of Gods, Goddesses, Heroes & Monsters.* Washington, DC: National Geographic Children's Books, 2011.
- Wilkinson, Philip. *Myths, Legends, and Sacred Stories: A Visual Encyclopedia.* London: DK, 2019.